XXIX.II.MMXII

MW01713737

and coolest people I know
and I'm glad to call
you my friend!

David

UNION

BY DAVID M. STERNBERG

UNION

Book One: *Union*

Book Two: *Galactic Union (TBD)*

Book Three: *Union's Origins (TBD)*

THOUGHT GENESIS

The Evolution of Reason

Edited By Jerine P. Watson

UNION

BOOK ONE OF UNION TRILOGY

A Novel By

David M. Sternberg

UNION NOVELS • LONDON

2012 Mass Market Edition

www.UnionNovels.com

ISBN-13: 978-1470083502
ISBN-10:1470083507

Cover design by David M. Sternberg

Printed in the United States of America

To Atalia and Yoram:

No son could have better parents,
No human could have nobler mentors.

This book is also dedicated to Marish and Ephraim:
For their heroic survival and victory.

Contents

PROLOGUE 10
ALLIANCE 16
Chapter 1.......................................17
Chapter 2.......................................21
Chapter 3.......................................35
Chapter 4.......................................44
Chapter 5.......................................48
Chapter 6.......................................56
Chapter 7.......................................62
Chapter 8.......................................74
Chapter 9.......................................80
Chapter 10.....................................86
Chapter 11.....................................94
Chapter 12.....................................97
Chapter 13.....................................106
Chapter 14.....................................109
Chapter 15.....................................112
Chapter 16.....................................114
Chapter 17.....................................129
Chapter 18.....................................135
Chapter 19.....................................142
Chapter 20.....................................150
Chapter 21.....................................160
Chapter 22.....................................168
Chapter 23.....................................187
Chapter 24.....................................194
Chapter 25.....................................211
Chapter 26.....................................216
Chapter 27.....................................227
Chapter 28.....................................234
Chapter 29.....................................246
Chapter 30.....................................261
Chapter 31.....................................265
Chapter 32.....................................268

Chapter 33..275
Chapter 34..283
Chapter 35..286
Chapter 36..296
Chapter 37..303
Chapter 38..311

BETRAYAL 315

Chapter 39..316
Chapter 40..325
Chapter 41..333
Chapter 42..343
Chapter 43..347
Chapter 44..356
Chapter 45..368
Chapter 46..372
Chapter 47..381
Chapter 48..397
Chapter 49..401

CONQUER 414

Chapter 50..415
Chapter 51..425
Chapter 52..429
Chapter 53..437
Chapter 54..449
Chapter 55..459
Chapter 56..466
Chapter 57..476
Chapter 58..479
Chapter 59..483
Chapter 60..490
Chapter 61..496
Chapter 62..503
Chapter 63..508
Chapter 64..512
Chapter 65..517

NOTES 520

About the Author 523

PROLOGUE

"Where is he?" Saul Eisenstein roared as he stormed into the hospital waiting room. From the crowded room, a man's voice answered the anxious father.

"He's fine, Saul. They've taken him for further examinations but aside from a few cuts and contusions, he is relatively unhurt. He's a strong kid, although I can't imagine what's going through his head."

Saul sat down on one of the waiting room chairs and curved his upper body as close to the ground as far as his ribs allowed. After a few moments he raised his head and spoke in a quiet voice filled with raspy undertones originating from a painful throat.

"Her mother, I think it was for the best she died, too. A parent should never have to go through his kid's funeral. It was a diversion, of that I'm sure. She was on her way from work to take her home. She was caught in the midst of that diversion. . .".

Danny Hayes, a research assistant to Dr. Eisenstein, walked to the water fountain in the corner of the room and filled a plastic cup with water. He made his way to the seat next to Saul's, sat down and gestured for him to have a sip of the warm water.

"I have to tell you something Saul, your kid…" before Danny could finish his sentence Saul interrupted him.

"Do we know what they took?" Saul reached for the cup in Danny's hand.

"They took everything. The papers, the servers, the computers and the three prototypes, Saul, one of the prototypes was…" Danny was again interrupted but this time by the voice of Marianna Young, the stocky middle-aged director of the research institute.

"What the hell were you thinking, Saul? Leaving two children to play in a lab my investors put hundreds of millions into. Internals informed me all the initial reports indicate it was your kid's stupid games that gave them easy access. We're lucky the mother of your little prick's friend was killed in that explosion or we would have had a lawsuit on our hands!"

Saul jumped from his chair, threw the cup of water at Marianna and back handed her forcefully on her cheek. Saul, who was an army pilot years before he was a scientist for the army's special tactical research team, still had quick and a powerful reflexes. The vigorous blow hit Marianna in the jaw, and made a crunching sound as his hand made contact. She fell to the floor, gasping in astonishment. The force of the blow was strong enough to frighten her into stunned silence, allowing Saul time for a follow-up speech.

"How dare you? That woman was a friend of mine and her daughter was as my own." He snarled at her, his face contorted with rage and his entire body trembling. "My wife and I helped raise her after her dad died while saving my wing in operation zero-nine. Take your selfish business school corporate ass out of here before, I swear, there will be another casualty tonight."

Marianna tried to stand up and nearly lost her balance, but Danny caught her and helped her to her feet. She cautiously placed her hand on her jaw. With a lisping diction forced by what was clearly a broken jaw and a few missing teeth, she spoke in obvious pain.

"You're finished, you're finished!" She wailed and left the room. Her sobs evolved into incoherent shouting as she hurried down the hall.

The crowded room was occupied by Saul's associates, both from the army and the research facility. They showed no intention of reacting to Saul's attack on Marianna since they all, in one way or another, felt like reacting in the same manner.

"Are you out of your goddamned mind?" Danny said.

"You're finished, you're finished!" Saul mocked Marianna's accusation. He paused for a moment and said, "I am finished, we all are. Do you know what she was talking about Danny? Is it true?"

Danny looked at Saul and nodded. "I've seen the security tapes; he somehow opened the lock for the inner lab. The problem is that whatever he did to hack into the inner lab was strong enough to open everything else. But the robbers came much later than that and were carrying high grade explosives intending to get rid of the blast doors. Right after they shot all of the outdoor security men. They planned a fully armed strike but had little resistance from the security and no alarms were set off."

In the far corner of the corridor through the door from the waiting room, a nurse pushed young Gustave in a wheelchair..

Both Saul and Danny were silent as they watched the approaching wheelchair.

"Saul, there's something you need to know." Danny was whispering, his lips close to Saul's ear. "After Gustave reached the inner lab, he got on the control station computer, connected to prototype two, and God knows how, got it to work"

" They didn't just steal the prototypes, they stole a working prototype," Saul said as he squinted in disbelief.

"He couldn't have, we never got them working, and how could he possibly know what to do with the…"

The nurse greeted Saul. Gustave's expression resembled the look of a lifeless carcass. Danny turned his head away from the empty expression of the thirteen-year-old boy and whispered, "He was preparing a surprise sign moments before they stormed in and killed her, and he did put up a fight."

All Saul wanted was to hug his son yet he couldn't bring himself to do so. He had never felt comfortable displaying emotions in that manner, but aside from that, now that the fear of losing his son had subsided, the full scope of the catastrophe began unfolding in his head, and the feelings of concern for his son were quickly substituted by the chilling reality of what had been lost in the raid.

"Mom should be here any moment," Saul said as an offering of comfort, and left the room.

"Now I am become Death, the destroyer of worlds"

Bhagavad Gita

Part One

ALLIANCE

CHAPTER 1

Gustave Eisenstein was not the type anyone else might have said they knew well or understood. He seemed to be capable of holding his first reactions tamped down as if under an invisible tarpaulin until he was absolutely certain of their being accepted and then he might release them as long as his insecurities could not be perceived as well. This control of his emotions seemed to be more important to him than which side of the issue he professed to consider championing. To an observer, he presented an enigma of contradictory vibrations, each vying for the full support of all his concentrated forces. No one, not even himself, was ever positive which viewpoint or side of the discussion he would eventually announce as a preference of his own. This he did as a defense mechanism, hiding his simmering hot temper from critical view as long as possible and thereby convincing himself he was in absolute control when in actuality, his behavior only delayed the exposure, which he did not realize in his conscious mind. He was also somewhat short and rather slim with no outstanding attributes or features.

His looks were not too appealing to the ladies, or so he assumed. However, he exuded a charisma that followed him whenever he needed to hide his uncertainties. And he needed to hide those most of the time, even occasionally when he was by himself.

He often chose to be left alone, and when spoken to, he would habitually respond with the shortest possible reply just to save time, which in his mind and from his point of view was all too precious. Of course, his other persona was nothing of that sort. A little short of outrageous, the charismatic character he presented to the public was outspoken and without a doubt elitist. He never thought being called an elitist was an insult at all, and enjoyed it quite thoroughly every time it was thrown in his direction to which he would always reply with a shadowy smile that exposed an otherwise hidden dimple on his cheek.

For his age, he found himself more comfortable spending time with older people. If not older, then those more mature than the rest. He couldn't stand the popular fashion, which in his time was composed of jeans or track pants and a raised collar of a semi-dressy tee shirt. No, he would put on a suit, every time he left his house. He told himself it was a matter of class, personal pride, and self-respect.

Other than watching documentaries or educational programming and the occasional sitcoms, he was obsessed with preaching about the destruction caused by reality TV. He was always taking the moral high ground. In his mind, something that held no educational value, and more importantly, something that gave the youth a presentation of augmented reality masquerading under the title 'reality' was immoral and against human intelligence. When he was asked about what he thought about this or that show he cheerfully replied, "It's art. . ." which satisfied the person who had asked. However, Gustave used it for its acronym, standing for Augmented Reality Television.

Gustave's daily routine was very straight forward. He would awaken around 10 AM, open his computers, boil water for a cup of tea, and occasionally substitute skim milk and hot chocolate then go right back to his computers. He would then navigate his way to his email host, and come back to the boiling water and poor in three quarters of a cup full, ready to mix with the powder or crumbled dry leaf tea, add some sugar and pour in enough skim milk just to cool it down. He would then reach for his cigarette pack, draw one, grab his Zippo lighter, and enjoy the combination of the two substances. It was very much a morning ritual, a ritual he knew all too well. He always knew exactly the amount he had to inhale in order to make it synchronize with the sipping of the hot beverage. If his drink ended before the cigarette or vice versa, he would feel slightly tense and discomfited.

After he finished with both his smoke and his hot beverage, he would go back to his computers and read a long list of emails. These emails organized his day in quite a remarkable way. His many various occupations required most of his time. Although he was a university graduate in both physics and engineering, he involved himself with little that had to do with what he had learned at school.

He developed Information Systems, worked on graphic designs, and had various personal projects each of which he thought might be groundbreaking once completed and perhaps could bring him the comfort of living to which he had become accustomed in his own little world, which was solely comprised of his vivid imagination.

He was still struggling with getting funding for his projects, even though he earned a comfortable living which he often spent on the latest in his adored field of technology. Most of his ideas remained as detailed sketches hidden safe within various folders of his computers. There were many, and they had continued to accumulate over the years.

Most of the time, he questioned his own abilities even though he had no doubt there was something different about himself. He often wondered if this notion originated from his imagination or from his elitist persona that had perhaps overtaken his exceptional capacities to reason.

Or he wondered to himself, at the age of thirty two, if his potential in many areas were beginning to falter. There was only one thing Gustave never doubted. He knew his ideas would take him somewhere sometime, but had he known how far they would actually take him he would have probably developed a resentful disbelief in everything that surrounded him, like the protective carapace of the dung beetle.

CHAPTER 2

The clock on Gustave's desktop showed it was quarter to four in the morning. He mumbled to himself it might be wise to stop his work and go to sleep. He was convinced however that in an hour he could probably finish what he had intended to do, or to be more precise, what he was supposed to finish, in order to be on track for the rest of the day, so he kept on working.

Sleeping, for what Gustave called 'maintenance', was just another habitual necessity he knew he could not ignore. Most nights he had to tire his eyes deliberately reading a book using a night light in order to feel any symptom of tiredness. He would have much rather not slept at all and just kept on living awake but he knew from experience, he would be rendered useless after three or four or even five sleepless nights. For that very reason, Gustave had given up on his second favorite drink, which was coffee, since the last thing he needed to metabolize was caffeine, so he adopted a caffeine- free regime.

After finishing what he started earlier that day, Gustave submitted his work to a server located in a room next to his work room, and then took the time to see if there was any news in the technology or scientific world since the last time he had checked. There was nothing new of interest, so he went to sleep.

Gustave awakened the next morning, shaken by a dream he had had. It was nothing he was unaccustomed to since he always had very odd dreams. As usual, he was quite satisfied with his imagination and told himself how wonderful it would be if computer-generated imagery could be as advanced as the brain's capacity.

"It will be one of these days, and most likely in my life time!" Gustave whispered to himself. He knew that to be true, because one of the sketches lying in a hidden folder in his main computer explained the exact way of doing it. If only he had funding, he thought again. The brain, as he thought of it, was nothing more than a colossal memory storage device with a very unique plasticity. Once we have the ability to retrieve memory very fast, and if we have an unlimited capacity of storage, my computer wouldn't need to calculate texture, shading, lights, or caustics, or worry about amount of polygons on screen. It would have it already there, but with the ability to be manipulated to any conceivable scenario and even that would be a memory of how to bend *another* type of memory. Just like the brain. Of course this was technically a process of calculation in a sense, but not exactly the same as the computers these days.

Wearing the same dark blue pants and long sleeved

shirt he had worn the day before, he got up quite dizzy and made his way to the electric kettle, pressed the only button it had and went to his office. One computer was still on from two weeks ago, working on a calculation Gustave had set for one of his new projects. He knew at what stage of calculation the computer has reached just by listening to the fleet of cooling fans spinning in that computer.

"There is no point waking up your monitors as there are still a few more hours for you to work," Gustave told the computer in his head. The vocal equivalence to his thought came out of his mouth as "nham" which was executed only by his tongue and the short opening and closing of his lips, barely discernible. If he had had any hopes the computer would finish his tasks by the time he woke up, they were attenuated right away. Gustave turned his other two computers on and went back into the kitchen to choose a mug for his hot chocolate.

"Wouldn't hurt having something sweet to start the day," Gustave told himself with a pleased smile. His mug collection was nothing out of the ordinary, just a few square-looking ones, which Gustave liked for how efficient they were to store, and a few regular round ones, all bright and creamy white. He opened a large container with low fat hot chocolate powder and scooped up a spoonful of the brown confection. He went back to his office, opened his email and went back to his kitchen. The water was boiling and he poured it into a square mug. While filling the water in one hand in a circular gesture, he grabbed a spoon in the other, and started stirring until he saw no powder clogs. He added a bit of milk, pulled a cigarette cylinder from its box and made his way to the garage.

When Gustave came back from smoking he placed the mug in the kitchen sink and quickly moved on to his home office. There were a few emails waiting for him to process then his day was off to a start.

He changed a feature this way or that way, adding a few conceptual artworks for some banners he worked on for a financial company and at the same time, he was keeping track of the calculations he had started working on one of his computers. His new project that had kept this computer working at full capacity was Gustave's latest brainchild: an impenetrable encryption system. The computer was simply testing out how impenetrable the system really was. The beauty in this system was the mere fact it was not using a fancy algorithm and was extremely simple to program. Considering Gustave was not an extraordinary programmer it was more a test of probabilities rather than an actual decoding attempt.

At its core, every time there was an attempt to try a key, the entire encryption would change. Not that the key would change but the actual rules the encryption was based upon. Gustave wanted to test to see if it was possible for a computer to predict the change after trying millions of attempts, and was anxiously waiting for a result. Even though his computer was quite a monstrosity of a cluster computer, where Gustav's time and much of his earnings went toward maintaining, he knew this cluster could give him some incentive to take it a step further if he was satisfied with the results. Of course that meant he would have to purchase and build an entire cluster in his home, a small price to pay for someone that will do anything to avoid doing his research in an established facility.

After a few hours of work it was time for Gustave to peek at the computer's monitors. The cooling fans were still running dreadfully loud but that was expected once the calculations were done. Gustave approached the computer with some level of nervousness, even though he was quite confident his encryption system was his ticket to riches. After pressing the monitors' power buttons it took a while until the visuals on the LCD monitor faded from existence. After waiting for more than two weeks, Gustave was quite upset that he did not have the patience of a few milliseconds to see the outcome and at that exact same moment, the phone rang.

Gustave looked at his phone and gazed with his peripheral vision at the fading pixels. He picked up his phone predisposed to have an antsy conversation with whoever was on the other line. With a short, impatient tone of voice, he began speaking.

"Yes?" He didn't bother looking at the call display, since that would mean taking his eye contact away from the monitors.

"Hi, Gustave!" A female voice answered. He glanced briefly at the screen, scanning the report.

The voice on the phone was that of Leanne Clark, a girl he had met through his friend, while attending a dinner with a few of his friends. She was an inch or two taller than Gustave and had a skinny physique. The mental picture that was now recalled to associate with that soft girly voice emphasized her best physical attributes. She had a long charcoal hair, fair skin that showed she was a person who doesn't mind being in the sunlight for a few hours a day yet still doesn't get tanned. And, of course the two enormous flashing blue eyes that always seemed as if they had their own backlighting. Gustave, even with his dedication to his work, all of a sudden shifted his attention to the voice that came out of the speaker of his phone. The encryption system became superfluous.

He spoke in a broken French accent. " 'Allo, I am currently away on zee vacashun and am unable to answer your call, pliss leave a massage, after zee tone. If this iss an emergency, you should conseeder calling nine-wan-wan".

Leanne broke into vibrant laughter. She was familiar with Gustave's phone humor, and every time she called he answered as a different personality. At times he even managed to trick her into thinking he was someone else.

Leanne slowed her laugh into giggles and then to chuckles. She was trying to gain some momentum to prepare a reply yet the time was not sufficient and all she could come up with was, "Gustave, I… I need your help with something…"

Gustave was very familiar with this sort of request.

He had many lady friends asking him for help with this or that after all, and many of them knew he could help them with their work, whether it was technologically based, artistically related, or even as a consultant regarding their private lives. He got accustomed to many of the requests, but that is not to say he didn't view them as feigned sexual extortions minus the sex. Although he did give a helping hand to many of the requests, at one point in his life he decided he would make the one in need work harder than usual to get what they wanted, and in doing so, make them understand the information or the time and work involved around their request was not to be taken for granted.

To carry on with his voice mail imitation, Gustave replied in the same French accent. "I said, if zis iss an emergency, you should conseeder calling nine-wan- wan!"

Leanne laughed again, only this time, her laugh rolled with a round and lovable voice, to which Gustave could not resist answering with a real conversation.

"Lady Clark! Yes, you just spoke to my rude French voice mail. I think I should fire him considering he is proving to be quite incompetent and I can't afford paying him the going rate of voice 'male' services." At first, Gustave thought how clever of him to have this play on words and have the opportunity to bring sexual connotation to the conversation, but a second later, his slip of the tongue in his mind cost him the association of his not being able to afford something.

That would not go well if he wanted to impress

her, he thought. Gustave was very cautious with words, so it took him by surprise that he allowed himself using two words that were associated with lack of finances: "Can't afford" in a sentence that involved the word "I". He quickly planned damage control and continued. "He charges me twenty five thousand dollars a minute and he has done nothing but be rude to cute ladies." Unfortunately Gustave had no idea if there was any blushing on the other end of the line, but Leanne replied with a quick response of her own.

"Oh…at that price, can he do other type of male services?"

Gustave was delighted the original joke did not go straight through her beautifully shaped head. In addition, she had managed to reply with even more of a sexual allusion, which pleased him very much.

This was enough for him to stop his belligerence against helping such a delightful lady and he was open to help her with anything she might have requested of him. But did she know this was his game? Or was it her game in the first place?

"What can I help you with, my dear, and what do I get out of it?" Gustave spoke in a jovial tone, to mask in his mind he actually meant his suggestive words.

"My laptop is not working, could you take a look at it? I have to hand in a proposal by tomorrow and my printer just stopped working. . . Oh Gustave, I don't know what to do. Do you think you can fix it?" Leanne's voice was high pitched, and sounded desperate, the equivalent of her dropping to her knees and begging for help

At that moment, Gustave lost interest, and looking at his own computer again, he replied, "It doesn't turn on, Leanne, or is it just acting up?".

Leanne hesitated for a moment, and said, "It just won't work, Gustave, I've tried everything! Can I come over with it?"

Gustave was jubilant her machine's little malfunction was going to give him an opportunity to take a break from work, but more so because he would have some time to spend with this attractive woman. "I don't see why not, Leanne. Come over around five today and we'll get it fixed."

Leanne seemed quite happy Gustave agreed to help, since it offered her comfort that no matter what, she would have her presentation ready by tomorrow.

Leanne was quite fond of Gustave. He was funny, and very talented. To her, he was a charming and fascinating man. She often entertained the idea of their dating, but her mind quickly filled with other types of men. He did not seem to be that interested in her in the first place. However, there was something quite alluring in that notion.

Gustave was wearing the hint of a smile on his face. It was the sort of smile that was a leftover after a phone conversation of either being polite or entertained, but in particular a smile that lingered perhaps a few more seconds than it was supposed to, considering the person on the other line could not see his facial reaction..

It was finally time to get back to his computer and the report of the encryption. The results were not exactly what he had anticipated. There were millions of attempts to break it, but it was never penetrated. He knew there would be some close attempts, but this? Didn't he need to change, or modify anything? Was it that perfect? This result made Gustave question the process with which he tested his own system. Could he possibly be biased enough to test his system or does he have to do the unthinkable and outsource it somewhere else? He would have rather given his first born to a stranger than give away such valuable information. He decided there had to be something else wrong. It should have penetrated through the main shield, Gustave thought to himself. The main shield is just the first level of encryption; there are four more after that, and they are meant to protect, or at least allow enough time to monitor and alert the system. The report showed him possibilities: either the system led to kryptonite or it shows he wasted two weeks from the computer's lifespan on faulty testing.

Angry and puzzled, Gustave grabbed the pack of smokes next to his computer, drew one lethal cylinder from the box, and lit it nervously. It was, after all, the time to comply with the dreadful longing of his body for nicotine, but there was no other way to calm his mind from the results he just received in the report. There was some sort of clarity that came with the fulfillment of an addicted mind and body. This gave Gustave a comforting and an outside view he believed helped him solve many of his problems. It also set the stage for cheerful thoughts reminding him he would later on today get to hang out with an attractive woman, even though she was just interested in a solution to her own computer problems.

When he finished smoking, he made his way back to his computer room, and it was time for his post cigarette break breather; reading the technology blogs, scanning for news of the day. He read a few gadgets blogs, found out what his next purchases would be directed toward, and then it was time for his share of real news: scientific journals. Instead of reading many different journals that each mentioned different areas of the scientific community, he made a quick visit to a website called "scientific weekly". This website collected the best of the each week's submitted papers of scientific journals and simplified them, while giving the option to go to the original paper they are taken from. This was Gustave's gold mine-source for new information. The website looked just like a standard news website, but was constantly updated with intriguing information that really had him glued to his computer screens. In a way, he thought it was quite a nifty idea its creators had had: to take the best from long and somewhat hard to understand papers, make them easy to read, and showcase them to the people who don't have the time to go through hundreds of publications.

There was some news regarding new developments in cancer treatments which Gustave always found himself reading to justify his smoking habits. And a few other featured articles presenting new methodologies of software development. The one article that in particular caught his attention was concerning a new research about black holes and the processes of the Einstein model of space and time. The blog post was fairly biased, especially since it only reported the ideas behind the papers it represented, but there were not very many concepts with which Gustave was a bit uncomfortable . The post reported: ". . .with this new understanding of our universe it is quite possible some day we will be able to distort not only space but also time, and perhaps even pave our way to time traveling." Time travel? This was a concept that was always a nice sci-fi concept for entertainment purposes but was now being looked at as an actual possibility. That alone disturbed Gustave. Not because there are far too many paradoxes and scenarios that have been for many years portrayed in films and books, and not because the idea that we will get that far ahead in technological advancement or even not because he felt envious with that generation of time travelers that will get to experience such wild ideas. It was simply the concept of time travel itself.

Now that they were really considering it as science fact, perhaps, Gustave thought, it was time to dedicate further self-investigation. What is time? Gustave asked himself for the millionth time. This clearly had to be the starting point of his pondering. For example, if he understood what an ocean was, he had a better starting point of thinking how to construct vessels to navigate through it such as boats.

Time is something we often think of when something moves in succession. Gustave looked at his watch. This is time. This is what we defined as a second hand, an hour hand, months and years, nothing but a definition.

In a sudden feeling of eureka accompanied by a sudden scream in falsetto, Gustave realized something. The notion of time moving forward is unsound. It occurred to him that in fact, there is no such a thing as time; there is only the displacement of matter in space. Even though one could argue time is the repetition of matter's dislocation in space, and our definition dictated by the perpetual movement of heavenly objects, it only further confirms time is not moving forward.

"What a strange thought!" Gustave said aloud, blinking rapidly at the dust motes dancing in a sunbeam from the window. "Well, how can anyone possibly move forward or backward in time, when other than just a concept, time is merely just another side effect of the nature of humans to perceive everything through repetitions of patterns, or to put it more eloquently, cognitive pattern association."

With his very newfound conclusiveness which he believed rose to him in a graceful curve, Gustave continued his reasoning process with exuberant conviction. "Time travel as contingent as it just might be, agrees with the law of conservation of energy. If I were to go back in time, this time-space continuum would have lost my particles, but another one will gain them. This works out quite reasonably. . .". Gustave rose from his chair, as if he was about to lecture a class. "Everything then, must exist at all times. If we were to move time backward or forward, we must move the location of all the particles in space the way they were before, in the desired point of past. Forward, is just outrageous since we can't possibly predict where they are supposed to be. There is no time, and there is no time travel, unless we undertake a major job of reconstructing placement of particles in the sub-atomic level. We might as well beam people from one place to another with the same technology!"

Gustave always found himself with a desire to comment on blogs or online news online although he never did as he never wanted to be that guy that doesn't have better things to do, other than posting some obscure comments only other people that have too much time on their hands will read, which oddly enough, of which he was one. With a plethora of complacency he looked about him with charming enthusiasm and posted his argument as a comment at the bottom of the article, and left it to simmer. He wasn't too keen on the idea that he had to sign up and leave his email to do so, but he always kept his garbage email address which he used for anything but work or social proposes. It was time now to get back to the temporarily abandoned routine of his day.

CHAPTER 3

Two hours of continuous work seemed to crawl slower than new grass in the spring could grow: unbelievably tediously. Other than the whirring noise of the busily spinning fans of one of his computers, there were no distractions. All that remained to finish and tighten were modifications here and there, a few new drafts to be sent for the client's approval and then Gustave planned to take a short break. He bent his head over a pack of cigarettes and pulled one free with his teeth since his hands were occupied, one with holding the box and the other with locating the brushed aluminum lighter that was safe in his jacket pocket. He was in the habit of never putting the two in the same place, reasoning if he misplaced his cigarettes he still had a lighter, and vice versa. His denim jacket had a rather deep pocket, and after he had clamped the cigarette between his lips, he was still struggling with reaching for the damned lighter. It was then he remembered he had posted a comment, of which he was quite proud.

Gustave was very curious to see what other people thought of his comment. He knew his comment would probably be disapproved of by many. He had planned to check the comments after his cigarette break, but in the meantime, while he was outside, he envisioned all the possible scenarios in his head with the intended purpose of wasting less time in the event he had to defend his idea.

In less than five minutes, Gustave was back at his computer. As he sat down he typed the address to the blog and navigated to the post. Surely, there were a few people by now that had had the chance to read his comment and a few of them surely would have voiced their opinions regarding his comment. Some might have defended the theory of time travel, some must have mentioned how he was not capable of understanding this sort of physics, but Gustave was all prepared to respond with logic to these comments.

There were none. No comments that had mentioned his comment whatsoever. By the time he had posted his comment, a dozen more had posted their own. Most of them referred to some specific movies, all were clever comments, but no one had taken him seriously. There were two options here. He decided either he was simply not seeing the big picture, thus no one had made any effort to look into what he had said, or perhaps it was all too much for those jokesters to deal with. Disappointed, Gustave decided he would not waste any more of his time and made up his mind to continue with his day.

It was almost five and Leanne was due to arrive soon. Gustave had always kept his place as clean and organized as he could. In a way, he was addicted to cleanliness so that was of no worry to him. He did however habitually enjoy an elaborate shower, a nice set of washcloths ready and perhaps even a nice cologne, the after-scent of which would merge well with that of his English lavender soap.

He chose a pair of tailored gray silk trousers still in the dry-cleaner's bag and a satin-striped black dress shirt with mother-of-pearl buttons. Elegant and classy. He laid the slacks and shirt on his bed and stood back, double-checking the blend of subtle colors. Nodding in approval, he chose underwear and silk socks to match his shirt, and hurried into the shower. He knew Leanne was never very punctual, but he wanted to be certain by the time she arrived, he was ready to welcome her.

At five-twenty the doorbell rang. By this time Gustave, had already finished dressing even taking the time to buff his patent-leather loafers and as he buckled his alligator belt, he checked himself in the bathroom mirror. He swiped his comb and cupped hand a couple of times across his clean hair and nodded his approval of himself. After tossing his used towels in the bin, he hung fresh ones and squared the edges of the bath mat, then made some final adjustments to his work area. He made sure it looked as if he was working on something important that might make her consider him an interesting man to be with, someone with a future rather than a superfluous entity to be disdained as a mere tech support man or a handy shoulder to cry on.

Gustave always strained to impress others, including himself, and this was no different than any other time. Knowing Leanne had little mathematical expertise, he had drawn many equations on the board that made absolutely no sense. He had chosen several books and carefully laid them on the table and around the work area to look as if they were there for some relevant reason. The doorbell rang again, rather impatiently, and Gustave made one last survey of his apartment and hurried to the front hall, opening the door with a smile.

Leanne looked particularly stunning to Gustave, with the glow from the streetlight giving her an ombre halo befitting an angel. He had to struggle to keep from gasping with pleasure as he smiled at the charming creature staring at him from the other side of his Welcome-mat. She had on very little make-up and was wearing a simple but stylish brown dress that clung in the right places without being inappropriate and her hair was styled in a casual bouffant natural coif that served to emphasize her natural beauty.

"It's an absolute pleasure to see you, my dear!" Gustave held his arms outstretched, ready for a hug from his lovely guest. She stepped into the circle of his arms with no apparent artifice whatsoever. He could sense the warmth of her body in his embrace and the softness of her breasts against his chest and he closed his eyes briefly, not wanting the moment to end.

Leanne was as cheerful as anyone would have been who was soon to have a computer-problem solved and her hug was as genuinely friendly as any friend's hug would have been. But nothing more.

"Gustave, I`m so sorry, but you're the only one that can help me! Here, I brought you an offering!" She handed him a bottle of white wine.

"Darling, you really shouldn't have! It is my pleasure to help you in any way I can!" In Gustave`s mind, "in any way" meant something in the lines of, "In case you are bored and want some guy to have fun with." He continued, " You brought my favorite wine! We`ll have to drink it together one evening. . ."

Leanne was thrilled Gustave approved of her gift. He could tell that much. He wondered if it was because she was now even with him, or rather she was happy she got the right wine, and he then he had offered for them to get together again for something more friendly than a computer breakdown. He wasn't certain. But he had hope.

"What is that enchanting perfume you are wearing, my dear? " Gustave asked in an exaggerated British accent. "And your hair looks lovely, too, I might add. . .". Gustave always made a point of saying nice things to a lady, either about the way she was wearing her hair, or her choice of perfume, or her clothes. "If I didn't know better, I would think you went the extra mile grooming yourself especially for me, but then you always carry yourself in a delightful manner, no matter what."

"I did pamper myself a little more than usual, all for you, Gustave. . ." Leanne spoke in a mellifluous voice as she looked up at him through her eyelashes and smiled demurely. This was just another way for them to act as if they had some sexual tension, when in actuality Gustave considered their relationship one of common courtesy without a lot of promise of anything more.

After surrendering her computer to Gustave's waiting hands, Leanne preceded him as he led the way through the small entry hall into his office area at the back of the apartment. He carefully placed her machine on a nearby console and removed the cover, gesturing to the arm chair adjacent to his work station indicating the best place for her to sit. She smiled up at him gratefully and then stared at her computer.

"Let's get on with this business!" Leanne sighed and shrugged her shoulders, trying to appear helpless.

"I've heard you are unable to work on your proposal?" Gustave tried not to sound like an angry parent but he couldn't disguise all of his impatience.

Leanne was not ready to drop the cheerful banter. "And who might have told you that, sir?" She chuckled, noticing his faint blushing.

"Well, I received a call today from a dreadful old woman who could not stop herself from yelling and crying on the phone as she told me she knew of someone who told her someone in her city broke their computer. . .".

"I didn't break it, Gustave, it just stopped working! And I wasn't crying on the phone!"

Gustave had thought Leanne was still in a humorous frame of mind. He had replied with his fictionalized answer, which had backfired and had immediately evoked a cautious but hostile reaction from her which he certainly had not intended.

It was a recurring thing between them. He often said something that was a bit more revealing than he should have said, since sometimes he would be too mesmerized by her striking features to weigh his retorts carefully enough. While under the influence of her beauty he would often slip some unnecessary over-the-top humorous remarks into his repartee. Blood flow, he thought quite humorously, is all too important to carry oxygen to my brain, yet in the company of a beautiful woman, it does not necessarily make its way to that organ but to the other one, with which I tend to think. It was a feeble acquiescence of his faulty persona.

"I know, Leanne. I was really just playing with you. So, can I get you anything to drink or eat? There is a fine selection and a variety of food. I could also cook something special for you! . . .ah, for us!" Gustave thought it was the opportune moment to bring up the fact that he could cook, and quite well. That did not seem to make any impression on many of the girls he met, even though some tested his cooking and were quite taken by the quality in which he executed exotic dishes. None openly mentioned anything about how good a catch he must be, however Gustave thought it worth bringing up.

"Unfortunately, no, Gustave, I really have to get

this thing working and get prepared for the proposal, but if I may have a rain check on your offer, I would be very grateful…"

It could have been that or because he in a way irritated her, but she seemed ready to get down to business.

The computer had shown no symbols of a breakdown. It was in a good shape, even though some dust was apparent. It failed to boot, and after opening it and checking output voltages Gustave said, "Would you like my professional opinion?"

"Yes, please!" Leanne replied with anticipation.

"It's not working," Gustave said, while trying to stifle a laugh. The humour might have been too one-sided for it to strike her as funny so he continued. "It doesn't look as if the hard drive is malfunctioning, though give me a few moments and I'll transfer the presentation files to my laptop which you can use tomorrow and until I get yours fixed, okay?" Gustave was carefully observing her reaction.

Leanne was not as happy as she might have been if Gustave had fixed her computer on the spot, but she nodded rapidly, like a very happy little bird, clasping her slender hands together in barely disguised joy.

"Gustave, you are wonderful! I really appreciate your help!"

After about ten minutes, the files were transferred to one of Gustave's laptops and he showed her exactly how to manipulate the controls so she wouldn't be ill-at-ease using it. She couldn't stop smiling at him as she held the borrowed machine to her bosom as if it were a long lost child and chattered happily all the way to the front door . Gustave closed the door behind her retreating figure and was overwhelmed by the sudden silence in the hall. A faint trace of her lovely scent remained on the top of the air, which he concluded was "Le Aire du Temps", a French perfume he remembered from an elegant woman in front of him waiting in line at the art museum's last exhibit. He closed his eyes and for a moment, was lost in reverie, thinking of several different endings to his evening with Leanne.

He knew the next morning, Leanne would be on her way to work, with his contribution making her day more pleasant.

Gustave thought he had given enough of his time to what was probably a fantasy anyway. He sighed audibly and got back to work.

CHAPTER 4

As was his custom and his indomitable nature, Gustave had been totally preoccupied with his work on the computer with carefully thought out predictions and prognoses as well as possible negative results to the point he had absolutely no idea how much time had elapsed as he slouched in his chair and peered at the monitor. The glowing screen lent an eerie suffusion to the skin of his face and neck of which he was completely unaware. He blinked rapidly and nodded, a faint smile hiking up the corners of his lips as he hit the "Save As" link and closed the document on the screen and then closed the remaining open files. He allowed himself to read and retain the time of day inexorably changing every second in the lower right corner of his monitor screen and was shocked to see it was four o'clock in the morning. His predictable reaction to this actuality was to feel suddenly and overwhelmingly tired. Gustave was ready for sleep. A pop-up screen appeared on his computer monitor screen accompanied by a soothing sound. It was an Instant Message, an IM, from an unknown contact regarding the post he had left earlier that day. Gustave swiftly opened the

IM , unable to suppress his excited anticipation. He read the message aloud to himself, in the pre-dawn darkness.

"Dear Gustave,

Your post is quite remarkable.

I apologize for any inconvenience; however it is the right time for us to meet."

There was no signature and no postscript. Gustave's eyebrows arched over his narrowed eyes as his brain's synapses became strongly alert again. The first thing he noticed was the email had been sent to his personal email address, and not the one he had used for posting comments. He noted the sender`s email address was his own! The outgoing box confirmed the email had been sent from his own email provider, or ISP, or was the work of a talented hacker. The back of Gustave's neck became as hard as plywood. He rubbed it with his palm as he mulled over the possibilities. Either both he and his work were vulnerable, open for anyone to view, or he had somehow completely lost it and sent the email himself, to populate the space created by the lack of replies to his comment.

He accessed his router. He could see who had accessed his computer as it was the only link connecting his computer and the World Wide Web. There was no record of any suspicious incoming inquiry. His firewall was state of the art hardware and software tools that kept him sleeping better at night. He could not allow himself to be vulnerable. He knew exactly what to look for in case someone had hacked into his system, but he could not find anything to indicate there was any infiltration. Gustave clenched his jaw and made a fist, then he hit the desk as hard as he could. The blow caused more damage to his hand than to the reinforced thick glass tabletop. After he made certain he had not broken the table itself, he went outside for a smoke but not before making his way to the liquor cabinet. He poured three fingers of a fifteen-year-old single malt scotch into a glass and tossed it down in one gulp. He usually did not drink alcohol when he was facing troubles but this time he felt like it was necessary. He slammed the empty glass down on the bar top, refilled it, and zipped on his windbreaker.

It was a bit chilly outside, but Gustave's heart was racing as if he had just run a marathon. He inhaled a heavy dose of nicotine while breathing as deeply as he could. He felt a familiar sting at the back of his throat and exhaled. The subsequent puffs from the cigarette were as deep as the first one, although the sting was not as sharp as it had felt earlier. Each inhalation of smoke was accompanied by a sip from the Scotch he held in his other hand. It was a smooth Scotch and filled the vacuum of his belly. By the time he had smoked half the cigarette, he was calm again, or at least as composed as he could have been in his situation.

"The damn power cord!" he shouted. "They can access my computer through the power cord!" He raised his voice, even though he knew there was no one around to hear him. Gustave realized even though it was not an ordinary maneuver, he could access the internet by simply connecting to the electrical outlet. Electricity in one frequency range and data in another. He crushed his cigarette under the heel of his shoe and went back inside. He shut all his computers down and then washed his face and brushed his teeth. Gustave was only now starting to feel the effects of the alcohol since the adrenalin that was rushing earlier in his blood was now wearing off, but the alcohol was still flowing through his body. It was definitely quite suspicious, he thought, but he reasoned his talented hacker would undoubtedly contact him again. With that thought, he turned off his lamp, closed his eyes, and fell into a deep sleep.

CHAPTER 5

Gustave's comfortable apartment had one bedroom but it was large enough to accommodate the one luxury he allowed himself – that of a a queen-sized bed with a well-made mattress that induced deep slumber whenever he crawled into it. He was a restless sleeper and this oversized bed allowed him all the room he needed to "travel" from one end of it to the other and never miss a dream chapter in the process. He loved having a bed large enough to have all the tossing room he needed plus he also delighted in having a "hidden agenda" no one else even dreamed he entertained, which was the potential of having an absolutely perfect place to enjoy a sex life with someone, some day, in the not too distant future. His perfect bed was ideal for two adults to sleep close together or a little distance apart or in any one of a myriad of convoluted positions he liked to imagine in his mind's eye, in Technicolor and black and white, depending on how much dessert he had eaten before bed or how much Scotch he had swallowed.

There were four large windows in Gustave's bedroom, which made it look larger than it actually was, especially in the spring and summer when the orbit of the sun angled warm golden light through the sheers hanging beneath the heavy damask thermal drapes. The custom-made matching cut-velvet bedspread in rich colors of bronze, burgundy, teal, and navy blue was too heavy to remove every night so he simply turned it neatly back until the foot of the bed was anchored by a two-foot wide fold of luxurious fabric. He had ordered silk bedding in a pale shade of teal which felt so cool to his head he stopped feeling guilty after about a week. The electric blanket was navy blue and had been a gift from his mother which he very much appreciated. He had framed five prints - two by Monet and three by Georgia O'Keefe – all five of which echoed some of the richness of the colors displayed by the bedspread. Gustave fervently hoped one day some innocent, charming, ingénue would be consumed with admiration for his worldly knowledge when he revealed the secrets behind those paintings to her, perhaps in soft whispers.

Gustave's bedroom also had a large walk-in closet with one side practically empty of hanging clothes and two bedside tables, one on each side of the bed, each with its own lamp and neat stack of books, plus a French china clock on one and a small FM-AM radio on the other. The glossy hardwood floor had an imitation white bear rug on each side of the bed, which Gustave loved feeling with his bare feet, just before he climbed in for the night. It wasn't a spectacular bedroom but it was more than sufficient for the length of time he was likely to be spending in it during each revolution of the earth's orbit. Gustave was almost smug about there not being a television receiver anywhere near his elegant bed.

When Gustave awoke, the French clock indicated it was six in the morning. The room was as bright as if it were a midsummer's day in a greenhouse and Gustave remembered he had not closed the drapes all the way when he went to bed the night before. He sat up and reached for his glasses on top of the bedside table and put them on very slowly, knowing the light flooding the room was not natural. He could tell because of the shadow cast by the stack of books on the other bedside table. The light was a sharp glow, very white, almost as if it were a large LED light. In the middle of the blindingly white light, was a sphere that appeared to glow of its own accord with a bluish tinge.

For a moment, Gustave thought he must be dreaming then he dismissed that idea and realized he felt very weak and his right arm lowered itself to the bed under its own volition and seemed too heavy for his torso. He tried to lift his arm but couldn't. He tried his other arm but it was as motionless and frozen as his right hand. His entire body was immobilized. Was he dying? The inauspicious thought had occurred to him, and if so, he had no intention of letting nature take its course. Gustave had an almost super human strength for self-help although it occasionally seemed to be ostentatious, alienating others against him. However ironic, it did prove useful as in the past he had suffered from depression followed by anxieties and countless other mental bumps yet he always found a way to treat himself with a wholesome dosage of logic. He knew he could have consulted with a psychiatrist just as millions of others do, and he knew he could get rid of some of these anxieties by dosing himself with medications but he feared the side effects and more than anything, he was afraid of losing his mental acuity because of those mood-altering drugs.

Gustave's eyes were beginning to adjust to the brightness that haloed his bed. He was still unable to see much, but he knew he was still in his bedroom. With every possible muscle he had, Gustave struggled against his comatose state. The harder he tried fighting, the more resistance his body manifested. He suddenly became aware of approaching footsteps. Gustave gasped for air and noticed that not only was he able to control his breathing normally but his entire head was fully operational as well. The sound of the footsteps grew louder. He began breathing rapidly as sweat trickled down his face. His heartbeat was pulsating against his eardrums. He needed to fight this but there was nothing he could do. Just as his computer was hacked into a few hours earlier, his body was now as vulnerable as his computer had been. He had no choice but to lay in a vegetative state. Thoughts churning, he began wondering whether whoever was responsible for his current state also perpetrated the attack on his computers.

The glistering light was interrupted by a movement of shadows. From the veil of the bright light, the shadows emerged into more distinguishable figures. That is not to say that Gustave actually recognized these figures but they now looked like solid moving entities. As he kept fighting his state of paralysis he suddenly heard a soft voice.

"Please try not to fight the temporary paralysis; it is a procedure for our protection."

The shadows morphed into complete figures. They were short and thin with silky gray skin, and had enormous deep-set black eyes, tiny noses and an even smaller proportional mouth. Their digits were longer than those of human hands; they looked just like the aliens people have been describing in countless accounts throughout fifty or so years of alien abduction reports.

"Are you out of your damned mind? Release me, I will not harm you!" Gustave's voice cracked from his desperation to try and take control of his body. On top of it all, he was now angry. This, he thought, was a direct insult, to be taken like that, when they could have asked him nicely. At that very moment, he was released. It was as if a wall vanished in the same moment a man was trying to break through it. His muscles, which were still under his control, or so he thought, suddenly released his body into an awkward fetal position making him look like a demented dried fruit. The sudden movement frightened the fragile-looking aliens causing them to jump in dismay away from Gustave's bed.

"I apologize! I was still fighting your lock when you released me. . . Why can't you announce anything you do beforehand?" From his tone of voice, it was obvious even now, free from their paralyzing force, he was still impatient with their way of approaching things.

"Gustave, we were asked to escort you to a meeting. . . Pleeze?" Their voices made it more apparent now than before. It was soft, almost childlike in timbre but nothing of the quality of the synthesized voices he had heard before. It was almost perfect.

A silent moment passed and he said, "I will." The light surrounding his room dimmed. His pupils that by now had gotten used to it, dilated to accommodate the new light conditions. Gustave's anger subsided and he now began shivering out of the sheer terror he had experienced. It was still odd that he was not panicked…It was odder still that calmness began infusing his mental state and his shivering stopped.

Gustave took another look at the group of aliens. There were three of them, each carrying different ropy instruments. He was going to meet with more aliens. "Not that it really matters, but where are you from?" Gustave asked.

Another alien spoke. His voice was identical to that of the other, and the only way for Gustave to know it was another alien speaking was the location from which the sound came. "We originate from this galaxy, the Milky Way, twenty-six thousand and thirty seven light years away from the center."

"So, you must have had more time to have evolved than we have had, and your suns in these areas are older than mine," Gustave said in an informative tone.

"That is correct, Gustave." Even at his state, Gustave felt it was necessary to impress these beings, otherwise he was afraid they would view him as a simpleton and handle him as one.

"Let's do this," Gustave said.

The aliens grouped into a tighter formation, and signaled with their hands toward the east window of Gustave's bedroom. The room filled again with a bright light.

Gustave approached the window and with a wry smile said, "So there aren't any doors on your planet?" The alien started speaking, but suddenly Gustave could not hear anything. He then realized he was being pulled upward, only the feeling was not of being pulled really, it was as if he had stepped into an elevator, only the elevator pulled his entire body from the top instead lifting him from beneath his feet. It was as if gravity was reversed. He experienced a slow fall, against earth's gravity. The inauspicious feeling resembled hanging upside down from a tree, where it feels as if the blood rushes to his head, only he was perfectly right side up.

What was above him now must have been an opening in the alien craft door, lit with a blinding light that emanated from inside the giant spaceship. The craft itself was colossal in proportions, comfortably larger than a few jumbo jets combined. The craft generated no sound while it was suspended in midair as if it was mysteriously and invisibly attached to the earth`s crust. Gustave wondered if it had something to do with the effect of manipulating the gravity around him, or perhaps the technology on which the craft manipulated space to accommodate its propulsion.

Gustave looked down, and he could see his neighborhood. It looked much smaller than he had expected, and while he looked back up he understood he had originally misjudged the size of the craft. It was much larger than he had thought. He looked back down and this time he became nauseated. It was strange enough being lifted in midair by a mysterious force, stranger was the feeling his body felt, which he could not fully describe, but this time, when he looked down to the shrinking buildings, houses and shopping areas it felt as if he was looking up to the stars. He quickly looked back up, and focused to gain his balance in the disconcerting vertigo.

CHAPTER 6

As usual when this occurred, Gustave found himself in the middle of a large bright room. He was aware his apartment walls and floor where he had stood only seconds before had vanished. He felt light-headed but strangely euphoric. The light glowing all around him was generated from within the walls and ceiling of the interior of the spaceship or whatever it was where he found himself. With sheer curiosity and interest, Gustave took a closer look at the walls of the strange enclosure to satisfy his fascination with these alien surroundings. He fought down the strong desire to scream for help, telling himself everything he saw here he had to absorb fully and remember, because one day, all the millions of details these aliens must have taken for granted would undoubtedly help him develop new technologies. He then asked himself if he thought he would in fact ever get out alive from this place let alone create new ideas and again, he had to fight down the urge to scream for help or at least, demand to be returned to his home and the relative sanity he remembered having there. Curiosity quickly overtook this feeling, however, and he reasoned the simple fact that he was still alive made it worth waiting to see what would transpire and how much he could learn from this experience – or imaginative fantasy hallucination, a type of mental "trip" - if indeed that was what this turned out to be. He had always been able to rely on his analytical, logical appraisals of enigmas, and concentrating on that reliable memory, his fear and basic survival reactions subsided.

He leaned to his right and touched the nearest glowing wall, which, like the others, was metallic to the touch and throbbed gently as if from a distant power source. He couldn't really explain it to himself, even as he experienced it. The curving walls functioned as if they were continuous blocks of LED lights although the texture and contour of the material told a completely different story. The nearly featureless room had a few round chambers but there were no apparent electronics, or control panels of any sort. There were no doors either. The room looked as if it was made with one solid glowing metal from which the shape of its inner space was carved.

Suddenly, an alien's voice reverberated in the area where Gustave stood, waiting. "Welcome to our command module, Gustave; we understand you must be anxious to learn why you are here. Pleaase, come with us; we must first go through decontamination."

Gustave turned toward the aliens and could now see them very clearly thanks to the continuous light emitted evenly throughout the room. The aliens wore no space suits; in fact, it looked as if they wore nothing at all. Either that or their clothing had fused to their bodies in a similar way in which the walls were constructed – framing, sheetrock, plaster, paint, all combined in one luminous material – and their bodies were apparently the same: bone, organs, life fluids, and luminous pliable skin-like material. Their bodies also seemed to lack sex organs. This seemed a bit strange, since they could not be all that different from humans.

"Decontamination is standard procedure, because you might carry with you some parasites or bacteria which the crew would like to avoid." All the aliens pointed in unison toward one of the empty walls.

"Diseases are best avoided, not fought," Gustave said, in a reaffirming tone, as he began walking toward the wall the aliens were indicating. As he approached the wall, it noiselessly opened to reveal a corridor. The parting in the wall was unlike anything he had ever seen before. He was completely speechless as he pondered the mysterious and bewildering impossibility. The opening in the wall resembled a sliding door, only the doors disappeared into the material the wall was made of and while doing so, emitted a hissing, high-pitched sound, as if a billion infinitesimal mechanical particles were working together at the same time. The aliens led the way into a smaller room.

"Gustave, you will need to take all of your clothes off. The solution we will wash you with is programmed to handle living organisms and your clothes will be washed with a different one, programmed to handle fabrics." One of the aliens gestured toward what appeared to be a type of laundry bin that had jutted itself out of the wall, with a hinged lid that opened, awaiting soiled clothing.

Gustave massaged his throat and brushed his fingertips across the stubble on his unshaved cheeks. "These solutions, are they based on some sort of nanon-ites? Is that what you mean by programmed?"

"Yes, we have a few general purpose nanonites with many different uses. Sometimes to save time, we hard wire them ahead of time instead of letting them collect-ively decide what task they need to do."

The alien who had performed as the spokesman and main guide for Gustave, walked to a corner of the room and joined the other two who were patiently waiting for him. Immediately, the wall shaped itself into a tube, the inside of which inverted in upon itself and formed smaller tubes within. A few moments passed and a flow of gray transparent liquid sprayed the aliens. The liquid seemed to stick to their bodies for a few moments then rushed itself downward into what seemed to be a hole in the ground, which opened up milliseconds after the strange liquid descended from their bodies. The liquid and all working parts of the ship communicated with each other in perfect harmony.

Gustave watched the process with awe and spoke almost in a whisper. "So, everything, including these walls, is made from these general purpose nanobots. From what I understand, the nanobots are able to rebuild themselves depending on the job they are required to do? Each nanonite communicates with another and positions itself to create a nano-mechanism or even a larger structure through clustered swarm intelligence?"

"Yes, Gustave, that is correct." The aliens spoke in unison. "Please, take off your clothes and step into the other corner." The alien pointed in the direction where he wanted Gustave to go.

Gustave took off his clothes and while doing so, he muttered to himself, "Mechanical stem cells!"

Oddly enough he was not self-conscious at all. The equivalent of taking his clothes off in front of these non-humans was like taking off one's clothes in front of a pet, yet with their high level of intellect, he surmised they must have felt sensitive toward him.

One of the aliens' slender hands stretched out to grab his clothes. Gustave realized this was the first time they had made almost a touching contact. The alien smiled reassuringly when he placed the clothes into the waiting depository, which closed itself and then vanished into the floor.

Gustave's heart rate seemed to triple when he realized the floor beneath his feet had changed shape and was continuing to do so as he watched. The pastel colors were mesmerizing and duplicated the most magnificent sunsets he had ever seen, for real and in prize-winning photographs.. Within seconds, the undulating morphing liquid forming the walls and tubes of all sizes began to leak from the walls onto his skin. It felt warm and soothing and even though Gustave knew it wasn't alive, he felt like it had worked its way under his skin and he was uneasy. At the same instant he felt uncomfortable, the liquid drained off his body and disappeared into the end of a waiting tube near his feet, then the tube itself disappeared as well. An alien appeared, holding out Gustave's clean clothes, all folded neatly and looking like new. There was a faint odor of ozone which Gustave did not feel was unpleasant at all.

Gustave took the clothes from the alien and smiled. "I certainly feel cleaner than I've ever been, that's for sure!" He pulled up his pajama bottoms and buttoned up his pajama shirt, smoothing it down with his hands. "Okay, I'm ready! Where do we go now?"

The alien said, "You are now ready for the meeting, Gustave. Come, follow us. . .we will take you to the one in charge."

CHAPTER 7

As Gustave and the three aliens approached the wall of the spaceship, it unzipped itself revealing a long corridor. Gustave noticed the walls of the corridor were beginning to change their transparency and it was then when the realization he was actually in an alien craft really hit him for the first time.

Through the metallic-appearing, glowing transparent material, Gustave intuited the full magnitude of the construction abilities of these sapient beings. He was aware of hundreds of aliens running to and fro with the help of countless gravitational lifts that ran both vertically and horizontally. On the lower level of the giant structure lay dozens of what seemed to have been flying saucer ships. Some of the crafts looked just like the ones that had been reported by numerous "crazy" people. Gustave laughed nervously. After a short walk, they came to what seemed to resemble an elevator. Gustave followed them onto to the platform and it began moving. The elevator was a marvel in its own right. Just like the gravitational lifts he had observed earlier, the elevator moved freely in the open space of the craft. Although Gustave enjoyed it, the speed with which the elevator and the other flying objects outside the elevator moved was a bit too fast for what he considered safe or comfortable. In a matter of seconds the platform stopped.

"Please walk toward the end of this corridor, the one who is in charge is awaiting you in his room. The door will open."

Immediately an opening occurred in the craft's wall and the elevator flew upward, away from its locked position the moment Gustave stepped off into the corridor. The thought of him going alone into this unfamiliar place was a bit disconcerting yet he knew he had no choice and he approached the opening in the wall. There was nothing else he could have done, and aside from that, his curiosity was stronger than before. He decided a cooperative attitude would be more useful to him than fear but he couldn't help being warily on guard as he neared the room at the end of the corridor.

The room décor was more shocking than Gustave could have ever imagined. Any evidence indicating the room was of alien origin was scarce. Along the right side of the room, there was a long conference table, comfortable executive chairs, and a few other items such as works of art from the early European nineteen century, a few objects that bespoke of the Byzantine period and a few others from Egyptian and Greek origin. Gustave recognized these objects inasmuch as he possessed a lifelong appreciation of the history and early civilizations of earth as apparently did this alien race. Gustave approached an Egyptian artifact. He recognized the artifact to be of Egyptian origin by the vivid colors used to decorate it and the careful yet precise technique with which the mason had used to carve it. Unable to resist the temptation, Gustave touched the statue very lightly, feeling its shape and glossy finish. The statue echoed the shape and form of the stone from which it was carved.

"From Neithhotep." The deep voice startled Gustave. He winced and a spasm caused him to open his hands almost dropping the ancient artifact. Gustave turned toward the voice.

"She was a friend to us, and a wife to Narmer, a pharaoh from the thirty-first dynasty BC. . . I have more collectibles from the Kefchu, which your historians call Minoan and also from Carthage. Quite the collection, wouldn't you agree?"

Gustave was expecting an alien but before him stood a human. The man wore a comfortable-looking suit. The suit changed colors frequently which seemed to blend with whatever object stood behind him. It was soothing to look at.

"I assume you are taking a less threatening shape for fear you might frighten me?" Gustave felt uneasy since it was the first question he had asked a representative of an alien race.

The alien laughed. Gustave quickly added, "I mean, I would like to give you the honor of presenting yourself in your regular form instead of needing to be masked for my personal well-being. . ."

"We are what you are looking at Gustave. Humanoids. We are from a different planet, far away by your standards of travel, but we look the same, and even used to share much of our DNA. . . Are you familiar with convergent evolution?"

"Yes, sorry, I didn't get your name?" Gustave moved closer to the man and smiled in a friendly manner.

"Where are my manners? It is Kta." The man reached out to shake Gustave's hand vigorously.

Kta's skin was soft. Gustave thought it was softer than the skin of a young teenaged girl who had never seen a work day in her life. He was unprepared for something so delicate, and he quickly loosened the firm grip with which he held the alien's hand. "This must be when two unrelated species evolve similar traits due to the physical constraints imposed upon them during evolution. But it can't possibly be that close!"

"I'm sorry, Gustave, but that's the best we've got. We tried for many years to understand this ourselves. There are many other planetary species that are different from us but we ended up very close to each other by chance."

"Did you know the accepted idea of aliens on earth is that appearance of your robots?"

Kta opened his mouth and for the first time looked surprised. "You still manage to fascinate me, Gustave! What confidence and trust you invest in your logical thought patterns!"

Gustave smiled for a moment; after all, he enjoyed being complimented. "It wasn't too hard to notice really, they moved like characters in our computer generated imagery, speak with a well-synthesized voice, and more than anything, were too humanoid to be lacking sexual organs in between their strongest organs. I guess you could say that pretty much told me what I wanted to know."

"Indeed, Gustave, you do understand convergent evolution."

"I guess you can say the idea is not so alien to me!" They both laughed.

Kta gestured toward the table and smiled. "Would you like something to drink? Water perhaps?"

Gustave was very thirsty. This whole experience was quite overwhelming, and it wasn't until now that he realized his mouth was very dry. "Yes, please."

As Kta's hand neared the table, two glasses sculpted themselves out of the table itself. The table did look as if was made of wood at first; however it seemed to be nothing but an illusion. A door opened, and an alien robot approached with a container. "We use them for pretty much everything, from repairing instruments, to doing some of our daily chores. You see, we started building them about five hundred years ago. And they were very useful to us when dealing with humans. We tend to avoid risking our lives at all costs. And these are pretty cheap to make. They are biological robots and very energy efficient, much stronger than you and I and built for various tasks."

Gustave was intrigued. Kta's race had managed to engineer its very own species. What were the implications to such creation? Do they have rights? Would they ever rebel? All this fascinated Gustave and he was eager to learn more.

Gustave approached the biobot that held the water container. Knowing that he was in the company of its creator so to speak, he felt like it would be safe if he examined the being up close.

With some hesitation Gustave asked, "May I examine it?"

"By all means, please do," Kta said while taking the water container from the robot. Gustave touched the robot in its joints, moved the robot's hands while trying to figure out how the thing was built.

"Kta, considering these are biological beings, do they have rights like you and your kind? Aren't you worried some of them will develop emotions by mistake, or rebel against the control? How intelligent are they?"

Kta didn't seem to mind the amount of questions Gustave was throwing at him. "Oh, they are very smart. But they cannot in any way rebel, or develop what you categorize as emotions. They go through thorough examinations before they leave the plant, and we developed a series of self-regulatory mechanisms to make sure they are safe for us. But I understand your worry. We had to go through hundreds of years of development and tests before they were accepted as an integral part of our society. And of course there were a lot of attacks from social rights organizations of the galactic union, until we authorized certain treaties to make everyone happy."

Gustave drew back from the robot. He reached for the glass of water. The water was a perfect drinking temperature, and as he drank it he felt like the water helped him swallow all the information that was coming to him, so rapidly.

"I suppose you would like to see our planet, Gustave?"

"Of course I would! You don't mean we…",

"Oh no, Gustave, I'll show you a reproduction. We can't travel to another planet right now."

"How do you travel to your planet so far away?" Gustave heard himself ask the preposterous question as if it was a common one proposed in a Monday morning office budget meeting. He continued. "You wouldn't be bending space using dark matter while encapsulating your ship in a space bubble, would you?"

Kta moved his head backward, silently repeating the words Gustave had just said with a slight smile. "Humans are getting closer. What humans refer to as dark energy, dark matter, and antimatter is something we know quite a bit about; there are much more complex elements working in the universe, and we used to call them with names such as dark or elusive energy as well until we figured it out a few hundred years after they were first imagined. Just as humans found out the universe bounced back in faster than the speed of light, we understood there was a way to move faster than light, and after that, it was only a matter of fine tuning to reach and control that force."

Gustave was now more intrigued than ever, and focused his thoughts preparing himself to ask the right questions. "By tuning to the force, do you mean like tuning to a vibration of a string?"

Kta paused for a moment and squinted as he slowly placed the cup of water on the table. "Not exactly, we entangle…" He paused for a moment and continued, "Please understand that I'd rather not say much more about our methods of transportation right now. . . Come, and let me show you my home planet!" He turned his head and as he did so, the air between Gustave and Kta filled with grey particles that merged with each other. Kta seemed to know exactly what Gustave was aiming toward, and it was equally apparent he couldn't work up the conviction to tell him more details.

The particles were now taking shape, and formed a solar system. "Our sun is about twice the size of Sol. We have eighteen different planets in our solar system, two of them are habitable. This is 'Gannedon' and the other planet is called 'Gennom'."

Gustave got up close to the planets. Impossible as it may have seemed, both planets were rotating in orbit at an equal distance from their sun which seemed farther than earth's orbit to Sol. He had never seen any model of a solar system that had two planets which stood equally in orbit to their star and remained stationary to each other. The two planets were not too distant from each other as well, of course, in astronomical proportions. Gustave was deeply focused looking at the planets and he didn't notice he was blocking the orbit of an enormous gas giant that now stopped its motion while keeping distance from him.

"The planet you are blocking is "Haa'm" Kta said, with a cheerful tone.

Gustave looked to his left and the giant planet was hovering not too far from his left cheek. He moved. The planet moved to adjust to the position it was supposed to be in accordance to the position of the other planets. "Is there intelligent life on that other planet?"

"Intelligent? Yes in some ways, the planet is abundant with big animals as we discovered when our first missions probed its atmosphere. Vicious animals, as we later learned in our manned missions. You see, our planet used to have large animals just like the dinosaurs on earth and on Gennom, and just like on earth they shared a mass extinction by a large meteor. Gennom was lucky, to some extent."

Gustave understood how it worked. The dinosaurs ruled the earth much longer than humans. And with the millions of years they had to evolve they did not developed into highly intelligent animals, since nature took its course differently and they evolved into bigger, meaner animals instead of smarter ones.

Kta continued. "We have a moon as well, but we were far more fascinated without neighboring planets, so it actually took us longer than humans to send a man into space, or put one on our moon."

Gustave laughed for a moment, and asked, "I assume that on your planet you didn't have a hard time proving the validity of evolution, or the existence of dinosaurs like we had on earth?"

"You would be surprised. Our historians believe we had religions as well, and they were as creative as your people in their foolishness. From our first direct contacts with humans, some say we did too much damage in perpetuating your religions."

Gustave had always thought about the mystery that religion was. There were too many books and movies that showed the relationship with aliens serving as god-figures to the ancient civilizations so he was not at all too surprised. He then replied, "I think we would have developed religion and gods whether you guys visited us or not. It's just a primitive means by which one can explain the inexplicable or just a powerhouse for the generation of wealth and power."

"I couldn't agree with you more Gustave, but we were actually punished for being responsible for the simple things such as the name Ganneden, which your Hebrews turned into Garden of Eden, or 'Heaven' in Christianity. We only tried to explain to them where we were from. There was a period of a few hundred years we were not allowed to visit or make contact." Kta was obviously passionate about the subject matter. It seemed as if there was a lot more to his frustration than he revealed.

"Who wouldn't allow for that?"

"The Galactic Union, you see, we were fascinated with humans all along. Although many of the other species are humanoids, they are not as nearly as genetically close a species to you as we are. It is still a mystery that remains unsolved, that is why earth was and still is an attraction to my kind."

Gustave's thoughts sprawled in his head. Just a few moments earlier, Kta had told him they were very similar in appearance due to convergence evolution, which made sense to some degree. Now, it seemed as if not only he, a mere human, was surprised by the similarities but also Kta's people were as bewildered as he was when the two species first met. Gustave asked in a soft voice, "Kta, may I sit?"

"By all means please do," Kta replied as Gustave made his way to the table.

The model of the planets fragmented in the air at the moment Kta made his way toward one of the chairs. Gustave noticed the disintegration of the planets as they were taken apart by what seemed to look like swarm of bees. He knew this technology was part of the same one being used in the door and walls and that the particles were the same as the ones that generated the shower modules. He was still quite impressed that the nano particles could also fly or hover in the air, but just *how* they did so was nothing Gustave could have wrapped his mind around.

The two sat down, each on the opposite ends of the table. The chair was much more comfortable than Gustave had expected it to be. The surface looked hard, but when Gustave's buttocks touched the material, the surface softened under his weight and it changed shape. "Kta, why am I here? What did you choose me for?"

Kta stood up almost as soon as he sat down. "I suppose I should tell you sooner than later; I brought you here to request something from you. You don't have to agree, and it is only natural you will have mixed feelings about it, but if you do agree to help, I will not be forced to reassert my prerogative."

Gustave was quite puzzled. What could he possibly be able to provide to this alien that he may not already possess? They had spaceships that ran on mysterious energy that has to do something with the string theory. Furthermore, they have self-assembling nano-robotic particles that can group themselves into any form, shape, or functionality. What is it that an earthman like himself could possibly provide this alien?

CHAPTER 8

Gustave raised his eyebrows and looked wistfully pleading, the same way a puppy would look at his owner if it had messed on the carpet.

"Kta, I assume you are not going to tell me to go on a mission to speak to my world telling them about how we need to be in touch with our inner power of love while trying to sell crystals at some new-age convention. How could I possibly be of any use?"

"No, I need you to steal something for me." Kta's expression was grave and he stared deeply into Gustave's eyes.

Gustave's eyebrows turned into a frown. "Steal? I'm not much of a thief, Kta. I imagine you must have a need for some field technology anyway, so why not send one of your biobots? What is it I'm supposed to be stealing?" Gustave spoke in a brusque manner.

Kta sat down, breathed deeply, exhaled through his nose, and said, "I can't do that ,Gustave. They will know, you see, they will be able to tell. And that is just the security. The thing I want you to steal was neither made by humans nor was it made by us. It was constructed by another alien race. They have a top secret facility where they develop advance technologies."

"Why would an alien race have a concealed facility on earth, of all places?"

"Two reasons: mainly, the location was convenient for them as there is a hub of resonator relays a few light years outside your system. The second reason is even simpler. After the Prometheus treaty, named after a story in your Greek mythology, the Union had decided no race in the galactic union was to share technology with the humans. The last place anyone would look is Earth."

"Makes sense, actually. . ." Gustave scratched his nose nervously. This whole segregation of the Union from other species was really not making much sense to him. He then reminded himself with the same thing people thought about on Earth. Some groups were trying to preserve a primitive tribe living in the Brazilian Amazon forest, far from the "madness," as they called it, of the new world. What good would that serve? Gustave thought it would be a crime to deny these people the free will to choose for their own good, but especially to deny them modern technology and medicine and for what purpose? To preserve their ways of living? This was excessive tree hugging. Humans did not get lucky to have developed such a brain to keep it away from exploration and development. Gustave always thought to deny a man of research and development was as unjust as to lock a bird in a confining cage. Both were limited to an environment built to control or suppress them.

"Why would they not share the technology with us? If we are as intelligent but not as lucky as some of the other races, why not make us creative partners?" Gustave's temper pushed his voice to a crescendo until it almost sounded as if he were shouting at Kta.

"I'm not with them on that matter." Kta's voice was controlled and calm. "There are others . . .there are others who don't share this notion with them. But the Union thinks you are still too violent for your own good, and for the good of the galactic Union. We are, after all much more mature as a species than humans. Given, we had our share of bloody conflicts in our histories but we survived them. It was so long ago our present civilizations know nothing of it other than to study what records we have from our own ancient history. The thought that at one point they were as violent as humans are, is as remote to them as you would compare yourself to a cave man. You are as intelligent as the men from the late Pleistocene period, give or take thousands of years of selective breeding, but I'll bet you would have a most difficult time introducing one to your modern civilization."

Gustave was not too eager to agree with Kta. A cave man would have a hard time understanding technology, and no technology existed in his time. Humans however, understood the nature of technology and were very well accustomed to its true nature of change over time. Gustave questioned how advanced Kta's race was for him to justify the crude comparison of a cave man. To avoid further conflict with Kta he quickly changed the direction of the conversation to a more pressing question. "What is the device you want me to steal? How will I do that? What..."

Kta had to interrupt Gustave. It was a way to avoid telling him what it was he needed to steal, but more so, he saw the human was beginning to lose his enthusiasm. "I apologize for interrupting, Gustave. . . please allow me to tell you what I can do for you should you help me."

Gustave knet there must be an exchange for services, as universal notion of exchange must co-exist throughout the universe, especially if there are unions which must have been initiated through trade of some sort. It all looked quite suspicious, he thought. Yet just as he expected something in return from most of the people he used to help throughout his life, the notion an advanced alien race would be in his debt almost tingled his spine. He was all ears.

"I represent a group that wanted to become strong allies alongside humans. We want to share some of our technology, and in time, all of it. We are surprisingly almost identical species except for the modified genes we changed ourselves. With our transportation, we have managed to visit most of the accessible universe. There are thousands upon thousands of intelligent species, and of all, we found you, an improbable and exact match. I can't tell you at what cost our civilization became non-violent pacifists but what I can say is that our numbers are low. My group would like to become more than what it is today. We are a considerably minute group of people, but we are like you humans. Just like you, we are held back by the Galactic Union." Kta reached to the water container and began twisting and reshaping it into different shapes. He was careful enough to conceal such information from a lot of people with whom he was acquainted. But sharing this information so openly, let alone with a human, made him a bit nervous. He continued, "The matter with which I am tasking you is something we have been perusing with far more eager ambition - and hope - than we would like to admit."

Gustave saw traits of himself in Kta. There stood a man who wanted more than he can get; a man who was oppressed, and wanted to leap forward for the betterment of his specie. "I am prepared to make you an ambassador of some sort; an ambassador to inject some of our technology in moderate periods into your own. We have to do it in a clandestine way, Gustave, it is of outmost importance we do so or our plan will not work. It could hardly be otherwise. I chose you because you were both the right candidate to introduce these technologies to your world, but also your talents will make it more likely for you to succeed with the theft. I can't tell you what it is you will be stealing as of yet. In time we will have to teach you how to understand what it is you are stealing. But we have agreed you will be able to infiltrate into the facility undetected and retrieve the device."

"And I, in turn, will get access to your technology?" Gustave asked with a dubious tone.

"Yes, Gustave, I can give you access to it all; in the right time, not all of it will be shared in your life time, or the lifetimes of your future generations, but you will be credited for most of it. Of that I'm certain. I am aware it is a hard decision you have to make, and I can give you a few months to think about it."

"There will be no need…I have your answer. I'll do it, but I would require some advance installments as an act of faith," Gustave said while reassuring to himself it was not a whimsical reply, and it was surely not obsequiousness that drove him to make such a request.

"I don't see why that should be any problem." Kta replied, beaming with enthusiasm.

CHAPTER 9

Kta walked slowly toward the room he usually assigned for general meetings with the crew. He couldn't help but feel complacent after his successful meeting with the human. He was also quite satisfied he was not disdainful or superior in their conversation, considering it took a conscious effort on his part. Most of his crew would not dare stand close to a savage and untamed specie such as a human, let alone conduct a meaningful conversation with one. It took a lot of fearless courage and confidence for him or other members of the union to involve themselves in interaction with a human.

Kta was born into a family of elite diplomatic standing. It was expected of him to carry on his family's name and represent the Angelonians at the gatherings in the Union's Agora, a massive artificial structure that served as the political and financial center of the Galactic Union.

Kta attended a school where he had been groomed for a successful political and financial career from a very young age. He was not affected under the hubris of his family title nor was he obliged to the school into which he was accepted. Instead he spent most of his time alone gazing absentmindedly at the path he was expected to take. It wasn't until further along in his education when he had the chance to be mentored under an Angelonian-Human expert, a swarthy Angelonian with hundreds of years of experience interacting with humans, that he began to take seriously his dutiful "calling." Alpha-Teacher Moor Sriclu was well respected in his field. His political skills, or lack thereof, brought his career to an abrupt slump after he tried to demonstrate his points against the Prometheus treaty in an act he thought to be mild innuendo, but the humans knew it as the explosion in Siberia's remote Tunguska region in the Earth year 1908. His demonstration was terminated by the Union's Intelligence keepers well before he could start his display. After that act, he was relieved of his field status, and was granted a teaching position in the Angelolian School for Political Infrastructure where he met the ambitious young student named Kta Virtues.

Kta showed a fascination toward the humans and Moor provided him with an abundance of detailed information about documented close encounters. Moor's political views naturally appealed to Kta's as Moor sought rebellion to the Union leaning strongly in favor of bonding with the humans. This is when Kta was brought into a secretive group structured around such volatile and dangerous ideas.

Making a strong connection with the separatist underground group that shared his ideas, Kta soon became a principal man as he showed a natural talent for diplomatic leadership. Kta's connection to both the elite society of the Union and the underground movement proved to be very useful for his secret double allegiance.

Awaiting the arrival of Kta were three of his trusted advisors. Milka Barzi, Kta's tactical officer, greeted him. A soft-spoken woman with a vast knowledge of ancient Angelonian military records, Milka's position, including her power and privileges, was a rank that had descended directly from ancient records. A practical knowledge of warfare had all but been forgotten through the course of history. Before assembling the team for the mission, the members in charge knew they might not have to use such knowledge and that the idea to introduce military tactics was revolutionary when compared to the previous missions conducted by the separatists but the risk of not having a tactical officer to a mission of such importance was unfathomable. To Milka's right stood Bor H'end, the Navigation Compiler and Nell Gurbo, Gustave's personal choice as a technology officer.

Where Kta's and Milka's positions were mostly strategic and political coinciding with the big plan, Bor's position along with Nell's were the backbone of its execution. Bor was a sharp shooter when it came to conducting a conversation, which was a necessary quality a Navigation Compiler must possess. He always spoke his mind and often was it crucial to take his arguments with the most serious consideration. He was a pilot of sorts. Although not operating flying machines as human pilots did, but the similarity of the sheer intelligence, lightning-quick thinking, and implementation of operating complex computers was uncanny. Operating and planning the ship's drive link to the resonator hubs, Navigation Compilers had to maintain a constant balance between consuming concentration and multitasking as their navigation machinery was operated by both hands simultaneously and they mentally connected wirelessly to it all through their brains'_neurotransmitters. Although much of the calculation was done through processors that translated the Navigation Compiler's thoughts into meaningful variables in order to calculate a spatial link, there was much logic and analytical reasoning required to achieve these thoughts.

Nell, on the other hand, was responsible for making sure everything on the ship worked as it should. She possessed a general knowledge of all technology on board, but most importantly understood Nanonites at a superior level. This allowed her to instruct them how to do anything they were required to do. Nell also majored in regenerative care, and although there were enough tools on the ship to provide care to the crew and the Biobots, her skill proved to be very handy. Nell's skills were only matched by her beauty. An intelligent and beautiful Angelonian woman with a strong-minded presence, Nell caught Kta's attention from the moment he saw her. She also shared with Kta the same ideas about humans, although solely for the sake of her specie. Actually, she was quite terrified by them. As a young girl, Nell stayed home when there were school trips to observe earth and their academy's spaceship floated unobserved and silent above human cities. She did, however, make a point to study humans just to overcome her human-phobia and somewhere along the lines, she became as fascinated as Kta was with the species that could give her people a more comprehensive understanding of original genomes prior to the genomic revolution of her kind. Or, perhaps was it fascination towards the childhood myths on the Human- Angelonian origins? If so, she would have never admitted to being smitten by these childish bedtime stories.

"How can you be sure it will work, Kta? He seems to me a bit. . . strange." Bor had a pensive frown on his face.

Kta sat down on a nearby chair and said, "We are not used to them, Bor, but it was both Moor's recommendation and my own observation to conclude he is the best candidate for a human Delegator. . ."

"You must know while he was speaking to you, calm as he may have seemed, his mind was busier planning a violent escape regardless of the remote neuro-sedatives. I monitored his brain activity from the moment we made first contact with him and noticed something strange indeed. Bor, his mind operates in the same manner of a junior navigation compiler." Nell's tone of voice was overtly skeptical.

"Impossible!" Bor snarled in anger. His tolerance for ambiguity was very low, as expected of a Navigator.

"Yes, I know, but I double-checked and double-tested it! Does it not seem bizarre to you, Kta?" Nell replied calmly, in contrast to Bor's temperamental outrage.

Struggling to find a suitable reply while trying to avoid undermining Nell's findings, Kta responded very softly, after clearing his throat. "Yes, it does seem very strange. . .but don't worry. I am aware of this anomaly. It will be taken care of."

CHAPTER 10

It was almost instantly later in the afternoon and Gustave found himself back in his own house. He did not turn his computers on and neither did he pick up any of the phone calls that kept interrupting his train of thought throughout the day. His mind was racing with nervousness. Could he tell any of his friends or family what had happened to him? Was he certain it was real or had he been imagining things? Although Kta had been quite specific about keeping things completely confidential, he knew he could entrust a few people with his experience. He was not sure whether or not he was being monitored by Kta, so he decided it would be for the best to keep his mouth shut. Besides if he told anyone, it was almost certain they would think he had finally lost it. Gustave felt overwhelmingly exhausted, both physically and mentally. He reached into his pocket and opened the tiny box Kta had given him. The box proved hard to open, and contained a grey liquid that displayed a viscosity resembling pudding. He looked at his desk for his laptop and at that instant he recalled Leanne having borrowed it, most likely at that very same moment. He looked at the box and said, "I was planning to buy a new one anyway, this is as good a reason as any." He always enjoyed buying new computers, and that notion gave him a second wind and he cheerfully went to take a shower, after which he dressed hurriedly and jogged to his favorite computer store a few blocks from his residence.

Gustave spotted what he wanted right away and picked up a ragged yet small mobile laptop. Not small to the extent of his not being able to type briskly, but compact-small with the strongest processor available in a notebook lap-top computer of that size. This was of course his second criteria. He could not stand wasting time waiting for a computer to open up a program, but he also preferred to be using something that would not embarrass him as he used it alongside alien technology, although he knew quite well there was little chance this computer or any other one on the planet would save him from that discomfiture.

Gustave returned home and changed into more comfortable clothes. He removed the little jeweled gift box which he had taped to the back of the night-light shade and went into the work room where the box containing the new mobile computer awaited. He opened it with force as he had no intention of keeping it, or of returning the product. The box contained a few user startup guides which he threw to the floor. Turning the computer upside down he glanced and measured the size of screws holding the computer's enclosure together and placed the computer on the table. From a toolkit filled with many instruments, he chose a Philips-head screwdriver and began to disassemble the new computer to expose the mother board. Then he opened the small gift box and paused for a few moments to be sure of what he was supposed to be doing. Then he emptied the grey material onto the CPU. Oddly enough, the material which appeared to behave like pudding easily dropped from the box onto the surface of the CPU. The material started vanishing in front of his eyes at a rapid speed until it was completely gone in seconds. Gustave's reaction was a nervous giggle, but as soon as a smile built on his face, he smelled burning circuitry and a white-hot spark shot out of the motherboard.

"Damn it!" Gustave yelled.

"Damn it!" He yelled again only this time with a much more meaningful tone. He raised both his hands to his scalp and yelled again and again while trotting in circles around the desk. He walked back and forth in utter frustration. He retrieved an electric meter from his tool kit and approached the computer. By force of will he checked the electric current flow from the main power supply and other key points on the motherboard. It all seemed to be fine. Something must have short-circuited but the computer was still okay. He closed the computer's aluminum enclosure and turned it upright. He turned the computer on, and the computer booted normally. He lit a cigarette and waited for the operating system to initialize. Following a few quick time and date settings the computer tried to find an internet connection for an update, but there was no internet connection available. In fact, it seemed as if there was no modem chip with the computer. Gustave found that a bit odd, and wondered whether that was damaged during the integration. He shut the computer down and following Kta's instruction, typed "PrometheusG" on the keyboard as the computer turned off.

The monitor flickered and a screen appeared. Gustave was quite overwhelmed. The computer was quiet and did not make any mechanical noise.

The message which appeared on the screen read: "Please wait as we synchronize with input and output devices, Gustave…Synchronization complete. Welcome to our communication termina, Gustave!". It appeared to be a terminal of some sort, unlike anything he had seen before. There were a few icons; one of them was called "documents" another "Communicate", others, "Compute" and "Destruct". As Gustave gazed at the screen a message dialogue appeared.

"Hello, Gustave, I hope this little program is running fine. It is programmed to test itself as it leeches into your computing device. As the nanonites fully adapted to your technology, they have taken control of some functions of your computer such as your keyboard and monitor, but the rest of the computer is turned off. It was crucial for us to communicate safely, so we deactivated any radio emitting devices from the computer. Please feel free to contact me once you are ready for debriefing."

Gustave was not ready for that just yet. He was more interested in what was written in the documents and what was behind the computer function on this alien parasite computer. The documents' folder contained Gustave's first imbursement — a complete set of elaborate three-dimensional sketches and renderings of a battery-manufacturing process that included high resolution chemical composition and structure analysis and explanations – Gustave was intrigued with the details of which he understood little. He was surprised to see the renderings were very photorealistic and had the ability to be modified as he moved the laptop's mouse. The parasite computer was able to calculate three dimensional objects with far more detail and speed then any of Gustave's big computers combined, some of which he retrofitted with the latest and most expensive video cards.

In earth terms, the battery was a marvel of science. Partially using what seemed to have been nuclear fusion, it was capable of storing and releasing constant energy to power any modern electronic device for very long periods. Gustave had always surmised battery technology never caught up with the unquenchable thirst for portable and mobile power. Having a battery capable of such power surely would make him very rich, he thought.

Scanning through the documents, Gustave also saw the aliens had included a complete set of instructions describing how to construct a complete and highly efficient manufacturing line for mass production of these batteries. It was quite obvious the aliens were keeping their word. By having his own manufacturing line, he would not have to outsource any of the work to engineers and designers with the risk of exposing how the batteries are made -- truly making him the exclusive recipient of the technology's benefits.

Gustave navigated his way toward the calculator. The program opened in a split second revealing a simple command-line design. On top of the command line it read: "Please use simple language to evoke the desired answer." Gustave took it upon himself to test the calculator. He pondered a few moments trying to find something suitable to ask, but decided he would first test to see if he understood how to use it. He began typing on the keyboard with enthusiasm. "One plus one equals…" He quickly noticed that as he was typing many different equations and formulas appeared on the screen below the command line. The more he wrote, the results on the screen appeared to be lessening as if this was merely a search engine rather than a calculator. The obvious answer appeared highlighted on the screen, although many other descriptions appeared as well, including logical equations using arithmetical expression such as: "one plus one doesn't equal 2" as well as "one plus one equals ten" which Gustave recognized very well as binary arithmetic expression. Fascinating as it was, Gustave decided he should test something more elaborate. He released the locking mechanism from his work chair, and with his feet, allowed himself to lean at a comfortable angle. He was impressed with the speed of the calculations which the three-dimensional sketches appeared in the documents program, but he really sought to test the limits of the parasite computer. He looked around his room as if he was looking for a piece of the furniture to give him a clue as to how he should test the calculator. Suddenly he leaned forward, causing the chair to rattle. The answer was obvious. He opened the computer he used to test his encryption algorithm. The computer took a few moments to load and Gustave took the opportunity to enjoy a cigarette and prepare some tea. When he returned to the room, the computer was running. Gustave navigated toward the program he used to compile his test. He brought the small laptop next to the computer. To test if his idea was possible through the descriptive language of the command line, he tried a few loops and conditions, was successful, then he started translating the program into a series of questions. It took him a while to get used to, but after a few minutes it became very intuitive to ask questions instead of showing the computer how to ask them.. As he was typing, many results appeared on the screen, just as before, but Gustave convinced himself not to look at them as they might cause him to make a mistake. When he finished he pressed enter, and nothing changed on the screen. At first he thought the computer was calculating. After all, it took his regular computer about a week to finalize an answer. He suddenly remembered the results under the command line, which by now extended to a large paragraph. The result appeared highlighted at the bottom of the screen. At that moment Gustave had a poignant moment of personal conviction.

He was not willing to wait years until these aliens shared the entire technology and methodology with him. Perhaps the alien race was too selfish, he thought. Maybe it was best for the human race if he was to contrive a plan to access all of their technology as soon as possible.

He must steal it if he had to. The thought seemed to have appeared too naturally to him, considering he had never stolen a thing in his life, but perhaps, after completing the alien's request, stealing would be something at which he should excel.

CHAPTER 11

"I hope you found the little computer to be of help, Gustave. . ." Kta's soft, melodious voice was friendly and concerned.

"Very helpful indeed, Kta. . ." Gustave's voice was transmitted clearly through his laptop's speaker. "This amazing battery will make a lot of difference to our technology, without a doubt. Are you sure this technology will go under the radar of Prometheus scrutiny?" Gustave was anxious about not breaking any "rules".

"Absolutely, Gustave. . . I imagine your race is only a few years away from this technology, anyway. And a battery is only a battery." Kta had always had the illusion of his own infallibility. He was certain of his plan. And the absolute magnanimity of his plan allowed him to concur with the notion that even if this technology was not meant to be in human hands just yet, it was for a very good cause. "Gustave, would you mind turning the video on? I'd like to see you as we converse." By having a visual, he was sure it would help keep a steady feeling of trust and confidence in Gustave for the suggestions and aims of the aliens.

Clicking on the visual button, a few screens

appeared. Gustave felt a sudden shift, like a condensed tone, between his ears, moving from right to left. An image appeared on the screen out of which Kta loomed. Kta was wearing a long-sleeved robe with a hint of color that glowed with an inner light. Although the image proved to be quite effective, it seemed a bit unstable.

"I don't think I have a video camera on my laptop; how is it that you can see me?" Gustave was unsure of his question. Kta after all had requested Gustave activate the visual, but he had not said anything about a two-way visual conversation. He corrected himself. "Let me put that another way: can you see me, or is it just one way?"

"Oh, I can see you, Gustave; we are using a different way to capture visuals other than the standard video transmission. The computer is able to pick up magnetic interference from its surroundings and together with the laptop's speakers it's able to construct an acceptable image which allows us to stay in reasonably safe and covert communication. It also allows for color transference, although there are a few disturbances that keeps it from being very stable. Please excuse the image if it's posing some discomfort to your eyes."

"I already know what I'm going to ask you next in our agreement, Kta," Gustave spoke with a cheerful tone.

"In due time, Gustave, in due time. This will involve a few things that are a few decades away from their implementation in human technology. Will you be ready to be picked up tonight? We need to address a few things and I'd like to make them more personal. Before you begin training in this facility I want you to meet the rest of my crew. . ."

Gustave was reminded of the last time he was taken to the ship. The experience, so freshly embedded in his memory, had left some emotional baggage. "Of course, Kta, and I hope we can please make it more pleasant than the first time. I'd like to be prepared well beforehand."

"The biobots will come at eleven at night; they will be instructed not to immobilize you in any way. Your safety will be their first priority and your comfort will be just as important. You have my word." Kta knew it should not be any trouble now that he could deduce exactly how Gustave would react to the contact. It was important for him to advocate the trust he was supposed to instill.

CHAPTER 12

Gustave blinked and was once again in the sleek room of the space ship. The journey to the ship was easier this time and he was escorted again by the group of three biobots, or was it another group? There was no way to know for sure. Gustave removed his clothes, and having had the time to get himself ready for the contact, he was wearing his best suit. He wondered for a moment whether or not his suit would be harmed under the decontamination process but he assured himself such a faster than light - technologically advanced civilization had probably figured out dry cleaning.

After his decontamination, Gustave followed the three biobots to a platform lift which had enough power to carry them all rapidly upward. Without the pressure of uncertainty like the first time, Gustave's eyes found much more to gaze at as the passengers were led toward the meeting room. The ship's giant mess hall was occupied with biobots from the many sections where they worked and lived. The architecture and the design was lavish, as much as any futuristic design he could conceive. Yet this time he noticed with all the lavish yet industrial feel the design resulted in offering a sense of comfort. The walls changed, rooms became larger or smaller as needed, all dynamically and in perfect sync. When a large group of biobots entered a room, the walls stretched and the rooms grew larger to accommodate the number of occupants. The lifter stopped.

Gustave and the three Biobots boarded as the platform of the lift docked in the corridor. The wall yawned open to reveal a large room that had a few odd-looking tables merging with what appeared to be plastic chairs. The design looked as if the table and the chairs were in constant argument over which was to serve which purpose. The three bots showed Gustave to a spot in the table-chair fixture. It was not at all obvious how to sit down in it. He looked back as he eased himself into the seat. The plastic- looking fixture changed its shape underneath him to accommodate the curvature of his body. As he sat down, the wall opened and Kta came into the room with two other human-looking people. Gustave stood, expecting to hit the table with his pelvic bone, but the table morphed and offered him reasonable space to avoid collision.

"Please sit down Gustave. . . It's a pleasure seeing you again in person. " Kta extended his hand in a welcoming gesture. "Behind me are my trusted crew Nell, Milka, and Bor. We are all Angelonian." Kta glanced behind himself once, then again. "Where is Nell? She was right behind us and suddenly disappeared!" Kta smiled apologetically at Gustave and the others. "Excuse me Gustave, I will be right back, Nell is a bit shy. Can you guys please introduce yourselves to each other? I will ask her to join us."

Kta left the room and the two Angelonian's sat down. Gustave leaned forward from the comfort of his chair and extended a hand. Milka imitated him and they exchanged the accepted earthman's salutation. Gustave couldn't help but notice her hand was as smooth as a rose petal.

"Hello, Gustave, I am Milka, the tactical officer of the mission. It is pleasure to meet a human."

Her accent was different than that of Kta. Her English did not seem as comprehensive as the English Kta spoke. "It's a pleasure to meet you too, Milka." Gustave glanced at the other Angelonian. "Bor? Did I get it right?"

Bor narrowed his eyes and replied with contempt. "Yes, you got it right". Bor seemed as if he did not intend to exchange the earthly custom of shaking hands. Gustave withdrew his hand to avoid further discomfort for him and the alien. He glanced at the opening in the wall, hoping for the arrival of Kta. He didn't hear any footsteps so he chose to try and warm up to the new aliens. "What do you do, Bor?" Gustave looked at the alien with a tentative smile.

Bor condescended to give him a haughty glance. "I fly."

Gustave's smile revealed more interest. "You know, I always wanted to fly aircrafts; that takes a high level of skills." Gustave hoped he could get through the thickness of the other's defensive personality and result in something resembling a friendship. His father had been a pilot, and he wished had it in him.

"I'm not flying human aircrafts. . . this is complicated," Bor said.

Gustave noticed an almost Russian like-accent in Bor's speech patterns. He wondered if Angelonian's had different languages instead of one universal. Why wouldn't they? In movies aliens from the same specie never spoke in diverse accents, probably due to the belief that different languages would disappear after many years of living under one intelligent economic state. There was a moment or two of silence. Gustave again tried to make small talk with the aliens. "Angelonian…sounds very much like.."

"Gustave, I'd like you to meet Nell. . ." Kta walked to the room and behind him was a female. She hid behind Kta at first, and slowly moved apart from him, exposing her striking figure. Gustave was speechless. She was undoubtedly the prettiest woman he had ever seen. She carried herself in a manner which Gustave thought was very appealing. Her luscious hair, succulent lips, and beautifully penetrating turquoise eyes took his breath away. He gathered himself together, swallowed a couple of times, and said, "It's a pleasure to make your acquaintance, Nell".

"Nell serves many positions on this mission; she is in charge of all technological matters including taking care of the ship, the biobot, and of course our health." Kta took the opportunity to emphasize the responsibility and trust he placed in Nell.

"Now that is quite impressive, Nell! A medical doctor and an engineer!" Gustave tried to show his admiration for her abilities while avoiding obvious expressions of flattery. And that, too, took quite a bit of effort.

Nell wanted to respond, still astonished to find herself in the same room with a human, and she took a few moments to gather her composure. "We, umm," Nell stuttered, blushed a dark red, then grew silent.

Perceiving it might be all too much for her as a first time being in a room with a human, Kta rescued her from having to speak, and answered Gustave. "We rely on machines and regenerative medicine, Gustave. A technology officer is responsible for all machines on the ship, including all nanonites. They just have to assign them to different purposes." As he spoke he realized he just undermined his initial introduction, quite possibly offending Nell.

"Nonetheless, it is very impressive, and quite a heavy responsibility, taking care of the most important things on the ship…", Gustave was compelled to defend Nell , even indirectly.

Nell smiled, which surprised even herself. She was afraid of humans. They were a brute version of Angelonians yet still, her first contact with one was nothing like she had expected; it was something else entirely.

Kta sat down between Bor and Milka, then Nell followed suit. "Gustave, as we discussed previously, we will have to debrief with the full intel you'll require for the mission. Milka, if you don't mind, please take it from here."

Milka nodded and looked at each individual in the group before speaking. "The device is located at a military research facility. Within that facility there is an underground compound that is not accessible to humans and is entirely run on its own. While some supervision is done somewhere at Agora, the Galactic Union center, we believe there are a few biobots conducting most of the experiments. Your job will be to locate the underground compound, disable the bots and retrieve the device. To do so, you will first require clearance to access the military research facility. It is a highly-guarded facility to which no Angelonian can enter because security measures have been installed unknowingly by the biobots. They can sense one of us thousands of kilometers away." Milka posed for a moment to let Gustave soak up the information. She was not sure to what length a human could follow her train of thought.

Gustave, on the other hand, had already planned a series of questions. "What measures have been taken for me to get clearance to the base?" He was impatient to ascertain he had full access to anything he wanted to know.

Milka smiled tolerantly and proceeded to answer his curiosity. "We have prepared you with a new identity, and a research paper under your new identity. We are certain this paper will impress them and they will request you to join them. The research conducted at the base is mostly focused on testing and development of light materials for armor. Your paper will propose a method to solve something they are currently struggling with. We have hacked into their computers, and listened to conversations held at the facility which is suffering from budget sanctions after failing to complete a working model."

Gustave froze. The aliens hacking into the facility reminded him of something he had tried to repress for many years. His dad had been a researcher for the army at one point as well, and his own hacking attempts had caused Gustave much grief as a small child. He disliked research labs but his loathing for military research facilities was far greater. He gathered his thoughts and with a soft voice said, "Kta, I. . .", and for a second he thought about telling Kta about his past. It seemed trivial to mention it. But over and above that he disliked this plan, however completing it was a priority for his own good, and that is what he chose to do. He nodded in affirmation and continued. "Once I get in the facility, how will I be able to locate the underground facility?"

"We will provide you with a detector of some sort. . ." Kta said.

A moment later, Gustave noticed an instrument materializing out of thousands of nanonites. It was odd-shaped, and with no jutting features, and seemed small enough to fit in a cigarette pack.

As the detector was shaping itself, Kta continued. "The experiments must yield some sort of energy that is otherwise not harnessed by humans; this energy is very likely to vent from the ground up. This instrument can detect it. How you are to locate the entrance to the underground compound, we cannot be sure. They would have built an entrance if they chose to do so. We imagine if the biobots were capable of installing security measures, they must have had some access to the outside world."

"Can you be certain the same bots that maintain the compound underground are also responsible for adding the detection defenses?" Gustave was understandably cautious, which the aliens admired.

Holding the rod-shaped instrument in her hand, Milka seemed excessively eager to answer Gustave's question. Kta noticed her obsequious gesture, and gave her a nod which was his permission to explain more. "It is unlikely for the Union to send more bots to achieve their tasks on other planets regardless of how disposable or extraneous these bots are. More so, since every mission is highly monitored by many different bureaucratic groups, and a mission with more than a few bots over the number needed is sure to raise undesirable suspicion and many questions."

Although Kta seemed satisfied with Milka's answer, her reaction did bear thinking about. The tactical readings made no mention of this, but it appeared elicited and rehearsed. He didn't quite catch on to how tactical ordeals worked quite as much as she did. The answer made enough sense for Gustave to ask what he might have considered the most urgent question he had.

"These bots, will they be easy to defeat? Do they

have those 'Do Not Harm a Human' sort of rules?" He realized he had made a mistake by saying humans but it conveyed the message just as well.

"We do not know, Gustave," Kta answered with a shudder. He took the rod-shaped instrument from Milka's hands and continued. "The Union has a policing force but it has long been ineffective. I imagine they must have some means of defending the project. In any case, Gustave, your safety means a lot to us. We will equip you with a dermal-skeleton, but you will need to practice how to use it."

"A dermal skeleton?" Gustave raised his eyebrows.

"Yes. . ." Kta smiled as he patiently explained. " A thin layer of nanonites will submerge under your skin to create a strong shield, capable of withstanding any small to midsized ballistic missile, although a direct hit would be unfavorable. They will mostly twitch your muscles in response to ballistic analysis and help you avoid any impact. They are also very capable of regenerating damaged tissue. It was developed by us for this purpose and although we practice controlling nanonites with our neural link from childhood, there was never a need to create such a protective tactical shield for over a thousand years – until now."

Gustave was not too pleased with the idea, but the prospect of being invincible was a visceral realization which he did find powerfully attractive. He took a deep breath and thought to himself, "In any case, this would work very well with the plan I have had in mind. . ."

CHAPTER 13

Kta and Nell were busy with preparations in a medical examining room. The space was efficient even though small and filled with many large tubes, instruments of sorts, and what appeared to be a fixed table. It only gave the visual impression of being fixed but the room was like any other room on the ship and could morph into anything useful in a matter of seconds. Kta noticed Nell was a bit tense and he wondered if she was again displaying signs of nervousness due to having to be close to a human.

"Nell, I assure you, he will be completely unconscious during the implantation and there is no need for you to be anxious." Kta placed a calming hand on her shoulder.

"Kta, that's not it... what if he doesn't respond well to the implants? I mean we have had a lot of experience with less intrusive implants in humans but a brain-board is something we have never done on them. I know there will be no physical complications but I can't possibly..."

"There shouldn't be any difference from our original brain-boards. If I recall they were successful enough to lead the way to further developments and eventually the introduction of genetic mods." Kta removed his hand.

"The genetic mods were introduced to allow for more natural and stable machine-linking, Kta." Nell handed Kta an spherically shaped device and grabbed for herself.

"If it goes wrong, we remove it and reset, and I suppose that will set us back some time but it shouldn't be longer than the anticipated regular curve of training".

Gustave had waited briefly in a small preparation room. The ceiling's soothing colors slowly changed. There was a comfortable sofa and a small table where a silky light blue robe lay folded. While still awake, Gustave had stroked the robe's material and felt a tingling sensation resembling that of an electrostatic force. The fabric had a silky-liquid feel to it and the color of the robe changed colors every place his fingers touched. The more firmly he pressed the more red it became. Gustave took off his clothes and changed into the robe which felt luxurious on his skin. The light blue robe immediately changed its colors, according to the temperatures of sections of his body. There was some text and data running on the fabric, but he understood none of it since it was all in an alien-looking language. He marveled at the robe, and tried to read the written script running on the lapels. He felt strangely light-headed and completely stress-free.

Kta walked into the room. "I see you found your way into the medical-robe, Gustave! We will begin the training shortly. . . please sit down on the sofa and relax. I will come back in a few minutes." Kta stood for a few moments then left the room, the walls closing behind him.

With nothing else to do, Gustave decided to give the sofa a try. He sat on its edge at first. Feeling how soft and embracing it was, he stretched out his entire body on the cushions until he was fully immersed by its nurturing embrace.

He immediately fell into a deep sleep.

CHAPTER 14

"The link is corrupted! It's not responding!" Nell shouted in her mother tongue. "Watch out, Kta!"

Gustave raised himself up from the operating table, leaning on one elbow. His eyes, flashed with anger as Kta started walking toward him. Nell continued shouting in her alien language distracting Gustave who turned toward her. "Quiet. quiet now, what have you done to Gustave!" Gustave oddly referred to himself in third person. The operating table started morphing into odd shapes and the entire room pulsated inward and outward in a silent visual accompaniment. The tubes and instruments rose to the air, some spun in blinding speeds.

"Gustave, please stop. . . You are experiencing incompatibility side effects. Please try to remain calm," K'ta cried.

Both K'ta and Nell were terrified. They cowered together in the corner where the walls met, but this offered them no comfort as the walls kept bending and pushing them closer toward the menacing state Gustave was experiencing.

"It hurts! Gustave is hurt!" Again referring to

himself in third person, Gustave shouted in anguish. He continued to yell as he placed his hands on his head, dropped to the floor, and curled into a foetal position. Within seconds, the room bent toward Gustave and the floating instruments and tubes smashed into him. The size of the room shrank to suffocating proposition as both Kta and Nell squeezed into Gustave's body.

Kta managed to locate a moment of clear thought even in the middle of his terrified state of mind. He called for rescue from all the biobots on ship. Instantly, all biobots abandoned their previous instructions and crowded onto lifters in an organized manner.

Gustave felt the pressure of the room pushing toward his body. For the first time he consciously noticed the chaos around him. He could also hear Nell's crying. He froze. The walls bounced and protruded back into their normal position and only a few instruments remained floating in the disorder.

"What's happening to me? What's happening here?" Gustave was frightened and confused as he tried to subdue his anger.

Kta, still trembling in fear, tried speaking but nothing came out, nothing but an incoherent stutter in his native tongue.

Gustave's temper subsided and his headache ebbed. He started realizing how terrified his friends must be and wasn't quite sure why or how he got there. A second later, he couldn't even remember what he had just said. A second later, he felt danger. A robotic hand extended toward his body and Gustave automatically moved his body to evade its touch. He yelled again and swiftly maneuvered his body to confront the danger. He grabbed the robotic hand of the biobot, lifted his foot and jammed it into the armpit joint and brutally tore the artificial ligaments, pulling the entire arm off. The artificial hand did not resemble a robotic hand. Liquid gushed, and muscle-like tissues continued contracting. The Biobot raised a rod with the hand that was still attached to his body. Gustave, remembering the terrifying experience with the kidnapping and the rod-carrying alien saw a potential for great danger. He understood little of what was happening and little of why this alien wanted to harm him. In a sudden moment of vivid terror, the walls, the floor and the ceiling collapsed instantaneously crushing the Biobot into the size of a small box.

Gustave fainted.

CHAPTER 15

Gustave's unconscious body lay motionless on a table. Kta was sitting in a chair looking at a computerized monitor that displayed characters, graphs, and graphics suspended in mid-air. Nell walked into the room.

"Nell I'm…" Kta couldn't say anything more. He stared down at his hands clenched in his lap.

"Sorry?" Nell answered with a shudder. "Sorry for almost killing me and destroying this ship?" She continued, her eyes started tearing, "I've never been so scared in my life, Kta. He's and animal, they are animals!"

"Nell, I had no idea it would turn out like this. He was not supposed to be able to regain consciousness and even then he was not himself; the brain-board interface was not designed for humans." K'ta attempted to apologize but he realized he was just repeating what Nell had told him prior to the implantation procedure.

"I warned you!" Nell was breathing rapidly in short gasps.

"His brain was not supposed to make the connection to the ship. He was so used to finding backdoors in code, he managed to do so without even trying. Neither of us took that into account." Kta said. He quickly corrected himself. "I meant to say, *I* didn't take that into account. I'm sorry, Nell."

Nell wiped the tears from her cheeks with her thumbs. She paused for a moment and raised a chair from the floor, the still fresh memory of the crushing walls lingering in her mind. She twitched momentarily when the chair morphed as she sat down. "Is he okay, can we still continue with our mission?"

"He will be just fine, there'd no need even for a rest, just some down time. I disconnected and encrypted access to his involuntary muscle movements; in the meantime, he is running in afterlife simulation. After a few weeks I expect his brain to have fully blended with the brain board. "If anything, we can now be certain he should be able to defend himself after we teach him to use the interface. He will remember nothing of what transpired in the medical procedures. I erased it all." Kta glanced at the monitor.

"We must make sure of that, Kta. . . no one should be allowed to remind him of that or he will become unstable again. He's not as powerful on earth without having so many objects to be connected to through the interface, but on this ship, a human, with this interface can cause our complete destruction." Nell's face was very pale and she was clenching her fists so tightly the knuckles were white.

Kta tried not to be concerned in the face of Nell's argument, but he knew she was right. "He will not be on this ship after we finished his training Nell, I can assure you of that. . ."

CHAPTER 16

Gustave awoke feeling well rested. He felt slightly weak when he got up from the sofa and was dizzy as blood rushed through his body. The feeling intensified and he found himself sitting back on the sofa before he decided to wait and stand more gradually. He wondered how long he had been asleep. He stood up again, this time with much less objection from his body and began walking around the room slowly. Something felt a bit odd in his movement but he brushed that feeling off.

The wall opened silently and Kta walked in. "I imagine you feel rested, Gustave. I did not want to interfere with your sleep." Kta smiled.

"I guess that sofa was more comfortable than I would have imagined it to be. I'm feeling rested and ready for the training!" Gustave was jubilant.

"Good, let's get you suited up."

Gustave followed Kta toward a larger room just down the brightly lit hall. Once inside the room, a tube morphed itself up from the floor. "Suiting up will feel just like a shower, only a bit longer and perhaps more intrusive

. . . I will leave the room for your privacy and will return once the process is complete and you are dressed. Is there anything you would like to ask me before we continue with this?"

"Is this in any way dangerous? Are there any side effects I should be aware of? Is this thing hundred percent safe for humans?" Gustave was wary and beginning to feel uncertain.

"Our implant technology is human tested, yes, the suit is not. There is very little risk of any harm, Gustave. You should not feel a thing once the process is complete as the shield is too thin for you to experience discomfort and since it works in perfect symbiosis with your nerves it allows for skin receptors to have free communication with your brain."

"Understood, Kta." Gustave nodded.

"Then I will see you shortly. . ." Kta said and left the room. The opening in the wall closed behind him as he left.

Gustave removed his robe and stepped into the tube, which closed softly around him. Gustave's body lifted from the ground. He was completely weightless which seemed to have affected the tube itself and not the entire room. Dark grey material gushed in through a smaller tube that appeared from the ceiling. The material started wrapping itself around Gustave's body. Little by little his entire body was covered with a thick layer of the material. Feeling a bit uncomfortable, Gustave felt himself breathing more rapidly. He tried closing his eyes to relax. The moment he closed his eyes, the thick layer encasing him like a locust's shell hardened instantaneously to a point he could not move at all or regain his sight. Gustave made a low humming noise, as if it was a natural thing to do. He felt a strange and fast-moving feeling that started at the base of his feet and moved its way up to his skull. The movement made the uncomfortable feeling bearable for him and the grip of the hardened material released. He opened his eyes and noticed the dark grey material gradually departing from his skin back into the tube from which it had emanated.

"Gustave, is everything all right?" Kta's voice sounded from the empty room.

"Yes, Kta."

"Everything looks good here as well; I should tell you we are now communicating through one of your armor's many neural connections, directly to your brain."

"I thought something felt odd. . ." Guestave massaged his neck and shoulder, twisting his head back and forth.

"You'll get used to it and learn to control, activate, and deactivate by yourself. The inner ear hairs are not moving right now, and this confuses your brain."

"Can I speak to you, using my inner voice that way? Is it possible to just think about what I want to say, like telepathy? " The whole notion was a matter of concern to Gustave. He might not be able to conceal anything from Kta if his thoughts were accessible to others.

"No, Gustave, my instruments can read only stress levels, anxiety levels, and other measurements that are very basic, such as blood pressure. It can take weeks to years before your brain patterns can be interpreted to a higher level, such as thought communication. And even then you would have to learn to speak silently, moving your tongue and mouth muscles without actually speaking. The system is specifically calibrated for low sensitivity to avoid noise and especially neural activity that is fired just because you think of it."

This brought immediate relief to Gustave. His plan was still safely tucked inside the comfort of his private thoughts.

"Try to open a rift through the wall, Gustave; we'll begin with that," Kta said.

Gustave stared at the side of one of the walls, and tried to imagine it opening. Nothing happened. He tried again and again until the beads of perspiration gleamed from his forehead. He tried focusing on different points of the wall and even looked at different walls with no success. Ultimately he gave up. "I can't Kta, could it be that it's not working?" Gustave was just not ready to admit failure.

"Now that you've attempted this your way, I should tell you that you need to use virtual hand gestures to apply commands wirelessly. Think about opening the wall with your hands and it will react to your command. The armor will interpret the virtual hand gesture and will combine the misfiring of the neurons in your hand muscles with other noise to be further processed and analyzed. In time you will not need to think about hand gestures at all. Give that a try."

Gustave waited a few moments to digest the thought about the technology involved with his armor. He was a bit nervous but excited to have the ability to control objects and communicate with technology through his mind. His anticipation grew more exciting when he remembered the armor was also a suit of armor. He was exhilarated by the idea but knew first he had to walk through the wall, unassisted by anything except his mental prowess.

Gustave lifted his arm and forcefully dropped it. For a moment he forgot he had only to *think* about the hand gesture rather than actually executing it with his muscles. He concentrated looking at the door and imagined his hand going through the wall parting a way through it as if it was liquid. The wall started dividing. The movement thrilled Gustave and he laughed with delight. The wall, of course stopped opening as his excitement caused him to lose his concentration. He tried again, and this time the wall appeared to be parting easily. He worked on closing it. He opened and closed it a few times, until the command gesture was comfortable to execute.

Kta's voice resounded through the communication link of the armor. "You are doing very well, Gustave, surprisingly well, actually. Please join me in the room at the end of the corridor. You will have to open the wall perpendicular to the one you are facing."

With some difficulty, Gustave did as he was instructed and found himself in a large open space. The room boasted an immense screen with the view of the cosmos similar to those transmitted by the Hubbell telescope years earlier but much more massive. It was the first time he had seen space and the view left him in tears. He remembered looking at space from earth on clear cold nights when he could identify the vastness of the Milky Way. Gustave was not prepared for such a view; he had never seen the glory from which so many galaxies were formed. Oddly enough, he felt a momentary terror but he quickly gave himself a good shake.

"Quite a view, isn't it?" Kta said quietly, smiling at Gustave's awe.

"The vastness of space is a supreme challenge to my limited knowledge, Kta. Can you even travel through it all?"

"No, we can't, Gustave. The infrastructure of our Throb-string Drive is not capable of tuning outside our galaxy; those who did try to venture off the galaxy with entangled jumps were lost. We can't establish reliable infrastructures in order to create tuning links."

Gustave tried to understand what Kta was talking about but was afraid to ask something that would immediately disclose his lack of understanding and comprehension of alien flight technology. Instead, he said, "It's funny, even an authoritatively advanced alien race has its limits, and those will be conquered in time like anything else. Well, that's not the funny part; the funny part is to observe how far away the universe is from being an intelligently designed system. In an intelligently designed system, an obstacle is created with consideration that solutions to the problem it poses might be ultimately found and thus need to be re-designed to accommodate and limit these solutions. Space isn't that easy."

"Everything is ready Kta. . ." Nell's voice came from behind. Gustave and Kta both turned to face her.

She was wearing a tight fitting white jump suit. The fabric appeared as if it was constructed deliberately to match the curviness of her body. She was a provocative vision and Gustave couldn't help but think she had chosen her outfit with hints of seduction in mind. "You look…ah. . ." he meant to say something witty, such as 'ravishing' or 'dazzling' but the confusion caused by her beauty caused his tongue to grow thick and any premeditated compliment dissipated in the air. "Stunning!" was all he could manage to choke out.

Kta inhaled, his chest swelling with resentful pomposity. "Gustave, we are not used to this sort of direct reactions toward our appearances. It's not acceptable in our society because you might offend others."

Gustave knew he would have to be more mindful of his manners by predicting how their society works. He certainly didn't want to offend anyone and he had thought he was giving Nell a compliment.

Nell, on the other hand, smiled albeit shyly. It was

still hard to tell exactly since she kept her fair distance from the human, so it was harder still to know what it meant.

Now that Gustave's attention was distracted from Nell, he noticed the floating container trembling in midair next to her. The room was quiet for a few moments until Kta spoke again.

"Now, let get to work, shall we?"

Nell made a few small steps toward the two. She still seemed like she was utterly afraid of Gustave despite his attempt to make her comfortable around him, even when they first met. It crossed his mind that she might be shy. That could possibly explain her behavior. A woman of such stature should never be shy, although it does increase the opportunities for them to get more personal at one point, should her shyness originate from insecurity. Again, he found it hard not to gaze in awe at that wonderfully crafted beauty of hers although he managed to gain a wider picture by also following the container that floated in the air above her while it maintained a constant distance from her as she walked.

"What we'll do now, Gustave, is to train you to control a few instruments. . ." Kta then approached Nell and the container and picked up a small cigarette-shaped object. The object was entirely grey and Gustave did not see anything especially strange in its appearance.

Kta stretched the palm of his hand open. As soon as he did, the rod rose to the air and floated about a foot from his hand "This may seem as a simple rod, Gustave, but it can be quite useful for your training."

The rod began spinning on its axis. First, it rotated on its horizontal plane, stopped, changed its rotation to its vertical plane, stopped and then rotated in an elaborate movement that included both axes. The rod stopped.

"You will now learn how to control with more delicate movements. You will find that since it is you that is in control of the object, you can command it to move in any direction you desire and even control the speed of its rotation and movement."

The rod now began spinning so fast it was impossible to discern its original shape. It looked like a plain metal plate. A few seconds later, the rotation changed, and it began spinning into the shape of a solid ball. An intense hiss filled the air as the rod burst upward into the air. The metallic-looking ball became astonishingly bright, as if the ball had become a giant orb of glowing lava. In a split second, the rod stood motionless and the bright light that emitted from it dimmed slowly.

Gustave looked at the little instrument in amazement. He couldn't miss the opportunity. "Can I give it a try, Kta?"

Kta smiled and commanded the rod to float slowly toward Gustave. Gustave opened the palm of his hand and extended his fingers, holding his hand still and flat. The rod stopped mid-air and floated just above Gustave's palm. "I'm going to transfer the control over the rod to you and you have to be ready to command it to float, Gustave."

"I'm ready!"

A second more and the rod plunged down into his hand and seared his palm. The rod was still very hot from the earlier display of aerodynamics and was hot enough that Gustave shouted a heartfelt curse and dropped it on the floor. He involuntarily made a fist which in turn injured the burn even further. Gustave opened his palm again and began shaking it and blowing on the angry burn.. Gustave looked at his hand. The wound seemed to have been entirely on the surface of his skin. His armor must have stopped the scorching rod from melting into his flesh. Embarrassed, he glanced at Kta and Nell. They both were chagrined as was Gustave.

Trying to recover from his embarrassment, and especially since there was no cause for solicitous concern, he squeaked, and said jokingly, "Careful, it's hot!"

Kta and Nell both looked at with puzzled expressions, not knowing how to interpret his attempt at humor. Gustave's sense of humor, and his casual attitude toward his injury, were probably not expected nor were they customary in their culture.

The wound began healing itself, and the pain subsided into a manageable, almost unnoticeable ache.

Gustave looked at the rod. He knew he had it in him to command it with his brain-armor interface. He focused his efforts and before too long, it rose into the air. He remembered he should have thought of mild hand gestures to control the object and he modestly acted out his intentions toward its movement. With an open palm and the rod floating above it, Gustave began moving his fingers gently together to simulate a rotation command. The object responded.

He changed the rotation, went sideways then up and down, at which point he discovered how easily he could control its motions and speed. Satisfied with his control over the object he decided to try something Kta did not show him. He made the object move in zigzag pattern reaching a speed that made it look as if it were a square plate. He continued with his experiment and from that plate, a brightly lit box formed itself. This was easier then he originally thought it would be. Sure of himself, he extended the width and length of the box until it reached a large size. This required the rod to move in incomprehensible speed as the little cigarette-sized object had to move up and down, forward and backward many times the speed of sound. Even still, the noise it generated was no more than the noise emitted by the high pitched sound of an air compressor.

Nell, surprised by the level of control over the object and the fast learning curve exhibited by Gustave, uttered a laugh which got Gustave's attention. He raised his glance toward her with a smile, and the rod followed his point of concentration. It almost hit her, until Gustave stopped it in mid-air when he noticed its movement. Not taking any chances, the tightly-fitted jump suit she was wearing calculated the odds of the projectile hitting her body and it lifted her from the ground, quickly gaining distance from the dangerous object.

"I am so sorry, I was distracted, but stopped it in time, Nell!" Gustave apologized with utmost sincerity.

Nell chuckled a nervously. "That's all right, Gustave, and I came prepared for that." Her reaction surprised Gustave, but not as much as it did Kta, who was curved on the ground in a foetal position for his protection from the now- distant danger.

"I think we'd better continue with less dangerous trials," Kta said.

He raised himself from the ground. Still shaken, he took little steps toward the floating container and slowly picked another rod. This rod had a brushed steel look to it, but it kept changing metallic colors.

He raised the rod toward higher ground, and said, "This is a detector and a computer, Gustave. . . You will have to learn how to use its interface. This exercise will teach you to connect into, gain access, and control different instruments. Your armor's wireless-neural connection to instruments allows you to do so using only your thought patterns."

Kta lifted the two fingers that held the rod. The instrument stayed in the air motionless as if there was an invisible shelf on which it might have lain. Kta continued, "You will soon learn that when you connect to devices they will imprint their identification along with lists of functionalities on the armor's memory, at which point you will be able to recall their use, without focusing, looking, or even being in the same room with them."

Anxious to experiment with the instrument, Gustave began focusing on the device before Kta finished talking. In a few seconds he gained a strange awareness for every feature of which the device was capable. He blinked and shifted his head backward.

"It's a strange feeling," Gustave said, barely waiting for Kta to finish his sentence. "Amazing! It's as if I've worked with this shift-transfer substrate particle detector for years!" Gustave caught himself in a moment of astonishment, because without any effort, he somehow already knew the device's name. The feeling resembled the sensation of using a familiar computer program where you mostly move your hand where the tools you want to be using are located, without the need to think where they are located on the tool bar. Muscle memory was acquired in seconds, but was applied toward different purposes when necessary.

Both Kta and Nell felt a chill creep up the back of their necks. Using his neural speech module, Kta vocalized his concern to Nell. "Did you enable him with access to the detector prior to my demonstration, Nell?"

"Yes I did, Kta, they are all open but the Nam stick. Look, he's already testing it out!"

Kta was displeased with the lack of precaution on Nell's behalf. He knew that there could be no room for error and some of the devices could pose great risk if mishandled without his supervision. He instantly ordered all the devices still hidden in the container were to be locked until his approval for them to be handled by others.

Nell realized her mistake and apologized silently over the neural com.

With a nod of acceptance, Kta shifted his effort to study Gustave's armor readings. His heart rate was beating at a higher rate than what was expected of a human, and his neural activity in the brain was spiking in extremely high levels of activity, caused by the interaction to his armor and head board. He would have to learn how to interact with his body. His head board was capable of inbound and outbound communications to his neural network.

"Gustave, I think I mentioned this before, but as you now know your armor's ability to connect to interactive objects, your final lesson will be self-interaction and governance of your armor."

Gustave held his concentration steady on the detector and allowed Kta to continue.

"Your armor is able to store information, calculate tasks at the same level as the little device I gave you when we first met, but is also capable of outperforming, with considerable strength, simpler functions such as running, jumping or anything you might require although you might find it a bit difficult at first to get used to it."

Gustave's curiosity grew stronger. He didn't feel all that powerful.

"Of course, you would have to learn to activate

each of these functions, and I encourage you to try and activate them yourself, using your own intuition. In time, you should be able to control it with little or no effort, although, as I said, it is an experimental armor and we have only tested it through simulations.". As Kta spoke, the room changed its form, the floor morphing into many different shapes, the ceiling extending in some areas to accommodate high obstacles and contracted in other areas to form delicate and awkward spots to allot Gustave room for practice.

"We will leave you to it, Gustave. Both the room and your armor are well-equipped to safely try out even the most dangerous jumps and falls. Concentrate, and try to feel your movements well before you act them out. Size up objects and obstacles in your mind. You will soon start being aware of their sizes within seconds, and receive intuitive intel from the armor's mechanics and calculator. You'll have no trouble whatsoever!"

Kta and Nell smiled broadly and left Gustave alone with time to learn his new self.

CHAPTER 17

In a quiet dark room lit only by a computer screen which emitted a glowing, soft green fluorescence, Harry M. Escher sat down on a large leather office chair and buried his head in his large hands.

There was a knock on the door.

"Sir, I have the full reports from NORAD, as you requested. Would you like to see them?" The voice was that of Liam Nicolson, Harry's personal assistant.

Harry cleared his throat and with a commanding tone said, "Come in!"

The door opened. "Turn the lights on, will you?" Harry's tone softened a bit, but was still rich with hints of irritated undertones. Harry squinted with both his eyes to try and shade the sharp light that instantly filled the room. That alone raised his temper even further, even though he himself requested the light be turned on. He was a tall man, with very little hair left on his head, which was brown and well-trimmed, but not shaven. He didn't like shaving his head because it would be too shiny and attract too much attention, but he was well aware growing it long and combing it in a bizarre comb-over was not the personal solution for him or for anyone in his line of work. His skin was rugged, but not too wrinkled and he was a well-built man for his age.

"Have you my FPM documents? Anything come up from the ground yet, Liam?" Harry now opened his eyes and looked at Liam, holding out a report folder. "We are working on it, sir. . . It seems like it was a clean in-and-out as far as public awareness is concerned. The planes were rejected from air very far from the damn E.T.V, a good thing if you ask me, or otherwise we would have had a few people asking questions about military jets flying over the city, sir, in the middle of the night."

Liam was wearing an outlandish tie with blue and yellow stripes, a pattern that offended Harry's preference for classic taste. Looking at Liam with his usual disgruntled impatience he reached for the report folder, scanning its pages rapidly.

"Pretty clean in-and-out indeed," Harry agreed.

"This case is laden with lack of information; these bastards usually like to play with our jets, and they even sent for the thirty-fives to let them have a closer look." Harry shuffled backward into his chair. His heavy sigh indicated his serious concern. "This belligerent silence makes this a new type of intrusion into our air-space. They were more interested with something specific in that city rather than making an observation. Is everything ready for the cleanup here?"

"Yes, sir!" Liam replied. He was quite happy the

three-day office lockdown was about to be over, even when it meant that again, he would have to undergo a few routine exit examinations.

Harry was anxious to return to the comfort of his home and especially back to Winston, his Great Dane. But his job was to collect intel for his superiors and there was nothing yet there to report. The feelings of belonging and home were overpowered by the feeling of failure due to the lack of information from this incident.

This was a routine procedure in the unit. Whenever there was an incident with a Non- Reference Target, or a fast walker, the offices would be under complete lockdown, their only connection to the outside world the field agents, but that was only one way into the compound. The facility included everything the staff required including a healthcare professional with a complete care unit, sleeping areas, which were rarely in use during the three-day lockdown, and a cafeteria which offered automated machines serving sandwiches and other foods that tasted like artificial chemicals. Following the lockdown, a special unit cleaned the place up from all the collected information, hot-swapped the hard drive with new ones, and lastly ran a complete check on the unit's personnel to be certain none had kept any of the top secret information. In the old days that would have meant x-ray examinations, but since the late nineties, the collectors began using sensitive metal detectors and a bit of manual probing into questionable areas. The initiative was understandable because if someone had gone to the trouble of devising a small storage pocket somewhere in their bodies, it was most likely information too important to risk having it erased or corrupted by x-rays.

"You may go now, Liam. . ." Harry spoke brusquely. There was no need for making further solicitous inquiries regarding the current incident with Liam. He would have to report to the officer in charge of the pickup team in a few hours. Perhaps he could elaborate more or even give him ideas about what might lay behind this particularly preternatural incident.

"Yes sir. . . Thank you, sir," Liam replied. He then left the office quietly, gently closing the door behind him to leave Harry to his work, which he had to complete under the utmost private and undisturbed conditions.

Harry's computer was the only one in the office connected to an internal database. No information leakage, or N.I.L for short, meant that his computer must have been contained in an enclosed magnetic safe with a few holes to accommodate the cables for the keyboard and monitor. The cables themselves were individually wrapped so as not to emit any sort of electrostatic interference. This ensured that no one could hack into the machine physically using some sort of wireless radio pickup. Following a lockdown, Harry, and the rest of his crew would get newly marked hard drives, to be inserted into their computers. While his team will get a simple hard drive with which they can write and compile their data, Harry would get a complete database from which he can retrieve all known and registered accounts of encounters with the E.T.V's. His job was to find similarities, mark them, and try to file the incidents in the correct categories. To his best knowledge, he was the last step before all the information went to the highest of unknown commands in charge. After all, his field agents wore the highest insignia on their uniforms. Admirals, generals and people in all posts with top secret, Majestic-12, and Cosmic Top Security clearance access through the military industrial complex reported to his staff, each assigned to their own contact, and his staff reported directly to him.

The system of hierarchy was well built to accommodate any sort of security breach. No individual knew exactly who's doing what and in particular, no individual knew or was allowed to share or even inquire about details from others. Harry, for example, didn't assign his staff their contacts; they received the assignments anonymously through a messenger. On the report, the staff filled in an identification number with the collected information and would submit it to Harry for final approval. This ensured no individual can have their identity disclosed, and if it so happened to be revealed, there was very little information available for disclosure.

Even though Harry was not connected to any government officials, he was certain the government did not run the top of this operation. There was no way of telling but it could hardly be otherwise. It was crucial he did not ask any questions into matters which did not concern his job requirements, but he knew if politicians ran the place, there would be budgetary cutbacks, or even less actions taken, since that's what politicians do best, or so he thought. His superiors' way of making sure people *don't* talk was also something he didn't think worked well with politicians. Harry himself had undergone the strictest of surveillance testing under these intimidating prerequisites. The threat would make anyone keep their mouth shut even on their death bed. They would simply murder the talker's entire family line and find a way to frame the killing on him or her. Locked in a maximum security cell, they would then watch continuously looping segments of pictures and videos of the well-documented murder and segments from local or national news covering their alleged crimes. To make sure the point gets across, anyone who agrees to join the N.I.L unit has to sit through videos documenting the entire operation as it was done on a randomly selected citizen who had nothing to do with the unit or the army. Harry remembered the two-hour long clip which was mostly a time-lap of the entire torture. The person, unable to move, was kept alive through tubes and was constantly fed visual and audio recordings of his entire bloodline twisted and altered until he lost his sanity. At one point the person became unaware of his surroundings, and was injected with different substances to keep him responsive and conscious during the torture. After a while, his brain became unresponsive to the drugs and at that point there was no need to continue the torture and he was dropped into a well filled with sulfuric acid.

Harry sublimated his inquisitive nature; it was leading nowhere in particular and he was still under a tight deadline before the collectors arrived.

It was time to attend to his work.

CHAPTER 18

The first obstacle Gustave chose to tackle to test his mind control ability was to try and jump up on a tall box, roughly twice his height. He tried his feet. A quick jump from the ground assured him he was not prepared to dabble with an obstacle of this height just yet. He must first try to run and try to learn how to trigger the armor's control over running. He began trotting briskly, running in place. Nothing felt different; he then began jogging faster, focusing his consciousness on his foot and the leg muscles, which seemed to be working at full output. Nothing changed, nothing felt out of the ordinary. He paused, and continued running, stopped, then began sprinting. There was still no change. He decided to continue running; perhaps something would trigger the controls. Gustave always found running to be a bit boring, and when his concentration finally gave up, he gazed at a rise in the floor which he was approaching and in a flash, he suddenly caught the notion of his distance from that mark, its height, and without conscious control, his legs felt as if they were pushed and pulled as the speed with which he approached the surface intensified. Wearing an amused grin on his face, he began convincing himself he could get to that mark faster at which point his body accelerated to a point where the armor caught up to the unfamiliar speed in the legs and he stumbled. Unexpectedly, it was a very soft fall as the room adjusted the projected hit points on the floor to become soft and spongy.

A bit shaken by the fall, Gustave rose to his feet and tried running again. He now chose a different target and began running toward it. With very little effort he was running faster, and he tried to control the speed of running. He was still moving his legs, although it felt as if he were achieving more speed with considerably less effort. Reaching his target area he changed course and began running to his next target, the first obstacle he had wanted to work with. The armor calculated for him the distance between himself and the object as well as the object's height. Gustave intuitively felt it. He now tried to envision where he should be aiming, which was on top of the box obstacle and then just try to make a well-intended jump. He was successful. And with little effort, he stood on top of a box 11ft high. His movements were still unstable; his armor was still learning to adjust to Gustave's body movements. But there was no doubt in his mind he was indeed getting the hang of it. There were many attributes to the armor which would require his exploration and study, still. But he now had a general idea how to command it.

For about two hours, Gustave kept training and exploring his newly found powers. With each step he learned how to control, manipulate, and even change his surroundings to create new obstacles and accommodate to them through the assistive movements of the armor.

"He will be ready in less time then we initially though, don't you think?" Nell inquired.

"Yes, Nell, this will help us when we give him a short sleep and inform him his sleep was longer to correct the time he might think he spent on this ship," Kta agreed. "I'll go inform the team we will be going into the next phase to allow them time to prepare so please stay with him and direct him to a sleeping room. . . You seem as if you are less troubled now by the human's company. . .". He studied her expression and was still shocked by her reaction to the Nam stick incident.

Nell was in no position to argue with Kta. As much as she didn't feel ready to be on her own in a room with Gustave, she had to try. Reassuring herself, she tried to calm herself down, thinking, "Perhaps these humans are not so terrible after all, just very primitive, nothing more.."

Kta left the room. He left the room puzzled by Nell's behavior toward Gustave which seemed utterly out of character, worryingly so. She was afraid of humans, of that he was certain, however she didn't display much emotion toward what had happened back in the room with the Nam stick. It could be that her personal protection suit helped her keep her cool, but that was as much as he would have expected of her, considering her nature. However, no matter what the reason, he had no choice but to let it go and focus on other things such as the report he had to make to his command.

Walking through a tight corridor he approached a floater disc and conducted it to his room. Entering, the floor began morphing into a desk, a seat, and a few other items he enjoyed. He sat down on the chair which resembled a fine ergonomic executive office chair. On the space above his desk, a user interface appeared in mid-air. He cleared his throat, prepared a few reference documents on the screen and made contact.

"Ah, right on time, and with much pleasure it is to see you, Kta"

The voice was of Pix Not, a high member of the Angelonian underground movement which was in charge of communication duties with the mission and especially with Kta. Pix was an opulent Angelonian well known in his community for security trades with at least a dozen members of the union. Of course, none other than the members of the underground knew his other certain skills. He saw the humans as a potential trading partner, of, course a long term investment but nonetheless a profitable one. He was amused with humans above all. His hair was silvery white and he always chose to wear imported garments, some of which he even acquired from earth— such as his Japanese kimono. In the spirit of their conversation, he found it humorous to be wearing a silky hard-to -acquire earth-made garment.

Kta was quick to notice of his choice of clothing and laughed appreciatively with Pix.

Kta spoke first. "A kimono! I'll have to ask Gustave to acquire one for myself. . . it's a pleasure to be in contact with you as well, Pix".

"Oh, if you wouldn't mind, ask him to get more than one, will you? I could trade them in for a sizeable profit considering earth objects are impossible to get these days. . . How is he progressing, Kta? Can we count on him to play a part of this mission?"

"I'm sure I can arrange that, Pix. As for Gustave's status, the circumstances don't permit an easy answer. I am certain of his capabilities. . . he has proven himself over and over again, exceeding Moor's predictions." Kta paused for a second to ready himself for his next bit of information only to be interrupted by Pix.

". . .Please go on, I can see you are slightly illl-at-ease"—

Kta continued. "His thirst for technology and knowledge is more than we can accommodate. It will take us some time to be fully calibrated with his armor, but we are getting some disconcerting information as regardes his behavioral patterns. I could say there are a few personalities hidden in him, and that makes him very hard to read, and not only that, his neural activity is more advanced than Moor had anticipated. I'll have to solicit him for more information."

"I'm afraid that would not be possible Kta. I agree that Moor could provide us with more information about Gustave's abilities but I'm afraid Moor has gone missing. He might be on one of his trips again and as usual he left no mention of his whereabouts and even blocked his identity. Do you think Gustave will be capable of doing what we request of him? We can surely deal with him later when we have the harp in our hands."

By dealing with Gustave, Kta knew Pix was insinuating the removal of Gustave's armor and brainboard. Killing was an unthinkable concept to members of the union and was considered a heinous scenario just as humans consider animal abuse to be inhumane.

Kta's mood darkened with the news of Moor's disappearance. He felt compelled to know more about Gustave's past to try and understand what he was dealing with and possibly spare him from s a drastic outcome, or to be more accurate, spare himself from having to commit such a gruesome act.

Trying to delay his thoughts, Kta spoke with measured and patient tones. "We can control him for now; he wants to help us and he is fascinated with our technology. I will certainly have to entertain him with some of our ancient achievements, which would keep him happy and our mission on track, Pix. I'm afraid we will have to consider removing his armor at one point, although I did not want it to come to that."

"I will consult with other members, Kta. We might find something that could be useful when the time comes, something that would ease the removal, and be less of an impact on him. Am I correct it is safe to assume you will be doubling your protection for now?" Pix asked with an inquisitive glance.

"Indeed so, Pix, I will only allow small portions of the ship to be exposed to his neural link. Although if he wanted, he will be capable of opening that at some point if my simulations together with Moor's predictions are accurate. But I plan to have him off the ship well before that happens, well before he is aware he does not have access to everything he desires."

Pix nodded his head. "Well done Kta, and I concur. I look forward to our next contact."

Pix's image vanished from the screen and a black silence took its place.

CHAPTER 19

About two hours had passed since Harry started putting the incident report together. During that period he found something he did not expect; a strong correlation to a two-decade old incident which had occurred at S-13 base. There was not much information other than a dozen death records of security guards and the testimony of one survivor. At the time of the break-in, two F-16 fighter jets were scrambled to intercept an unidentified object. The report stated the two jets were immobilized as soon as they were airborne. Soon thereafter they were diverted to a different course at which point the pilots regained control over their aircraft. There was absolutely no reason to relate the interception and break-in but Harry's inquisitive mind saw something very interesting in common, two extreme oddballs. He tried digging deeper into his records, locating radar images, eye witness reports, and even found death certificates of a few physicists who had died in an explosion not far from S-13. It occurred to him to test the sizes of the unidentified blips located on the radar images of the two cases. They were a match in speed and size. Finally, He had enough information to place them under a new category which he named "S-type Incident."

Harry buzzed Liam on the intercom. "Liam, may I see you in my office?"

"Yes sir, Right away, sir," Liam responded respectfully.

Harry finalized his report, then shut his computer down. After two short knocks on the reinforced steel door, Liam entered the room, shutting the door behind him. He stood at attention and waited for Harry to speak.

Harry cleared his throat before he began. "The report is complete Liam, and we have ourselves a fine case even with the lack of data from our agents. I want you to inspect everyone's station. Make sure they are clean of dust and other dirt. The team members will be coming in ten to fifteen minutes. Once everything is clean, I want everything ready to go for the inspection team before they arrive. Please request them individually to take their time once they go for inspection; they have already waited three days here, so a few more minutes won't kill them."

"Sir?" Liam was puzzled. He didn't really understand Harry's request.

"I require some more time with the Superior. If I can have her just a few more minutes to talk, I'll do so any way I can. She always leaves the moment they check all the staff, and I need some time with her myself. . . Do you understand, Liam?" Harry was in no mood to explain.

"Yes sir. . . Understood, sir," Liam replied.

Harry sat back in his chair. "Oh, and Liam, don't

make it seem as if I requested this, okay?" Harry's tone changed to more a soothing level, almost as if he requested a personal favor. The 'on a privileged basis' tone made Liam very happy, which Harry knew it would.

The collectors had arrived not long after the entire complex was cleaned to the superior standards the unit was trained to achieve. The floors were shiny, all files, documents and records were straightened into neatly organized piles. The light in the office was luminously bright; the specially installed Halogen light bulbs made sure of that. There was a luxuriant feel to the rooms sowed by the level of neatness and orderliness in which the compound was displayed as it awaited inspection..

An alarm was activated, whereupon the entire staff rose to their feet and walked into the large checkout foyer, with the exception of Harry, whose duty it was to remain in his room and await the short talk with his superior. He was excited about discussing with her his findings and the possibility of being rewarded with a nod or any form of a stilted reply made his entire stay of three days locked in this place well worth it.

A few minutes passed by and the door opened. Harry rose from his chair, a smile lighting up his countenance as he extended his hand.

After the superior, another man dressed in a black suit entered, followed by a third person, a woman, who wore a custom-tailored navy blue suit. Harry felt uneasy. This was not the usual procedure to start; he also did not recognize his superior's two companions. Harry could not help but think if he ever thought he'd had a chance to talk a little more, he now was sure it was neither the right time nor the right place for a friendlier chat with the one he did know.

The three sat down. Harry remained standing for a few more seconds and slowly lowered his hand that had been ignored by the touch of another. He sat down.

"Harry, there are a few pressing issues at hand, but even so, these are two of my associates," the superior spoke. She was a dark-haired woman with wavy hair that was neatly held back from her high forehead by a burgundy-colored velvet head band.

Her skin was pale and smooth. Her lips, eyes and other facial features looked as if they were never meant to attract any attention. Her voice was as nondescript as her appearance and left no memorable impression.

"What have you found for us, Harry?" She sounded worried.

Her two associates stared at Harry as if they were examining his every move. He was well accustomed to being scrutinized by a group of superiors during his long military career. But these circumstances were a bit different considering the magnanimity of his superiors, especially now that things were not going according to the usual procedures.

"Well, it's not the first time it happened, I can tell you that with certainty." Harry straightened his shoulders and looked steadily at each of the inspectors in turn. "You see, I found a strong resemblance to another incident about twenty-five years ago. I filed the two under a new category I called S-type after the break-in incident at S-13 base."

"The break-in at the S-13? What connects the two, Harry?" This time another person spoke, the man who stood to Harry's superior's right. He had a commanding baritone voice well suited to his physical appearance.

Harry wasn't sure to whom should he speak first. Moving only his eyes, he looked at his superior, then back to the man who had spoken.

"The jets were diverted as soon as they took off. This was an indication the two cases show a strong relation – a similarity of procedure."

The man to whom Harry spoke, clenched his fist and let it go almost as if to not reveal any signs of stress. Clearly, however, it seemed as if he knew more than he gave away and this was simply a confirmation.

Harry was intimidated about revealing the second reason the confirmed cases seemed to be similar. He dreaded the disclosure because he did not have the stamina to withhold any information from these people.

"There is more." Harry said in a quiet tone. "My intel shows there is more in common with the two cases, a person actually, a civilian." Harry paused and opened a folder containing documents and a few photos. He went through the pages until he found the paper he was looking for.

"Gustave Eisenstein." He said out loud and placed it on the table facing the others. "Eisenstein was reported missing yesterday. It so happened both he and his father Dr. Saul Eisenstein were involved with the break-in in S-13. His father worked at the base, and his lab was the one from which, as the report says, important equipment and research data was stolen. Gustave himself was in the lab at the time of the break-in." Everyone became motionless as Harry continued, almost whispering.

"I reviewed the surveillance video; it doesn't look as if the kid was involved with the break-in. He was resistant to the intruders and even severely injured one of them using a high temperature soldering tool he had been playing with before they entered. The report was filed by Gustave's parents, so I can't tell whether the family is up to something or not. But the strong connection is there."

"Wait outside, Harry," a female voice shattered the deathly quiet. It was the voice of the second woman dressed in the dark suit. Harry now got a better look at her, and saw that she seemed a bit older, but not much older than his superior or her male colleague.

"M a'am?" Harry said in a fearful voice.

"Wait outside, Harry!" the woman insisted, only this time with a much more meaningful and assertive tone.

Startled, Harry rose from his seat. "Yes, ma'am!" and left them alone in the room.

The corridor next to his office had a grey carpet and there were no chairs or any other pieces of furniture in sight. Even if there had been seating arrangements, he was too jittery to sit down. Instead, he walked back and forth keeping a close distance to his office door. The door was blast proof, and with that came the security knowing nothing in the room could be heard, including the conversation taking place in his office right now. A few moments passed by and Harry paused his strolling to lean against the wall opposing his office door. He looked at his watch, which was a fine time piece that encompassed a large black dial and two silvery day and date dials within it. It was eleven past seven. Anxious, Harry resorted to the only thing he imagined he could do to keep himself helpful: he began thinking more deeply into this particular case, trying to piece together some of the anomalies that had captured his attention to connect the recent incidents together with the incident at S-13 base. The only incidents involving civilians with the unknowns were abductions. Otherwise it was mostly hovering over military bases with the occasional nuclear disarming, for what he called the alien equivalent of tree hugging. Other occasions were the leisure flights which mostly consisted of the accompaniment to test flights or even other types of military and commercial traffic.

Before he managed to continue his train of thought the door opened. The three came out, first the man he didn't know, second was the woman who seemed to be in charge and third came his superior who closed the door as she left the room.

"Harry, you've served us well for some time now. We believe this situation calls for a person with your skill set to move up the ladder in our organization. A few hours from now there will be an accident in which you will be declared dead at the scene. Everything will be arranged so as to make it seem you have died in that accident. Some of your possessions will be transferred in about a week to our compound. In the meantime, you have to come with us; we have a lot to talk about. You are now to be involved directly with us. At a much more prestigious level, I might add."

Harry's face turned a warm reddish tint. He was feeling as if someone had suddenly turned on a heater and aimed it directly into his face. His training as an order-following soldier and the accompanying anticipation eventually kicked in, and he felt no negative reaction to the order. Now he was prepared to go to any length if it meant finding out what he had yearned to know all these years of service. Now it was more palpable than ever before. . . and almost within reach.

CHAPTER 20

Nell was feeling very anxious about entering the room where the human was training, but she knew she had to brave the dreaded one-on-one confrontation. She took a deep breath, held her shoulders rigidly erect, and caused the wall to open so she could enter the human's room.. Her neural heart rate grew faster, but it was rapidly lowered to normal again after her neural-regulators took charge.

The Angelonians had a much more advanced system than that which they had armed Gustave with. Their bodies were injected with self-regulating module monitors a few months before their births, which accepted unfamiliar controlling modules anywhere needed. These numerous and varied locations were bio-engineered to accommodate the module's two way communications with the body's own neural networks. There were hundreds of different modules, each with its own unique set of functions, from simple tasks such as regulating blood flow in a more effective way to monitoring and regulating cellular regeneration and even chemical analysis. If, for example, a chemical analysis revealed a nutritional or chromosome imbalance, the module would contact other locations with pertinent modules to remedy the imbalance either by introducing more or by limiting hormonal production. There were other more general mother-posts where communications and pattern analysis modules activated functions that communicated with perception, memory, and learning. This alone ensured a very long life, as there was no room for failure of organs as a result of natural or external means. In a sense, this was merely correcting a few evolutionary mistakes. The simpler the organism was, the less likely it was to have failures, which is equally true of artificial devices.

Gustave sensed Nell's presence as she approached the room cautiously and as stealthily as a wary feral cat. He couldn't understand completely what it was that he felt, but he was hyper-sensitive to her presence. His armor was equipped with very acute sensory systems to which he was not yet accustomed, but as he trained by modifying the room, changing the floors and walls, his nervous system became more and more accustomed to communicating with the armor; in turn, the armor learned the pattern recognition behavior from his neural network. The mapping of his neural patterns grew larger and larger and that helped the armor feed his biological neural network with clearer messages.

Being the man that he was, he felt compelled to demonstrate his newfound capabilities for Nell, of course, trying to pretend he was unaware of her presence.

He looked up at the tall ceiling and back at the ground. He morphed the ground into an elaborate maze that resembled a painting by Asher that rose to the top through vertical and horizontal perpendicular surfaces. Satisfied with how difficult it seemed, he made a run for it.

Jumping here, climbing there, hopping great distances over impossibly twisted shapes, he made his way to the end of the three-dimensional labyrinth. He wanted to make sure his observer was watching, so he glanced in Nell's direction. He would have probably made it through the maze if it hadn't been for the armor's interpretation of his glimpse to the side, which was rendered as a destination to which a route was calculated and then transmitted into his body movement. He fell, and his maze morphed into a soft, spongy like material.

Even knowing he would not be in any life-threatening situation because of the safety of this specially programmed training room, Nell screamed. She was not accustomed to seeing such kinds of accidents.

Gustave recovered himself, although he was slightly chagrined. In a jubilant tone of voice he said, "I'm quite all right, Nell! Did you like my sculpture?"

Nell was still a bit stressed about being in the human's presence, even though her body synthesized calming remedies. Her throat felt as dry as sand but she managed to create some saliva and swallowed to sooth her epiglottis. "I don't think I can say I had feelings toward the structure, Gustave, but I am very impressed with the level of your control over the nanonites in such a short time. If you weren't so ignorant I could probably find good use for you with my work." As she answered, she managed a brief smile.

Enraged by the insult, Gustave clenched his teeth and glared at her with an angry expression. The clenching was strong enough to reveal dimples on both of his cheeks. He had always been very patient with people who possessed less knowledge than he did and until not too long ago, he had come across many. He never insulted someone right to their face in matters of knowledge or wits. There were only a few things that angered Gustave deeply—an insult to his intelligence was probably the least favorable of them all.

"Did you invent most of the technology of this ship, Nell?" Gustave's eyes were slightly narrowed as he awaited her answer.

Nell did not see where Gustave was going with this right away, but she noticed his tone of voice, and the aggressive signals that undulated from his armor readings. She stepped backward cautiously, her throat even drier than before and she sensed danger. Her face turned pinky-red. She wondered if she had done something to evoke such behavior from the barbaric human, but she couldn't imagine what.

"I, no I did not, Gusta.."

Gustave cut her off in mid-sentence. "So you have had the privilege of being taught about all this technology from another, were you not?

Tears filled Nell's beautiful eyes. Almost whispering, she replied, "Yes I have. . ."

At this moment she understood that she had translated her sentence incorrectly. She had not meant to call him ignorant, but just lacking in advanced knowledge.

Gustave was not done, however. His anger was building up more and more. "Then does that give you the right to insult my intelligence? Is it because I am an idiot or because I have not had the hundreds of years, wait a second, did I say hundreds, I meant thousands of years of studying knowledge that has been accumulated by the works of others?"

Nell truly did not mean to insult Gustave, however, now that he was behaving aggressively, she began to wonder if he was less intelligent than she had hoped, and just like the other humans, governed by aggressive tendencies. She tried speaking and found it difficult. "I was confused in language. . . Please..." she grasped for air, and seemed to be tottering. Her body was not accustomed to such feelings of confusing danger. It was unnatural to be yelled at in her culture.

When Gustave noticed Nell's distress, he also realized she didn't mean what she said and she might have made a translation error. Ashamed, he began apologizing. "Nell, I'm so sorry, I didn't mean to frighten you, I'm not going to harm you in any way. Please forgive my behavior." He approached her very slowly, and comforted her with a soft pat on her shoulder. As he comforted her, Nell released her emotion into a soft cry.

Gustave wasn't too sure how to react to her crying. He only understood how to deal with human distress. There she stood, an alien, a very pretty alien female and he had made her cry.

Nell sniffled and wiped the tears from her face. She looked at Gustave with her big turquoise eyes and said, "Thank you Gustave. . . I didn't mean to say you are ignorant. I wouldn't like to be called that either!. I meant to say . . . there are many things you don't know about our technology, but if you did. . .ah. . . you could be useful."

Gustave continued stroking her shoulder in soothing and very soft pats, He then said, "I just realized even before that, I was being more sarcastic then angry, I didn't mean to…"

"That's okay Gustave, I understand. I think I'll have to try and read into your behavior more carefully".

Nell was comforted by Gustave's touch. She felt a warmth which she had not expected. She was petrified by humans before the mission and now, especially following this incident when she should have been more scared than before she suddenly began understanding humans shared with Angelonians more than just basic genetical structure but also emotions, even when these emotions were expressed in a much less refined way than her own species would have done.

Nell's charming smile caught Gustave off guard

and as a result, he stopped stroking her and his hand remained motionless on her shoulder. She removed his hand with her own and said, "Gustave, we shouldn't waste any more time. Your body and armor require a respite. . . I will take you to a room where you must rest for a few days to allow for the new networks to set in."

Gustave was not ready just yet for sleep; he did not feel tired, and on the contrary, he was still overwhelmed with excitement. Besides, sleeping or resting for a few days was something he thought was less likely to happen to him than this entire adventure.

He was just about to voice his opinion when Nell continued. "I can see that you are not experiencing any discomfort or tiredness, that is a very good sign that everything is connecting and communicating well, but we must not risk damaging the new networks; they do require further processing while you are less active."

Gustave suddenly realized he had spent quite a long time on the ship. People must be looking for him. He pondered for a moment and asked, "Can I sleep at home? I can't be gone for too long without having people looking for me."

Trying to conceal the fact that Gustave had missed more time than he was actually aware of, Nell smiled reassuringly. "Unfortunately that would not be possible, Gustave. We must monitor you for a while until you can get back. Kta informed me of a technology he used to contact you, something you call e-mail, perhaps you can connect to your home network and send a message back to your contacts?" Her answer was premeditated. She and Kta had figured out every strategy that would help them to avoid telling Gustave the truth about his lost time.

Gustave paused to think for a moment. Even though he wasn't ready for complete obsequiousness he understood there were too many unknowns involved with what he desired to do, which was to continue his training, and get back home. After a few moments, he agreed contacting a few people would be a good idea since he was not the type that would disappear for a few days without making sure everything, and everyone around him, knew he would be gone.

"I understand, Nell. That would be fine. . .but how can I contact my computer back at home?"

"Your armor is capable of doing that for you. You must find the right process to do so. We have programmed your mobile computer to connect with electronic devices on earth. I would suggest connecting to it and using it as reference."

Gustave was still unclear as to how he could achieve that. The devices he connected to so far were physically in the same room as he was, so how could he connect to the little laptop he left back at home? The moment he thought of the laptop, a specific image of the computer flashed into his memory. It was at that moment he realized he was able to access it without even trying to find a connection, a network, or a workgroup. Unlike any other computer on earth, he was able to locate a device just by recalling the connection to himself and a visual input. He was very confused as to how it worked so fast, but he had no doubt he was connected to the computer.

"Nell, that's incredible! I'm connected to the little computer! I can even connect to my computer in the office through the power grid. Although I'm not sure how my armor did all that, I just envisioned myself connecting into my computer and it did just that. Would it be possible to receive the technology of this type of connectivity, just its core of identifying remote devices in a network with such ease?"

"I think that can be arranged, Gustave. I promise we will look into it."

Gustave smiled and was certain this was something he could make good use of. The implications of being able to find a device with just a vague description with such ease were not extended merely to networking devices but also in the implementation in ultimate search engine technology and even advertisement. He tried to think less of the technology, and the more he thought about it, the closer he got to the plan of getting it all, which he tried to surpass as hard as he could. Instead he focused on writing an email to a few clients, family, and friends apologizing for not being able to be in touch and saying he would be back soon.

After writing the emails, he joined Nell in a room where a large brown sofa materialized next to a small table where a water container and a few odd-looking nutrition bars lay invitingly on the surface.

"You must be hungry, Gustave; these are very healthy flavorless food supplements. We are not accustomed to the victuals on earth so we brought you this bar we like to eat. It has very little taste. Please try it!"

"I will in a moment, Nell, but if you don't mind, first I would like to take a shower." He summoned a shower module into the room. Nell did so at the same time only in a different corner. Half way, they both looked at the showers that were constructing themselves from the material of the floor and the ceiling. They looked at each-other and smiled. In an awkward moment of trying to decide whose creation would be instructed to regress and whose would continue to materialize, Gustave thought that alien or human, it would have been nice to see beautiful Nell naked.

Nell quickly turned her head toward the shower she constructed and with a wry smile, she said, "I will leave you to it, Gustave, and will see you after your rest."

They exchanged goodbyes and Gustave was left to himself, his solitary shower, and the odd-looking nutrition bars.

CHAPTER 21

Harry left his office building accompanied by the older woman and the man he had just met. He noticed a large black bus near the front entrance in the parking lot, obviously awaiting members of his staff who were still standing around in the foyer on the first floor. Harry and his two escorts made a quick exit and none of his staff even knew he was rushed out of the building.

A few meters from the bus, two average looking metallic grey SUVs were parked, awaiting Harry, the older woman and the other man. Harry had expected a bit classier transportation, something that would fit a high profile politician, and initially was a little disappointed, but on second thought, he understood unobtrusiveness was exactly the point. As they approached one of the vehicles the doors opened. The inside was as plain as the exterior sporting no fancy gadgets or leather seating. What did impress Harry as unusual was the enforced plating of the car at key points, as well as the back seats, which were luxuriously padded and faced each other.

Harry climbed into the car, found a seat and buckled himself in. The woman followed him into the car and sat down across from him. The man got into the driver's seat. When the doors closed, the car emitted an irritating warning beep, which ceased within seconds.

Harry did not hear a sound from the engine but he felt the car move as it left the curb. He assumed the hum of the motor was blocked by the heavy layers of steel armor.

"My name is Terra, and his is Norm." The woman spoke softly and extended a gloved hand.

"Nice to meet you, ah, Terra. . .I'm Harry, ma'am. . ." He shook her hand gently, then realized he probably didn't have to introduce himself. He smiled awkwardly and sat back in the upholstered seat. He attributed his anxious behavior to his proximity to the truth of his situation, which he was inordinately curious about and eager to know. Nothing in his demeanor revealed his overwhelming curiosity, a deliberate tactical mask he had perfected over a period of many years. He also knew his persistent questioning nature would be obvious to someone who knew him very, very well.

It was rather dark in the car, and the tinted windows did not allow for much light into the interior. Terra, who was merely a shadow in the seat nearest Harry, emitted a faint aroma of a delightful French perfume, tantalizing with hints of jasmine and attar of roses. She leaned forward slightly so Harry could hear her subdued voice more clearly.

"Our organization is called the Agency for Monitoring Extra Terrestrials, or AMET for short. We were established in June, nineteen thirty-seven, under President Roosevelt's administration. Our intended purpose was to monitor and estimate the threat to national security specifically in matters of extraterrestrial activity on U.S soil. You were given access to many early reports of unknown flying objects back then, Harry, and at that time, those reports were all we knew about them. All of that changed in early nineteen thirty-nine when there was a crash near a military base in Colorado where the US War Department carried out various experiments based upon the long distance power transmission experiments of Nikola Tesla. An observing extraterrestrial vehicle at the time of the test was unguarded by its standard defense mechanism and crashed after temporarily losing all its power from the interference - the vehicle including four alien bodies was brought to us - and we have done our best to examine the bodies from the wreckage, all of which disappeared shortly afterward. Following that year, we had a more successful retrieval when we captured another ETV using a different test facility in Missouri in nineteen forty-one. We secretly transported the craft to an underground base in Los Angeles and we managed to keep it until February twenty-fourth, nineteen forty-two. That day was a first full air-to-air combat between us and the ETs. We were unsuccessful with our counter attack against their crafts and the retrieved alien craft was again, gone from the base following that battle.

"In forty-seven, another crash happened near

Roswell, New Mexico, only this time we captured two live ETs. At this point we began understanding we absolutely could not let them die, otherwise we might create a much more severe situation. We have tried attending the aliens and at the same time keeping them under unsecured space so that they would be easily found by retrieval attempts. This was the first time we had managed to reach an open understanding between us. This was also the first time we had to deal with trying to cover our tracks that were left open to the media, to allow for the aliens to be rescued. That's where we created several divisions to control leakage to the public. One of the divisions is NIL, where you worked until a few hours ago, where we collected and destroyed evidence.

"In late May, fifty-two, we were contacted by an alien group called Angelonians. They were purportedly a humanoid specie that said they wanted to help us by giving access to their advanced technology. Two days later we were contacted by another alien specie called the Krills which warned us that the Angelonians were very dangerous and not to be trusted. The Krills said they would help defend us. We were at first unsure of what action we should choose, and delayed our reply. A month later, without warning, we have observed hundreds of crafts above Washington. We understood immediately it was the beginning of an invasion, something which the Krills had informed us. We had unanimously voted on contacting the Krill for help. About a week later, on June the second, nineteen fifty-two, we held the first assembly with the Krills. The assembly was held in the New Mexico desert, attended only by members of AMET and representatives of the Krills. You see, we reached a sort of mutual consensus. . .They would be allowed to continue browsing our skies without interruption such as occurred in Los Angeles, and they would also report on a certain quota of humans they were allowed to take for medical examinations and in turn they would give us access to technology.

"The Krill's were very specific with their demands, though. They insisted we discontinue our nuclear weapon programs.

"Our immediate response was in agreement to their demands. But since this was at the height of the cold war, we did not intend to comply with these demands. For one, at that time we did not consider ourselves within the military industrial complex and the Russian threat was nothing we could turn our back on and ignore."

Harry nodded in agreement. Even though he was quite taken by the scope of the unknowns which stood hidden from the general public and kept secret even from himself, a person in a position that he thought to be with Need-To-Know privileges. He tried not to look too surprised or show any emotion.

Terra continued, "The Krills left us with a few gifts as promised. These new technologies kept us busy for some time, but after a while, we wanted more. We met a few more times. As they kept pressing us toward nuclear disarmament, we tried explaining to them that the human race is not yet ready for ending all wars, much less be open to exposure to alien technology. . . Primarily because the confirmation of life on a planet other than earth could bring down the church, as well as cause massive public panic. They agreed with restraining the disclosure of their existence. It wasn't hard, as they happened to have observed the public during the radio production of H.G Well's War of the Worlds in thirty-eight.

"Following that meeting, we have had no success in any further contact attempts. They have been completely ignoring us. And other than the information we received from NIL and some other resources, we were left in the dark. There have been a few more natural crashes, and we managed to salvage a few more items during the years, although all have been stolen by them or their associates. A few of their items were sent to the S-13 facility for reverse engineering, but those have been stolen, too. We still have a lot of records they did not confiscate, such as schematics for a device which Dr. Eisenstein was in charge of and one which was impossibly activated by his teen-aged boy, Gustave, right before they took everything they could find from the lab."

Harry felt uncomfortable in his seat. He was afraid the agency was playing with Greek fire. First he found out they were taking more than an active part with the aliens, then he was reassured they had reached a peaceful understanding with them, and now, he learned they were still under a very 'generous friendly' approach that was keeping humans alive on this planet, but that generous approach was solely based upon a one-sided patience exhibited by this alien race. He then asked, "Ma'am, if you don't mind my asking, how many aliens are out there? What was the device function?"

Terra didn't take long to answer. "There are probably more than fifty different races that we know of, and you will soon find out what their technology is capable of, and what our understanding of that device's purpose was. Harry, I would like to continue this talk when we get to headquarters. In the meantime, tell me more about what you dug up on that son of Dr. Eisenstein."

"I haven't had the time to study his file in depth but what I did manage to find out was nothing too impressive, other than his academic achievements." Harry wiped his perspiring forehead with his right hand.

Terra snorted, indicating her haughty disapproval. "I'm not surprised. . . well, we'll continue this discussion when we get to headquarters. We have all the tools we need right now to find out more."

Inside the car, everyone grew silent as the automobile turned onto a curving two-lane country road. Harry had no idea where they were going, but he was certain he would soon find out much more. In an attempt to make the drive less tense for himself and the others, Harry leaned forward, addressing Terra. "Ma'am, may I ask you one more question?"

"Yes, Harry."

"It seems neither the government nor the army is involved with this, so. . .why have I, an army man, been assigned to this operation?"

"You have started piecing together very important and delicate information, Harry. At this point, we would normally terminate and replace. But we believe this incident is involving something larger than we have encountered before. So we have decided this calls for unusual measures. Consider yourself lucky."

"Yes ma'am, I do, ma'am!" Harry cleared his throat nervously. The way she expressed the normal procedures with which their organization usually worked reminded him of horrible torture videos he had watched in disbelief. He had to respond affirmatively and with as much respectful acquiescence he could muster in his tone of voice.

Terra looked at him silently for a beat, blinked, then smiled and said, "Good."

CHAPTER 22

The faint blue glow of the walls of the post-op alcove where Gustave had been sleeping began to change into the brilliant rosy pastels of a mountain sunrise. Objects in the room were beginning to have shape and form: the 2-drawer bedside table where the water pitcher stood , the tri-fold moveable screen about 6 feet long shielded the patient's bed from any nursing activity that might emanate from the front of the room, a cushioned arm chair against the far wall, the changing colors of the translucent tiles of the floor as the internal heating system adjusted the warmth of the floor to a comfortable temperature, and Gustave's clothing folded neatly on the seat of the chair. Gustave wiped his eyes to clear his vision and sat up, looking around cautiously, trying hard to remember everything that had preceded his entering this room. He felt heavy and stiff, and his head ached dully, as if he had a hangover. He stood up slowly, holding on to the edge of the cot's mattress but that only intensified his dizzy symptoms. Gradually, he began stabilizing and became fully aware of his surroundings. He felt the mattress move strangely and he jerked his hand back. The bed was making itself up.

Gustave realized he was very thirsty and hungry, and wondered how long he had been asleep. Somehow, he knew he could contact Nell through the comm-link of his armor. Instead, he decided to summon Kta because he wasn't sure he had enough mental alertness to respond favorably to Beautiful Nell.

"Kta?" Gustave spoke hesitantly.

"Yes, Gustave, I see you are awake. Please wait, I am making my way toward your room."

Looking around, Gustave noticed his clothes and began to dress. The wall zipped open and Kta entered. The whole time, Gustave instinctively knew the distance and speed Kta was traveling through the ship to get to this room. The armor had calculated every move and translated it into a simple awareness of how much time he had until Kta arrived.

"You must feel a bit tired ,Gustave. We had to hold you under suspended animation for longer than we had initially expected. The armor fusion to the body had a few complications but they were all resolved. What you are experiencing now is a small side effect but it will soon diminish and be gone. . ." Kta was wearing a vibrant silk-like overall that changed colors as he moved, like an iridescent oil slick on a quiet pond . Its colors reflected the light of the room, as if they had been copied from the Northern Light displays above the Arctic Circle.

"How long did I sleep?" Gustave pulled on his trousers then placed his hospital gown on the wheeled tray bridging the foot of the bed.

"You were under suspension for three days and twenty-one hours; please understand that there was nothing we could have done to make the process any quicker... Your body is unexpectedly resistant to change induced by external means."

Kta knew flattery would soften Gustave's reaction to the news of his lost time.

"But everything is working fine, right?" Gustave's impatient tone was gone.

"Everything is working flawlessly now, Gustave! Please join me. You must be famished. . . let's enjoy a meal before one last briefing with the crew." Kta didn't want to linger too long in a conversation regarding the supposed lost time because he knew that might lead to more questions and worse yet, more mistakes while answering them. Kta had made every effort to be prepared, including inducing the mild effects Gustave was experiencing, which simulated a mild hangover.

The two left the room, Gustave carrying his vest and tie slung over his shoulder. They entered the corridor leading toward a floating elevator. Gustave couldn't understand why but it seemed as if now he had a much more familiar understanding of the ship. They stepped aboard and immediately were whisked upward as if they were dandelion seeds lofted by a soft breeze. As he noticed the work areas of the passing biobots speeding by, he was amazed at how much he was aware of, intuitively. He knew the speed at which they were zooming, he even knew the unit numbers of the biobots as he focused his attention on individuals. It was almost as if he received the information through an invisible heads-up-display, but it was extremely faint and diaphanous, almost as if it was there just because his mind was expecting this information to appear thus compensating for the lack of one.

He took the opportunity to try and understand his surroundings better but he wasn't able to retrieve any information other than the very surface of things. Unlike other parts of the spaceship, this part was unresponsive to his inquiries. That's when he discovered most of this information was encrypted. He continued searching for other information, and kept being denied communication. Gustave was too busy concentrating to notice the amused look on Kta's face.

The floating platform came to a halt. They reached a section of the ship Gustave had never visited. A corridor leading to a large opening in the wall was decorated with many unfamiliar objects. He noticed statues that changed shape and color as he looked at them from different angles, and the walls interacted with the statues by glowing in different hues so the atmosphere around the objects was in a state of constant flux. It was a gallery of some sort.

Gustave followed Kta's steps through the large opening of the wall into a room where Nell, Milka, and

Bor waited. He felt their presence well before he entered the room. He even sensed Nell's position; she was seated at the right side of the table. Gustave smiled and greeted everyone.

The table was constructed with the same morphing-smart material as the rest of the ship. At present, it was in the shape of an oval that was stretched on one side as if it was forged from molten glass. Following Kta's lead, he sat down on a chair which morphed into position, perfectly leveled to accommodate Gustave's height and shape. Breaking the silence, Gustave addressed Milka who was wearing a silky-looking fabric that wrapped around her body, then stiffened in appearance as it approached her neckline, ending in an accordion-pleated collar.

"It's good seeing you again, Milka!" Gustave couldn't what caused it, but something in his spine moved. Ignoring the rather odd yet short-lived spark of inconvenience he waited for her reply.

"It has been a few days, hasn't it?" Milka said with a wry smile.

Bor immediately felt the need to interrupt. "You play with your suit good now, I see. What else do you do?"

Gustave was unsure how to respond to Bor's sarcasm.

K'ta felt the need to intervene. "Gustave is a super combatant now, Bor, our own super soldier. Let's eat!"

Robots swarmed around the table with an array of dishes. The table morphed its surface to accommodate plates, strange magnetic cutlery and drinking water. Still finding it a bit difficult to get used to, Gustave found it easy to find out what was in the dishes that were brought to the table. The plates were embedded with enough technology to have both the ingredients and recipes embedded within them. Each time Gustave looked at a plate mentally inquiring what was in the food it held, the information was fed instantaneously via his wireless link. It wasn't as if he actually asked a question; the information autonomously floated toward his consciousness as he thought the question.

"Gustave, as our guest we have had our kitchen make you some of our delicacies." K'ta nodded toward the plates as they floated up, down, and sideways, like a futuristic anti-gravity highway.

"Thank you all, it is much appreciated!" Gustave said. In the split second after stating his gratitude, he reminded himself of his ulterior motive. Was he doing the right thing? They have been more than accommodating to him so far. With an effort, he diverted his attention to something else. Using the closest object in his eyesight he focused on the utensil that lay next to his plate. Although it resembled a simple rod, this piece of technology was yet another alien gadget: a spot gravity fork capable of both lifting and slicing. Gustave raised the instrument and grabbed it with his right hand. Bringing a plate of food close to his hand he navigated the rod toward the plate and chose a serving of food from the plate he most preferred. The gravity fork automatically adjusted its beam and strength required for the lift. Of course, most of these calculations came directly from Gustave's own muscle memory of lifting normal food with a standard fork, a human's use. The feeling of satisfaction sticking a fork or a knife in something that is about to be eaten was missing. Humans, with their violent nature, obtained a disturbing amount of enjoyment from that sensation. But surely enough, for sanitation purposes, it would have been irrational to stick to the old barbaric patterns of eating food.

The food was delicious but even though Gustave was extremely hungry he restrained from eating too much because he wasn't certain about the eating habits of his hosts.

Instead, he ate slowly focusing his prior fascination with the cutlery now to the main course. He noticed the group was keeping close track of his movements. To counteract negative comments or other disapproval, he said, "The food is delicious!"

Milka nodded in agreement, and it seemed as if she enjoyed the meal hugely herself. They continued eating until the plates on the table were empty.

K'ta, picked up his glass of water, sipped from it and grinned at Nell. Gustave wondered whether Kta's smile was of satisfaction from the food or perhaps, just like man on earth, his smile filled the empty gap of what man liked most, third after food and expensive toys, but not necessarily in the same order.

"We have arranged an alias identity for you on earth, Gustave," K'ta said. "Your name will be changed as well your appearance so you can penetrate the army research facility more easily. For the next few months you will be Dr. Steven Monde, a clever particle physicist from the University of Pittsburgh who published a paper on a theoretical particle which is of great importance to the research institute. We have arranged it so the appropriate departments on the army base will take notice of your published paper and are expected to ask you, or should I say, Steven, to join their team." K'ta's eyes twinkled as he observed Gustave's astonished reaction.

Gustave found the transition from eating to technically complicated matters almost too abrupt for his taste.

"I'm not sure I follow, sir. Is Steven Monde a real person?"

"No, not at all Gustave. . . We have been observing their work for a while now, and we know they are struggling with their research to the point where they think they should just, as they say, kill the switch on it. The solution is very simple, only they lack the right intuition. We easily created a fake identity and submitted a paper to a journal that is periodically sent to several people in high positions at that institute. The paper will be answering a few pieces of the puzzle they are currently stuck with, all while neglecting to mention the full solutions. . .This will most likely cause tremendous interest in Dr. Monde's research."

Milka waited until K'ta had finished his sentence

and added, "My probes show it has already stirred up quite a lot of curiosity and interest. . ."

"Precisely!" K'ta confirmed her statement with a firm, assertive nod... "Your expertise, Gustave, as Steven, will be needed there to complete their research and this will in turn give you access to their high level security facility. We will equip you with several detectors to locate and penetrate into the underground Union facility, and this is where your training and quick thinking will be put to good use. . . You see, Gustave, we are unsure where it is, and to what extent the facility is guarded."

Gustave was again reminded he would have to go into the belly of the beast. He was beginning to look forward to his infiltration of the alien lab facility as an exciting adventure. His negativity was toward the monstrous institution, a grandchild of the cold war ideology military family, raised by corporate types and to make things worse, maintained by academic people whose social skills resembled those of a rattlesnake. Not a safe haven for a man like himself, a man who for his entire life had deliberately avoided a career amongst such people.

"How do you expect me to make it seem like myself, or Steven to be more exact, is capable of being a man who has been studying particle physics for a lifetime?" Gustave was sincerely worried he couldn't pull off the charade.

Bor mumbled something in his native tongue. Nell gently placed her hand on his forearm and said, "Please". Her touch and soothing voice calmed him down. Looking at Gustave, she said, "Your direct connection from the armor to your mobile computer will handle this, Gustave, all you need to do is just maintain an open connection."

"The computer will instantly feed you the information you will need." K'ta rose from his chair and walked toward a large statue.

The statue, which had no obvious structure, began morphing into the shape of a four-legged furry animal, changing color to vibrant shades of scarlet, with enormous green-gold slanted eyes. Resembling the likeness of a Bengal tiger with the exception of an elongated mouth and a less intimidating set of claws and teeth, the statue took into a life-like animation, omitting deep purring sounds.

"Magnificent isn't she?" Kt'a said with admiration.

The giant cat brushed her nose in K'ta's palm. Suddenly she stopped, open her eyes wide, and began walking towards Gustave, her huge paws moving silently and confidently.

Gustave was so overwhelmed by the cat's life-like gestures he completely forgot it was a lump of bad art just a few moments earlier. Gustave loved all cats, and this was the most beautiful animal he had ever been near. He slowly extended his arm toward her. With majestic grace the animal approached more closely, nose first. He could feel it breathing, smelling, and expressing curiosity. He leaned forward to pet her but she quickly retreated a few steps backward, keeping her eyes locked on his.

"Our planets resemble each other very much,

Gustave," K'ta said. Gustave was enjoying the interaction with the animal yet he managed to glance at K'ta to indicate his interest. "We have plants that are very similar to those on your planet, and animals similar to the animals on your planet, with the exception of our cows, which are not only similar in shape and size, but are identical in all respects to the cows on your planet. We think it has something to do with our ancestors, but we are not certain."

This really caught Gustave's attention. "So we do have mutual ancestors?" He held his hand up in the air and the cat took the opportunity to come closer and rub against his nose and his cheeks. Gustave enjoyed this feeling. The sensation of the rubbing with the animal's fur felt like a nice pelt of a domesticated and well-groomed animal. Gustave was only able to express his joy with high pitched tones in broken English. Clearing his throat as if to clear himself from the embarrassment of the feminine tones he uttered to the cat, Gustave grew silent and returned his attention back to K'ta's face.

"We are not certain, Gustave , but we intend to find out, and in time we hope to be able to find out working as an open collaborative effort with the humans and our species."

"And when will that be?" K'ta motioned to the cat with his hand, and although her attention was at that moment focused on Gustave, she shifted her attention to K'ta and made her way toward him.

"In due time, Gustave, but first we have to focus

on getting the device from the secret lab. . . which will give our organization the leverage needed to openly share technology and information with the human race, regardless of the Union's say on the matter. It will all fall into place thereafter."

The device. Gustave wondered what "the device" was. Their technology was already advanced in ways he could not have imagined far beyond that which he had witnessed in the spaceship. He wondered what more there could be to invent, after instantaneous interplanetary travel, smart particles that changed and grouped to whatever material object was needed and sources of energy unknown to humans, even those scientists whose entire life was dedicated toward theoretical physics. In the days of the steam engine, would we have anticipated an inventor to have thought about nuclear power? The whole concept of something from a creative imagination becoming a reality was exceptionally difficult, to put it mildly, considering the only link between the two technologies was the use of heated liquid.

Gustave realized considering the superior intellectual level of the advanced civilization he had witnessed in the Galactic Union, weaponry must have been perfected to such destructive means it had become expedient not to have any at all.

As a human, the first thing that came to his mind was some sort of an advanced weapon. What else could possibly give the Angelonian separatists enough power to act openly and flaunt their disagreement with the Union?

Gustave rose from his chair to show K'ta he was prepared to be his equal and share some of his Angelonian knowledge and without hesitation asked, "What is this device, K'ta?"

"Ah yes. . I did promise you this information. . . ." He paused for a moment then pointed at the small tiger-cat. "This Lirish is a fully automated statue. It is capable of simulating the same movements as the original animal or a clone; it even feels and sounds like the original animal. If we wished for it, it could even produce the same odors the original animal emits. Yet it is just a simple robot controlled by our wishes and commends. The nanonites can group together, into any shape or structure we choose for them to be. You yourself, with the help of your morphing suit, can change it into anything from your memory, although it works best if it was preprogrammed into the database. It isn't a living creature. We create living creatures all the time, changing their biological structures; we are even capable of breathing life in animals long dead. This Device…" K'ta paused. 'I am finding this attempt to explain this ability we have in a simplistic manner very difficult, so if you will bear with me, I'll make a sincere attempt not to be patronizing...What if you had the same sort of ability and control you have over nanonites over real objects, real materials, and real subatomic particles?" His voice became animated and full of excited anticipation. Gustave, however was still unaffected by that enthusiasm. He was still uncertain about what the device could do. His silence signaled K'ta to give him a more explanatory illustration so he would be able to absorb the entire concept more comprehensively.

"For example, consider this statue,. . . I would like it to become a thin layer of metallic- looking sheet." In a matter of milliseconds, the animal flattened and became a reflective sheet of thin metal floating in the air. The sound it made as it morphed resonated long after it became motionless and floating in mid-air.

"Imagine what you could do if you had that kind of control over everything in this universe on a micro and a macro scale. You could rearrange the molecular structure of elements and you could re-form and move planets, rearrange, or completely freeze solar systems and even galaxies. With such power and scale, you could also bend time however you like"

A cold shiver ran down Gustave's spine. K'ta was referring to skills cited from religious dogmas, skills that were only mentioned when describing the power of the all-knowing god of the monotheistic religions. And there was an actual science behind this?

"How is any of this even possible K'ta, how can you communicate with everything?" Gustave asked, a detectable concern apparent in his tone of voice.

The entire team looked nervous because of their deep-seated fear of giving away knowledge beyond what they planned to give when they formulized their mission. Even K'ta was under strict restrictions decreed by the council in charge of monitoring the underground movement.

Everyone on the team looked at K'ta with uneasy anticipation. Even they questioned how skillful K'ta could be explaining this without breaking the mission codes.

K'ta, however was well prepared to answer this, which was one of the prerequisites necessary for his appointment as the mission's highest command – the C.O.O.- Chief Operations Officer. "No, we can't talk or communicate with sub-molecular particles, Gustave. We can, however, sync, for the lack of a better term, with structures that can. Humans, for example, have been toying with magnetic resonant coupling although they are completely unaware what magnetic energy actually is. The technology behind the device has a common ancient ancestor shared with modern technology used by humans as well as our instantaneous Quantum-Throb-tone drive." Finishing his sentence K'ta waited for this information to sink in with Gustave. Only Bor, misunderstood K'ta's explanation and was uncertain how the reference was applied to the Harp. With aggressive over-confidence, he capriciously decided to continue where K'ta left off.

"Only instead of a jump tune it uses a structure tune!" Bor's expression was that of a smug know-it-all.

K'ta, Nell and Milka all three glared angrily at Bor. He was not supposed to mention any of this. Giving away the fact that there was a lot more behind what he said.

Milka laughed too loudly and without humor. "If it

was only that simple, Bor."

K'ta joined in on the illusion. "We wouldn't need to steal it, now would we?"

They might have been highly intelligent species, but they were not very capable of deceptiveness or duplicity. Gustave perceived there was something more behind what Bor said, but decided to play along, and give them the benefit of a doubt.

"I guess if it was that simple, I would have invented it myself" Gustave smiled mischievously smile, and to add to the humorous disguise, he started laughing as if to make it clear he was laughing at himself.

The group was highly entertained by Gustave's comment and the mood changed to a more favorable and relaxed one.

Milka and Bor rose from their chairs. The table shrank to a different shape to give them walking room.

Milka placed her hand on Bor's arm and said, "Come Bor, we should be getting to our duties. Gustave, it has been a pleasure. When we meet again in a few months of your earth's time, I will be delighted to have another conference with your company." Smiling, she extended her hand for a gracious farewell.

Bor bobbed his head and the two left the room.

The flattened Statue-tiger returned to its original unformed mesh of a motionless abstract piece of solid matter. The dining table morphed and minimized into the size of a small coffee table, by earth standards. There was no doubt the banquet was over.

There were a few moments of silence before Nell walked toward a featureless part of the room and summoned a comfortable-looking overstuffed wing-back chair from the floor. Her dress changed to different shades of magenta as she sat down making herself comfortable. The colors of her dress continued changing until she finally settled herself and let her head fall back resting on the thick damask cushion of the elegant chair.

"Gustave, please join us. . ." K'ta made his way toward the new lounging spot. An equally comfortable-looking seat rose from the floor and he too gracefully dropped into the seat cushion to rest.

Gustave walked toward the area and gazed at the floor. He was concentrating too fiercely, trying to ask the floor for an ordinary seat to try to match it to the nicely designed sofa chairs Nell and K't had arranged for themselves. Instead, an earthly-looking standard TV sofa appeared.

Nell found the addition to be of some charm, ignoring the mismatch to the micro-climate formed by stylish modern design.

Without waiting for Gustave to be seated, K'ta said, "We will watch you closely, Gustave, and try to provide you with any support necessary to complete the mission. We originally planned on settling close by in orbit, in an air base from which we could monitor and direct the operation. Once the device is in your hands we will have a very short window of retrieving you as there will most likely be some form of alert to the union's authorities. Nell was supposed to take an important part of that but seeing you are almost fully capable of handling yourself with the armor, I don't think that will be necessary anymore."

Nell looked surprised. This was the first time she had heard of this deviation from the original plan. She was in no position to question K'ta on this move, especially not in front of humans, so she kept any display of surprise to a bare minimum.

Gustave was disappointed not to have the opportunity to spend more time with Nell. It was equally true he was more afraid his level of interaction with the armor would get to the point where they became comfortable observing him from a further distance.

"What if I had to ask you something from a situation where I couldn't engage in an actual vocal conversation, K'ta?" Gustave was exposing his fear with this question, hoping he would know more about the armor and find out if the aliens could fully understand and probe his thoughts.

"We still can't read your thoughts, Gustave, so you would have to dictate them to your computer while an open link to us is maintained. In return I can send you answers via your internal auditory interface or perhaps send you the required information as packets to your armor's memory."

Gustave was relieved to hear this reply, yet had no assurance it was the truth.

A bio-bot zoomed into their lounging zone and

handed K'ta a black box.

"These will be the only tools available to you for completing the mission. I have uploaded a run program for you to test it out. Please make sure you have a very good understanding and muscle memory buildup before you use them." K'ta then extended his hand which was holding the black tool box, roughly the size of a cellular phone.

Gustave took the box from K'ta hands and observed it carefully without opening it. Whatever lies within the content of this box, couldn't have been cooler than the magnetic cutlery, Gustave thought, especially as he was holding in his pocket both the magnetic knife and fork lifter which he had managed to confiscate before their disassembly. In any case, he felt he would be in need of any help he could get. And, of course, other things came to his mind.

"We are good for our next phase of operation!" K'ta was enthusiastic.

Not spending more than what seemed like half an hour engaging in further exchanges of words, Gustave finally found himself on his way back home. Only this time he vowed to take a more active part in the entire operation. He could barely contain his excitement.

CHAPTER 23

After what seemed like a long drive the car slowed to a stop. Terra unbuckled her seatbelt and said, "You may leave the vehicle, Harry. . . We have arrived at the landing pad."

"Yes Ma'am." Harry released himself from his own seatbelt.

Harry stepped out of the car and noticed the well-lit army base. A few cargo planes were visible in the distance as well as a few smaller aircraft. To his right, a black Bell 4 series helicopter was poised like a gigantic metal insect. Harry could see the pilots doing their pre-take-off checks in the cabin. There was always a sense of adventure going up in these things, no matter how often he got to ride one, and it was always a pleasure. This time, he was more focused on where he was going rather than how he was getting there.

The car's door automatically closed as the chauffeur drove it away. Harry watched the car drive off.

"It's a short flight to our final destination for the day, Harry." Terra led the way toward the helicopter as one of the pilots nodded in her direction and opened the door. The interior was luxurious. In comparison to the standard-looking car, the four large dark leather seats and brushed steel trim made Harry a bit uncomfortable. He was not used to such lavishness. He followed Terra into the passenger cabin and settled into a seat directly across from Terra.

Terra removed some documents from her briefcase and began making small notes. She wasn't too talkative, but Harry didn't mind that at all. It gave him some time to digest and collect his thoughts, although seeing her doing work made him feel a little uncomfortable as he felt like he should be doing some himself.

The aircraft began its take-off procedures. He could hear the electrical components booting up, followed by the sound of the engine and the rotating whirr of the blades which started at a low pitch and became higher as the blades gained more and more speed. He was well accustomed to the sound of helicopters after many years of serving under various black ops missions. These were not military people, however. In an army operation, the helicopter would have been already running well before the team reached the landing pad.

Terra paused from making notes and put on a headset located next to her seat. She signaled Harry to do the same.

"It will be a short flight to our final destination, Harry" Terra said and then she took off her headset.

The helicopter rapidly gained height and speed. The airbase below was mostly comprised of various hangers, a flight control tower, and a few other buildings. The ground dropped farther away as they climbed away from the base.

Terra, after placing her headset next to her seat, dived back into her paperwork. Here and there she took out her mobile phone, or what looked like one, and quickly typed on its small keyboard.

Harry left his headset on. There was not much else he could do other than looking at the pale, grey clouds in the distance. The ground below was too dark to make out his whereabouts and discern where they were headed.

About twenty minutes after take off, he began seeing lights in the distance. The aircraft was approaching a large city. Harry could make out tall buildings by the flashing lights emitted from the antennas on their roofs.

Down below, roads were beginning to take shape, and he could make out houses on the outskirts of the city. It wasn't long before he saw the central area of the city. Harry wasn't much of a traveler in the states. His life was spent mostly in army bases, or close to them. He never had much time for television, either. He regretted he was unable to know which city they were approaching by looking at the land marks. He decided he would not ask something that could be embarrassing but also that he must get himself familiar with more cities, once this was all over.

The helicopter made its descent toward a rooftop of a tall building. There was a visible landing pad marked by proper symbols and lighting right in the center.

Immersed as she was with her work, Terra only noticed the descent when her ear pressure began changing. She glanced at Harry and started gathering her paperwork and putting it back in her briefcase.

The helicopter landed. They both came out of the helicopter running from the noise while crouching, as if the blades were close enough to harm them.

Beside the pad, a group of well-dressed people came to greet them. Terra gave her brief case to one man and received another set of documents from another. They all began walking towards the building's entrance.

Harry followed them into the building.

The door led into an elevator room. Once in, the door closed and the sound of the helicopter was muffled by the strong shielding and insulation of the interior of the building.

None of the men carried any identification. Unlike a regular agency, they remained dressed in expensive suits without tags.

"Welcome to Peterson Financial, Harry." Terra said.

The group walked towards the elevator. There were four of them besides himself and Terra. Entering the elevator, one of the men began pressing numbers in sequence on the elevator's keypad. After completing a sequence of ten floors in sequence another man began a different sequence on the second keypad to the left of the door. Harry never understood why some elevators had two keypads on either side of the door. It wasn't until now that he saw a legitimate reason for having a duplicate set of keys.

After completing the sequence, the elevator closed its doors and began moving downward.

A few moments later the elevator stopped. A third man entered yet another sequence to the elevator's keypad while the fourth man entered his own sequence at the same time.

The elevator doors opened.

"There are other companies working in this building. We have a few ways to enforce they never make a mistake getting to their floors. Security cards that each worker in this building carries with him, make sure an elevator knows what floor they are supposed to be going to. Once they pass through the lobby they wave the card through the lobby's reader that sends that information to the elevator." Terra was very proud of a security protocol she herself had engendered. "We on the other hand, have these cards but there must be the accompaniment of four other top security guards with good memory of sequences that change by the hour."

"Wouldn't it look a bit suspicious when there are

keypads for the floors in this case?" Harry asked trying to take a proactive part in the welfare of the secrecy of the organization.

"Not at all, we added these later," Terra replied hastily.

The floor`s lobby was ostentatious in interior design. Harry never remembered visiting anywhere with so much money spent on lavish wall decorations and shiny marble floors that shimmered with tiny lights encapsulated inside the marble.

Except for a few eagle-shaped statues as well as other sculptures of various shapes Harry was not too fond of, there were comfortable-looking modern seating arrangements, tables and chairs. It looked like the lobby of a fancy hotel or even a high-tech, overly successful company.

There wasn't a reception desk as such, but rather, a large contraption built from various mechanical and digital devices Harry had never seen guarding what appeared to be the main entrance door.

It was no surprise that this was yet another security mechanism, the use of excessive security measures was the organization calling card although neither they nor Harry had become accustomed to such precautions.

The door opened after a complete scan by the mechanism guarding the door was complete. Harry felt a little nauseous and dizzy following the scan. Walking slowly, he tried combating his momentary sea sickness induced by the electro-magnetic scan and focus on what lay in front of him.

The grouped walked into a tall-ceilinged room fitted with lavish lights suspended in mid-air. The room also had a few terminal computers and some other odd devices Harry had no idea as to what their purpose could be. Terra stopped her march in the middle of the room and turned toward the group.

"Peter, Jack, get the monitor prepared, please. The rest of you know what to do. Harry. Harry!" Terra raised her tone. Harry tried focusing too hard on the interior of the room in order to ignore his nausea. He was not paying attention to anything else. His vision began crumbling and it was difficult for him to focus on anything specific. With his greatest effort to block his dizziness, he couldn't keep from losing his balance. He collapsed to the floor. A calm and fuzzy quietness fell on him as he lay on the floor, motionless. The air became thick, or so he thought, and the sounds muted until the room noise or Terra's screams sounded as if they were in another room, or outside a pool, while he felt submerged underwater. For the first time in his life Harry had fainted.

CHAPTER 24

The first thing Gustave did when he got home was to charge his cellular phone. He assumed many people had tried to call him in the past few days, and the constant ringing must have drained the battery. Going to his office, he turned on his computers. As much as he was used to opening them in a certain order while not even looking at the switch button, this time was different and he navigated around his equipment with a little clumsiness, having to think before he acted. Still hungry, he took off his clothes and changed into a pair of comfortable fleece pajamas. He didn't bother hanging up his suit, shirt, and tie but instead, he threw them all on the bed that was still tousled, as he had left it.

He decided it would be best if he ate something then with a full stomach and a cigarette he would be able to confront his family and friends and disclose where he'd been and why a man that had never disappeared before, or taken many vacations, was gone for almost a week without so much as leaving a note. A cigarette! He hadn't indulged himself in a single smoke for his entire stay on the ship, yet he didn't feel a craving for nicotine. It wasn't until he had to deal with something he'd much rather not face that he was reminded of his bad habit. The craving returned.

He should have probably kept himself busy with other things to stall the craving but he went to his kitchen pantry where he always kept a carton of Benson & Hedges in stock. He took out a new box, tore the protective plastic, opened the box and ripped off the health warning together with the foil lining. The smell of the tobacco was as good as the scent of a beautiful woman. He desired it, even knowing it would be unhealthy for him to have one. He was addicted to both.

With his eyes closed to increase his sense of satisfaction, Gustave inhaled, and felt the soothing smoke filling up his throat and completing a void that was the result of several days off nicotine. The cigarette did not, however, subdue the feeling of hunger. Opening the freezer he dug around in the frozen foods until he found a pack of frozen chicken. Hungry as he was, he wasn't in the mood for cooking. A quick fix was all he craved.

He grabbed a container of rice, a leftover from a past dinner a few days before he left for training.

The rice didn't smell right from the moment he opened the lid of the container. The stench of food that had been sitting too long was overwhelming. With a look of dissatisfaction Gustave held the plastic container as far away from his nose as his arm could reach. Holding his breath, he opened the cabinet door under the kitchen sink and tossed the rotten food, along with the container, into the garbage container.

The door of the refrigerator had been left open which made it easier for him to realize his entire supply of vegetables were in bad shape, along with other prepared dishes.

"There must have been a power outage. . ." he muttered, which was possibly the only logical explanation, perhaps even more logical than the actual reason. There was an abundance of spaghetti in one of the kitchen cabinets as well as a large selection of canned tomato sauces. He grabbed a large pot and heated some water.

It wasn't long before he felt well rested, with his stomach full of carbs and another cigarette in his mouth. He almost nodded off to sleep, but decided it was probably best if he called his parents and let them know of his return. What feeble excuse he was going to come up with, he had no idea.

He tried to wrap his mind around what would cause him, a person who doesn't leave the house too often to go away for a few days without saying anything to anyone, then he remembered he had sent an email with a short explanation. He could not remember what the email said, but at that moment, his armor connected to the computer which he had turned on earlier. The feeling was strange. So strange that he felt as if the training he had just undergone was not enough to prepare him. He asked himself to remember the email he had sent his family and friends.

The memory, together with typeface and even paragraph organization, came back to his mind. It wasn't that he suddenly remembered; there was too much detail in the memory, almost as if he was looking at it right now, although he was in a different room. The email was not much help for inspiration. All it stated was that he apologized for not being available and he would return shortly.

Had he run off with a strange woman he barely knew and had fallen in love? As nice as he thought that might be, his friends and family knew him not to have a great track record when it came to women, or falling in love and many other things that would cause him to act in such way. He did meet the beautiful Nell. Indeed, he spent some time with her, away, to some galactic extent. But she was an alien. Which one of the more ridiculous sounding stories should he tell? That he was contacted by an alien group or that he ran away with a woman? He might as well tell them both since no one would believe him anyway.

The phone battery charger beeped in acknowledgment that the charge was complete.

"The battery!" Gustave shouted out loud. A perfect excuse, and one that would fit him well. He had come up with an ingenious idea for a new battery, and had gone to seek investors for it. Of course, he wanted to keep it quiet because he didn't want to jinx it. This was suitable for him, he thought. Coming up with a new idea, one of his many to which he would follow with pursuing investment that would often fail. Only this time he did get an investor.

He didn't have much time before he had to submerge under a new identity. He decided he should first call his best friend and ask him to help him out with the launch of the company to start making the batteries. After that, he would go see his parents rather than calling them which would surely be a pleasant surprise and much more favorable than an apologetic phone call.

* * *

In a busy office churning with people wearing business suits stood Chris Timpelton. Chris was an associate researcher for a company that provided other companies with information they could have gotten themselves if only they had possessed half a working brain and a little extra time on their hands. Chris was a very capable young man although he didn't get the job because of his potential for being put into good use. That was not a necessary prerequisite; instead he got the job because he was a friend of one of the exec's daughters who was quite taken by him. Chris carried with him an animal magnetism leaving a smoky trail through female admirers. Chris was very comfortable with his way of life, although he was always disappointed none of his personal projects had succeeded so far. He loved going out to clubs at night and the early mornings that followed were nothing he favored. The job paid well, and it kept him satisfied since he didn't have to work hard to make it seem as if he did.

As a general rule, Chris couldn't stand working hard for someone else other than himself. It wasn't his dream he was working toward fulfilling, it was someone else's. It wasn't his office, his desk or his chair; it all belonged to someone else.

Still, the company and the clients were very satisfied with his work for which international clients from the far reaches of the corporate world paid exuberant sums of money.

This particular day started off just like any other day. He got to work a few minutes late, after spending a few extra minutes in front of a mirror while getting ready for work. His appearance was very important to him, just as a working athlete would exercise his body to stay fit for the game, Chris took good care of his body, his mind, and his clothes. It was almost lunch time and Chris made his way towards the lunch room only to be stopped by two men hauling new equipment to an office that was to be retrofitted with new furniture.

Miranda, from accounting, together with Jeff, from shipping, walked down the corridor that lay next to the new office and passed Chris. Miranda, who was in her early thirties was, like the rest of the ladies in the office, infatuated with Chris`s charm. She was a little shy, although the opportunity to say hello to the alpha male of the group was too inviting. She smiled at Chris, and kept her smile bright long after she passed him. Chris was somewhat oblivious to the fact that women saw him as a sex object. He had not been a ladies' man in his early childhood. He was the exact opposite, rather chubby with very thick eyeglasses. To complete the picture, he was also a nerd in the full extent of the word. In university, he met Gustave and their friendship grew very strong. They both shared a passion for technology, money, and women, often enjoying the three in succession. Invent the technology, get the money, and attract the women. It wasn't until Gustave felt comfortable enough with his new pal to let him know he should change his appearance in order to feel more comfortable about himself, when Chris started realizing he was better looking than he had thought. He started cleaning up his bearded look, after getting a few lectures from Gustave about how he should talk to women, and how to eliminate the shy-mouse persona he often had. Gustave was never good at taking his own advice, but Chris absorbed it as if it he were a sponge. Growing out of his teenage appearance, he lost his extra pounds, started playing tennis and got a laser treatment for his eyes. A changed man, rather a ladies' man, was reborn. With his looks and over-confidence that compensated for the lack thereof, Chris started seeing girls, going to fun parties and attending important events.

That is not to say Gustave and Chris were no longer friends by this transformation. Gustave often joined Chris and was always welcome as his corky and a slightly crazy friend. Gustave himself molded his outgoing personality to accommodate his quiet, shy self whenever he went to a function or a party with Chris.

They were both full of ideas about how to make it in the world yet neither made it where they wanted to go. Only Gustave was more persistent with the dreams or perhaps it was his obliviousness to the fact that the reality of a stable career rather than continuously looking for a holy grail is a more persistent solution.

The path was clear for Chris to make his way to the lunch room. Looking at his watch, he estimated how slow he would have to walk to make it seem he got to lunch on time and not earlier. He gradually made his way toward the cafeteria. The room was spacious with large tables, vending machines and of course a few pretty ladies Chris knew quite well. He had slept with all of them except one, which was something of an anomaly. He knew he would get through to her eventually and the challenge was something he smugly enjoyed.

"Well! Hello there, ladies!" he called out in a playful tone.

"Good morning Chris", they answered, giggling like chattering squirrels.

Chris smiled, opened his arms wide and said, "Ah, my angels!" This was somewhat of a daily ritual they all followed.

Chris went to the vending machine and bought a plastic pack of sweets. He then went to the coffee machine, poured himself a cup of black coffee and sat with the girls. Placing the pack of sweets on the table for sharing, he sat on a chair facing the three lovely faces. "You're so sweet!" one of the girls said. He sipped from his coffee cup with a confident smirk on his face. While the mug was still close to his mouth he muttered, "These young ladies are sweet. I'm a little salty, you know!" and he laughed.

He had discovered a good rule for dealing with being in the same room with a few girls with whom he had spent the night. The rule was simple; to make it seem obvious he was fine with it. That would rub off on the rest, and in turn make them feel at ease with the situation. The girls laughed, even Kim, the only one of the three to still have any ground for such awkwardness. More people started swarming into the lunch room until the room was loud with their chatter as they talked about the coming weekend and other matters. The table where Chris was sitting filled up with more ladies, and a few of the other alpha males in the group.

"Hey there, champ!" a man's voice spoke out in Chris's direction. The voice was that of George Baldween, the head of International Communications and his fake enthusiasm was obvious. Shaking Chris' hand firmly, George placed his hand on Chris's shoulder and said, "nice work on the FanTech account buddy! They just secured a five-year subscription with your name on it as the head of the account. Apparently, you hit them with a tip that got them very rich, and we will be sharing some of that wealth, so congratulations!"

He started clapping and the rest of the room joined

in. Chris enjoyed the attention. He looked to his left and right and made a "me?" face and with his fingers, made a fake gun pointing toward others that had helped him with the account.

George approached Chris and whispered, "Now, I want you in my office at three PM. We have something we have to talk about. . ."

His tone was serious, almost as if Chris was in some trouble. He respectfully answered, "Yes, sir!"

Following the rather short lunch break, Chris returned to his office a little worried. Even though he didn't liked his work place, he did enjoy the casual flirtation with the girls, and had even grown accustomed to his morning routine, the anticipation of getting home after a hard day as well as the simple mind-numbing work he was assigned to perform. His taste for good things in life had also grown since he first started working at the firm. His salary allowed him to get a nice car, a bachelor's apartment where he could bring younger girls for the purpose of researching their nocturnal habits but above all, he never wanted to be placed in a position where he would be fired.

"I didn't do anything wrong, damn it!" he said to himself, chewing on a cheap plastic pen. "He's probably joking, that imbecile!" Reassuring himself, he put his suit on, straightened his tie and made his way to George's oversized office.

A large cherry-wood desk monopolized Patrick's huge office, upon which sat a beautiful computer that broadcast little more than the latest online videos.

Also prominently displayed on his desk was a portrait of his wife and two kids. The frame was slightly twisted toward the guest chairs and was meant to depict him as a family man, a team player with core values. Another frame showed him in faded khaki fishing shorts holding a large fish in his right hand. The purpose of this picture was simply to depict him as a man who enjoyed life and his masculine hobby. These were modest personality traits on the blank canvas of his being painted with prefabricated concepts of a fulfilled life.

Chris knocked on the office door. George shouted, "Come in!" Pretending to be concentrating on his work, George raised his hand in a gesture to let Chris know he would be right with him. "Have a seat, buddy," George said, still gazing at his computer with a fake frown as he pretended to be in deep concentration. Chris sat in the chair, crossing his legs and trying to be patient while he was kept waiting. His cellular phone, in vibrate mode, began quivering. Curious, he carefully reached into his pocket and withdrew the phone. It was Gustave.

Chris looked at George who was still busily pretending to be working. "Would you like me to come back, later today, when you are less busy, sir?" Chris asked, hoping he would take him up on his offer which would allow him to answer his phone.

"No no, no need, I'm good to go." George smiled at Chris, interlacing the fingers of both hands behind his head and stretching backward in his chair. "Chris, it is no secret that you are one of our top guys here. You have exceeded every expectation we had of you. But we received a third sexual complaint against you and unfortunately you're going to have to…" He paused, looking very serious, then he closed one eye for a moment. "You're going to have to sleep with McMire's wife, because she keeps complaining he's not like you!" He broke into laughter, then added, "You old dog you!"

It took Chris a while to understand he was a casualty of another one of George's ideas of having fun in the office. It was humorous nonetheless, and he joined in the loud laughter while pointing his finger as if to say, "You got me there."

George stood up and reached for a glass of water that was on a table facing the windows. He laughed again briefly and said, "Chris, the reason I called you in was to let you know we appreciate the work you do for our company. Our clients love you and your work, the people in the office respect you. You've got what it takes to move on to the next level. . ." He expected some reaction from Chris but when he saw none, he continued. "We would like you to take a bigger part in our family. Put in more hours, work a little more, but the increase in your pay will be worth it." He paused again, on his office wall there was a picture of his fishing yacht which was his pride and glory. He flicked a few particles of dust off the picture and said, "In a year or less, you'll be able to buy a yacht just like my

Katherine." He had named his yacht after his wife, which also happened to be the same as a natural disaster which he considered humorous and especially ironic, considering his history with the 15-foot luxury boat.

Chris loved money, but he hated having to spend more time in this place. Now that his job security wasn't on the line anymore, he was reminded how dissatisfied he was with going home to his comfortable apartment every day, a little earlier than the rest of the employees. Speaking hesitantly, he said, "

"George, it would be an honor to take a larger part. I'm just not sure I'm ready. . ."

George turned to faced Chris. "What are you talking about? You're more ready now than you should be. . Come on!"

Chris tried to find a reasonable excuse. But there wasn't much he could add. He always saw this job as a temporary thing. A few minutes ago he was scared of losing his position, and now, he was scared of getting pulled in more deeply.

"I'll give it a try, Boss," Chris said, extending his hand.

"I knew you do the right thing, son!" George shook Chris`s hand with vigor, smiling broadly. "Now get outta here!" He placed his arm affectionately around

Chris's shoulder and Chris knew the meeting was over. Leaving George's office, Chris wondered what exactly he had gotten himself into. This was a big promotion, yet he still felt like something wasn't right about taking it and by doing so, putting yet another nail into the coffin of what just might end up being his routine.

"Gustave!" he said out loud, remembering the call that had come in earlier. He looked at his phone and decided he'd better delay calling Gustave back until he got to his office.

* * *

The corridors in the building were very spacious. The floor was covered with a strange material that looked like wood, yet had the shine and sparkle of marble. There were seats, sofas and tasteful décor that was incorporated in the interior design of the place. The walk back to his office reassured Chris the company had the money to pay his salary and therefore he shouldn't feel guilty because he had never tried working hard for them yet still received a premium cut of their revenue, considering many other ant workers. His phone buzzed. It was Gustave again. "Must be something urgent," he thought to himself.

* * *

As soon as it was convenient, Chris dialed Gustave's number.

"Gustave, how are you?" Chris was concerned. The phone was silent for a second or two. Afraid the connection was broken, he spoke again, "Gustave?"

"Chris! We must meet as soon as you can. . . I have a really large project..."

Before Gustave was able to finish his sentence Chris interrupted him. "Hey, not even a hello? How are you?"

Gustave was too excited to tell him about what was going on that he put all phone manners off to the side. "Sorry Chris, it's just that we..."

Chris was highly stressed with his promotion. He had been given an opportunity here that both assured him a very comfortable living on one hand and on the other, destroyed all hope of trying the next big thing in which he might want to invest. Gustave was a very strong reminder of that side of him. Perhaps it wasn't the right time to appear considering all he was trying to digest.

"Chris, how are you, is everything all right?" Gustave detected his friend's hesitancy.

Chris waited momentarily to give himself time to calm down. There was no need for him to take his frustration out on his friend. "I'm all right, just had a strange day at work, sorry, what were you talking about earlier?" Chris was now calm and interested in a normal conversation.

"Chris, I have in my hands a new idea. This one will make us very, very rich. . ." Gustave tried very hard to keep the excitement he felt out of his voice.

Chris put his hand on his forehead. He was used to getting calls like this from Gustave, always about new devices or technology he invented or had heard about, followed by helping him with trying to get it out there, only to have their dream shattered when they couldn't get an investor or they found that there was already something like it on the market or in development.

Chris wanted to say something but Gustave interrupted him as soon as he heard the first "no" coming out of his mouth.

"It's different this time, Chris, I swear it is," Gustave stood firmly behind his words. Intrigued as he was, to Chris it was all repetition: Gustave saying that this time his idea was groundbreaking, it had never been done before, and most importantly, that they should have no problem getting investors for their start-up.

Gustave had a good hunch Chris was not in the mood for games, but more than anything, Chris was not interested in being involved in any business-type adventure again and every time the venture not going through.

Gustave responded in a serious tone of voice. "I have ten million reasons in my bank account from these investors to show you this one will not fail."

Chris was taken aback. Remaining quiet, he tried to test, no, he anticipated screeching laughter coming from Gustave's end, as he did tend to joke with him quite often, yet there was silence. He was almost positive Gustave was joking.

Gustave waited for Chris to say something, but the line remained silent, only to be filled with some textural background sound that poorly reflected the office ambiance of Chris's work place.

"Chris, I swear, I have ten million dollars in my bank account, I need you to help me open it up and run it until I come back." Gustave was a little irritated by the silence, however, he began to understand that for people like himself and Chris this would sound like a fairytale.

Chris was beginning to think Gustave was serious about this whole thing and considering he did have an unexplained absence for the past week or so, there must be something behind all of this. His heartbeat accelerated as his thoughts began whirling with hundreds of questions. What would he do with his promotion? If this fails, would he be able to return to this place? At the same executive-salary level? He never expected to consider a new business venture as a threat to his well-being.

"I am shocked, Gustave. I need you to tell me right now, I have a very important decision to make today at work. If I tell them I'm not coming back to the office tomorrow and thereafter, after telling them I will gladly accept the new promotion, I have to be sure you are not kidding around with me here." As excited as he was, the previous failed attempts at fame, glory, and riches taught him not to trust anything that sounded too good to be true.

Gustave laughed. "Chris, come to my place tonight. I'm going to visit my parents briefly then come back home. Trust me, this is it, this is what you and I have been waiting for. And I wouldn't be able to do it without you."

After a long, pulsing silence, Chris swallowed audibly and said, "I'll. . .I'll be there at ten.

CHAPTER 25

Harry struggled against the strong undertow, swimming as hard as he could, convinced his life was at stake if he didn't. The water was warm and slick and suddenly changed into a soft material, leather, that's what it was, what was he doing swimming in his clothing without shoes on but now on top of something slick and warm? Harry fought himself awake, gradually recognizing he was sleeping fully clothed and stretched out on a luxurious leather sofa. He massaged his temples, attempting to remember details part of his mind wanted to forget. He sat up slowly, looking around the large study, appreciating the muted glow from brass lamps on each end of a library table at the back of the sofa, the original oil paintings on the walnut-paneled walls and the rich colors of the Oriental area rug extending from under his feet to the river-rock fireplace across the room. A few sparks snapped and popped as the dying fire burned itself out.

As he stared at the glowing coals, his memory of the night before jangled into clarity and he began to feel humiliated and embarrassed at having fainted.

He saw his shoes on the floor and he bent over, pulling them closer and put them on. Behind the sofa, there was a large table serving as a desk, where a computer screen and several unfamiliar instruments stood, including a machine that looked like an arm with many tiny cameras resembling the compound eye of a fly. His embarrassment because of fainting turned into humiliation and as he tied his shoelaces, he heard approaching footsteps. He stood up inhaling deeply and holding his shoulders deliberately erect, turned to face Terra as she walked into the room,

"I forgot about the scan, Harry. It's been a very long time since we added a newcomer to our team." Terra spoke calmly. "Do you feel all right?" She checked the monitor screen on the table.

Harry walked toward her, clearing his throat. "Yes ma'am, I feel perfectly fine, what was that..."

Terra immediately interrupted him. "We've lost enough time as it is, Harry. . . Are you certain you are fully functional?"

"Yes Ma'am!" He started to click his heels then thought better of it.

"Then let's go to the command station, we have a long day ahead of us!"

Terra walked out of the room, with Harry right behind her.

* * *

The command station was imposingly massive. Seeing the building from the helicopter, Harry wasn't certain how something so large could fit into the structure. At the end of the room a giant monitor hung on a wall, massive in size, almost encompassing every inch of that wall. There was a white opaque glass table positioned at a comfortable distance from the colossal monitor. The table had a see-through keyboard that merged nicely onto the table; its keys were brightly outlined in blue strokes that shaped them as well as the fonts and some extra keys that were circle-shaped with silhouettes of knobs superimposed on their top surfaces.

Terra sat in the comfortable-looking command station chair. Harry moved in closer, yet kept a comfortable distance. The keys, he noticed, flickered and adjusted their shapes in response to her hand movements. She was a fast and accurate typist, which caught his attention, because he didn't understand how she was able to navigate across the keys without even looking. He gazed at the screen in front of him to observe the result of her typing. The screen flickered through various user interface menus zooming through extensive chunks of data. He realized the speed of this computer had to be record-breaking. Looking back at the keyboard, he noticed the keys changed whenever Terra navigated to different menus, each adjusting itself to the new shortcuts and features.

"Gustave," Terra said, pointing to the screen. Harry saw a giant image of a somewhat short young man appearing on the screen. Terra pressed a few more keys. The screen responded with a flickering of many pictures from the internet, bank machines, and various other public cameras. Each had many dots accompanying a picture. A status bar indicated a quick calculation of all these pictures and yielded a three dimensional rendering of the suspect in question.

"Is he still reported missing?" Harry asked.

"No," she answered.

Harry squinted at the screen trying to see where she got that information so quickly. There was too much information displayed there and he felt as if he should try to make himself more useful than just asking questions. "I imagine with his father's clearance and past he has some sort of bugs tracking his movements?"

Terra's fingernails clicked on the keyboard. Saul Eisenstein appeared on screen, along with his military records and his research among many other attributes. "He was a seventh party recruit for us," Terra said.

Harry knew what she meant: Saul was seven top security levels away from knowing the entire bigger picture.

"Saul was working for us to reverse engineer alien technology recovered in one of the crash traps. The last crash trap to be successful. . . His lab was broken into and all data was stolen. This was one of our biggest disasters.

Wait. . .what?" she screamed, staring at the monitor in disbelief.

"What's wrong?" Harry responded.

"All trailing has been called off! We have never let anyone slip through our hands like that. There is no surveillance on him anymore, it was sanctioned to be dismissed! I can't believe this!"

Harry tried to reason with her, calm her down. There was nothing special in having to find a man not guilty and having him removed from being observed. "Could it be that I was mistaken and he really isn't the guy?" Harry asked.

"Oh no, he isn't our guy! It's his kid Gustave we're after, but this is not how we operate around here, not under my command, not under our codes. He should have been terminated already. Let's bring him in and finish what we should have done many years ago. We'll get to his son this way. And there won't be any reason or evidence to suspect us, if we're careful. . ."

CHAPTER 26

Gustave parked his car in the driveway. He was looking forward to seeing his parents but was still undecided as to what he should or shouldn't be telling them about his unexplained absence. One moment he considered telling them all about his adventure and the next he assured himself it was not the right time or the right way to break such unconventional news. He rang the doorbell which was immediately followed by the barking of Allegro, their West Highland terrier. Allegro recognized Gustave's familiar scent and the barks abated almost immediately. Sarah, Gustave's mother, opened the door.

She immediately started yelling. "Do you know how worried I was? How could you put your mother through such a thing, Gustave?" Her eyes watered and she began to cry. She grabbed him in her arms and hugged him close.

Gustave returned the hug and said, "I know, Mom, I'm sorry, but it was for the best. I'll tell you all about it. . ." Seeing her in this emotional state gave him second thoughts about revealing the real reason for his disappearance. But he knew it was for the best, considering he would be putting them all at risk if he said anything. If it wasn't a risk of jeopardizing the mission, it was the risk of her thinking he was some sort of an idiot inventing a story about alien kidnapping and extraterrestrial beings from another planet.

The house exuded a warm and welcoming feeling. The layout of the house was the same as many other standard suburban middle class residences: one main floor with a basement and a back yard. The kitchen was the central gathering place for anything that was family-related and they naturally made their way there.

Sarah Eisenstein was in her early sixties. She was a petite-sized woman, and even though she tried taking care of herself, the physical labor of taking care of a family and a house as well as working for most of her life, showed on her aging, freckled skin. She was a natural brunette with streaks of gray beginning to soften the remaining shine and color of her youthful brown hair. She always spoke in a soft voice, except times when she argued with Saul, which was quite often as they both were diversely opinionated about most matters. The arguments often resulted in an agreement to disagree and there was no doubt Gustave had inherited some of their temperamental argumentativeness and the need to prove a point, which inclined him to take things a little farther than he should. For that reason, he tried avoiding arguments.

The kitchen was filled with the appetizing aromas of home cooking. A few pots simmered on the stove, whetting everyone's appetites. Gustave sat down in a chair at the kitchen table.

"Can I get you something, Gustave?" Sarah asked.

"No thanks, Mom, I had lots to eat when I got back home today. Where's Dad?" Gustave replied. Seated next to Gustave, Sarah looked at him, with worshipful eyes as if she hadn't seen him for years. "He's upstairs. . .I'll fix something to drink. . . should I prepare some tea?" She stood up.

"Only if you're making some for yourself. . .and for me, anything without caffeine, is fine. . .please."

Gustave knew very well he couldn't get away with not having anything to drink or eat. Sarah filled two cups with boiling water from the kettle on the stove and added mint-flavored tea bags from the tea canister in the cupboard.

Saul came in smiling at his son. "You put her under stress, Gustave. So, where have you been?" He was never good at showing his emotions.

The father and son shook hands affectionately. Gustave knew his father was probably under stress as well because of his son's disappearance but he never backed down from confronting any issue.

"Dad, you wouldn't believe. I'm working on some revolutionary technology for batteries and went abroad to receive the terms from my investors."

Saul was always fascinated by his son's newest ideas. He saw a lot of himself in his son and his way to bond with him was always to offer some help, and of course, his opinion and advice. That didn't go so smoothly at times, but was engaging nonetheless.

Saul waited a few moments to let Gustave explain his concept, although inside his head he was analyzing every possible theoretical concept of battery technology he knew of so he could compare notes with what he thought was already done, or was being tried. Gustave was well prepared for this, only this time he instead continued expounding on his grander plan.

"I have many more things coming up very soon, and my investors have already given me all I need to open up a factory, purchase materials, and market it. We're wealthy, Dad, and this is just the beginning!" Gustave was about to burst with enthusiasm.

Sarah glanced toward Gustave when he began speaking of investors. She had heard too many stories of her son's pipe-dream attempts and was weary of new endeavors. Only this time it seemed different. He seemed to have accomplished the first stage successfully. She wasn't happy about the money, but because her son finally seemed to have a positive future, that alone filled her heart with an overwhelming feeling of relief. She approached him, her arms open in welcome. Her eyes were watery again with happiness. Before she was able to give him a hug, the doorbell rang. Allegro started barking loudly while running to the door. The barking was a little more intense and aggressive than usual.

Saul went to the door, with Gustave and Sarah following close behind.

Sarah gathered Allegro up in her arms as Saul

opened the door. There were very bright LED lights pointed toward the three standing there and they could barely make out the shapes of the people outside.

"Saul Eisenstein?" a deep voice said. Allegro's frenzied barking almost overpowered the man's threatening tone. Saul nodded affirmatively and shaded his eyes, trying to identify the persons behind the blinding lights.

A large, swarthy man elbowed his way into the house, and following closely behind him was another man and a woman, both holding what appeared to be .9 millimeter Glock revolvers. Allegro's barks became frenetic. "Take him!" the woman commanded. Gustave, standing beside the door was hidden from their vision but he could hear every word.

Saul knew these were not policemen or agents of any government unit. Having worked in advance secret departments for the military, he was familiar with all war machines and tactical maneuvers, but this was unlike anything he'd ever seen before.

"Take me? Take me where? What for?" The larger man held him by his arm. Saul tried to resist but the man was much stronger than he was. The woman stepped into the light, closer to Saul.

"Terra?" Saul was bewildered.

"Hello Saul. . . it's been a while, hasn't it?" and she slammed her gun into his jaw, causing him to cry out in pain and duck his head against his shoulder.

Gustave had been focused on one of the men,

trying to place his face which he thought for a moment was familiar. The minute he heard the sound of the handgun striking his father and his father's cry of pain, he became someone possessed of inhuman strength. The man holding his father was twice the size of Gustave but it was as if he was merely a temporary nuisance not even as threatening as a mosquito. Gustave grabbed him from behind, his fingers cutting into and through his reinforced armor as if was sheer fabric, and then into his flesh as if were thin air. The man's pain was so unbearable that he released a long screaming guttural roar that echoed through the walls of the house. In his agony, he released his grip on Saul who scrambled back out of the way. Gustave's hand was like a robotic steel-grasping mangle, and had ripped into the man's torso through his back, gripping his lower spine as if it were a teapot handle. He pushed the screaming man forward then with roar he threw him backward, and released the dying man. Like a rag doll the man was thrown several meters into a back wall. Gustave's highly attuned warning system sensed something and his armor maneuvered him away from the path of a bullet.

"Don't shoot him!" Terra screamed. The men were highly trained to follow orders, yet the mutilation of their unit member had caused them to panic. A few stray bullets managed to hit Gustave, who screamed in pain, but he never lost control. The bullets tore through the layers of Gustave's skin revealing a gray, lead-colored undercoat. He grew angrier instead of surrendering himself to the pain. Sheltering his face from the bullets, he snarled like an angry Bengal tiger and ran toward another man shooting at him. In a mere second he grabbed the man's automatic rifle and broke it in half. The gun was scorching hot, yet he took the two pieces and shoved the burning metal inside both of the man's shoulders. The man screamed and lost consciousness, falling to the ground.

"Enough!" Terra screamed. The gunfire ceased.

Gustave's skin wounds healed instantly. His pain was almost gone and with it his rage. "Who are you?" Gustave yelled. "Why have you attacked my parents' home? Who sent you here?"

Terra moved in front of her guards. "I should ask you the same thing, Gustave."

"You are in no position to ask me anything, Terra!". His mind was beginning to clear, and as he spoke, his armor tapped into the electronics located in the van parked outside. Bits of information pertaining to the mission flew at him as if they were chunks of memory. "You came here to terminate my father! Who are you?"

Saul was still unconscious from the blow to his head.

"We were actually looking for you, Gustave. . ." a man spoke from the shadows. It was Harry, who, surprisingly, was more restrained than anyone else. He couldn't read Terra's true opinion of their current situation. He knew, however, they would not get out of this alive by more yelling, shooting, or Terra's antagonism.

"You came here for my father, don't lie to me!" Gustave said. He moved closer toward the man. Terra's bodyguards pointed their rifles towards Gustave.

"Lower your guns, men!" Harry commanded. He continued speaking while cautiously moving closer to Gustave. "We came here to arrest your father in order to find your whereabouts, Gustave, I'm not going to lie to you. And here you are, so there is no need to cause you or your father any more harm."

Gustave, checking the bullets holes in his torn armor, looked at Harry. "You really think you can cause them any more harm? I can kill you and your guard dogs in mere seconds, or at the very least before any of them could even raise their guns at me . . ." Gustave said, pointing at Harry.

One of the guards raised his rifle. Gustave's armor alerted him to a trajectory lock on his location. In a split second, the man who was standing a few good meters from Gustave was on the ground, as if he had been violently thrown. His scream was blood-curdling and filled the other interlopers with fear for themselves. Gustave was nowhere to be seen, but the man lay miserably twisted, his arms bent painfully backward around his weapon.

"Did I not make myself clear?" Gustave asked, standing behind Terra. The guards shifted their attention respectfully back toward Gustave. They did not bother raising their weapons.

"Good. . ." Gustave said. "Now clean up and

leave!"

"We request a word with you, Gustave,", Harry pleaded. "We will leave and clean up. I apologize for my colleagues' approach but we believed this was a matter of grave danger to our national security." Harry was trying a different approach, attempting to get closer to Gustave. He thought to himself Gustave should be immediately examined. He wondered if he was an alien. Were they a family of aliens? But that could not be, since his father was taken out easily.

"I'll come." Gustave said decisively. "

"What?" Terra couldn't hide her surprise. She was a little annoyed by losing command of the situation, but she was still relieved by adding Harry to the team.

Although they planned on using Gustave, once he was captured and with the advantage of having him on their home turf, Gustave had his own plan. He had a bigger mission at hand and could not have them on his back, slowing him down. He decided to infiltrate their command area which location he had already pinpointed by tapping into their car's GPS memory. Once there, he planned to grab every record they had and release them to the general public. It would, for one thing, have them in hiding from an ocean of media frenzy and conspiracy aficionados, but more importantly, the undeniable evidence of the existence of extra-terrestrial life would make his ultimate goal much easier to achieve.

Although Terra considered Gustave's rapid agreement a small victory, Harry was suspicious and was struggling to understand why it went so smoothly. Was Gustave's young age misleading him into thinking he was infallible? He clearly seemed to be susceptible to injury, even though he healed very quickly. He was beginning to wonder if he was indeed tractable by whatever equipment they had back at HQ. The situation obscured his comprehensive understanding of Gustave's reason for coming with them, but through the mess he saw a reasonable entity which really did not mean to harm them any more than they pushed him to react.

"Clean up first, everyone. . . I have to attend to my parents." Gustave gave the order, making sure to speak in a voice showing no hint of fear. He helped Sarah guide Saul back inside and ushered them into the kitchen, along with Allegro who was very relieved to be back inside. He scampered off to his feeding bowl and Sarah stood wringing her hands, fighting back tears, as she gently rubbed Saul's cheek with salve.

"Mother, it's all going to be all right. I'm going to go with them and make sure they don't bother us again." Gustave patted Sarah on the shoulder, trying to reassure her that he was in control and they were safe.

"Gustave, you killed a man!" she screamed loudly. In the moment of quietness that followed, her state of panic seemed more strident.

Gustave put his arms around her and pulled her close. "Mom, there is no time to explain how I know, but they came here to kill Dad and you. And they wanted to capture me. The man was the most aggressive out of them and I had to set an example to show them they are in no position of strength here." She gave him a hug and held him close. "Take Dad, and Allegro, and check into a hotel, and tell no one, no relatives, no friends. No one. I am going to be making sure they can't track you where you go. I will call you in a day or so, after then they will be of no bother to anyone. They are bad people and will receive justice through regular means. I will spare them their lives, something which they very likely may eventually regret."

"Gustave, what really happened to you?" Sarah whispered, half afraid to find out.

"I'll tell you one day soon, but not yet, okay? It's for the best. . ." Gustave kissed her softly on the forehead and quietly left the house, closing the door firmly behind him, a resigned expression on his face.

CHAPTER 27

Rather than taking his own car, Gustave joined Harry and Terra in theirs. It would be easier to assess and control the situation being close to them. Before they left he made sure his parents had departed safely to an undisclosed location. The group communicated to another one for an immediate satellite recon of where the car was headed. Gustave, with his armor connected directly to any input and output of their communication devices, approached Harry.

"Harry, I don't like you playing spy games here. There are no three strikes before I retaliate. I thought I made myself quite clear not to follow my parents and you went after them anyway."

Gustave was beginning to think his plan of keeping them away might be more difficult, as they were both decisive and strongly opinionated.

Harry tried to speak, but Gustave did not allow him to continue, and interrupted him. "You're sorry, yes". Using the armor's interface was starting to become second nature to Gustave. It wasn't the ease of operating it, but the sheer processing power and connectivity gave Gustave access to every electronic device within reach. Once inside, disabling it, changing its programming or just destroying it was a mere two intuitive command lines away. It was helpful that he was a programmer, which sped things up as far as knowing what to do with the earthly devices, but the actual armor anyone could manipulate with some practice.

Gustave accessed their communication exchange server and placed it under a complete black-out.

"You might notice you have no communications with headquarters, or any other device for that matter, Harry."

Harry looked at Terra who was frantically trying to get a signal from her phone in the background. He was beginning to question if they could really capture Gustave seeing the ease with which he accessed and controlled their entire gadgetry in split seconds.

"What are we waiting for? You said you wanted to take me in for some questions. . . I don't want to waste too much of my time." Gustave was growing impatient.

He waited for everyone to get into their cars, before he got in the back seat, next to Harry.

Gustave wanted to understand their purpose and the only way to do so was to question them and try to break their silence. He really didn't care what they were to ask him because he didn't intend to give them any valuable information at all.

"Well, what is it you wanted from me, even if it

meant risking your lives?"

Terra was quick to answer; she had planned on asking the questions, but not with herself at a disadvantage. "We can't talk here, it's not safe."

Gustave laughed. "Really? No, it's safe all right, no one can hear your unimportant mumbling. . . The only thing making this situation unsafe is if you were to do anything stupid, which I can assure you, you are quite prone to do."

"Please, let's be civilized here, no need for insults! We are both very sorry for the trouble we've put you through. We are accustomed to dealing with humans, and sometimes the use of force is necessary to achieve the action. I'm certain you understand, sir. . ." Harry interrupted, trying to defuse further conflict.

Gustave wasn't sure whether he should be humored or worried about the fact that the man thought he was an alien. On one hand, they might be less prone to act in a violent way if they thought he was an alien, especially if they were acting out of concern for national security, however, that would put him at a disadvantage he was not willing to accept at this time. It was probably best he keep his mouth shut for the time being and change the subject.

"That's quite a way to make a point. I read the order code from your devices, and the order was to execute him. I, on the other hand, acted in self-defense." Gustave said as he moved closer toward Harry.

"We believe he had something to do with the

disappearance of an important technology that belonged to us. We also know of your part in that event. What would you do if something as important to you was stolen and you knew the thief, Gustave?"

Gustave knew what the man was talking about -- he could not have forgotten that dark night when the burglars killed his friend. He felt his blood pressure rise but considering his situation, he decided to try and calm himself down.

Gustave sat back in the seat and smiled. "I would have probably been a little aggressive about it; you have a point. My dad, however did not steal from you. And although both of us were involved we are not the ones you are after. What did you say your name was?" Gustave wanted to give the man the impression that he was willing to abandon the antagonism. Calming them down by giving them a false sense of security would give him the element of surprise in case they did plan on trying to execute a capture, for which he was prepared.

"It's Harry, Harry Escher"

"And you, old woman?" Gustave pointed at Terra with his finger half erect. He knew she was the more irrational of the two and wanted to test how far he could go with her. He wasn't sure who was calling the shots, but he thought it might be Harry, considering how more capable he was to deal with a hostile situation.

Harry placed his hand on Terra's shoulder, knowing that he probably should try to restrain her from replying. Harry knew he was not in a position to take charge over, or even touch, his superior, but the concept of communicating with an alien was much too exciting for any formalities on one hand, and worth the risk of losing his job, even if that meant termination. Although he had a strong feeling things were about to change radically now that such communication was taking place.

The rest of the drive was made in silence. None of them wanted to talk much so as to not give away their personal agendas.

Gustave asked for their location through his armor. The armor connected to the GPS system and reported his position. Gustave knew his city well. They were not headed toward the headquarters he had found in the database.

Gustave asked himself what the possible destinations could be and although his thought was nothing but a very short spike of a collection of words, the armor calculated everything precisely and instantly, finding data in the electronic devices of the people who came with Harry. The armor checked registered and unregistered locations in the city logs and police records as well as cross-matching these calculations with the car's onboard computer to try to project trajectories, speed, and even fuel consumption. Gathering all this information in split seconds, it gave Gustave feedback naming all logical destinations. Gustave learned the probabilities of their going to one of three locations. There was no need for a virtual head's up display as the information flowed from the armor directly into his brain as if it were an ordinary thought process. Two of the locations were soon dismissed.

"We're not going to headquarters, are we?" Gustave said in musing tone of voice. After a few more moments of steady driving, the car stopped.

Gustave saw Terra nod to Harry as she unbuckled her seatbelt. It seemed as if they were preparing for something, some procedure.

Harry didn`t recognize the place. From the nod, he understood he was to follow Terra`s lead into the warehouse.

The door opened to the musty odor of a long-abandoned storage building which was rapidly showing signs of obsolescence. The rest of the team were dressed in construction clothing in which they seemed very comfortable. This was obviously not the first time they had changed into more incognito clothing, especially considering the location was remote and civilian. Keeping close to each other, Gustave, Terra, and Harry, and the men approached the building in a casual formation.

The building doors seemed to be of some heavy metal material. There was nothing too strange about them as they resembled all steel doors located at factory entrances.

Harry knew there must be some form of heavy security near these doors. His first impulse was to protect the security into the building. However, there was no way of knowing with what ease the aliens could discover and penetrate their security measures which relied heavily on technology. He asked Terra to go ahead and lead them on a clear route into the building and by doing so, perhaps take Gustave's mind off of worrying about their security measures.

Terra moved forward together with a few of the men. The first door required a standard-looking key, which she pulled out of her pocket. Opening the door, she rushed right in, with her group following.

"Gustave," Harry said, as he noticed they were alone. "I haven't been here yet, I'm new to this but they do have some technology which knocked me out in seconds. I don't know what they have against you but Terra was confident enough to invite you in. You might be in trouble." Harry whispered in a torrent of words. "We managed to take several of your ships down, and I imagine it is something that has to do with magnetic energy."

Gustave placed his hands on Harry's shoulder. "You are a good man Harry, I appreciate your honesty," he said, with a wry smile.

He knew he had to finish this opportunity. Of that he was certain. However, it was only now that he began second guessing his moves. Was it possible that they sent him on a mission without knowing the strength of their defenses against humans? If so, could they even begin to estimate what it was they were dealing with to resist the Galactic Union? Maybe that was the reason they sent him.

Before entering the empty but perilous warehouse, he sent a distress signal to K'ta.

CHAPTER 28

Nell was in the midst of a system update for one of the engines of a support vehicle. The tiny ship was floating, suspended, without movement. It's shape gathered rays of light and reflected them unobtrusively back into the room. The machine was built for quick pickups and was capable of unimaginable speeds in human terms. It was not of Angelonian origin, however, and no amount of precaution could hide the serious danger of handling it, especially since the machine's interface was known to be tricky.

Frightened of humans as she was, Nell was considered to be a brave engineer among her peers. She was starting to enjoy their company, if Gustave was any indication of the rest of them. Whereas before she viewed humans as hostile yet fascinating creatures, she now began to see there was more to them. Such as the ship she was working on, a little rough and dangerous but quite capable nonetheless. Perhaps Gustave's beguiling personality helped calm her fear of the unknown. Indeed their mission was focused, at this stage, on one man, but he was all she could think about, even while she was working on this ship. Her mind replayed her experiences with the human and she smiled, remembering.

The engine was finally updated, and Nell signaled Bor to double-check the modifications.

A few moments later Bor arrived holding a mug in his hands.

"What is that strange smell?" Nell asked. Bor, who usually ignored what he considered aimless questions, answered cheerfully.

"Ca'fe. Human drink. Freshly brewed from beans I sent for. . ."

Nell looked surprised. The aroma of the coffee hung in the air, filling her nostrils with a symphony of colors and taste. The delightful smell almost caused her to overlook his answer but was grounded quickly by her chemical balancer.

"What do you mean, 'sent for' Bor, does this have to do anything with one of my biobots sitting in the bay waiting to be cleaned after examination?"

"Damn humans!" Bor's tone was one of anger. "The robot went at night to a village where I had sent it. I searched on their Internet and found in that particular place they produce the best beans. The robot followed all procedures well. Humans tend to keep their best things in hidden or locked places and that is exactly where I sent it. I looked at the entire extrusion operation. I didn't intend to wait and see how things went, but to monitor and oversee it actively."

Nell raised her voice. "But the biobots are…"

"Please don't interrupt me. . . There were brown bags of different kinds, and another door, locked. I reasoned that was where they kept their prized selection. It was packed differently, much tighter than the loose packaging of the other beans. The bot left a gold brick as payment for it as I instructed it to but then there was gunfire shot from some mechanism, causing the powdered coffee to spread all over the biobot which went into a frenzy. Strange, I've never seen them react this way. I sent two others to go after it, and one of them grabbed a bag of the regular coffee and a bag of the special one which I'm saving for a special occasion. Would you like to have a taste, Nell? It's the best this race has to offer. If we start trading with them, I will be in the business of distributing coffee all over the galaxy!"

"You don't say!" Nell smile, still a little taken aback by her disapproval of his methods.

"Yes, they have coffee shops, thousands of them, on one overcrowded planet. I can bring them with me to Planet Chama'ama and have it grown there, same climate. Now let's take a look at her. . ."

Bor removed the coffee mug from his hand, which remained floating in the air, at the spot where he left it, even with the slight tilt of its axis. The mug did not float from the lack of gravity, on the contrary, it rested on a personalized axis that was projected the moment Bor took his hand off the mug.

Placing his hand on the ship, he immediately connected with the ship's computers. This was a traditional approach pilots usually took each time they got into a ship, a unique pre-flight check-up procedure. Of course, he could have done it at a distance, but as tradition goes and for meditative purposes he preferred a more personal touch.

With his guidance, the machine ran simulation tests of all its systems plus stress testing of mechanical parts, and navigation scenarios usually dictated by the pilot. Each pilot developed their own personal stress test on top of the standardized ones which were necessary for the log records.

"You've done well!" Bor said. Satisfied, Nell smiled.

Her smile quickly vanished. They looked at each other as they recognized the signal for a mission critical emergency. Following procedures with a little less accuracy than that which they had been trained for, they gathered their equipment and rushed to the emergency-designated room.

The room was filled with large moving images floating in the air as if they were embedded in the fabric of the space surrounding the room. Key objects and some structures appeared to be in three dimensions. K'ta, sitting in the middle of the room surrounded by the moving structures, was controlling camera movement and several other mechanisms. Milka stood next to him, working in unison, helping him prepare for a defense mission for which she was trained, especially since that was one of her main purposes and an important addition to the mission.

Nell zoomed into the room. She had already been briefed about the situation on her way up. The details of how they would proceed were still unfolding as she came rushing in.

"Nell, Milka and I have to stay here," K'ta said, still focused on the screens which were showing him tactical information and imagery. "If they get hold of Gustave our entire mission is at risk; you and Bor will have to go in there and rescue him, there is no other way, and we can't send the bots in daylight."

Nell didn't know quite how to express herself. She was not ready to go down to a planet surrounded by particularly hostile denizens. Her breathing became labored with her frustration.

K'ta knew she was not quite ready for such a mission but there was no way he could control the situation from anywhere else but the specific room. He was, after all, the leader of this most important mission and could not be compromised.

Bor was not too keen on taking on the role of an escape pilot but he did join the mission for the action and to honor his belief in the mission itself. He did, however find it appropriate to question the heist which they were undertaking at such high risk. In a sardonic tone of voice, he said, "I thought he would be capable of dealing with such danger, because the suit is built for..."

K'ta interrupted him. "The armor was built from ancient sketches and drawings from a war database which we barely got our hands on, Bor. We cannot be certain of its effectiveness against human intuitiveness for warfare which we have all but forgotten." All members of the team wore a bewildered look. K'ta's raise in tone was in contrast to his usual demeanor and especially not typical of their race in which a deferential behavior was the core fiber of their culture.

They both quickly retreated from their positions. K'ta, admitting he was spending too much time accustoming himself to human behavior which was beginning to affect his own, and Bor, understanding it was not the appropriate time for technical questions.

"We are going to create a diversion to draw the attention of the locals toward something more important than gazing at the skies, at which point you will use a transport vehicle to reach this section." Milka acknowledged the two needed some time to cool their adverse tempers.

K'ta, still gazing toward Bor, shifted his attention towards Milka and looked back at Nell and Bor. With a calculating, unemotional smile he said, "We are going to orchestrate an earthquake in the city, which should give you the proper cover under which you can enter the skies and not be seen."

Nell, understanding that there was no time or room for frivolities found herself thinking out loud: "Most of the citizens will surely be interested in what's below them, but some will look up to escape possible structure fails from tall buildings. And considering the landing site is in the middle of the city, would that be a wise place to be?"

Milka nodded. "We considered that, Nell, however, the earthquake will resonate at the same frequencies as the visual disturbance of the vehicle will display in the air."

The team members nodded their approval. This was a brilliant idea. Such use of their tools for deception was the excitement they had wished for when signing up for this mission.

"We, of course," K'ta added, "have to thank Milka for her strategic training in deception and defense." He moved toward a screen glowing in the corner of the room, and pointing to an aerial map which flickered into existence he added, "Of course, you will have to position yourself so as to cast no shadow."

"Once we're in, do we know what they've got in defense of his armor?" Nell asked.

"Humans like to play with electricity and other types of energy. . . The best things they have are primitive devices that channel electricity with very brute and powerful force," K'ta said. Nell knew considering the old technology used for the armor, there might be a risk of breaking the swarm network of the nanonites which were mostly built for endurance against impact. She unexpectedly began to fear for Gustave's safety. Not wanting to divulge her emotions toward Gustave, she asked, "K'ta, what would happen if we're too late, can we replace Gustave with someone else? I'm sure there were other candidates. . ."

For personal purposes, K'ta was somewhat satisfied by her question, however, he did not want to give her the idea of minimizing the severity of their situation. A little hesitant to bring it up, he answered, "Not very likely, Nell. We had interfered with his family many decades ago." His tone was clearly noncommittal.

"Interfered?" Nell grimaced.

K'ta understood her reaction to which he quickly replied, "Nell, as you know, we have quite the history of testing humans in the past, and several things, few of which had the success we hoped for showed to be quite useful at a later stage. You could say that he is, structurally a little bit different than we would have expected from his great grandmother, who was not introduced to a certain procedure. Some of that intellect and quick thinking derived from her, but mostly his resistance to our own protection against humans is as a result of that. You picked up on it yourself when you first examined him, did you not?"

Nell recalled when she first scanned Gustave upon his arrival to the ship. The human seemed to be hostile yet calculative. His mind was churning with violent thoughts that should not have been there considering the influx of behavior tempering devices that should have kept him from causing them any harm. He had the mind of an untrained young navigator, often seen in carefully tempered promising young Angelonian children. It made sense. But a human? There must have been something else about him or his family to have made his abilities resemble that of Angelonians, of the post-singularity genomic revolution yet with very little genetic tempering.

Seeing that his point was made and time was of the essence, K'ta ordered, "Bor, suit up and prepare for descent. Nell, please join me before you get suited up.". He placed his hand on her shoulder. They left the room leaving Milka at the helm of the interspersing monitors in the emergency room.

K'ta waited a few moments for Bor to gain some distance as he made his way through the corridor back to the descent vehicle. Until now, he refrained from showing his feelings toward Nell, however, realizing the mission was of a risky nature, he let himself open up a little.

Still in the corridor and Bor out of sight, he paused and turned toward Nell.

"Nell, I really don't want to have to send you there. I can't imagine the emotion of bereavement I would feel if anything happens to you. You are important to me." He paused then continued, "You are very important to our organization."

Nell stood there quietly letting K'ta finish his words of encouragement. She saw K'ta as egalitarian in nature but she smiled knowing he felt there was more to her than the others.

Her smile was all the confirmation he needed to acknowledge his message got across, although perhaps not as encompassing as he had wished for. Raising his arm, he handed her a small sphere. The sphere had distinct features of any energy device, its body glistening with a fluctuating bright light. It was almost difficult to make out its shape. "If anything goes wrong," K'ta handed the device to her as its color turned murky dark, "create a short parameter shield and throw it away from you."

Nell stepped back and retracted her hand from the sphere. "Is that a bomb? You want me to carry a weapon?" Starting off in a whisper the words progressed in a crescendo, again, she stopped herself from speaking too loudly. "I did not sign up for doing something I can't do, something none of us can do, K'ta! I can't believe you would expect me to. . ."

K'ta raised his hand. He found it nerve-wracking to be in a constant state of needing to explain himself in front of her and Bor. "Just what did you expect? That we will need not worry about such things? You signed up for a mission that was unlike the rest of the failed attempts in that it was an affirmative action instead of those other feeble attempts. Why do you think we have Milka on board? If any of you are caught, we cannot risk the entire GU knowing about our operation. I need you to understand this, Nell, and I ask you to cooperate with me on this.

You have been briefed on the procedures; there are only a few armed guards which you will immediately control the moment you get there. Gustave was instructed to have them stay outside for that purpose. However, the man and woman, might require a closer contact for the suppressors to work so you should come to no harm, but in any case, if all goes wrong, this is your last resort and most important final step. The device will not release its energy until you throw it to the floor and activate it. You should not worry about carrying it! Do you understand, Nell?"

Holding a weapon. Activating a weapon. Protection. She was uncomfortable with all of this. It was against her entire raison d'être. It was against the core belief system of her entire race. Her mind congealed under a cacophony of voices preaching to her against going on. As quickly as it developed, the choir of these dark and opposing thoughts she was struggling to grasp suddenly stopped. She grabbed the sphere from his hands and said, "I'll hold on to it, but I'm not going to use it unless I have no other options."

K'ta was comforted. He saw some faint submission in her otherwise angry features. He knew it was a behavior regulator that prevented her from opposing too aggressively to a higher ranking officer, but this must have been initiated by a stronger personal force defined by her character. Holding the sphere in her hands, she nodded farewell to K'ta, and made her way to a ready room where the same suit she used to protect herself from Gustave in the practice room stood after going through careful maintenance stress tests. The suit, unlike the armor Gustave was fitted with, was not meant for forceful and aggressive counterattacks. It was built solely for the purpose of initiating complete protection, and was much better at that. However, it was important for her to have it examined and tested well before she wore it to a planet, and especially a race of savage, rapacious species she found to be completely uncivilized.

* * *

The escape vehicle was ready to go. Bor sat inside comfortably, at the controls. Nell, fully suited, only this time carrying an explosive, entered the bay doors. She always found descent vehicles to be too simplistic in their entry, and she had never taken a liking to traditional doors. As she walked in, the doors closed. She signaled Bor when she was buckled in and ready.

The ship took off blasting its way through space.

CHAPTER 29

"Stop right there" Gustave shouted. The group that was still outside the building stopped

from entering its door.

"You there!" Gustave pointed at one of the guards. "Call your other man back outside and bring the woman with you."

The guard looked at Harry for validation. Harry, surprised, remained silent but nodded with his head in confirmation. The man moved toward the building and entered through its doors. A moment later the entire group emerged from the building.

Terra, wearing a disgruntled look on her face looked at Harry and said, "What?"

"I want your man outside. I'm either coming in without them, or I'm not coming in at all. . ."

"What difference could it make?" Terra said abruptly.

Gustave smiled while deliberately ignoring her. Speaking under his breath, he responded. "Exactly my point, what difference is it going to make? I can take them all out and get to you before your slow mind registers the threat. I just don't want them in there when you ask me all the questions we came here to get answered. To put it in layman terms so you can understand, I don't like them. It's either they stay outside or they can accompany you to wherever you want, only without my presence. It's rather simple when you think about it, is it not, Terra?"

The men felt anger simmering inside them. They were usually considered elite soldiers, chosen through many years of service and selected by their ability and performance. Nonetheless, they were also chosen for their ability to switch their warrior's uniform off, and pay attention to their command, regardless of the issue.

"Stay outside and guard the area!" Terra commanded. The guard regrouped themselves into formation. They all glared at Gustave showing their disapproval of the situation. They ached from not having anything to do with the security of the situation and they felt completely useless as a result.

With some apprehension, Terra turned her back and walked back into the building without saying a word. Gustave followed.

The doors looked heavy and sturdy. Voice activated, hand-print readouts activated security as well as many other features to protect the entrance to the actual room. The more Gustave tracked the lines of construction, the more it seemed as if the building was so heavily reinforced there could be no room left inside other than a small rectangular space. That space, however, opened up the moment they walked through the last automatic security check.

The room was as high inside as the building itself. There seem to have been no specific reason for it to extend its ceiling right up to the top of the building's roof, other than that it was probably easier to secure, having no levels and sections to allow for intruders room to hide in or to avoid flying bullets. The oddest thing yet, was that the room was in the shape of an elongated tube. There was a glass table at one end on which a keyboard and a large screen stood. The room was mostly empty, except for several extra chairs, and it was then Gustave noticed the walls were heavily covered by something that resembled brushed steel, and it just might be the entire structure was reinforced by steel. The floor however was softly carpeted with a disturbingly brilliant shade of scarlet that felt strange to walk on. Gustave thought to himself that if they meant this to be a way to impress guests or even to intimidate them, it was a rather over-the-top way to do it. He tried to avoid, as much as he could, making too much of the design. Next to the table stood one sturdy chair, which more than anything, looked comfortable enough to sit on. Gustave felt a little lightheaded, which he thought was the result of the energy that must have been drawn from his body to the nanonites in his armor. It was a feeling of fatigue which he was unaccustomed to but he made no acknowledgement of it.

"Harry, could you grab those three chairs?" Terra

asked.

"Three?" Gustave asked. "Expecting someone else are we?"

Terra hesitated to answer. She punched a few key strokes through the keyboard and said, "I would like to have an important member of our command present and he is on his way, do you mind?" Her tone was noncommittal.

"I don't think of it as an issue," Gustave said, he sat down in the bulky arm chair.

"I mean, do you mind opening up our communications, so I could contact him?"

That would take quite an effort Gustave thought to himself. On one hand he wanted to make sure their communications were limited however, this would give him an opportunity to hack into their entire infrastructure, considering this was a terminal connected to the main hub. They couldn't know where his parents were which was important. They must have lost communications with them when he made sure of their safety. The risk seemed to be worth it.

"You have my permission. . ." Gustave said. Terra was unhappy with his tone, and she even silently repeated the "permission" with her lips with a resentful frown on her face.

As she typed a few commands to the computer, Gustave released their communications satellite from its frozen state and cleared the scrambled frequencies. He quickly engaged in an interception of the signal and traced it back their hub. The armor without a doubt was capable of copying information simultaneously as it accessed all the files from their massive server. Gustave instructed it to remember the information 'by heart' rather than making a file copy considering he instantly found a protection mechanism preventing copies being made as a large transfer. He had to keep his mind, however, from glancing into the information being copied in order to keep track of the communication traces Terra was leaving behind her. He was amused to see she typed a short message reading "Captured an s-type extraterrestrial, need to engage in R level procedures."

The moment she sent her report to her associate, Gustave instructed his armor to forbid any attempt on the server. He did so to secure his file reading and prevent the server from receiving a command to wipe or lock itself, even-though he did not question that he would be able to access through whatever they threw in his direction.

"I wouldn't go as far as to say you've captured me, Terra; the gentleman you've called in, Mr. Omaha, will find that out quickly since he will be here in, in oh," he looked at his watch. "about ten minutes; he lives very near."

Terra's face turned red. The system, which she always thought of as being impenetrable, was as open to the alien as if there were no security measures at all. She was thankful, however, Gustave did not have the means to understand the order she issued, as it was never written down into the system.

She tried to cover her embarrassment by trying to approach him in a nicer tone while changing the subject. "Gustave, I would like to ask you a few questions before we start." She sat down next to the computer and retrieved a digital questionnaire to the monitor.

Gustave remained silent. She looked at him briefly, then turned her attention back to the computer screen. She posed the first question. "What is your real name in your language?"

Gustave was unsure how to respond to that. Should he give her his real name, or should he have a little fun? He did need to stall her after all. "Vingaluktrapst" he responded with a smile. Terra was too busy trying to type it into the computer to notice his amusement. She quickly gave up.

"Do you prefer a special way to spell it?" she asked. "No, I have none. But you could spell it as it sounds- V..." he repeated each letter slowly.

The form she was filling, Gustave learned, was a form that was made up during the sixties in case an alien was in custody and was to be detained. Gustave thought it to be a little too quirky for his taste. His thoughts quickly navigated toward old references from the time this document was forged, especially as it back-referenced to other encounters and the procedures taken to deal with them. The more his thoughts shifted, the more he accessed the memory that was retrieved from the server.

The information was overwhelming, which he absorbed as if it were brand new. The alien encounters, cover-ups at the highest levels of military and governments, killings of innocent people. The information zoomed through his mind as if he were skydiving toward an endless landscape of information. He lost his focus and with it the concentration of his surroundings. It was almost as if he entered a catatonic state. Eager to learn more and more, to look into the finest of details all in the name of understanding the larger picture, which was almost too much for him to fathom considering the short time he tried to retrieve it.

"Gustave!" Terra yelled. A few moments had passed. She had asked him a few more questions

but he replied to none of them. His eyes moved in rapid fluttering as if he was trying to focus on a display of fireworks on a TV screen running at hundred times their original speed.

"Gustave!" She yelled again. Only this time, she approached him, and extended her arm, pushing his shoulder. The armor would have none of it.

Gustave, oblivious to his surroundings, grabbed her hand with extreme force. He folded her wrist, breaking it in several locations until finally twisting it down onto the table with enough torque to shatter the table. Glass splinters entered her broken hand. Screaming in agony, she tried fighting with her other hand but the pain was too excruciating for her to function. Gustave awoke from his day-dreaming into an awareness of the database which by now completely stored itself onto his armor's memory. Unsure what was happening, he was quickly updated by thought processes. Not moving much he shifted his head slowly looking down at Terra's hand which was still in his powerful grip, flattened into the shattered glass table.

Noticing he was awake, she begged. "Please let me go, please, let my hand..."

Startled by what had transpired, Gustave raised his hand almost in disgust of his own power, or rather the lack of consciousness he was under. Terra slowly moved her hand from the table. Her sobbing became louder as she tried moving her hand. Gustave rose from his chair and looked at Harry. Harry looked as if it wasn't the first or the second time he was forced to watch a human undergoing a disturbing amount of pain. He was quiet and controlled in his composure.

"Harry, you've been helpful. I suggest you go home. I will take care of the res..."

Harry's eyes shifted from Gustave to his right. Something was happening. Gustave saw the look in his eye and turned back. Terra, standing next to a control panel looked as she was activating something with her free hand. Before Gustave had the chance to figure out what it was, a deafening sound as loud as a jet engine filled the room. From the ceiling, rays of light began lowering in rows at an alarming sequence which descended down to the floor. Gustave ran from the room. But as soon he began running something hit him.

The pain was unbearable. It felt as if million tiny needles punctured through his skin in unison, tearing his flesh from the inside towards the surface of the skin and out from his body. The strong magnetic force from the room caused the nanonites to change their shape to a thin string-like figure disrupting their connection to each other as well as their molecular bonds they erupted out from his body just like quills are raised in porcupine when threatened, only much denser. His entire body changed to a grey color. The armor was almost completely outside his body, yet still connected, half inside, while the other half was exposed. Except for his eyes, which remained unchanged, he looked as if he was a mechanical being —a robot, enclosed by a mysterious alloy — He could not move. Still conscious by the awakening pain, he fell to the floor. Not even his lips, or his eyelids were able to move as they were also covered by the nanonites which were fixed in a locked state. He felt alone. Unable to communicate with the armor, call for help, or even scream in pain, he realized he was running out of air. He tried, as hard as he could to inflate his lungs and gather air. With extreme difficulty he slowly began to breathe.

"Shoot him! Shoot him now!" Terra yelled. Harry was too busy looking at the transformation of the creature in front of him. He had never seen anything like it and never expected to in his life time. The sound of a fired bullet sounded from the room. Harry glanced toward the location of the nozzle flash. His hearing was almost obliterated, from the deafening sound of the gun shot, but after years of experience he was well trained to rely on other senses in case one was crippled. A grizzled man wearing a uniform of a high ranking officer held a Desert Eagle in his hands. Gustave did not move. He didn't feel much of the bullet's impact as the millions of tiny spikes naturally stopped it from entering his body. Instead they absorbed it while enclosing it.

The ground of the room began shaking underneath them. It felt as if there was an earthquake. Harry was not sure if this was the result of whatever it was Terra activated but he felt safe in the re-enforced room.

Both Harry and Omaha stepped closer to Gustave, trying to find any damage to the creature. Unable to see anything they both moved in closer and closer while examining the body. Harry, feeling safer than the uniformed man but also much more curious about the odd texture of the composite from which the alien seemed to be composed of, moved closer to the body. The shaking ground made it difficult for him to be certain what he was seeing, however, he could see millions of tiny needles almost invisible to the normal eye. He then noticed the bullet in perfect condition as if there was no sign of an impact. It was embraced and encapsulated among the odd texture of Gustave's skin. Standing closer to Gustave he noticed that he was still breathing. Suddenly a strong shove startled him. It was Terra, holding in her left hand a fire distinguisher. She forcefully shoved Harry aside and tried hitting Gustave again and again, but the fire distinguisher bent to the point that Harry moved again even farther away out of fear it would explode at any given moment. "His eyes Omaha, shoot him in the eye!" she yelled. Stumbling, she stepped a few steps backward.

Aiming at the center of Gustave's pupil, Omaha tightened his grip to secure his shot. His index finger began squeezing the trigger.

It suddenly stopped, the strength left his hands, and he lowered his weapon. He entered a dreamy state, conscious but utterly relaxed. The room around him was quiet. A feeling of calmness invaded his body. He looked at Terra with a smirk on his face. Both she and Harry were also quiet. Smiling and relaxed. They all stood there motionless as if they were frozen under a spell. Which they were.

* * *

"There is not much time, Nell, we have to make it quick" Bor said. The ship had stopped in mid air over the huge structure on the planet. Nell was scared to leave the safety of the vehicle. She was afraid, and had for many years visited this planet, observing it from high above at safe altitudes, but she never imagined herself having to step on the ground of that planet, let alone be up and close to humans. She was breathing heavily.

"Nell!" Bor tried to shake her out of the state she was in. Nell, felt she would need to conquer her fear with measures she preferred not to use. She would have to set her body to a more regulated state, risking that she might not end up as sharp thinking as she should be. But there was no other way. She issued a command to her interface to override regulatory releases in the brain to reduce her fear. Her mind quickly softened and the claustrophobic feeling of being trapped under a very small windowless room full of danger gradually left. Self-preventive medication was a very common practice in many of the species of the Union. Nell, however tried to live her life with as much self-restraint as she could, while trying to deal with everyday life without needing to rely on the internal machinery for mental and physical repairs. For her generation, it was much easier than many that had preceded her. This time, she was unable to cope. Her specie was modified to become less aggressive, to avoid arguments and welcome tolerance. This was nothing she could have prepared herself for.

She grabbed her paralyser and the device K'ta gave her before they left. Her suit indicated a group of ten people in the proximity. They were the body guards that were seen from the images on the screen in the emergency room. The paralyser quickly adjusted to the optimal levels and execution parameters required to deal with the guards. A moment later, she received a reading that they were all completely under it's effects. Their suits informed them the area was secure to enter the building.

Nell and Bor deplaned from their ship and running inside, Nell was quickly informed of Gustave's condition. He was on the floor, his armor completely dysfunctional; his life signs were of more concern to her. The room contained three other humans in it. A trajectory alarm came to her attention. She issued an order to synchronize with the proper settings for the room and the four humans. The device received a failing test signal from the human on the floor, but Nell, knowing why it did, overrode the telemetries, and immediately turned the paralysers on to full action.

She ran toward Gustave who was lying on the floor, frozen at the same position. "Bor, look at this, Gustave, can you hear me?" she yelled. "Gustave!" Her eyes were glassy from tearing after seeing Gustave in such a fearful condition, one she never imagined seeing anyone in. She was not used to seeing injuries. The entire floor was stained with blood which was oozing from his wounds through his armor.

Bor was examining the room to look for any potential danger. Hearing Nell's cry he looked at Gustave. Horrified by the view, he turned away to look at the body of the wounded woman. He did not expect to see any other injury, but her hand was unimaginably twisted, bruised, torn apart and shattered in many places. He turned away and vomited onto the floor behind a chair.

Nell extended her palm towards Gustave body. She tried rebooting the nanonites. They were unresponsive.

"We have to get him up. . ." she said. "Bor?"

She looked to her side, Bor was still crouching, trying to adjust to the fluids gushing out of his body. She looked away in disgust. She would have probably reacted the same way had she not taken the pre-emptive measures.

"Let's get out of her, Bor!" she said, while picking up Gustave's body. His body and his armor were fairly heavy, even with the help of her suit which provided most of the strength in her arms to pick Gustave up. Bor wiped off his face with the fabric of his suit.

Nell could hear Gustave breathing with much difficulty. While they were running to the ship, he grunted several times in pain. Bor commanded the ship to be lowered to the ground for an emergency departure. There was no time to use an anti-gravity field to pick them up. They entered the vehicle. Nell placed Gustave on the floor of the ship and signaled Bor to take off.

When they were out of range, she activated another set of earthquakes on the planet below them. She waited until she saw the buildings in the area shake in sync with the tremors in the ground, and the visibility cloak adjusted itself for a movement that would also be synchronized with the shaking of the ground, which would yield a better chance of no one seeing them, or rather would appear as only a dim flash of light in the sky as they took flight. "We are bringing him up," Nell said.

"Well done Nell, well done," K'ta signaled through the speaker on the instrument panel, speaking from the mission-control room.

Gustave lay on the floor still unable to move. Nell gathered a few instruments she brought with her onboard the ship. “I will need to restart the nanonites, Gustave, while giving them an instantaneous command of their assignment. Each nanonite has to recall its memory.” Nell said. Gustave did not reply. He was beginning to lose his consciousness as very little air flowed to his lungs.

Nell waved a small tool. A sharp and powerful tone that resonated throughout the ship’s hull was released from the device. There was a rising pitch in the sounds, almost as if the resonating wave was recharging and leading toward a climax. Suddenly, a banging flash hit Gustave’s body, and in that moment his armor retracted back to its regular position. The pain was excruciating to the point that Gustave screamed with whatever little air he had left in his lungs, and he was finally able to move his lips and able to voice the severe pain he had suffered from earlier. Nell, unprepared for being responsible for inducing pain in another creature, screamed louder than Gustave.

When the last of his air was depleted by the scream, Gustave fainted.

CHAPTER 30

Everyone in the room was silent. K'ta, Nell and Milka stood around the examining table on which Gustave lay unconscious. They waited for a complete analysis to report the full extent of damage caused by the electromagnetic discharge. The real danger was not to the armor itself but to any neural damage of the mind interface which was particularly vulnerable. It was never designed to be subjected to such radiation. Humans, in their brusque attempts to try and figure out the universe by exploding things, managed to create weapons that were effective against defense mechanisms which was, in a way, rather naive.

The report was fed straight into their receptors.

"What do you make of it Nell?" K'ta asked.

"The damage to the neural connections is extensive," Nell responded.

K'ta pressed a fist against his mouth.

"The good news," Nell continued, "is that Gustave was afraid during the time of the discharge pulse, afraid to the point where his brain bypassed every possible link, rerouting it to a flight only instinct. He wasn't even able to run fast enough to get away, as the armor was not controlled by his brain anymore; it was just superfluous weight".

"I'm not sure I understand," Milka said. It was her group that had managed to retrieve the ancient schematics of the armor. Defending her findings, she tried to learn more about what went wrong. A weak link in the mission would undermine her authority as the chief of strategic ops. She could not afford having such vulnerability as it would risk the dependence with which she had been entrusted. "Could you please speak in terms we could all understand, Nell?"

Nell sighed, indicative of her growing impatience. "We have regulators controlling extremities in our emotions and behaviors; they don't allow us to get too angry or too scared as those extremes often result in unimaginable acts. Humans can train for decades to control their emotions, but they are still predisposed to the natural workings of their brains. Like all of us, you studied human violence, have you not?" Nell looked at Milka.

"But of course I have, Nell!"

Nell summoned a computer screen showing several motion images. "The regulators are capable of entering a human subject into a state of trance where they are completely disconnected from reasoning thought. Most of the time, they will not even be aware of what they are doing. A strong, emotionally impending event can trigger such a state. Fear, for example, or hate. They will, for a brief moment, act as if they are controlled by some puppeteer forcing them toward an act they would otherwise not do. They can be pushed toward extreme heroism, or even more extreme violence and sometimes tap into a uni-subfield without even knowing of such a thing, let alone train in controlling it."

Milka became very thoughtful, as Nell continued.

"It is for these reasons and the fact that it's easier to achieve on earth that we believe the Union conducts its research on the device at that location."

Milka replied, "Are you suggesting Gustave did that?"

"No, not at all, nothing of that sort, on the contrary, he behaved more like an animal rather than an enlightened being. That, simply, is what saved him by disconnecting him from the nano-network. . . I dare say, it was an organic fuse. The strange thing is that Gustave does not test as the type that would be easily subjected to a trance-like state, or hypnosis, for that matter. In fact, as K'ta suggested, it would be impossible as we saw to induce such a state using external sources, so something must have triggered the reaction within him."

"We got lucky" K'ta said sullenly. "How long until he is able to function again, Nell?" He spoke as if he was anxious to change the subject.

"The nanonites took care of everything once I re-started them. I can wake him up now," Nell studied K'ta's expression but did not allude to her concern.

"No" K'ta said in a noncommittal tone. "Milka, please take him home and wake him up there. . . we don't have much time."

K'ta left the room. Nell lingered for a moment, uncertain about why K'ta displayed a less than hospitable disposition toward Gustave, a man who had endured much pain, risking his life for this cause. She looked at Milka, nodded her head and hurried to catch up with K'ta.

CHAPTER 31

Chris sat on his living room sofa sipping a glass of twenty-year-old single malt scotch. He had just returned from Gustave's house after waiting in the driveway for thirty minutes. He tried ringing the doorbell, tried calling his phone, but nothing yielded any evidence as to Gustave's whereabouts. It was not like him to disappear without notice and this was the second time he had pulled such an act.

The phone rang. Hoping it might be Gustave, Chris leaned forward in order to reach the glass table on which his cellular phone stood. It was Leanne.

"Leanne, how are you?"

"I'm great Chris. . . How have you been?".

"I'm fine, although our friend Gustave has given me a few reasons to be a little annoyed..."

"Do you know where he is? I've been trying to reach him for over a week!" Leanne sounded like a petulant, spoiled child.

Chris, being closer to Gustave than to Leanne, was

displeased by her obvious self-centeredness and knew how much help Gustave had been giving her just for the purpose of having her around. Nonetheless, he was angrier yet, as Gustave's location remained an unsolved mystery. He was beginning to wonder if something bad had happened to him.

"Have you seen him this week?" Leanne asked, after the long silence from the other end of the line.

"I have spoken to him. . . he was away for a week or so, but we were supposed to meet at his place this evening. He wasn't there. I tried calling him but there was no answer. I tried him at his parents', but there was no answer there either."

Leanne had always liked Chris. He was a handsome man, and had many other attributes to which she was very attracted. One of those happened to be he never showed her much attention, as if she was nothing special. That alone merely drove her to the edge of her seat, especially whenever someone mentioned Chris was going to be at a friend's gathering or some other event, then she immediately planned to attend. Interestingly enough, it was Gustave that taught Chris back in the university residence that women tend to like guys who don't consider them attractive, either for the purpose of the challenge or something else that kept them from understanding their female psyche. Gustave had difficulties exercising his own teachings, had very little success with the opposite sex compared to Chris, and his willingness to help her through every small crack, made him an easy target in her eyes. She was quite happy contacting him, or at least finding a good reason to contact him, even in such a situation. "I really need to return his laptop and I need his help with something. . . do you think he'll come see you?"

"Unless something has happened to him, I would imagine so, Leanne." Chris replied in a sardonic tone.

"Well, then, can I come and wait for him at your place?" Leanne hoped he would agree to her proposition.

Chris did not sense any hidden motive in her suggestion. He wasn't in much mood for entertaining anyone but was intrigued despite himself. "I don't see why not. . . okay, I'll see you then. Have to go." He hung up the phone.

CHAPTER 32

Gustave awoke and immediately focused on his surroundings. It was obvious to him he was in his own bed, in his own home, but was not sure how he got there. The thought of not knowing exactly what had happened to him in the immediate past caused him great distress. He tried poking into his memory, but nothing came up. Not even the armor which was certainly active giving him readouts about his surroundings gave him any other pertinent information. Milka was near, he sensed. He got out of bed and looked into a large mirror, noticing he was dressed in tightly fitting attire which didn't compliment his figure very well. There was no point in changing though, considering there was a more pressing issue on his mind. He walked slowly into his kitchen, deciding to brew a cup of coffee or perhaps steep some orange pekoe tea.

"Good evening, Gustave. . ." Milka was standing next to the toaster in the kitchen. She seemed fascinated by the device.

"What happened?" Gustave was so eager to know details he couldn't remember, he dismissed any formalities, not even asking her how she got there.

"These are electric wires slaughtering energy to produce heat, just for the purpose of warming up two pieces of bread! How clever! You humans love to play with energy transfer, don't you?" She smiled broadly and continued playing with the appliance.

"Milka, what happened to me back there?"

Milka looked fondly at the toaster again, than pointed at the microwave, retrieving her finger rapidly. "I was just about to say, you have a lot of knowledge enabling you to play with things you don't fully understand. I assume my race, and many others, were just the same way, many years ago. You were hit by some sort of energy disruptor. Same as the ones used on earth to take down our old crafts. The technology used for your armor is predating the refinements to our shields used against such weapons. It was an oversight on our behalf, and we apologize."

"Oversight?" Gustave was angry. "Oversight? Do you realize how much pain I suffered? I could have died there had I not. . .",

". . .called for our help, yes I know, that was a very smart decision you made." Milka smiled sweetly at Gustave's frustration. "Your foresight corrected our oversight." She tried to console him by patting his arm. "Gustave, we can't change the nanonites to shield from these immense energy transfers, but we have advanced them to look for such danger. You will have plenty of time to disarm such weapons or get away from their trajectories."

"I lost a lot of valuable information Milka, a lot of very sensitive information which would have helped our mission. . ." Gustave spoke through clenched teeth. If anything he was more angered with the loss of the information he was unable to retrieve while being connected to the server.

"I wasn't aware of information important to our mission," Milka said.

"What do you mean? You were able to salvage it?" Gustave eyes lit up.

"I didn't say that. . .".

"No, Milka, you did however say you saw no information you found of any value. . ."

"What was it in there of interest to us, or our mission, Gustave?"

"It was a collection of historical records and vicious acts." Gustave was growing annoyed. "Surely, you of all people, must see the value of historical records, Milka, considering your entire position in this mission was the result of the little you managed to scrape up by your own historical records. . ." Gustave realized immediately it wasn't a very becoming remark and it wasn't in his nature to alter his stance. He chose to explain himself instead of apologizing. "Having this information will allow me to avoid them, or to defend myself in fight, if I encounter them again. We have a saying, 'know your enemy'...There is no better way to be prepared."

Milka enjoyed this remark. As a tactical officer not

very accustomed to the way of war, she cherished such adages. Smirking, she said "I could probably learn a lot from humans and their hostile way of thinking."

She knew the value of information Gustave had gathered, and hesitated to retrieve the data, especially as K'ta had not ordered her to do so, but there was a hidden value there. A hidden value of which only she was aware of, and it would certainly be more useful in Gustave's hands than not.

"Very well, but Gustave, can I ask you for the right to use that war adage you told me about as if I said it myself? I would like to tell it to K'ta at some point. Just please don't mention to him we had this discussion, because then it wouldn't look as if I had thought of it myself."

What a strange request Gustave thought to himself and a part of his eagerness to get his memory back he saw no harm in doing that. "I don't see why that should be a problem, Milka"

Happy she found a way to convince Gustave to keep this quiet, without causing any alarms to go off, she was satisfied and executed the memory transfer immediately to Gustave's parasite computer sitting on his laptop.

Gustave, connected with his armor to his computer, instantly recognized the information was there.

"Thank you," he said. "Can I fix you something to drink?"

"No, Gustave, that won't be necessary, I have overstayed my time here. Success to you. . . " Milka smiled, waved her hand slightly and went out to through the window. Still finding it odd her kind didn't understand what doors were for, Gustave shook his head, and turned around to hunt for his cellular phone.

There were several messages and more missed calls than Gustave wanted to attend to or even look at. "Chris!" he yelled, followed by some obscenities. He left the phone on the counter as he tapped on to the device and called Chris through his armor.

The phone rang several times. He was just about to disconnect when Chris's voice answered. "Gustave? Damn it, where have you been?"

Gustave felt sheepish, and knew he had neglected his friend. "Chris, I am deeply sorry, I had some emergency at my parent's house, but everything is good now. Can we please meet soon?"

"I am sorry to hear that. What happened?" Chris knew Gustave's parents very well, and his mood switched from anger to worry.

"I will tell you soon, Chris. . . I have to leave again for some time, but we have to meet before I do. I have very big news and a very big venture for the both of us!" Gustave said, trying not to get into too much detail on the phone.

"I have to work in the morning, Gustave, and I have already waited for you for very long time!" Chris had grown impatient and was close to anger.

"Chris, I have millions in a bank account from my

investors. That will take care of your work. I'll be there in twenty minutes."

Chris mouth fell open. He looked at Leanne. She gazed at him as if he were the only attraction in the room. After a moment or so he replied "Sounds good to me Gustave. . ., see you in a bit." He disconnected the call. Chris looked at his phone, still disbelieving Gustave's tale of huge funds. At the same time, he was beginning to feel quite excited and a surge of adrenaline began flowing through his veins.

"Was that Gustave?" Leanne asked.

"Yes he's quite all right; had some emergency at his parent's house, but everything seems to be in order. He'll be here soon." He made his way to the Scotch bottle, and poured himself a drink. There was reason to celebrate although he was still uncertain what reason that might be. More than anything he was happy he didn't have to wake up early and go to work tomorrow, unless Gustave was pulling his leg. Which he was quite certain would not be the case.

Abruptly, he remembered he was not alone. A good host should offer his guest a drink, but he didn't want Leanne to be there when Gustave arrived. He knew the new project must be discussed in secrecy, and Leanne should not be part of their duo. However, he didn't want to celebrate another drink alone. Raising his glass he asked, "Can I get you a drink?"

"I can't, Chris, I have work early in the morning,

but I'm glad to see everything is fine. Could you please give the laptop back to Gustave?"

Chris couldn't help but notice she seemed a little more distant than she was before, at least a lot less forthcoming. He figured out her game and didn't hesitate to say, "It's probably for the best actually. Gustave and I have to talk business, and he probably wouldn't want you there; this is a very big one."

He somewhat knew that Gustave had had his eyes on Leanne for some time, even though he never mentioned her much. He knew Gustave helped Leanne through many projects and other things that anyone with a schedule as busy as his would have not give up their time for …unless they wanted something in return, especially if it was a woman. He was oblivious to the fact she used Gustave and was more interested in him, and now it seemed the right time to insult her a little, play his game, and perhaps by doing so help Gustave out.

She smiled a confused smile, although it was quite clear she took his comment to heart. This would be a side of Gustave she had never expected. "I'll see you soon, Chris" she said, while grabbing her purse and car keys.

Chris raised his glass in a farewell salute and smiled.

CHAPTER 33

Gustave parked his car as close as he could to the entrance so as not to waste any time. Through the rather short walk to the building's lobby he had to lean into a chilly gust of wind. Either that or it was his excitement at the thought of sharing at least some of his plan with a friend with whom he had always hoped to work in their very own company some day. The moment was finally about to arrive—the definite "we made it" moment. Even considering that the moment was the result of very unlikely circumstances, it was still something he had yearned for most of his life.

His excitement caused a straining movement against his armor. He wanted to walk faster, and get to the elevator sooner, but still wanted to look less conspicuous. However, the ambition to get there faster, which was translated by the armor to move along his muscles faster, clashed with his motivation of attempting restraint. Almost stumbling, he finally made it to the lobby entrance and buzzed Chris's apartment.

Chris released the lock on the apartment door instantly and Gustave rode the elevator up to his floor and hurried down the hall where Chris stood in the open doorway, waiting.

"Chris!" Gustave said with a jubilant tone and extended his hand.

"Can I offer you a drink?" Chris said, gesturing with his glass from which the sweet and pungent aroma of Scotch arose.

Gustave asked himself if that would be a good idea, considering his nervous system was interconnected to sophisticated alien hardware. His query returned a neutral answer which made it clear that the armor would not be harmed by the alcohol, however it would not correct the effects of the alcohol either. "Sure, we have a good reason to celebrate with a drink, too!" Gustave smiled at his friend.

Reaching for a glass, Chris asked, "So, where did you disappear to?"

"Chris, I can't tell you just yet. I agreed with our investors not to expose their involvement until they approved for me to do so, but I can tell you all about it, very soon."

Chris was not very pleased with the secrecy.

"Are you joking? What do you mean, you can't tell me?"

"Let's focus on the project. Trust me, Chris, this will be worth it, more than you can imagine." Gustave attempted to avoid answering, but knowing Chris, he realized he would be better off telling him a lie than not giving him any answer.

He lowered his tone almost to a whisper. "The daughter of a very reach industrial family is trying to make her own fortune without the knowledge of her family, until her investment has come to a successful fruition. We must respect her wishes with the utmost confidentiality, as she would pull out if they heard about it before the proper time. It's really important we keep this quiet."

"Is it Japan? Are you sure you're not messing with some laundering money scheme of the Yakuza or something like that?"

Chris seemed worried; he was never overly cautious, but he never took large risks, either.

"No no, I always make thorough inquiries about investors at first. She happened to look over my submission. She was quite tricky and told me my idea would either not pass their minimum requirements, or would come to light, but only on her terms. I didn't care. She promised me it was her own money she was investing and that she could back up the project financially just as easily as her company could. Chris you should have seen the luxurious way these people live."

"And she transferred you money, just like that?" Chris asked, still very curious about the sources of the financial backing.

"Not really. . . she had me sign all the regular paperwork, it took some time for her to find people to help her out with the legal aspects without the knowledge of her family. I now have eighty-seven million dollars in a bank account! We had ninety at first but she arranged for me to have a private and secured factory lease."

Chris's did not quite know what to make of all of this. "Factory? What are we going to make?"

Gustave raised his glass and silently toasted Chris with his drink. After a sip, he grinned at his friend and his eyes were shining with excitement. "Imagine the most efficient, reliable and safe source of energy —miniature, the size of a very small battery—you get the picture. . ."

"What do you mean?" Chris asked. "What sort of battery are we talking about?"

"We're talking about a battery that can operate a car for about three years before it needs recharging, or can run a house in a larger form, or a mobile computer for, Darwin knows how long considering its size, although the size is really a funny thing. . . When I say in a larger form, I mean the size of a triple A battery."

"Gustave, you're telling me you found the Holy Grail of energy production?"

"Worth a dollar or two, wouldn't you agree?" Gustave laughed.

Chris placed his glass onto the table, and sat down. "This would make us very rich. . ."

"Correct."

"This will make us richer than all the fuel companies in the word, combined."

"Correct."

"Are we nuts?" Chris' voice was full of wonder. "This will make us the richest assassination target in the world, Gustave, they would have us killed before we could even launch the product."

"We can take precautionary measures. We create and manufacture the devices, we then approach the public with our products, while at the same time taking care to defend ourselves. In any case, I would imagine them going after me instead of you, but before we go public, I need to go away for several months. I need you to oversee the production."

"Going away? I don't think I can oversee something like that, Gustave, wait. . . where are you going, now that you finally made it this far?" Chris was bursting questions. He could not, for the life of him understand what it was Gustave was really up to.

"The production will be completely automated. We don't need to hire employees or factory workers. Everything's automated as I designed it."

"So, what do you need me for?"

"Although the production will be automated, the construction of the facility will not. When people are assembling the equipment, I need you to make sure everyone is doing what they're supposed to do. Most of the workers won't know what other teams will be doing, what other equipment is coming in. You'll have to periodically close sections of the factory using layman workers, to prepare for other teams and equipment the next day. You'll have to find an engineering firm that will be able to keep everything quiet, because they are responsible for connecting the almost self-assembling pieces. Think of it as if it were sets of IKEA furniture. Many pieces will be coming from different places in the world, so we'll tell them we are performing an experiment on the impact of high velocity lasers on organic tissue. That should cover our tracks for the time being. Also you'll have to hire security to make sure no one takes any photos, documents, or anything from the factory. I need you to run the most secured place you can possibly think of, and I know I can trust you to do your best in that respect."

Chris seemed to be overwhelmed. For a few moments he was speechless. "I don't know Gustave, I've never done anything like this before. What if I screw up? Then the entire thing is gone!"

"I trust you with this Chris, but don't worry, by the time the crew is done, I will build the final, most crucial piece of that factory. . . without it, this whole thing is just a really messy- looking particle accelerator. The secrecy is a smoke-screen, mostly to buy us time."

"Gustave, I know you to be the most brilliant man I have ever met in my life, but, are you certain this is going to work?"

Gustave, always enjoyed receiving compliments indicative of his genius, but he never quite knew how to receive them seeming over-confident and unbearably vain, but he was certain that this would work. "I have no shadow of a doubt, Chris. This will work"

"Where do you need to go?" Chris was not sure he could fulfil what it was Gustave was asking him to accomplish, at least, not on his own.

"I am going to work on something much larger than that. The money from the energy devices will sponsor this new project, but I must take myself off the grid to allow myself the time to concentrate on developing it. . ."

What could possibly be larger than the solution to humanity's biggest problem? Chris wondered to himself. His arms were crossed over his chest and he looked at his friend with a dubious yet hopeful expression. "And I don't suppose you can tell me what it is. . ."

Gustave raised his glass and smiled. "You suppose right my friend. Let's drink to our future success!"

For several hours the two sat, talking over all the details of their future endeavour. They discussed and plotted ways of making the new factory a truly impregnable facility. They talked about distributions, and marketing of the products. Detail by detail they uncovered every possible angle of the project without dismissing even the smallest details such as company colors, or forgetting to bring up the risks, and the many enemies they were about to make. It all seemed to have been worth it. Realizing the job might be too big for just one man, Gustave brought up the idea of bringing a security specialist into the picture, who he identified only as' Harry' and described to Chris as an extop security man. Surely a man such as Harry would be very capable of handling a very highly classified project. Above and beyond that, Gustave envisioned a much greater purpose for him in the future knowing the man was soon to be out of work.

On his way home, Gustave realized he would be putting his trusted friend at risk, more so than himself. Through proper security measures, he knew it would be virtually impossible to kill either of them by conventional means, which these enemies would most likely try to use. He must think of a way to guarantee the protection of all three members leading this project. Surely, he could not ask K'ta to equip Chris with a suit of armor. Maybe some sort of mobile anti-projectile device which Chris could have with him at all times. He wondered how his armor figured out projectiles at such tremendous speeds. Surely such a device could be modified to use the same technology, only with a counter-acting projectile of its own.

It was in that very moment he realized as he was thinking about the technology of his armor, he intuited its information being retrieved. Alien sketches and writings with three dimensional schematics came rushing to his memory bank as if he stood in a room observing them first hand. Something was utterly different. He somehow had access to nanonites' technology, and to the programming of these incredibly fast molecular swarm networks.

He had access to all the alien technology that was used to construct his armor. But how, he did not know.

CHAPTER 34

Nell's footsteps left soft impressions in the corridor's soft floor as she trailed behind K'ta. K'ta, noticed he was being followed by Nell and continued walking but wondered about her reason for following him. "Is there something on your mind Nell?" He asked, without changing his speed.

"What is going on, K'ta?" Nell's tone of voice was animated and indicative of her mood which was contrary to her nature.

K'ta felt uncomfortable. "Need I remind you to keep your temper, Nell?" His comment was the equivalent in earth terms of informing someone they were being idiotic. The personal attack only alienated her even more. She told herself she needed to calm down, and at the same time her neuro-link adjusted her mood. Controlling behaviour was a very common practice throughout the species of the Union. The new generations evolved after many years of adjustments in positive and negative feedback towards rude, or aggressive behaviour. But that did not mean they were incapable of displaying any of these emotions, except when piqued to preconfigured aggressive levels.

"I could have used more time to observe him on the ship, and perhaps run several more tests." Nell was trying to find the reasoning behind K'ta's behaviour toward Gustave.

"You? Out of all people I thought you might welcome having the human gone. . ." K'ta said sullenly, trying to buy some time.

"I am pleased to report that I have adjusted to working with the human. And considering the extraction mission, I am no longer as terrified of humans as before."

"Well then, I have made a dire mistake, Nell."

"I don't understand . . ."

K'ta turned towards Nell, his angry expression exposed his disapproval.

"You should be nervous around the presence of a human, Nell. It will do you no good to trust them."

"But we entrusted Gustave with our future, why should I not trust him?"

"We trusted him because we have no other solution, but that does not mean we should be comfortable around him. The more comfortable we are, the more vulnerable we'll get. The report showed a complete recovery and considering we are running low on time, it was the best judgment." K'ta turned and began walking again toward his destination. Nell followed.

"I am well aware of the report, and am well aware

of his condition, but we are in uncharted territories here. " Nell realized she was, after all, under his command, and she began explaining her reason for questioning K'ta's decision.

"You are correct. But we have no time for standard procedures. The circumstances with his capture by AMET endangered the mission greatly. I am not certain how to deal with them. It seems as if they will try to hunt him down again."

"The human agency?"

"Indeed. The Union had intervened before when we tried to contact them decades ago, and if you recall, that mission has ended up quite badly for both the humans and ourselves. "They might contact them again. Although Union, pretending to be the Krill's, haven't had contact with them for a very long time, you see, and if AMET contacts them again, requesting some information about Gustave, our entire mission is at danger."

Nell began to understand the issue at hand. "But AMET has tried contacting them again and again for decades and they never reply."

K'ta stopped. It had never occurred to Nell that even though the 'Krill' never reply to the humans that did not mean they never listened. He knew he had to contact command immediately.

"Please excuse me, Nell. . ." He opened a rift in the wall of the corridor leading into a separate room, one of the only places in the ship where he alone had clearance.

Their conversation left Nell with a bad after-taste. There was more going on behind the scenes, more than she had imagined, but knowing K'ta as well as she did, she knew he was hiding something.

CHAPTER 35

Gustave awoke early. The morning sun was turning the glass in his bedroom window to glistening gold. Perhaps it was the sunlight that woke him up earlier than usual or it was thinking about what was on his schedule for the upcoming day. He jumped out of bed to prepare himself hurriedly for things to come. He was determined his plan for getting AMET off his back would work, or even more, he was determined to destroy AMET and bring their activities to an end. His stomach, however got his attention and he knew he had to eat for strength and energy or else he would not be as useful as he could be. He usually didn't ingest much food and it felt odd to be that hungry. His armor reported it was normal for the nanonites to use up the body's own energy, and it was them causing the hunger pangs. Cautious of his weight, he wasn't too happy about eating more than his usual daily rations. But he then reasoned it is most likely to make no difference in his size. As he was thinking about his size. a new memory was triggered about actively controlling the nanonites around the body. The armor, it seems, was also intrigued and tempted with several, more covert ops type luxuries. Ignoring his hunger, he took off his shirt and approached the mirror next to his walk-in closet. His belly was a little flat, slightly curvy, indicating he never concentrated on working out, yet at the same time, a healthy eater. He flexed his stomach muscles as hard as he could. There was not much change, other than the very subtle appearance of the shapes of his normal muscles. He tried it again, this time he envisioned a muscular toned body. It worked. Consequently, entertained by his new body, he began laughing a villain's cackle like a character in an inadequately produced movie. After releasing the shapes, he tried getting creative with the sizes of his six-pack and moved them around a little, up and down, replacing them with triangle shapes and even tried creating the contours of his face which left him a little disturbed. The feeling accompanying his playfulness was of skin being stretched and wasn't very comfortable but his zealous concentration at making the changes kept the uneasiness secondary. He wondered if he could change the rest of his body. His nose to begin with, and it moved a little, then his cheeks changed form; it all worked. He wondered how long the armor could keep a shape. . . indefinitely, he decided, as long as he stayed away from mirrors or very reflective surfaces. The report came back to him with a recommendation to either practice in front of a mirror in order to train his brain to the self- projection of his new figure, otherwise, looking at a reflection would recall the old features the brain expected to see, triggering immediate reassembly.

He put his shirt back on and made his way to the kitchen where he decided to make some hot chocolate and perhaps a piece of cinnamon toast and scrambled eggs.

Luckily, he did have several eggs left in the refrigerator. And a loaf of bread was kept in the freezer.

Thirty minutes later, he felt well fed and satisfied. It was time to start what he had decided to get done that day.

He looked for Harry's contact information through the immense data retrieved during his meeting with the AMET. With not much effort and very little time, the number was recalled to his memory as if he had dialed it a thousand times.

Too lazy to retrieve his phone, he connected to Harry's number through the interface. The phone rang several times before Harry, sounding a little agitated picked up.

"Is this. . . this..." Gustave was trying to buy some time to ascertain whether or not there was a trace on the phone.

"Who is this?" Harry asked

Sure enough, the line was bugged. Gustave prepared a signal-lost false read for the trace program.

"I'm sorry, I dialed the wrong number," Gustave said, and jacked the false feed through the system.

"Hold on, Harry, I imagine AMET is on the fritz?" He asked before Harry had managed to disconnect his phone.

"Who is this?" Harry asked, only this time with a more assertive tone.

"It's Gustave. I wanted to thank you personally for saving me the other day."

"Are you nuts? They..."

"They can't hear us talking anymore," Gustave interrupted.

"They have been pretty quiet about this. Well, Terra is still in a bad shape; heavily sedated; she, too, is very quiet."

"Harry, there's not much time. I need to ask you to get out, get all your necessary belongings, your dog, and leave to a location I will text to your phone. It is imperative you do this as fast as possible. . .""

Harry didn't know what to make of it, but he had a hunch he should be doing just what Gustave had asked him to do.

"They might follow me, or think something is wrong, can you take care of that?" Harry, had no sympathy for his new colleagues or the organization in charge of for the new mission ahead.

"Harry, in a few hours, these people are going to be worried about a whole lot more than your whereabouts. However, if I turn off their satellite communications they will sniff the danger. I can't have that in my plan. I will see you there in approximately four hours."

He transmitted a text message to Harry's handset, and included a personal note, stating "this world will benefit by your service to my cause, so try to make it there without getting yourself killed."

The entire database of all of AMET's operations through its bloody history was in Gustave's computer and he was very sure of his next move. Set up a server, lock it up through various encoding algorithms that will take a millennium to break and then let it loose on the Internet and the World Wide Web. He purchased a domain name and arranged for the hosting paid by a synthesized credit card number and identity newly-embedded into the credit union's authorities. The upload should take some time, but he sketched a small program that attached itself hidden under layers of code in an email that would in turn catch a ride onto another and so on. Once the upload returned an acknowledgement of being complete, the small program would direct every one infected into the website, and then release itself from its grip; not very malicious, but certain to reach the news and the authorities. There were incriminating documents, on missing people, torture, cover-ups, more UFO video footage than anyone can imagine, and of course, documents detailing the ancestral tree of hierarchy of secret operatives working from within the government, the military, and it's industrial complex.

This should not only send them on the run, but expose something much larger, something that would help his ultimate goals, which were far nobler than causing the destruction of dangerous people with more power than they should ever hold.

Observing the time, which moved rapidly through his hard work, Gustave made a conscious effort to finish everything so he would be free to meet with Harry when he said he would.

The drive, although a short distance outside of the city, was rather brief. Dressed in a striped dark blue silk suit, he left for his destination.

Traffic was not very accommodating. Gustave knew Harry's life was at great risk if he were late. Frustrated, his patience ran low and with it the armor began to work its magic. Calculating surrounding cars' trajectories to avoid impacts, he drove almost as if he were not human, faster than the speed limits, ignoring traffic lights, and incoming traffic. His hand movements on the steering wheel acted as if he were a precognitive Formula One driver. At the same time, he managed to block all the police traffic reports and calls. He had never broken the law before, however, and considering the magnitude of the situation, there was no room for comfort or doing the right thing. The road zoomed under his vehicle's wheels, until less and less traffic appeared in front of him. He was getting closer to the meeting destination, which was a lake where Gustave and his parents used to visit every few years or so when he was a child.

His headlights picked up the colorful lights strung along the bank of the deep blue water encompassing a vast area. It was almost hard to see the far side of the lake. There were several local restaurants and shops, and the air was filled with the scent of fresh seafood.

The docking area, where small, thirty-something-foot yachts were berthed calm in the lake's water, also accommodated several tables with benches for people picnicking before their leisure ride. Harry, sitting on one of them was accompanied by his colossal Great Dane. The dog looked at Gustave and raised his pointed ears. Gustave smiled at the dog, at which point it began wagging its sizeable tail.

"Come here!" Gustave said in a jubilant tone as he tapped his knee. He knew the breed very well as he had grown up around them. To his dismay, his parents never accepted one for very long due to allergies. Gustave, however was very fond of the gentle giants and always knew how to enjoy them and evoke their pleasure with him as well.

The dog trotted toward Gustave, his huge paws slapping the deck. Harry stayed motionless, watching from his seat. He found it a moment to be proud of his dog's behaviour or perhaps it was also the shared fondness for dogs the alien seemed to have.

"You made it. . ." Gustave spoke in a musical tone to the dog. He was glad to see Harry and the dog had made it safely to the rendezvous spot.

"I tried not to be seen, I did my best, but I can't tell if there is anyone watching over us..."

"Oh, I wouldn't worry about that, Harry. . ." Gustave jostled the thick shoulders of the dog playfully. The dog raised his head and produced a snorting noise, responding to the game. "Let's just say your old company went public, and from now on, things are not exactly in their hands."

Harry seemed surprised. After many years of seasoned secrecy, his life's work was breached to its core. He was about to say something but Gustave stopped him.

"Relax Harry, your files have been omitted from the public eye, you are safe from the media circus that is about to come. I need your help, I need you to work for me, and they..." Gustave paused for a moment, ". . .they need to be destroyed."

Harry felt tremendous relief, seeing that he was not at risk. Now the objectives to which he had dedicated much of his life would finally be paid off, climaxing with the destruction of that very organization of which he had grown more and more resentful.

"At this very moment Harry, a factory is being constructed in a remote location. Not many know what this factory is meant for but I am about to reveal that information to you because I trust you can help me secure its purpose."

Intrigued, Harry kept very still as he listened to every word.

"I am about to release an energy device that will change the course of human history. That factory has two purposes; one you might view as a noble cause to clean up our dependency for fossil fuel, and the second is to make me the richest entity on earth."

Harry seemed confused, as to how an alien could care for earthy finances.

"I should probably tell you now that like yourself, I'm a human, not an alien."

Harry had to interrupt, "But I've seen you..."

"I am, however, equipped with alien technology, and not only that, my purpose is to adapt some alien technology to our culture. To produce more of it, to manufacture it and introduce it to market is very expensive considering I will not have anything but exclusivity on the technology. I'm not a saviour of any kind, but I do want to see a change. What you've seen me do is what I was equipped with to protect myself for my mission, and we both know it was well worth it to be so equipped. I have bigger plans Harry, but for safety reasons I will not disclose them to you at this point."

"You are telling me, if I'm hearing this right, that you would like to become the richest man in the world and profit from technology that was meant for humanity's sake?" Harry's tone of voice was very close to anger.

"Yes Harry, you must think of it as a ridiculous ideology, but let me remind you that your previous employers tried getting this technology and keeping it from the general public. As I said, it costs a lot of money to produce new technology, as everything, every small part has to be fabricated. While I will most certainly become the richest man in the world, I will release more and more of the technology that was given to me. It's a very simple concept for which there is no alternative. And as I said, there is a greater purpose for it all."

"Who are these aliens, why didn't introduce it themselves?" Harry asked.

"They would like to keep themselves anonymous, or perhaps silent partners, until the moment is right."

"Why?" Harry asked again, only this time with more insistence.

"For some reasons I cannot explain to you at this moment, but in due time you will know all the details. That, I promise. . ."

CHAPTER 36

K'ta was alone in his own room. The walls slowly changed into the color of smooth golden-brown of sleek wood. He sat on a comfortable seat that curved itself around his body. The seat which was fairly low stance from the floor began raising itself, morphing in to a curvy stool which helped K'ta stand up. Next to him, millions of tiny particles began floating in what seemed at first a chaotic fashion, now formed into a more organized structure that began producing moving images, clear and sharp tones of colors and with them some of three-dimensional depth.

"I am most pleased you've answered my call, Pix" K'ta turned toward the screen.

"You seem to have a problem with Gustave, K'ta" Pix said. He was wearing a custom-tailored suit, blue in color yet with an orange tint.

K'ta began speaking. "I'm afraid so. He..."

". . .Solved your problem? I apologize for interrupting you." It would have been easy to dump the information into K'ta's memory, but out of mutual respect, and with a little sense of playfulness, he wanted to keep K'ta from knowing exactly what happened, at least until he released the information to him, bit by bit.

K'ta, considering the critical nature of the mission, did not appreciate the approach; he was more impatient to receive all the information at once. However, he knew it would be rude of him to request it. "He did what?" He was trying to speed up the process.

"There was no attempt to contact Union from AMET, they are too busy hiding. Humans, destructive and obnoxious creatures that they are, do tend to amuse me, especially with their ingenuity when causing harm to anything that stands in their way. Brilliant, if you ask me."

"Sir, could you please explain?" K'ta begged for more information.

"He unloaded all AMET's database into a computer and linked the entire earth through an internet mail to it. AMET are on the run. They should provide you with very little trouble anymore."

K'ta felt relief that the mission was still on track, even though it bothered him how comfortable Gustave was being so independent, which, after studying humans, K'ta had discovered there was a thin line before crossing into some form of recklessness. With the help of his internal computer, he ran several scenarios in his head, corresponding to what the humans might do in such situation. "What if the Union finds out about this? They know how secretive and well-guarded AMET's facilities were. They might become suspicious."

"You may be right, but in this case, they have an army of analysts, and committees through which this information will have to go through for a very long time. A lengthy bureaucratic process that will yield results well after you should be back here with the device.

So far, the news traveled to the initial processing facility on Tuty's moon." Pix said.

K'ta didn't want to ask for verification of that information. He knew their organization had ears and eyes in many places.

"But Kt'a, it is very important to persuade the human to do what he was asked to do, with no more delay."

"That is firmly understood Pix," K'ta nodded. "I will see to it myself" he added.

"K'ta, if I may suggest, Nell might have a more convincing touch; my records show Gustave seems to respond to her very well. . . He's attracted to her and we've both seen him do more than enough to help an attractive woman." Pix had a small grin on his face. It was no secret that Nell was astonishingly beautiful. K'ta, however did not find the idea too appealing; after all he was himself attracted to her, but any feeling of anger was quickly sedated by his regulator.

"Excellent suggestion; it will take some convincing to send her back down, but she will follow orders," K'ta responded.

"Until next time, then. Farewell and success!" Pix

said and the connection was broken.

The video screen began self-disassembling into millions of microscopic nanonites vanishing equally across the room's walls. K'ta issued a message to Nell through the neural link ordering her to see him for a quick briefing. His reaction almost seemed automated and also calculated. Perhaps he believed in the mission more than he saw to matters of his own heart, yet there was the possibility the regulator injected a little more than the usual amount of calming agents into his stream, indicating he was in fact, not at ease with his position.

Nell received the call to attend the briefing. The call was quick and to the point. Nell, was in her lab working on a private project, trying to teach the Nanobot how to configure themselves automatically to co-produce an evolved state to any given problem. The Nanobots were much more sophisticated than electronic stem cells and since their conception and their mass production stages, the major advancements were in the creativity of their usage, perhaps similar to an intelligent putty. Anything can be created with these intelligent building blocks, yet it was more important how elegantly, or how efficiently, it was executed.

Nell got up from her chair and began walking toward the wall. The Nanobots gathered themselves into a tiny grey tube as the wall opened, allowing Nell a comfortable exit.

She wondered about the whereabouts of her

colleagues. Her interface instantly gave her a pinpoint position of everyone. It seemed she and K'ta were the only ones to attend this briefing.

The ship's corridors were busy with Biobots running about completing tasks. It was important to keep them busy at times, to let their mechanics stretch to their maximal ability. She passed through several units, until she arrived at the room. The entrance was open.

"Nell, how is your project coming along?" K'ta asked as a friendly gesture.

"It is going quite well, although I wish I had more resources to test against. . ." Nell seemed a little concerned as to her abrupt summoning.

"Nell, I spoke to command. They have requested me to..." He paused. "Gustave, and the mission itself, as you may know, was in great danger. However, our fear has diminished since Gustave took it upon himself to clear his way through considerably insightful means. The council fears he may have a few more resources to his disposal to cause harm to himself, the missions, and to us. He will require a little push toward completing his task without further distraction."

Nell didn't understand exactly to what K'ta was referring. She made sure to transfer her bafflement through their link, at which point K'ta quickly dumped the memory containing the information on Gustav's approach dealing with AMET. She found it quite entertaining and chuckled. Her smirk quickly turned upside down when she realized

Gustave had somehow gained access to memory which she was certain had been deleted from his armor. "How did he..." She paused.

K'ta waited a little and decided to interrupt her. "Exactly, none of us could have predicted such use of this ancient technology, but it seems his flair for reinventing himself and the resources available to him serve him better than we expected."

"He needs reprogramming," Nell said, understanding the severity of giving too much power to a human.

"I'm afraid that would be equally risky. We don't have much time," K'ta said. It was the first time they had somewhat reversed their positions, although it might have well been because she arrived fresh from her nanobots and was ready to reprogram and test anything put in front of her.

"What would you have me do, K'ta?" She asked with a hint of disappointment.

K'ta looked at her, then looked up toward the ceiling. "Oh, some superficial behavioral conditioning and a little guided direction toward a more specified purpose, I suppose"

"You want me to spend more time with him on earth?" Nell asked, not for clarification purposes, but to try to let K'ta realize how offensive his request was.

"Outside of having the right protection, it is merely for a few days. Your courage will be profoundly rewarded."

K'ta tried easing his way through a proposal of

incentives, at least incentives he would have considered worth the risk, however, she had no need or lust for leadership or such ambitions. She only wanted to be known for her work rather than her heroics.

K'ta didn't reply. His silence was enough of an indicator to show her he was not in any position to negotiate her new travel arrangements any further.

"I'll get ready. I suppose I'll be well equipped, I won't worry about much other than Gustave having another breakdown, but I'll be well prepared for that."

CHAPTER 37

Gustave left the new compound after introducing Harry to Chris. The factory space was still empty, and except for a dozen security patrol cars, which had been stationed around the area, there was not a soul anywhere near the newly formed Centre for Unconventional Technologies (C.U.T.). The area was well guarded, but was yet to be secured. The group had selected a company which erected huge re-enforced concrete walls as opposed to electrical fences. Each section was fitted with seismographic scanners which would respond even to the slightest movement near the walls.

Gustave, knowing he left the project in the hands of a capable team, left to begin his mission. He planned to go home and prepare for traveling to the army base research center under his new identity. During the ride, he studied his armor technology. After finding a translating program of English to the Melech dialect, it was only a matter of asking the right questions to receive a full reverse compatibility for Melech to English. The formulas, however, proved to be a little more difficult, as the signs were completely different and there was no glossary. Again and again, he tried plugging in things he knew, converting into formulas using some of the alien constructs which revealed their secrets one after another. The more he knew, the easier it was for him to dig deeper.

After an hour of driving he learned of Nell's arrival. The way communication and transfer of new information through which this alien technology worked still left him amazed. He suddenly remembered Nell was expected to arrive for a visit at a given hour. It was as if he had known all along, had the date planned but forgot about it, and then suddenly remembered. Strange as it was, he knew this was a transfer of new information since he did not remember arranging such a visit. He was very excited.

While he usually drove moderately slow on his way home, he now accelerated as fast as he could and began listening to police reports, noting any keyword referring to speeding and the road on which he was speeding. Here and there, the few police cars which managed to try to chase him experienced a complete electronic shut down which left them capable of only steering and braking: a thrilling ride.

He did question Nell's visit, but his best guess which was somewhat egocentric, was that she had come to congratulate him for his cleverness in dealing with AMET, which surely they had noticed. Studying the records, he knew very well there was something going on between the

Union and AMET. Extremely confident of his achievement for helping the Angelonians, he began envisioning his reward. Perhaps it would be a more personal reward, which would explain Nell's visit rather their taking him up into the ship again.

Gustave arrived home, dropped his keys on the table and ran to the shower. He was usually only briefly in the shower although lately he had often started taking longer ones to soothe his frequent headaches. After drying off, he chose his nicest clothing and straightened up the house which was not in bad shape to start with. Nell was scheduled to arrive at quarter after eight and he had just enough time to take care of his immediate surroundings. Again, he arranged his computer room and areas of the house in a way he thought represented an intellectual human being. He knew nothing he had would impress her considering her origins, but nonetheless it was important for him to at least make an effort out of respect for her, if for nothing else.

The house rattled. It was like a very mild earthquake. Gustave's armor indicated Nell was approaching.

Making sure his hair was in place in the living room mirror, he prepared himself for her.

A few moments later the door opened clumsily. Nell was not used to doors, or door knobs for that matter, and although she got the meaning of the handle, it took her a while to figure out it had to be pulled closed right after entering. There was nothing in her human studies to prepare her for using such a basic contraption as they mostly concentrated on human psychology, history, and social interaction.

The technology section still categorized humans as in "the beginning of the digital age."

Nell appeared dressed in stunning evening wear: a floor-length black chiffon dress with an elegant and flawless mix of modern and classic romance. The neckline of the couturier gown was twisted lilac organza, which framed her lovely face and echoed the brilliant color of her eyes and the mysterious pendant glittering from the silver chain around her slender neck. She knew her purpose was to keep him on his mission by suggestive means, so after profiling him, she had fabricated a dress that was both to his taste and one that would cover the battery of protective equipment she had brought with her.

Gustave did not expect such a stunning vision. Although he thought her to be a striking and exquisite beauty before, he now realized that there was more beauty hidden within her still.

They both remained silent, studying each other. Of course, Gustave didn't think it would be a very smart move if he kept his mouth shut too long.

"Going out for a dinner, are we?" He asked. Nell didn't seem to understand why he said that.

"Hello, Gustave, it's good to see you again, too. . .What do you mean by 'out to dinner'?"

"You are dressed for it! Are you hungry? We could

go out, if you wish. . ." He would be proud to be seen in public with such a mesmerizing creature.

Nell realized she had put off eating to prepare for her visit to earth. For some reason, now that she was with Gustave, her anxiety about all the bad things that can happen to her among humans moved to the back of her mind.

"I wouldn't mind eating, Gustave. . .". It was only fair she thought to herself. Gustave had eaten with them on the spaceship, and it would be rude if she refused taking him up on his invitation.

"I did not have the time to prepare anything , Nell, I'm sorry! I've been keeping too busy, but we can go to a fine restaurant, where at least you'll get a good impression of our local cooking."

Nell had watched a lot of human movies. The aliens tended to watch them often to understand humans better. It was much less risky and a whole lot more revealing than walking amongst them to observe. Many movies, some from which she got the idea to dress as she did, did portray a dinner among well-dressed people. No harm would be done. She knew she was making history by being that close, and that public, with the humans. She was amused how previously she was afraid of being in proximity to earth, and now, she was not afraid to involve herself in activities that would be considered too risky among her colleagues. Of course, the equivalence of how safe she was while encompassed by every possible protective gadget, would be the same as sitting in a heavily armored army tank moving along among cavemen who could do no more than throw wooden spears at it.

"Yes, eating would be acceptable. . ." Nell said.

Gustave did not expect that response but he smiled broadly.

"Yes, you would like to go, or yes, you are hungry?" He wanted to clarify as well as give him some time to think of the best place he could take her to. Nell looked around. She was admiring the prehistoric look of the place.

"Yes to both, Gustave" she chuckled. "And why do you keep so many things, does it not feel cluttered?" She was used to rooms that accommodated themselves to the immediate needs of their visitors instead of rooms that could attend to many needs, whether they were used or not.

"Unless you want to help me manufacture nanonites here on earth, we'll continue to decorate with many of our needs in mind."

Nell caught his humoristic tone, "Yes, I did think that would be the first thing we'll do," she laughed.

"I guess it's sort of like those statues you keep where we had dinner in your ship, only we keep more things, pictures, art, and functional furniture...Would you care for some wine?"

"Alcohol?" She asked. "No, I think I will be just fine without perception-changing substances, but thank you, anyway. . ."

" You are with a good friend..and if I can handle

several men carrying automatic weapons, I can probably save you from a waiter with a bad attitude."

Protection? What a barbaric way to talk, she thought, although someone willing to fight for her safety was comforting and new in a way. Not that there was ever any need for such a concept, but she wondered if any Angelonian would have done the same.

"And if I may add, you are probably more well equipped than I, judging by the electronic footprint of your underwear. . ." He coughed. "I mean what you wear under that dress. . ." His face turned red.

To avoid any further embarrassment she changed the topic. "Gustave, you adapted to your new abilities sooner than I thought you would!. I see you've made some modifications of your own?"

She knew Gustave wouldn't mind her poking around his armor.

"You've noticed have you?"

"Yes I have…".

"I've modified a few things here and there; I've had the chance to test it quite a bit, as you may have noticed. I'm just trying to be sure I'll be ready for things to come."

Nell liked his approach. In a way, Gustave was practicing her line of work, only at the same time not really understanding the material he worked on. Very typical of human behavior she thought to herself, but nonetheless a formidable effort.

"Shell we proceed with dinner?" She realized that

up until he had asked her, she was not hungry, but now was quite famished, and the thought of experimenting with human food, which she read quite a lot about in her cultural studies, was exhilarating.

Gustave was trying to think of a place. The options were many, especially since he had already set up an approximately limitless budget for dining. There was, however, one restaurant he knew that would be the most magnificent place to could take her.

"Indeed, Nell, shall we?"

Gustgave offered her his arm and she paused at first, then remembered an etiquette book she had scanned months earlier. She smiled demurely and slipped a graceful hand through the crook of his elbow and they walked out of the apartment looking every bit as handsome as any other sophisticated earth couple, going out to dinner, thoroughly entranced with each other.

CHAPTER 38

EXCERPT FROM LOCAL NEWS BROADCAST ON 'POLITICAL UPDATES':

Hostess MC: *In recent developments in the AMET Scandal, the Supreme Court has set a date to begin its investigations in what they called the most unlawful undertaking of a government-run organization in U.S history. A press conference was held an hour ago at the White House. Our White House correspondent, Jeremy Short reports:*

Jeremy Short: *Thank you, Liz. About an hour ago, White House spokesperson Mr. Daniels Griffith disclosed very little information and said the administration had no knowledge of the existence of the organization. Mr. Griffith emphasized it still remains to be seen if there is any validity in the leaked information and said they are planning to cooperate fully with the committee. After being asked about the suicide of Senator R.N Mitchell and whether or not that was enough of an indicator of the validity of the disclosed documents, which contained hundreds of references toward his involvement with the organization, Mr. Griffith declined to comment and left the stage.*

'Thousands of demonstrators have gathered here in Wash-

ington to demand the immediate removal and arrest of key people in the government and the military. It is reported that among the crowds are families and friends of victims listed in the disclosed documents.

"The FBI has reported the location where the documents originated still remains a mystery. FBI Director, Renwick B. Gould said he cannot comment in regards to the involvement of officials in the FBI, but they are treating this as a national threat, considering the information was spread by spam with the use of a very sophisticated virus.

We do know many officials mentioned in the documents are currently in protective custody under the supervision of the NSA. We are not sure just how long they will be maintained for safekeeping, but we are certain they are indeed under investigation and a tight watch, 24/7. Back to you, Liz.

* * *

Hostess MC: *"Thanks, Jeremy. In light of recent events, many anti-religious demonstrations have been held throughout the world. One man was left dead after being shot several times in the head at a demonstration held in Michigan in front of the Cathedral of St Andrew. The man, a father of two, was seen carrying a sign saying, "We have proof they exist, you've had nothing but lies" and he was rushed to the hospital, later succumbing to his injuries. The Church has posted a formal request calling people on all sides to remain calm. And condemned any sort of violence. The search continues following witnesses' reports that the gunshots came from a firearm held by a Caucasian male driving a white Ford Taurus. No arrests have yet to be made.*

"Joining us live are Tiffany Andrus, author of The Other Cover-Up and Chief Editor of The Report, as well as Lee Foster, former national affairs advisor for President Randall.

"Ms. Andrus, in your book, you've mentioned there are immense amounts of funds being earmarked for Black Ops' operations. Would you say that AMET was funded through these instruments?"

Tiffany Andrus: *"I have no doubt projects like this, were funded under the Black Ops umbrella."*

Hostess MC: *"Considering the origins of funding and the involvement of key officials within the government, would you say the involvement is deeper than what the government has so far admitted?"*

Tiffany Andrus: *"Well, Liz, the government has yet to confirm anything. If indeed these documents are liable sources, we have to remember most of the Black Ops funds are passed through many hands before anyone knows their final destiny. Ninety-nine percent of the administration does not know where these funds go, which is by itself nothing short of a tragedy for the American tax payer."*

Hostess MC: *"Thank you Ms. Andrus. Comments, Mr. Foster?"*

Lee Foster: *"Thank you Liz for letting me participate. . . The public must remain calm and we have to remember there is no direct evidence the information from these documents is not the work of madmen with access to death records and other data. I can safely say that in my entire career I have not heard of such an organization let alone approved or advised funding it."*

Hostess MC: *"Clearly! You are not mentioned in these documents."*

Lee Foster: *"Ms. Andrus, my position has allowed me to gain full access to most of the projects you've so conveniently titled Black Ops and I can assure you, none were even remotely connected. The accusations rising from these documents are severe and must be taken very seriously, however, at the same time, this all seems to be too disorganized, and excuse my saying so, but all of it seems too far out there for it to be considered valid. The FBI is still trying to track down whoever spread these rumors as he or she not only spread malicious software nationally but has caused catastrophic damages on a national security scale. . . I would also like to add that I was a close friend of Senator Mitchell. It is very important to know that many of the people involved are under a lot of pressure. Some know they are going to be ridiculed and haunted by the media, some are under stress because of the investigations. It is not indicative of proof the documents revealed a month ago are valid. Senator Mitchell was a very self-confident and reserved man. I can only blame the stress and false accusations brought by the media for causing him to take his own life."*

Hostess MC: *"Thank you, Mr. Foster and Ms Andrus, for joining us. After the break, Perry Cooper will be joining us to discuss the latest events affecting our economy. Stay tuned for the KPW's weather forecasts at eight-thirty. . ."*

Part Two

BETRAYAL

CHAPTER 39

Gustave looked in the car's mirror. It was still hard for him to look at himself without being a little spooked by the transformation visible in his reflection. His jaw was wider, his nose was much flatter and his cheekbones were a little more prominent. During Nell's visit, he learned a lot about how to control and reprogram his armor's nanonites, especially when working with his new identity.

He approached the army complex. The gated entry to the base was heavily guarded by an electrified fence, topped by razor wire. The other side of the gate was secured by two armored vehicles and about a dozen armed guards.

Gustave slowed the car as he approached the gates. In his mind he rehearsed the details of his new identity. A uniformed soldier approached the driver's window and saluted him smartly. "Mr. Monde, you are expected; please leave your car here and an authorized vehicle will take you into the base."

"Certainly, but what about my gear?" Gustave hesitated.

"Everything will be taken to your new quarters and arranged for you. Please, sir, step out of the car."

There was no room for argument. Gustave, turned off the engine, grabbed his bag which contained his laptop, and stepped outside his vehicle, but not before he made sure he had his cigarettes and lighter.

The soldier gestured for him to stand still, then he removed a small metal detector from one of his pockets. The nanonites! Gustave was alarmed. He wondered if they would register on the detector.

The soldier held the detector very close to Gustave's body and moved it from his head down, until it started beeping. Gustave was trying to think of a good explanation why his body was filled with metallic objects. The beeping intensified until the soldier retrieved the device and said, "Please remove your belt."

But of course, the belt! He had been certain it was the nanonites which had triggered the device.

He tried to remain calm. He remembered times during his childhood entering army bases and many of them involved security checkups upon entry, so he was familiar with the routine.

He stretched out his arms while holding his belt in his right hand. The soldier gave another quick scan across his body and cleared Gustave for entrance.

In the distance, a glistening reflection of light from a flat windshield of an approaching armored vehicle caught Gustave's attention. It was most likely his ride to the base.

The vehicle stopped. The door opened and from inside a slender man dressed in a lab coat climbed out, and obviously was not used to getting in and out of tall vehicles.

"Mr. Monde! Pleasure to meet you. . .I'm Dr. Jeffery Finch." The man extended his hand in greeting , and was out of breath, as if the physical activity of getting out of the car was too much for him. He wore thick glasses and had dark hair with traces of silver and his smile was stiff and forced.

"Pleasure to meet you , too, Mr. Finch. . . Please call me Steve."

"Very well! Steve, welcome to Base Seven-Nine!"

"Thank you sir. It's an honor to be here, although, I'm not sure why I am . . ." . It was very important for Gustave to play his part perfectly

Jeffery smiled. "Come, let me show you around. . ."

Gustave got into the car. The base was very similar to the many he had seen in his childhood. The starkly simple buildings were for the most part comprised of offices, with carefully maintained lawns. Large hangars filled the landscape not too far away. Gustave memorized the peripheral and panoramic glimpses of his surroundings in order to study his environment. Of course, in his briefing, he was provided with most of the imagery and very detailed layouts of the base but it was much more vivid seeing it with his own eyes instead of through the artificial memory that came from his armor which only gave him the comfort of virtually remembering the base as if he had been working there for many years. More specifically, he paid close attention to the surroundings and readout of the road to try and locate the secret underground complex which was kept at the base, unbeknownst to the humans.

"Here we are!" Jeffery said. The vehicle stopped in front of an entrance to a hangar which seemed to have been converted into an office building some years earlier. The external layout suggested it could have housed several large planes at one time or another.

"Please follow me Mr. Monde. . ." Jeffery mumbled, "Steven". Certainly not a man with well-developed people skills, but he obviously tried.

They entered the building and walked down the hall toward a small room guarded by two security guards. Gustave noticed the ranks and name tags of the guards and realized the level of security to which this division of the base was assigned. At some levels, even guards were handpicked to serve for several months as security officers in very high profile, highly secured areas. At some places the security clearance of standard soldiers would not be sufficient for delicate secret operations. The two guards here were highly ranked Special Ops members. Judging by the behavior of Dr. Finch, they were treated with the highest respect, and not to be reckoned with.

"Dr. Finch. . ." one of the men nodded his head in greeting. Just like his counterpart, he was wearing a black protective bullet proof vest, carrying what may have been a heavily retrofitted P-90.

Dr. Finch approached the glass door and swiped his security card through the mechanism. The other guard didn't speak much. He didn't seem the type for much conversation. He just looked at Gustave, studying every movement he made. Gustave, noticing that, tried keeping a stooped-over stance as if he was a hard-working scientist, a man that preferred sitting in front of ten computer screens rather than any other type of physical activity. There was no doubt he could drop these two sentries if he wished, but then again, that would lead him nowhere. . .

The door opened into a comfortably large hall from which many corridors and stairs led throughout the structure. Dr. Finch led the way down one of the corridors. He was a little short of breath but managed to speak. "There is a certain smell in the building, which you'll get used to soon."

"Yes, I can smell it. . . what is it?" Gustave hated certain lab smells, and the thought that his lungs were inhaling fumes and particles used for chemical processing didn't make him very comfortable.

Dr. Finch decided to avoid answering, and instead he started asking Gustave several questions to save time rather than waiting until they reached the lab.

"Mr. Monde, I mean, Steven, I've had a chance to read a paper of yours published in one of my favorite journals. You published a paper called "Novel Applications of Quantum Mechanical Theory – Van Der Waals Forces in

Density Functional Theory. When did you come up with the idea?"

Gustave wasn't prepared for that question. However there were other ways to respond. "Some time ago, well before that paper, only it wasn't until we involved Iridium in the study that this really took off from a passing thought to the research and the paper."

"I see," Dr. Finch said, followed by a mumble. "Yes it is most certainly a key element, isn't it? I'm intrigued, how did you arrive at putting it together? I would have probably tried Osmium first, although I can't say I would have thought about it myself, now that I'm thinking about it."

Gustave quickly assessed the question. He retrieved the information from his interface and compared other dense metals to Iridium. "It's funny you mention it, Dr. Finch. To start with, we needed a stronger compound, something dense but not to the point we wouldn't be able to use. I also noticed for quite some time our feedback sensors were affected by corrosion very easily and very frequently. We needed to replace them quite often to receive clean results. My lab partner who always kept a fountain pen on her gave me the idea for using Osmium as their tips usually utilize the element. But I made an assumption that it might be a better to try Iridium first as it might solve two problems at once, I just didn't know how well it would perform. Osmium ended up being too dense, so there was a soft spot which the Iridium tests were able to demonstrate were superior and when combined in a proper manner, more effective than stronger elements."

"It's the simple things," Dr. Finch laughed.

Gustave agreed. "Yes, it is, Doctor."

Finally making it to their destination Dr. Finch opened the door into what seemed to have been a brainstorming room which was the equivalent of a boardroom, only with a flair of scientific touches to accommodate the spontaneous creativity of methodical brains. There were several men in lab coats and an army official waiting for their arrival.

"Mr. Monde, I would like to introduce you to the team."

All eyes were focused on Gustave. The group remained silent except of a few who nodded their heads and muttered a friendly greeting. Gustave, who usually enjoyed commanding attention, felt uneasy, considering he was there under false pretenses assuming someone else's identity, not to mention a 'Dr. Monde' didn't actually exist. It was also required of him to keep a low profile until he secured some level of confidence among the others on the base.

"It's great being here among such talent. Thank you for inviting me," Gustave said quietly.

The commanding officer, a woman with a striking voluptuous figure stood up. "Please sit down," she said, pointing to a vacant chair. She had twinkling brown eyes and long, straight glossy black hair that framed her heart-shaped face very attractively.

Gustave eased his way onto the chair while keeping a shy smile on his lips and eye contact with the woman.

"Dr. Monde, we think we can use you here, not only for this project but also to serve as part of the team. I'm aware you were called to come in with only a few of your personal belongings however, if you agree, you will be required to be here permanently."

Her attitude already wasn't very friendly by Gustave's standards. However, he was here to complete a mission, and whatever it took he would do what he could to fulfill her request. Yet, of course, he could not make it seem as if he was too agreeable as that could be regarded as suspicious.

"Thank you for the offer, Commander…" He had made a mistake, and he let her know he understood army rank protocol. However, since they were all very familiar with army hierarchy they made nothing of it.

"Angela Antoinette. . ." she said, filling in the blank, letting him know her name.

"Ma'am, if you don't mind my asking, what are you doing here? What will be my duty if I sign on?"

Commander Antoinette nodded at one of the team members and sat down.

A man wearing a white lab coat cleaned his throat and stood up. "We are in the business of shielding Dr. Monde. We develop and design lighter and stronger armors for vehicles and impact- resistant vests for soldiers."

Gustave already knew that. If they had known he was wearing a piece of technology under his skin they would most likely not be able to get their hands on for at least a millennium, they would have probably tried to cut him open. "Then my experiments would have been pretty useful for you I imagine; you are probably wondering if I have the methodology to implement my ideas?"

"As a matter of fact, we were."

Gustave leaned forward and smiled. "You do realize how expensive implementing this on a large scale would be, let alone bringing this technology to mass production?"

"Dr. Monde, have you heard of DARPA?" the man said.

"But of course" Gustave replied, leaning back in his seat.

The man paused for a moment and continued. "DARPA has budgets, we don't. We simply work."

Gustave laughed nervously. It amused him to realize that for most of his life he had had no funding, and no access to funding no matter what project he had in mind, yet there he was, living two separate lives, both equally different from the one he had lived through the past thirty odd years, each with unlimited financial backing. Of course, the team didn't share his enthusiasm, whether they were serious or not, or perhaps it was that they had heard a similar joke too many times. Gustave swallowed and said, "Understood. . . when can we start?" looking directly at the man then shifting his glance toward Commander

Antoinette he smiled with satisfaction to show he was ready to begin work.

The commander rose from her chair. The rest of the team stood as well.

"Right away Dr. Monde", she said, extending her hand.

"Dr. Cassidy, Dr. O'Donovan, show him to the labs."

"Yes Ma'am!" the two men said.

CHAPTER 40

After walking through several sections of the building, the team reached the HR office. They explained to Gustave he would need a special access card that would allow him to move freely through the different labs on the base. Dr. Cassidy explained most employees had to work hard for several years to be eligible for the privileged clearance authorization such as Dr. Monde was to receive and immediately, Gustave knew he had inadvertently evoked animosity in his first job. There must be some way he could rectify this, but he was not very accustomed to inter-office quarrels. Instead he assured Dr. Cassidy he understood he was fortunate and that he was more than willing to respect the people who had worked hard and were more deserving of the privilege. At the same time he also assured him that he was looking forward to working with him and hoped that he would be able to show he was worthy of working alongside him.

Although Gustave was quite satisfied with the way he treated the situation, it seemed hollow, like a fake response of acceptance. Dr. Cassidy was still quite contemptible toward him. Gustave knew he would have to keep an eye on him and do whatever was necessary to complete this mission.

The administrative office resembled a standard army office just as he remembered from his childhood. There was a large wooden desk where a receptionist was seated, and the rest of the room displayed countless cabinets against every wall with the exception of a door leading to another office, off to the left. The receptionist was concentrating on her computer monitor but finally glanced toward the men. She was blond and tall and wore dark blue glasses that served only to emphasize the emptiness of her stare.

"Hello, Patricia," Dr. O'Donovan said in a cheerful tone. From the very little time they had been together, it was quite clear to Gustave that he was friendlier than his partner. His body language indicated he was undoubtedly a man of integrity and charisma, yet still capable of seeing the good side of life.

"Hello, Dr. O'Donovan. . . Do you have a meeting?" Patricia was noncommittal, but efficient.

"We're here to set up our new friend, Dr. Monde, with his ID; is she in?"

"Yes, the sergeant is in, Doctor, let me check with her, one moment please. . ."

Gustave realized something rather odd. He remembered that when he had visited with his father, the scientists who were all high- ranking officers, were treated with great respect, unlike the way they seem to be addressed here. He remembered going to several offices here and there and being treated the same way by assistants to directors and executives, who considered themselves higher in the food chain than they actually were. He was still learning the ropes of proper procedures in this place.

"Patricia Dorogoi. . . That's a Russian surname, isn't it?" Gustave said, trying to please her. He specifically spoke with Russian inflections.

Patricia smiled. Both the men were a little surprised as neither one had ever been able to receive even the slightest acknowledgment from the female automaton throughout their entire career at the base.

"Yes. . ." She nodded her head in affirmation.

Gustave instantly accessed a translation from English to Russian from his armor's language database. "Zdravstvujte?" He asked, trying to effect a proper Russian pronunciation.

"Ahh," she giggled, "neplokho!" She answered, "Dabro pozhalovat, Dr. . . ?"

"Monde, Steven Monde," he said. "I'm sorry my

Russian is very amateur; I tried to learn it for several years. What a great language!"

"That's very sweet of you to say that, Dr. Monde," She smiled. For some reason, despite her smile, he still couldn't detect the faintest sign of animation in her facial expression. But it was clear she was pleased with the small cheerful break in routine.

"Yes?" A voice came from a speaker phone.

"Dr. Monde, Dr. O'Donovan, and Dr. Cassidy are here to see you, ma'am. . ."

"Let them in, Patricia, and thank you."

Patricia struck a few keys on the keyboard then looked at Gustave. "You can go in now." After a brief smile she resumed concentrating on the computer screen. The door made a clicking sound.

"Thank you," Gustave said. He looked at the men and nodded, saying "After you, please" to show he was courteous and letting them lead the way.

The room they entered was much larger than Gustave had expected. There was a large machine that resembled an MRI scanner. Next to it stood several other smaller machines which were all connected to a set of computers. The room also had a desk where a pleasant-looking woman dressed in civilian clothes was seated.

"Ah, Dr. Monde, welcome to the team! I'm happy you accepted the invitation!"

"It's my pleasure, I'm very excited to be working here, ma'am," Gustave replied.

"Gosh, where are my manners. . . I'm Kayla Bernard."

The woman had a striking figure. Her dark brown eyes radiated a calm and assuring persona. She appeared to be in her late forties and was beautifully groomed. She extended her hand revealing a handsome, diamond-encrusted watch. From her outfit it, was evident that she was being paid generously.

"It is a pleasure to make your acquaintance, Kayla," Gustave said. He shook her hand and hated releasing her fingers from his. Her soft touch fulfilled his anticipated texture of her skin.

"Okay, let's get to work shall we?" Kayla leaned back in her swivel chair, twisted to the side and gazed at a document propped next to the computer monitor. Graceful as she was, she was not a fast typist, stroking one key at a time painfully slow. "All right, I'll just get these printed." Clicking on the mouse while squinting at the monitor she then stood up and made her way to the printer, which began printing as soon as she started walking toward it.

Gustave noticed the paper had an odd texture to it, almost like that of a certificate or foolscap parchment but more elaborate, with some specialized water marking for extra protection.

"These are consent forms, Dr. Monde, nothing out of the ordinary, just several liability clauses, compensation agreement as well as non-disclosure agreement. Please read them carefully before you sign. Gentleman, I can take it from here, why don't you leave me here with Dr. Monde while we complete the paperwork and codes."

The two men nodded. Dr. Cassidy smiled and said, "We'll wait for you outside, Steven."

"Steven, may I call you 'Steven'?" Kayla asked as she handed him the paperwork.

"But of course, ma'am!"

"Please have a seat, and call me Kayla. . ."

Gustave smiled and sat down in the chair that stood in front of her desk.

He had no intention of reading the forms, since none of them applied to the plans he planned to put into effect. However, not reading them might indicate carelessness, which was not something a person likes to do when he needs to evoke trust from others, and not look like an idiot. The ever-so-carefully worded forms were standard as she had said and Gustave muttered to himself to make it look like he was reading them carefully nonetheless.

"May I please have a pen, Kayla?" Gustave asked, holding the last page of the forms.

"Of course. . .Please grab one," Kayla replied, pointing to the end of the desk where a desktop organizer held a dozen or more colorful pens.

Signing the forms he handed them back to her. "All done!"

Kayla took the forms from his hand and skimmed through his signatures.

"Very good! Now, I'm going to need your

impressions, finger prints, corona and palm veins."

Gustave was quite surprised. He had heard about the use of veins for authentication but he had yet to see it in action. Instead of gazing absentmindedly, he decided it was probably expected of him to ask as if he didn't know, "Palm veins?"

"Ah, of course, I thought it might make you curious. We have included this new thing. It is much faster at reading and is more accurate, I am told." She took out a small device from one of the drawers. It was a semi-spherical device that connected to the computer. "Now, place your hand here. . ."

Gustave noticed the spherical part of the device had comfortable grooves indicating where to place his hand and in what specific position. While placing his hand he noticed Kayla taking the forms and inserting them into what seem to have been a paper shredder which seemed quite odd. Inserting the first paper from the top of the machine it began feeding the paper downward while emitting bright light. The paper came down, completely empty, as if nothing was written on it.

Gustave's puzzled look was quickly replaced by that of an intrigued person, "Is that a scanner and eraser of inked paper?"

"Yes, we don't use regular paper anymore. It scans the paper, using some special print that is easily traced into the system then the UV light cleans it. I'm not sure exactly how it works, but it does. You can probably figure it out yourself more than I can. . ." She laughed.

"I wish I could! I would probably have made millions from it," Gustave laughed with her, enjoying sharing a moment of amusement.

He could not help but think to himself he just recently come from an alien space ship, and inside his body there was technology that was centuries away from human discovery and here he was genuinely fascinated by something as mundane as paper. He wondered if Nell was right that day on the space ship, maybe humans can be compared to cavemen, in comparison to their differences in technology, considering a cave man would have probably found a bow and arrow to be quite more intriguing than, say, a computer, as he really would have not known what to do with the latter, or have the social-collective capacity to grasp its potential. The thought quickly subsided, since he was certain he knew very well the potential of the technology he was equipped with. Especially now, after the several unforgettable nights he had spent with Nell, stealing technology from her even though she had lain in bed naked, curled in the warmth of his arms.

"All set Steven. You are now ready to move around in the base labs."

CHAPTER 41

Gustave was lying on the bed in his room. The day was over and after several hours of familiarizing himself with the rest of the staff, as well as visiting several labs and seeing his own work space, he was quite tired. He felt as if he had been robbed of his freedom. Regardless of how temporary his new accommodations might be, he had no idea when exactly he would get to walk out of the place and begin his real adventure. He was more determined than ever to find the secret facility somewhere underneath the earth on this property.

His quarters were quite small, smaller than his house. There was a bedroom which featured an interior design comparable to a three-star hotel at best. The bed was of medium size, a night stand to its left on which a lamp stood and a large wardrobe that was suitable only for storing bed sheets and minimum articles of clothing. The bedroom was connected to the living room through a small corridor from which there was a doorway leading into a fairly small shower area.

It wasn't that he was unhappy with his

accommodation but he was full of anxiety for the next day when he was to begin his work on an unimportant project, for unimportant people whose vision was rather lacking, especially the stilted old Cassidy with his constant referrals to out-of-date adages. He was certainly unprepared to be working with that man as this would be a constant challenge to his patience and offend his sense of dignity.

He must stand up to the challenge. Of that he was sure, although the thought of guns blazing throughout the base did cross his mind. He was given a new laptop for personal use. The meaning of personal use was quite different than what one might consider as personal. While some would consider this could mean personal emails and browsing the web for the occasional alcohol-driven pornographic website stroll, the army reasoned everything must be restricted, or at least monitored. The computer was crawling with spyware restricting movement or reporting to an IT support division which Gustave, after several minutes, found its exact secret location. Oddly enough, it was not in the database provided by the Angelonians.

Using the laptop, he browsed through the web, gazing through several peer-reviewed scientific publications. He needed to leave some sort of trace behind him, because undoubtedly as a new employee they would check every move he made.

Following a quick shower and a change of clothes he made his way to the mess hall. The living accommodations at the base were very similar to the ones he remembered from his childhood. Located at a reasonable distance from the hangars and offices there were larger complexes where families of army personnel lived, and other complexes where single personnel, such as himself, called home. They were all concrete structures that looked as if they were designed in the architectural concrete rush age. Clean, triangular lines, exposed grey structures that had an almost strikingly modern look, even though they were indeed designed back in the seventies. While family houses had their own kitchens, there was a larger community-like cafeteria here available all day and night throughout the week where people found the opportunity to mingle a little. He couldn't explain much how he felt about all of it, there it was, like an arm built to protect its capitalistic body. At its core, the arm was structured very much like a communist colony, then again, there was a lot more structure needed in the hierarchal nature of an army but with communal bonding attributes.

Gustave knew his way to the mess hall quite well. The architecture of the base was embedded in his memory, well before he put a foot into the place. However, he could not help but think he must make it seem as if he didn't know his way around. In turn, he made his way to a map which was located in a nearby juncture outside his complex. He briefly studied the map, which was embossed on a bronze panel lit by a flickering yellow street light above it.

The way there was very pleasant. The walkway was quiet and filled with neatly organized and well-cared for gardens. In the distance the paved walkway led to a well-lit building which housed the mess hall and recreational facilities including a large swimming pool, sports courts of all kinds, and several other amenities. The building was enormous and just like the living quarters, it was built using large exposed concrete blocks and brightly lit large glass windows throughout.

The closer he got, the more he noticed people walking in and out of the building. There was a large paved area where several groups gathered to play games, exchange stories, and generally enjoy the cool evening summer breeze. This brought him a few happy childhood memories, playing with other kids who had also grown up in an army base environment.

"Dr. Monde!" Gustave looked to his right where the call seemed to have originated.

"Dr. Monde, right here!" A hand beckoned from a shadowy patch near the concrete beach. It was Dr. O'Donovan.

"Dr. O'Donovan! How are you?" Gustave replied and began walking towards him.

"I'm great!" Dr. O'Donovan began clumsily striding toward Gustave. The two shook hands. "I was just about to get something to eat. I'm glad to see you made it! Would you care to join me?"

It seemed a little strange that such a friendly man was about to go eat alone— strange enough to raise Gustave's curiosity which automatically brought Dr.

O'Donovan's background to his memory; he was single, and in comparison to his other colleagues the majority of whom were married, he was quite shy, regardless of how good he was with people he found to his liking. At least so his psychological assessment suggested.

"You know, I started working at the base not too long ago myself, Dr. Monde. It certainly is nice to have people showing you around and keeping you company."

"I certainly agree," Gustave said looking at him with amusement.

"The food is actually not bad, once you get over the strange motion sickness that comes with it. . ."

Gustave was startled and suddenly on guard. His facial expression revealed his reaction.

Dr. O'Donovan flicked his hand in a friendly manner on Gustave's shoulder. The armor, of course did not like the physical encounter, and accommodated itself for soft impact response.

"Gotchya!" O'Donovan said as his hand hit Gustave's shoulder only to be greeted with a hard and rather painful equal force.

"Wow, awu! I was just kidding about the motion sickness. ." He shook his hand trying to relieve the pain then held it with his other hand. "You work out don't you?"

Gustave was quite embarrassed. The armor was not accustomed to all everyday scenarios and considered all objects moving toward it as violence intentioned, especially from the hand of another.

"Strong bones; you hit one of them," Gustave said, trying to recover. He began rubbing his shoulder as if to show it did in fact also absorb some of the pain. His explanation might have seemed a little odd but it worked.

"Sorry, Dr. Monde! All right, let's go get some food!"

* * *

The mess hall was quite large. Gustave estimated several hundred people could easily fit inside. The eating area, which took up most of the room, was furnished with elongated tables surrounded by metal folding chairs. Although the room was big enough to host many of the base's residents, there weren't many people eating when they arrived.

The food service area was set up like a buffet with several long tables on which platters and bowls of different kinds of foods awaited diners.

Dr. O'Donovan pointed at the plates. "You see, Dr. Monde, there is a wide selection of breakfast, lunch, and dinner plates in many variations. Some units work night shifts and only wake up now to eat their breakfast; others are just going to lunch, and others like us will eat dinner. I think it's the best thing I've found since I came here! I get to eat breakfast whenever I feel like it, or dinner whenever my stomach desires."

There was no doubt the many varied selections of the buffet were certainly more substantial than what Gustave could remember as a child, but the avaricious look of satisfaction on Dr. O'Donovan's face struck Gustave as strange. Surely he wasn't from around here locally, or perhaps he came from a less fortunate family, Gustave wasn't sure.

Picking up a clean plate still warm from the hot steam of the dishwasher, he approached several inviting selections and chose several appetizers. O'Donovan, on the other hand, headed straight for the main courses and piled up as much as he could on one plate. First roast chicken, then barbecued pork ribs, then filet mignon, then lamb shish kabob and each time, he gazed at Gustave, smiled and signaled what he had just chosen was a delightful culinary experience he must try.

These scientists are goofy, Gustave thought to himself. But they did have the charm of innocence. Gustave admitted he did spoil himself with five star restaurants, often criticizing them as he compared one to the other.

"Find us a seat; I'll be right with you. . ." Dr. O'Donovan said, trying to balance just a little more on his plate.

Gustave began gravitating towards a secluded area, then out of courtesy to O'Donovan, he ended up choosing a table with less distance to travel, balancing a very large plate brimful with hot food.

Dinner was satisfying. After the meal and a pleasant conversation with Dr. O'Donovan, who proved to be a lot more knowledgeable then Gustave had anticipated him to be, they left the dining room. Dr. O'Donovan had shared his experience of arriving at the base not too long ago and gave Gustave pointers about how to get along with the staff and around the base, information which he would have not gotten through usual channels nor would have been able to learn before arriving.

Gustave, curious about his new surroundings decided it was too early to retire and instead of heading back to his room, went on a stroll around the building, but not before he had a cigarette to help digest the food and ease the constant nervousness from being around a friendly person who was inclined to ask many questions.

There was a large gym, several lecture areas, one of which was showing a movie. The smell of the pool intrigued Gustave. He saw it from the outside, but the smell of the chlorine enticed him to pay a visit from the inside. He knew he was close as the scent got very intense, but also knew the schematics of the area quite well once he retrieved them from his simulated long term memory.

Something felt strange. And odd alarm went off as if it was inside his brain. It was then he discovered the underground secret Union base was hidden underneath the large swimming pool.

The Rod was signaling his armor. Of that he was certain. It acted as if he had some sort of mythical six sense, but Gustave knew quite well it was picking up on the special radiation. Just like K'ta and Nell told him it would.

"How on earth am I going to find my way underneath this?" Gustave muffled his inner voice.

He had expected the underground installation to be somewhere on the outskirts of the base, where he would have probably been required to dig some sand at night, but this? There must be something underneath this pool, some support system that would give him a clue.

He mentally called for the digital blueprints of the area, focusing on the pool support system. It yielded nothing. It was utterly useless for him at this moment.

He gazed at the swimming pool. It was massively built and by Olympic standards. It wasn't the size he was worried about but the water. Digging underneath it would require too much effort, not to mention time and much risk as someone would be certain to notice tunnel work. No, instead, he must penetrate through the pool. For that, Gustave reasoned he needed to get the water out. Surely penetrating through the floor of the pool with water can cause some unexpected issues, among them, being noticed by anyone who happened to be below in the facility, or damaging sensitive equipment such as whatever it was the alien lab used as equipment.

A diversion; Gustave somehow needed to cause the pool to be closed, emptied out and deemed unsafe for several days. The answer was fairly simple although Gustave was quite amused with his solution. E. Coli bacteria would be sure to be noticed by the facility caretakers. A flock of people suffering from diarrhea would trigger a search for the source of the bacteria, and once they all reported swimming in the pool they would be sure to close it for several days, drain it, and wait for a special team to sterilize the pool.

The question as to where he would get the bacteria was still unanswered. The last time he took part in any biological research was farther back than he cared to remember. Perhaps it was the right time to have a little chat with Nell, but he wouldn't be able to get any sort of communication while still at the base. This enigma would take a great deal more deep and careful contemplation.

CHAPTER 42

The factory looked almost complete. It was a massive structure retrofitted with giant pipes, conveyer belts, automated machines, and every possible scientific innovation Harry could have ever imagined. Every day more and more teams were going in and out of the compound, each being scanned thoroughly for camera equipment, recording mediums, and other materials which were not on the permitted-items list. There were time restrictions and a battery of security personnel which governed the operation. However, Harry demanded each and every worker be examined personally by himself. Each day, he coordinated the work to be achieved with Chris, and at the end of the day they met again to summarize and prepare for the next day's schedule.

Despite their differences they became more fond of each other and it became apparent Gustave had made the right choice to have them work beside each other. Since the new security measurements were installed, they felt more comfortable taking an evening off, and hanging out at a pub. Of course, considering the remote location of the compound, they had to take the helicopter which Chris was quite adamant about buying after learning Harry knew how to fly one.

"Yesterday was the last of them, right?" Chris asked.

Harry, drinking a cold dark beer sipped slowly before answering. "I believe it was."

"Did Gustave mention what we are to do next?" Harry placed the pint on the table.

"To wait for his return I presume. It really did strike me as odd he came up with this magnificent technology and has extremely rich investors, then he goes away. That's unlike him. He is usually fully involved in what he does."

During their time together, Chris had shared many stories about Gustave with Harry. Harry's first impression of Gustave was that he was an alien, after that, that he was an extremely lucky man. But after hearing about his history, he wasn't sure if he was just lucky, or human, or both. However, he instantly recognized Gustave had kept some information from Chris. Was Gustave the inventor or was he a Prometheus-like alien-man delegator. There was no point in digging deeper just yet, or even mentioning anything to Chris. Harry was certain considering his past and the several encounters with Gustave's abilities, it is best he chose not to disclose some information which Chris would have otherwise thought he was a mad man.

There was a moment of silence. Both men sipped their drinks quietly.

Chris finished his Scotch and went to the bar to

fill his glass with another round. Coming back to the sitting area, he made himself comfortable and asked, "Harry, Gustave told me you were in the army for many years, and that you were at a very high level of security facility. What did you do?"

Harry lowered his drink while keeping it close to his mouth, smiled at Chris and began shaking his head.

"You can't tell me, can you? Yeah, you can't tell me."

"Correct, Chris," Harry said.

Chris wasn't about ready to give up. "Well, you can simply nod your head like you just did, only tell me if I'm right or wrong"

Harry broke into heavy laughter. "Oh, I haven't heard that one since I was a kid!" He wiped the tears off his eyes with his fingers.

"Oh come on!" Chris laughed. "All this news lately, some heavy stuff about secret government agency, aliens, and what not. Is this all an elaborate hoax like everyone says it is or is it not?"

Harry did not find his questions amusing anymore. This was a personal matter which he had hoped would not come up. He remained silent.

"You were high up there, you must have seen or heard about some stuff, right ?"

Harry didn't want to reply. However, he thought, considering Gustave did intend for a disclosure to occur sooner or later, he would probably not mind if some information got out.

On top of that, Harry had a good hunch that Gustave will hear this at one point or another so it would probably be for the best not to be fully guarded.

"I have heard and seen some really bizarre things, Chris, and I'd rather not say any more."

Chris's had a long face. He did not expect such an answer, let alone any answer at all. But this was a confirmation there was a lot more going on than he could have possibly imagined, and although he could not put his finger on it, it certainly smelled like he was taking part in something big. He knew that if that were the case, Gustave would have done so for a good reason.

CHAPTER 43

Several weeks had gone by since Gustave had become a part of the group on the base. Each day brought with it new set of frustrations. It wasn't that he found his tasks difficult, it was simply that he found them to be a waste of his time. There were protocols on top of other protocols which were governed by yet another set of protocols. He was only allowed three breaks each day, including smoke breaks which he found to be an absurdity. After years of working very efficiently from one project to another he was suddenly dealing with procedures that were contrary to his work methods. Everything he did had to be reported and summarized in plain, watered down descriptions so his superiors would understand. Some of them were highly decorated army personnel, yet none had any scientific background. He cared very little about the three breaks they did allow him, designating them mainly for time to eat and smoke. Another frustration resulted from the use of specific formats of language which particularly angered Gustave: ALL CAPS emails, as well as the excessive use of A.S.A.P, which usually meant As Soon As

I Want It regardless of the task, which did nothing other than constantly raise Gustave's blood pressure to the point the armor began regulating it. All he wanted was to talk back to these delinquent idiots, but the most expedient way to his goal was by remaining calm.

Morning requirements were a whole other story. Gustave, who was used to staying up and working until very late, was never much of an early riser. The workplace on the other hand, had restricted times when he was allowed to go in and out of the labs only by special permission.

It seemed as if no one had any objection to starting their day early, on the contrary, they were very much morning people and were smugly vain about their ability to fall asleep early and wake up with the sunrise. Gustave on the other hand was realistic about the need for structured hours of work, but he was not prepared to take part in following the others' pattern.

In the first week or so he managed to wake up early by force of will. Later on he would not go to sleep just so he'd be on time in his lab, but that proved to be a hindrance to his psyche. The thought of programming his armor for sleepwalking, or bathing, or dressing and other morning rituals did cross his mind but he knew he was being constantly watched and that would be a tough trick to explain. He did befriend Dr. O'Donovan. They regularly exchanged words during work, and walked together to the mess hall where they enjoyed engaging conversations.

Dr. O'Donovan was an anomaly to Gustave.

He was very quiet, soft spoken with a great amount of knowledge, but he was tremendously naive, a virtue to which Gustave was never able to relate. Every time they met was yet another opportunity to understand the doctor yet Gustave was always left with the strange feeling that he had gained no further knowledge of the man's persona or his background. His true self remained a mystery.

From time to time, Gustave made trips to the swimming pool to try and spot the exact location of the entrance to the underground structure, but to no avail. It would have to be with force at the right moment as there was no other way he could see. Being a public place, it was difficult for him to bring any equipment to assess the structure using any standard means. It didn't matter much, because he was about to finish his project for these idiots and was hoping to request a few days off from the base for visiting his parents and he was counting on the fact they would have to grant him such a bonus, considering they had been working on this technology for years and he was about to single-handedly crack it down in matter of several weeks. They would have to start taking him very seriously after he achieved that kind of result.

Gustave woke up in the middle of the night. Something had startled him awake. It felt like a sharp pain crawling through every fibre of his body. His armor triggered an immediate wakeup command. In less than a second, Gustave was alert for an attack.

There was no one in the room other than himself

and his computer which had been on since the night before. Gustave, wondering if this was a malfunctioning in his armor, began running diagnostics but he received no pertinent information. Everything seemed to have been working properly. And he was quite certain there was no one in the room, especially considering he could detect hidden entities as their electronics gave off distinctive traces. What if they had a more sophisticated technology that could counteract his armor's abilities?

There was no straight answer to that. One thing he learned from Nell about the Union was that everyone had stopped inventing, in its purest form, new technologies. They had reached a point where everything of value was very close to having been invented, so it was really a matter of sending the right instructions for fabrication via molecular communications of the nanonites. This was one of the things that made the device they were after incredibly valuable. They believed they had been completely successful in conquering most technology but had yet to have a controlling grasp of nature, without which nothing could be. Scholars spent most of their time training tiny robots while they maximized how they are arranged and communicated to others via standard Union link protocols.

His armor's concept did come from an older age, however Nell had informed him there was nothing old about his defense as it utilized the combat and defense tactics from their barbaric days which were in turn combined with the elegance and efficiency of the new generation of micro self-fabrication.

Rising from the bed, he made his way toward the washroom to splash his face with cool water. There was no point going back to sleep, not while he was wide awake and his mind seethed with theories.

After several minutes spent gazing in the mirror, he went back to his bedroom, put on a raincoat and went outside for a smoke. The damp cold atmosphere of the desert night made him more relaxed. He remembered when he was young, he always feared being outside alone in the wee hours of the morning. The sounds of night insects and other animals made him extremely uncomfortable. Plus, the combination of watching too many horror movies and being a child with a large imagination never helped. It was different now. He had seen aliens, real ones, and there was no more room for a fear of being abducted at night, as that had already happened to him and turned out quite well. He felt very strong, as if he could beat anything that came to his direction but his mind was never completely at ease with the thoughts of what lay ahead.

It was to be an important day today. He was to demonstrate the new material for the group. Not only that, he had designed a prototype armor for them, complete with an entire analysis of fabrication and manufacturing instructions. As far as they were concerned, he not only fulfilled what it was they set out to do and failed in the first place, but also he provided them with a turnkey solution to manufacture the product which was nothing less than a full army personnel suite capable of withstanding direct ballistic hits by bullets yet was completely flexible. An entire army equipped with that suit was sure to become a defining force. Of course, there were specifically designed backdoor errors in the fabric, yet not ones they were able to discover. There was no point making things hard until the time was right. All he cared about was if they were pleased with his work, they would allow him some well-needed time off the base which was inextricably linked to his mission.

The sun rose, and with it the fleet of army personnel, workers, and their families swarmed toward their daily activities. There were many in-base transportation vehicles taking people to and from one place to the other. The base, as usual, was quite lively during the mornings. Gustave, who was awake during the better part of the night and early morning now began feeling tired and was ready to drag himself back to bed. The upcoming presentation however kept him struggling to stay alert. He showered and dressed to leave for the mess hall where he was to meet with Dr. O'Donovan for their morning catch up. It wasn't that Gustave was much of a breakfast eater, but he enjoyed the company of Dr. O'Donovan who was undoubtedly a morning person.

Waking up early gave him the chance to ride the bus to the mess hall which he had missed every previous morning. There were several intriguing young women on the bus that caught his eye, some were office workers, some worked in other positions on the base. He somehow managed to offend a particularly attractive blond by winking at her playfully. After she reciprocated with a disapproving sneer, Gustave flushed and quickly looked at the floor of the bus. He never understood why most women rejected his presence, except when they required help, but then again, he was quite lucky attracting an alien woman who had more substance, intelligence, and beauty put together than most of the humans he knew. Or was it that she was simply attracted to the idea of some fantasy, or the equivalent of playing with an animal at a petting zoo? He didn't care, he missed her touch, he missed her soft skin and he missed the adrenaline surge he had when they kissed.

The bus stopped conveniently next to the mess hall. Entering the compound, Gustave knew where to find Dr. O'Donovan as they had their usual spot where they could have a conversation without any need to raise their voices yet were also able to people watch, something they both found to be a pleasurable pastime. Dr. O'Donovan's tray was, as usual overflowing with everything the morning table had to offer. He seemed to have been enjoying a round cup of rice pudding, gnawing each spoonful with much delight, very much like an old man treating himself to his favorite dish which he hadn't been able to enjoy for many years. That was another characteristic that fascinated Gustave about him; he had the wonder-filled stare of a small child along with the wisdom and composure of an older person yet he was neither young nor was he anywhere close to being an old man.

"Ah, Steven, good morning!" Dr. O'Donovan stood up. His smile lit up the room.

"Good morning to you too, Morris," Gustave said as he shook O'Donovan's hand. During the past few weeks they decided that calling each other by their first names was perhaps not the standard around here but otherwise suitable for the two.

"Big day today. . . excited?" Dr. O'Donovan asked. He sat down, and continued making love to the rice pudding, although he did keep an eye open in Gustave's direction.

Gustave set his tray down, on which stood a cup of coffee and a slice of toast with nothing on it. "I suppose you can say so, I'm not nervous or anything I'm certain it will work, I'm just hoping they will like it and give me some time off."

"Time off?" O'Donovan froze as if they were both jail inmates' discussing options for an escape.

Gustave didn't quite know what to make of O'Donovan's reaction. He decided to elaborate. "You see, there is a woman I would really like to see again, I miss her very much. I didn't know it would be such restrictive accommodations where I would not be able to leave the base for extended periods of time. Are you telling me you haven't left the base since you came here, Morris?"

"Can't say I have Dr. Monde" O'Donovan replied. Gustave noticed the change in tone, especially considering

Dr. O'Donovan using his formal name. Some time ago, Gustave had told him he never liked to be called Doctor, as unlike many with a PhD who liked to be called doctor, he felt only medical doctors were deserving of that title. He knew that Dr. O'Donovan, who was in fact an MD, called him so to irritate him for some odd reason.

"Do you have no one on the outside?" Gustave asked.

"No, I'm sorry, where are my manners, you are entitled to some privileges, they couldn't have done the project without you and now it's completed and is more than they could have ever expected. But Steven, I really think it might be too early to ask them something like that. . . perhaps you should delay for a while?"

"I'm afraid I can't do that my friend, I must see her and their absence of consideration for my well-being will not serve them well."

"That they lack care is something we are both aware of, but they neither have any obsolescence to their silly protocols. In any case, I do hope your request will be granted Steven. . . come, we have a full day ahead of us!" said Morris with a chilling aloofness.

CHAPTER 44

The room was crowded with Gustave's colleagues and several high ranking officials. Among them were Commander Antoinette, which he hadn't seen since the day he began working at the base.

Dr. Cassidy was there, too, although he made it quite clear he was there with the hope that something would go wrong. His expression was supercilious which was emphasized by his attire, and enhanced by colorful yellow shades. He took his seat in the show room.

Gustave had arranged the seating in the visitors section which was protected under heavy, thick blast-proof glass. The room behind that glass had a dummy retrofitted with the armor. It was obvious many demonstrations had taken place in that room as there were bullet holes in the ceiling and walls, and the ground showed the markings that had obviously been made by explosives. Gustave had arranged a table facing the crowd on top of which stood a laptop and a monitor.

"I would like to welcome my esteemed colleagues and high-ranking members of the combined forces and thank you for taking some of your valuable time to attend this short demonstration." Gustave swiveled the computer mouse to shake the screen saver off, and continued. "I would like to present to you IBAS, the Impenetrable Ballistics Absorbing Shield."

The screen showed the initials as the logo of his invention.

"I have here all the documentation and a set of instructions showing how to produce the materials needed to manufacture it, as well as very detailed manufacturing instructions, costs, and pertinent facts which I thought would make this demonstration more complete however, I know you are here to see it in action and I, more than anyone, am looking forward to it just as much as you are." Gustave pressed a button that was a part of a very simple command module to give instructions in the other room.

"Before we begin shooting at it, I would like to know if there is anyone who would volunteer to replace the dummy?"

This was, of course, a joke he had thought of the night before when he couldn't asleep, however his audience did not seem to favor his brand of humor. Instead of laughing, a hand rose.

"Was this tested before we got here?" It was a little dark to see who asked the question.

"I'm afraid not, this is the first time."

The voice answered back, "Then I think it best we leave it for the dummy for now. . ." The room filled with laughter. They were naturally skeptical, which was expected, especially as he was new to the operation.

A side door opened and the lights were turned on. An army man helping Gustave brought a second prototype to the room. It was important to show the skeptics among them the features of the armor up close. It looked like a rubber divers suit, only there were several features engineered into shapes that resembled a sea shell. Up close, it seemed as if it deflected light the same way a stealth aircraft deflected radar. It was fairly lightweight, looked like it was breathable but there was something very odd about it when touching it; it felt like a strange combination of a water bed and melted chocolate.

The members of the audience began to talk quietly among themselves. Several moments passed while they all got a chance to hold the prototype. Gustave, seeing everyone got their turn, raised his hand and waited until the room quieted down. He dimmed the lights to indicate the demonstration was about to begin. Moments later, a man in uniform walked into the test zone. He was dressed in combat uniform and protective head gear and made his way to a mark on the ground, stopped, and saluted the visitors.

"You may commence," Gustave said. The man drew a desert eagle from its holster and fixed his body in the proper posture of assault target shooting.

A shot was fired. The sound, even through the protective glass, resonated through the room. While the army personnel visitors did not flinch, several managerial types jumped from their seats.

The bullet, clearly visible against the dark color of the protective suit, remained within its fabric. Slowly, it bounced off and fell to the ground as the unique material rejected it.

There was a distinctive metallic sound as it hit the ground. Within seconds, another shot was fired, and then another one right after that. The two bullets, rejected by the fabric that had earlier absorbed them, fell to the ground.

The room remained silent. Everyone remained quiet, with many mouths hanging open in astonishment.

"Proceed!" Gustave ordered, still looking at the crowd and glancing into the adjoining room.

Another soldier entered carrying a semi-automatic magazine-fed M-16 rifle. Following the same procedures as the soldier before him, he made his way to the mark, saluted and began shooting at the dummy in bursts. The bullets were all absorbed, and then rejected just like the larger caliber bullets of the desert eagle.

The dummy, affixed to a heavy stand, shuddered slightly from second degree shockwaves, however, the suit remained intact and it was clear any harm that could have been caused by either the penetration of the bullet or the direct shockwave were all negligible.

"You see, my calculations were correct to assume that all energy from the hit will be rejected outward. Not only is there no penetration but there is very little if any damage done like with standard armored suits and shielding. Now, who wants to give this a try?"

The demonstration was a success. The army officials praised Gustave for his triumph, a gentleman from the Pentagon also approached Gustave, honoring him for his innovative accomplishment. Gustave basked in the admiration of the entire team.

Following several Q&A sessions with both the visitors and the team, it was decided to give the suit an immediate full beta trial production run. Gustave made certain to give just enough information for them to take it over without any need for him to participate in the production process. He didn't want anything to restrict him any longer to the base.

Gustave calmly approached Commander Antoinette to request a private audience with her. All smiles, she did not seem to flinch when she answered any time he would like to see her she would be glad to arrange a meeting. That seemed somewhat promising, considering she was a rather busy woman and yet was still willing to give some of her time to a rookie scientist.

After a very quick lunch break, Gustave made his way to her quarters where she gave him permission to enter.

"Come in," Commander Antoinette stated. It was clear the many cameras scattered throughout the building as well as access protocols had informed her of his arrival.

Her office was meticulously clean. Bright blonde wooden tiles complemented the room which featured unique space age curved white furniture. There were no papers lying around, neither were there any books, simply a computer which in its own right looked like a centerpiece from a fashion magazine. The commander wore a couturier red suit which complimented her lipstick and light olive complexion. "Please, leave the door open," Antoinette said with a smile.

"And have a seat," she added.

In front of her desk was a retro-looking egg chair. It was then he noticed the odd but striking shape of the sculpture on top of her desk. It resembled an aluminum artichoke. Whoever she was, Antoinette seemed to be a woman of his liking. He had a keen eye for design and always enjoyed noticing the value of art in functional form, however he couldn't help but question why an army base would allow such a radically anti-establishment expression in its confines. If anything, it reassured him that there was some room to wiggle protocols around here, which gave him hope that they might let him out for a few days.

"Steven..." she paused, "may I call you Steven?" Antoinette asked. It was clear she wanted to convey a more personal impression of herself.

"But of course, Captain Antoinette." Gustave was certain she would reciprocate and extend the offer for using a first name on her own, but she didn't. That did not go unnoticed. He was reminded of the many occasions where people he had worked for in the past, had the audacity to assume they were above conforming to standard human courtesy, wrapped around a self-perpetuating false notion of self- worth. Usually, these were also overblown egos.

He reassured himself about the commander, thinking it was not because she was truly narcissistic but because her feelings of self-worth were a result of battered self-esteem. This would explain the ostentatious display that was her work area.

"Steven, we are very satisfied with what you've done. It has taken us years to try to arrive where you caught up with in a matter of days, then completely revitalized the project. On behalf of the entire team, I thank you."

"Thank you Commander, I really do appreciate your acknowledgement." Gustave smiled noncommittally.

"I have a new project for you, Steven. This one is not going to be as easy for you, although seeing your ability, I think you will be able to pull this off. It's another project we've buried, since no one was capable of doing it. . ."

Fascinated as he was, he had more pressing issues; however, not displaying any enthusiasm would be utterly out of character and could be considered rude. Coerced, he smiled and moved closer to the table. "Please, tell me more!"

The commander rose from her chair slowly. "We were working on an invisible shield. . ." she began.

Gustave couldn't help himself and fought to hide an outburst of laughter. All those sci-fi movies they must have been watching for years while trying to emulate them with tax dollars!

The commander glanced at him, and noticed his giggle, which was more of a huffing sound. Gustave corrected himself by repeating the same sound pretending he was clearing his nose.

She continued. "We tried to create an invisible shield that soldiers would be able to shoot through, yet not be shot at."

Gustave smiled, unable to contain himself. "Like a force field? He asked to show interest. His armor brought up perfect schematics on alien technologies using graviton particle structures to bend light. But what could possibly make them believe that without any knowledge they could construct anything of the sort? Preposterous!

"Indeed, just like a force field, Steven. Needless to say, nothing came out of that project. You think you are up for the task?"

Gustave thought for several moments. He needed to come up with something viable, even a keyword to satisfy her and get on with what he came here for. "How much do you know about metamaterials, Commander?" Gustave asked. It was the only thing that made some sense to be of any use going forward with such an outrageous technology in earth terms.

"Not much at all, but do you think it's possible?" Antoinette asked.

"I think this is going to be an expensive project that will take some time. . ." Gustave replied. He closed his eyes for a moment as he spoke. He tried to convey a very serious and believable picture.

"I think you know by now that cost is not an issue here," Antoinette laughed.

"Very well, Commander, I'll get on it first thing when I come back," Gustave deliberately alluded to his imminent absence.

"Come back?" Antoinette looked confused.

"Commander, that was my reason for coming here. I would like to request a few days off for personal matters."

"Impossible," she responded.

"But Commander..." Gustave tried to reason with her.

She shrugged him off and said while pointing at him. "You are not to leave the base until I tell you to, understood?" she yelled.

Gustave's nostrils flared. "Commander, I don't see why this is an issue. I need some time off for a day or two, what difference could it make?"

"I do not have to explain myself to you, now leave!"

Gustave felt a tingling feeling in his spine. His nerves were tightening up. He had reached his limit dealing with these people. He calculated his attack routes. He was in an army base filled with every possible experimental weapon known to man. Plus the finest soldiers who knew how not only to operate said weapons but they knew how to fight well with their bare hands if needed. None of that seemed matter. "Who the hell do you think I am? Your damned slave?" he shouted.

"In several moments there will be a few men here to take you away from here. You have two choices: one is to apologize for your rude ill-mannered behavior or let them throw you into a locked cell. Your choice."

Two men came in to the room. Gustave's armor showed him an instantaneous readout of possible ways to attack them. There were many more options for certain death than for any lesser disablement ones. The selection was wholly engendered by his mood, which quickly dismissed any non-lethal means inappropriate to the current situation.

Morris came running into the room."Wait, please wait, please!" he begged. "Commander, please, he is new here he didn't know and he just solved our toughest project. Please show him some mercy, I'll have a talk with him. . . "

Gustave had no idea what was going on. He did not want to hurt Morris but as it was he was standing in the way of his objectives. What on earth was he doing in the room anyway? Unless...

"Fine, take him out, but I want a full apology." Antoinette sniffed arrogantly.

Something felt odd. As hard as he could, Gustave fought the urge to tear the place down. The armor in turn requested his brain ease up his anger by releasing stress-relieving hormones.

Morris raised his hand in protest and requested from the soldiers, "Please, just leave us alone a few minutes, we'll be right back, I promise, no harm done. . ."

The two left the room. Morris closed the door behind them. "Are you out of your damned mind?" Morris spoke in a soft tone, but it was clear he wanted to be more aggressive.

"She has no right treating me like a damn slave!" Gustave was furious.

"Shhh! Shut up for just one moment, Gustave!" Morris said.

Gustave? Morris knew who he really was! "Who are you?" Gustave replied. His hand grabbed Morris by his neck, ready to snap it as if it was a toothpick.

"Gustave, stop, I'm with them!" He tried breathing forcefully under the grip of Gustave's hand. "I'm here to help, let go!" He said with what little breath he could squeeze out of his lungs. Gustave released his grip.

Morris took a few moments to get some air back, while massaging his throat. "You think you'll kill all of them without their noticing?"

Gustave was slowly becoming more calm.

"No, I wasn't sent here by K'ta's team, but rather from high command." Morris was still finding it difficult to speak plainly.

"Why are you talking about this? They can hear us back there!" Gustave whispered.

"Oh, no - temporal arrest, they are on auto pilot, I tried to put you on one as well, but big surprise...it didn't do much on you, now go in there and apologize, it won't hold them for too long!"

"They must learn their..." Gustave began only to be interrupted by Morris.

"Sacrifice your ego's emotions for once, Gustave. It will do us no good. . ."

"Sacrifice?" Gustave looked at Morris in contempt, "Sacrifice?" He repeated. "You have no idea..."

"I went through a gene mutation to get here; do you have any idea what that takes? Shedding yourself from your specie, human?" Morris said. It answered his first question as to how an Angelonian would be able to enter the base without being automatically recognized by the alien detectors.

Gustave had no idea what it took. Nothing in his armor's memory related to anything he was talking about. Of course, that didn't mean much as most of the alien technology was still unknown, only the things he was able to extract from Nell in those moments of her vulnerability as she reached climax.

He gave it a thought. Even though he would have no problem attacking the entire base, the implications of his action, although unnoticeable by the rest of the population, would surely destroy the entire mission, and of course his ultimate goals.

"This conversation is far from over Morris, but I'll do as you suggest." Gustave returned to the commander's office with Morris right behind him.

With sincere penitence, Gustave apologized to

Commander Antoinette.

CHAPTER 45

Morris, or rather as Gustave had recently been informed, was actually known as Alpha-Teacher Moor Sriclu and was the brain behind the entire operation. As the founder of the group against the Prometheus treaty, he remained an active member, only operating for the most part in the shadows of the organization. Without the knowledge of the rest of the team, he volunteered to help the operations on the ground. Being among humans on a daily basis was something none were capable of comprehending much less actually doing but he was different and had the true spirit of an explorer. The procedure to turn himself into a human was an extremely dangerous physical undertaking. Not only that, he now had a shelf life of no more than several years. Several years which he hoped would be used to enjoy the fruit of his labor.

He was given the choice to be carbon copied to After Life's servers or continue as he was, but he chose to remain on earth and die with the rest of humans, who he believed to be the closest and purest form to whomever it was that had initially fathered and fostered their specie. Of course, it was genuinely believed there was no such thing, but he remained true to his beliefs.

"I know where it is Alpha-Teacher," Gustave said. They were sitting under the artificially lit evening just outside the mess hall.

"That is wonderful. I assume you have no way of accessing it without the help of the team?" Alpha-Teacher asked. His eyes shone excitedly with the news, his old bewildered child-like expectancy returned to his face.

"You are correct, but that wretched commander-woman wouldn't let me visit them, and that is why I needed to get out." Gustave was not in a very good mood considering everything.

"The access array is under the swimming pool. I need it to be closed for several days in order to enter unnoticed. The only option is to infiltrate some bacteria into the water in order to label it unsafe until a team arrives to clean it."

Alpha-Teacher smiled jubilantly. "We chose you well; that is a very creative solution, but you will inflict pain on children and their parents, there must be another…"

Gustave decided to interrupt him. "Some stomach pain and other unfavorable bodily experiences but they are only temporary, so I don't see why I shouldn't go ahead with the plan, it's for their own good. Well, yes, in the long run, for their own good."

"Humans never fail to amaze me. You can do unimaginable things to one another for a just cause!" Alpha-Teacher said.

"Of course, we are going to argue about what is a just cause now, are we?" Gustave was unwilling to enter into such an argument as it had been hashed over many times in history classes.

"No, Gustave, where we come from, every solution must come without harming anyone else, it's a basic principle we all live by. . ."

"But you deprive species of access to technology that can save them, and is that not causing them harm?"

Alpha-Teacher smiled gently and said, "And so you see, we are here to change that aren't we? They say new species are not ready for our technology since most are still violent but I think our technology can change this for the better, I believe we all have evil engrained in ourselves through millions of years of natural selection but we, they, all have the capacity to become good. With the proper means."

Gustave, touched by this notion, sat back in his chair and crossed his arms. He had a pleased expression on his face as he knew he was indeed in the company of an incredibly compassionate humanoid. They waited a few moments, enjoying the silence of the evening.

"Any other plans?" Gustave asked. He meant was there another method Alpha-Teacher had come up with.

"I'll provide you with what you need...although, we'll change the bacteria a little, give it a shelf life of several hours, no need to cause too much pain for these poor people, is there now?"

Gustave nodded in agreement.

They both knew the invasion into the alien base would commence in just a few more days.

CHAPTER 46

Catepet stood with his hands crossed behind his back, a posture befitting his august stature. Through the transparent wall he watched the docking of his newly constructed ambassadorial transport. The site was awe-inspiring. It looked like a giant bubble, out of which several thousands of tentacles protruded. It had a fluid yet mechanical motion about it, which was the latest in fashion. The ship was fairly visible considering it needed to be seen by other oncoming traffic but it had it been out in space there would have been no way to detect it. It wasn't because politicians had any need to stay invisible in order to escape any threats. There were no threats, nor did anyone even have the capacity for silencing any threats. It was merely a fashion statement that postulated giant ships distorted the natural beauty of open, uncluttered space.

The ship finished docking. Catepet immediately felt it as well. Had he not seen the docking in action, he would have intuited the process as it was being carried out.

There was nothing with which the many different residents among the Galactic Union didn't resonate on several levels. At any given moment, all statistics about the whereabouts, schedules, and all other information about an individual or their belongings was distributed along the main data network. The few that were lucky enough to have some of their information blocked from publication were political officials. No one, other than their peers, had the luxury of being privy to their daily activities and sometimes a few had the clearance to be relieved of exposing even that.

Average citizens of all species couldn't fathom the idea of not being connected to the network they simply called the Link. They enjoyed all its benefits and understood none of its risks. The thirst for information was so strong it was impossible to be tempted out of the link. However, officials knew very well several seditious groups had arranged for scramblers and were capable of accessing restricted information and were quite active outside of the Link. Catepet was in charge of the committee responsible for studying them, which was the Committee for Aberrant Activity.

The committee served as a place for studying and bringing these renegades to order, although most of their activity was data gathering. However, since there were several Angelonians to be quite proactive in their resentment to the Prometheus treaty, Catepet had undergone several changes, one of which included a newly assigned division for counter intelligence.

Through a very large corridor, he walked toward a room where a meeting was scheduled to start. New information was received, just as expected. The members were all handed packets of information to process well before the meeting began. The gathering was simply to discuss the information and choose proper ways to act upon the information which they had received.

It wasn't necessary as everyone could have just created a secure link between themselves, however they did not want to have the burden of sustaining the link at the same time they were processing new things.

Not that anyone was aware of it, but there was a very big flaw in the Link, in that it was too easy to have information widely available. Most of them no longer had much capacity to remember things without the link, neither did they have any clue to what the mental capacity of remembering actually required. They were extremely good manipulators of information yet did not know very well how to store it without the help of the Link and any of the post-singularity interfaces to their brain. To bring into memory a set of very complex equations was as simple as breathing, in that they didn't have to think much to do it, yet had the option to inhale or exhale at will.

Most training and schooling was primarily concentrated on methods for utilizing information, or as they often called it "info-bending" to fit different purposes.

The Angelonian underground movement made every effort to help restore some self-sustained mental capacities in that they often trained their children from a very young age using memory games.

The beauty of it was that no one could have known someone was capable of the gift of increased memory capacity. There was never any test issued to examine it.

* * *

The corridors were filled with officials, their assistants, and other visitors and scholars. Although the place seemed vividly alive with bustling activity, it was quiet. It was considered rude to discuss matters in corridors except in simple, basic proximity exchanges and greetings, which were often transferred via the link. Of course, this was created out of courtesy and in doing that, there was no need to translate some of the more undecipherable accents.

Catepet passed by a Bordonian official. He nodded his head. This time there was no need for a conversation as they both quickly matched their updates and correlated them to the last time they had met. Seeing there was nothing new or noteworthy to discuss, they both continued on their own way without any interference. The Bordonian were most likely one of the stranger species the G.U. had acquired and they were the newest members of the G.U. They had hundreds of tiny digits on each of their two hands. Each hand was capable of constant movement as well and was all tiny bones and a lot of muscles that moved any way they desired. Their entire body was translucent, but it wasn't anything evolutionary, merely the way they perceived beauty in nature. The inner workings of their neural network was indeed a unique site, and with the odd shape of their hands and legs, they somewhat resembled a squid or a jellyfish.

It was not the reason why they were considered different but it was for the way they accomplished an incredible array of technological achievements, including the introduction to the Huhsh race which was strangest of them all; they were void entities who lived in a theorized existence undetectable by any instrumentation. How the Bordonians found them and constructed the bridge to communicate and interact with them was the latest marvel of the G.U., which earned them a place not only as a G.U specie but as one of the enlightened ones.

The room resembled an auditorium. Once the opening in the wall closed after the last member of the committee entered, the room transformed its shape into a perfect circle from which symmetrical shapes extruded to create sitting arrangements.

"He is a menace. But we must wait and see how this turns out. . ." a speaker said. The room was too dark to see the features of the members but Catepet was intuitively aware of each one.

"I agree. Earth's media is calmly nonplussed about this. I think this is good, as this whole thing will be discredited very soon, and AMET is out of the picture. We have wanted this for a very long time, and the operation is progressing quite well. They chose him for whatever reason, but it is we who are benefiting. . ." Catepet's tone was reassuring.

"Did we perceive any way to warn them? It's just a matter of time until he finds the base. . ." The voice was that of Ganuk Hirsgs, a representative of the fasbina space.

"No Ganuk. . . We have no communications with them. However we predict no harm will be done. We can shut him off when we please. We will be able to monitor and counteract without stepping foot on earth. . ." Catepat could afford not to mention this, as a breach of the treaty was an extreme offence against the G.U. Once a law was instated, it could not be removed or bypassed for any reason. Citizens of the Union knew it well, and politicians were under even heavier restrictions to pass any law.

"The situation is quite favorable. Once this is over, we have exposed their plan, and will be able to re-assign all members of the underground organization." Catepat paused, a thoughtful expression on his face. "Although this wasn't included in the report, Senator Posh informed me the crew is currently under no communication with Gustave, but they are expecting a contact once he's found the base, after which we will let him inside and transmit to the workers to deactivate him and inform us of their progress. I, for one, can't wait to hear back from them."

The room filled with the ebb and flow of joyful murmurings. The Matter-Speaker project was a very sought-after technology. They anticipated it would take several years to construct, but it had begun several years before the treaty was signed, after which all communications to and from earth were shut down, and with it by mistake, so did the communication with the base. It wasn't until now that they had such a wonderful opportunity to regain communications with the base and the workers, as this was manipulated for them by the renegades of the Union. Therefore, their hands were clean and subsequently they cleverly had nothing much for which to atone.

The meeting concluded after several discussions in regards to other matters. There was an anomaly reported in After Life. Several residents rejected all communications with their families and fellow residents. They were still there. Un-erased from the storage, but it was still hard to track their whereabouts. They behaved like an elusive virus that whenever it was called by the system, its location was instantly copied to another undisclosed location on the mainframe. Finding any information in an extremely large array of data was something the G.U was very capable of, however it required identity tags used in storing and retrieving each entry. These residents had their tags somehow removed and were free-roaming the After Life universe.

The committee members concluded this was a result of a failure and named a sub-committee to locate and rescue those poor souls. It was yet to be determined how this could be done, however experts from the After Life Institution were selected to advise the members and work with them to have the matter resolved.

After the meeting, Catepet made his way to his new ship. He was anxious, but more than anything, excited to test it out and arrive home with it to show his family and friends.

He signaled his assistants to prepare for his arrival with his new toy.

"There she is," he said to himself. The dock station lit up the ship in blue and pink suffused glows. The colors served a different purpose than just shining colorfully on the ship. Instead, they held the ship in its current form, guiding its shape through complex transformations of positioning data. Where the light shone, reflective parts constructed themselves along unique patterns, where the extrusions of the ship caused shadowing, the expected level and position of these shadows gave away corrections necessary to form a stable outline. The entire construct had memory form, however the engines caused extreme spatial turbulence that required constant guidance for corrective shape amendment.

The ship's interior was just as he had seen in the catalogue. It looked like a pool of liquid mercury. There were subtle waves moving the liquid in different directions.

Catepet made a sighing noise and fell to the ground. The liquid quickly took shape and caught him mid-air. It raised him up high and while doing so, the entire room formed into place. Controls morphed into complex shapes and colors. Smoothly lifting Catepet into a comfortable location near the controls, the liquid froze, and the entire ship was ready to begin flight. Catepet felt as one with the machine - the overwhelming feeling had an orgasmic resonance.

Catepet, who had his eyes closed during the feeling of euphoria, smiled with the utmost delight and opened his eyes. He calibrated his link and gently instructed the ship's computer.

"Let's take you home!"

The bright orange flashing of the enormous engines filled the launching area with a light bright enough to compete with one of the planet's suns. As the ship lifted off the pad, the shuddering roar humbled the men who had themselves developed such powerful engines. The spectators were silent as they watched the result of their combined creative imaginations leap impossibly forward on a journey toward the stars.

CHAPTER 47

Gustave felt trapped in his cubicle. The day featured all the mundane activities one would expect working for an old-fashioned company. It was aggravating to know all the while he was working on projects that could be categorized as high-tech, there was no such atmosphere in this place. He couldn't understand why the people were so comfortable working here. While they were expected to produce much more than all those fancy new start-ups elsewhere they have been treated with an iron fist as opposed to comfortable hours, fun activities, and daily activities which were usually considered standard. Although his fledgling experience working in an office was not enough to differentiate from one place to another, he knew this was not the way things should be conducted to keep employees happy. If they were content with this workplace, they were either desperate, or were simply not deserving of anything better, he thought to himself.

The fax machine constantly emitted horrible chirps that were accompanied by a duet with the network printer, which was even louder and at times even noisier.

In the background, the sound of secretaries and

assistants filled the hall with the repeated lyrics of morning greetings, followed by the division greetings, and followed by "Please hold while I transfer the call." Then afternoon greetings, followed by the division greetings, followed by, "Your party is on a lunch break, may I take a message?" This didn't seem to end. Perhaps it was because he was still new that he didn't have this background noise canceled, but he couldn't see himself getting used to it. Especially as perceptive as he was: nothing passes by, nothing passes through. Every sound, activity, and movement was a matter for concern, or at least attention. The only thought that kept him from losing his mind was that he probably wouldn't be there for too long. Alpha Teacher was working on the gene mutation of the bacteria and should be completed with it any day now. He was ecstatic with the idea that some of these noise makers he had to call co-workers had the habit of visiting the pool every day after work. They would most likely have an encounter with his bacterial-virus friend, which would in turn provide them with a glimpse of how he felt about them.

It was a wonderfully impish, devilish feeling. Having someone treat you with far less than the respect you deserve then looking at them in the eye and knowing one day they would be in a position so far below you, they would have nothing but regret for the rest of their adult lives.

That kept Gustave from losing his mind.

An email appeared on his screen. It was from

HR. Gustave didn't bother reading it too soon as he usually received emails from the department, announcing unimportant promotions or the ever-more annoying ones that were titled: "Congratulations, Mark & Melissa on your baby girl," which often included pictures of the new-born. Gustave couldn't stand the look of the babies who all looked the same, freakishly red, eyes barely opened, some hairier than others, some fatter than the others. Why they felt the urge to send these emails Gustave did not know, but he felt obligated to look at these since the people involved had a silly tendency for quizzing one another, "Bill did you see Karen's baby? Isn't she's adorable, what did you think of the little shoes?" What a waste of time!

After pondering for a few moments delaying reading the email, Gustave made himself open his email application.

"HR: Important safety news – MUST READ!

The use of the swimming pool is forbidden until further notice due to severe health concerns. If you or any of your family members suffer from stomach pain, please report to the medical center immediately!"

Alpha Teacher did it! It won't be long before the pool would be closed and emptied. Just in time! He thought. It was Friday and the cleaning crew would not be able to come any earlier than Monday. He had the whole weekend to finish and once and for all leave this place and start his life. His mind filled with a certain prodigious feeling of things to come. Not a moment too soon, he was reminded that the biggest unknowns lay ahead him. He was about to encounter some very protective, very powerful beings. Was he ready to fight with them?

After a moment of trepidation, he calmed himself down. He had to look past the mission and remind himself why he was doing this. The fruits of his labor on which the entire future of his race depended! Good reason as any to get yourself killed, not that he was ready to die. With the inevitability he would most likely injure himself, at least he knew he was ready to fight them with everything he had.

Gustave hurried to his apartment and was trying to decide what to wear and what he could leave behind. He knew he would not have time to come back to collect his belongings if he wanted to escape the base in a hurry, without leaving traces of carnage and disarray. He wanted to wear a suit for dinner. It was Friday evening, and knew it would not be too suspicious if he dressed in moderately casual attire, especially if others did the same.

Not knowing whether or not it would be the last time he would have a chance to dine with his new friend, Alpha Teacher, he thought it would be a nice gesture if they enjoyed one last meal and a conversation together and he would have the opportunity to show his respect for all his help. He packed a small bag with a few changes of clothes as he expected to begin his extraction operation right after their meal.

After showering, he dressed and picked up his wallet and watch. A little distracted by the thoughts of the events to come, he absent-mindedly tucked his wallet in the right-hand pocket of his coat which was usually reserved for his cellular phone because it provided an easier access to his right hand.

He felt a small object in the bottom of his pocket, as he put the soft leather wallet inside.

It was the practice rod from the ship. In theory he was supposed to know about its whereabouts the moment he was close to it, but the practice rod was so simplistic as far as technology goes its earthly equivalent would have been like a wooden bat compared to a carefully forged Japanese sword. It did not keep a constant communication link open with the armor or any grid.

"This will most certainly be useful as a weapon," Gustave thought to himself. He was left to walk toward the mess hall.

The evening was pleasant. The setting sun, created a display of magnificent colors that engulfed the desert horizon. Higher stars were beginning to emerge beckoning the observer's eye to the limitless space beyond. A cool breeze gently caressed his skin which was very welcome because he was extremely nervous. The walk to the mess hall was difficult. With every step, Gustave grew more and more wary of the impending danger.

Arriving at the mess hall, Gustave made his way to Alpha Teacher's table. As usual with his voracious appetite, his tray was filled to capacity with assortments of dishes. Mooris was focused on his food, enjoying every bite. It looked as if he had indulged himself more than usual, knowing this might well be the last time he ate at the base. There was no way to tell.

Gustave sat down.

"Mooris. . . ."

Alpha Teacher, who was just about to take a prodigious amount of food into his mouth, stopped and looked up. "Ah, what a nice suit!" Mooris announced perfunctorily. It seemed as if he was more interested in enjoying his food than making conversation.

Gustave smiled and said, "Thank you!"

"You must try this dish. It taste better and better every day, and gets better and better with every bite."

Looking at the plate, Gustave couldn't help but ask in a confused tone, "Mashed potatoes?"

Alpha Teacher hummed and chewed loudly, swallowed and said, "Yes, yes, mashed potatoes! You know, I would dearly miss this if I had to stop eating here for any reason."

"I can imagine that, but, you know, they are very easy to make. Do you think after our work here is done I could invite you over for some of my own cooking? I can teach you how to cook. . ."

Alpha was very interested in that offer, and he stopped chewing. "I want nothing more!" Alpha-Teacher smiled, his eyes shining with delight. This dinner was quite possibly the last time they would meet but apparently Gustave would not be the only casualty if the mission failed, all the more reason to push himself to succeed. It was time to go their separate ways.

Gustave made his way to the public washrooms adjacent to the swimming facility. He knew all the facilities would be closed to the public, except for the dining room which was always open. He automatically programmed his work computer to hack into the system and create a diversion which would keep the base internal security occupied while he was working in the swimming pool area. The diversion was to shut down all video surveillance while fake multiple underground entries proceeded. It would be a field trip for security at the base as they would be forced to send all security personnel to several fronts while each tried to figure out a way of digging under the surface. He knew that explosives would be used and alarms would force people and their families to hide in the network of nuclear shelters. This would not only ensure no eye witnesses, but also no security around him as the intrusions were all faked to seem to come from the outskirts of the base while the mess hall facilities were located right in the middle. A redundancy, of course, but he wanted to be certain his plan succeeded.

The second hand of his watch, which was calibrated with the internal clock of his computer, ticked loudly. There were ten more seconds to go until the alarms would go off.

Then the alarms sounded throughout the base from several watch towers. The deafening sound rose slowly in pitch until it reached a certain tone at which it remained for about a minute. All throughout the base, more and more alarms began singing one after the other. It was difficult to hear anything else. It created a chilling feeling down Gustave's spine. It was the sound of war. Adrenaline pumped through his veins and he was ready to begin. He changed clothes and tucked the old ones into his carryall, but not before he removed the rod from the suit and held on to it.

The corridor to the swimming pool was littered with signs of warning against entering the pool. His movements were precise and agile. The armor was primed to recognize a distinct end point which Gustave set as he approached from the distance. The locked doors yielded no resistance under his strength. The training rod had the strength of a single artificial molecule no matter what shape or form it took, Gustave jumped high up into the air while instructing the rod to flatten into a micro-thick surface which zoomed into the bottom of the empty pool. The paper-thin structure slid into the concrete of the pool, destroying all piping and metallic foundations underneath, producing almost no sound until it reached the outer edge of the entrance to the secret base. In seconds, it curved itself and lifted all materials up in the air exposing the opening beyond the outer rim. At that point, Gustave was at the apex of his jump, reaching up to the extremely tall ceiling of the facility. The rod's now flattened structure, holding a fair amount of concrete, pipes and giant steel support foundations quickly extruded another two thin walls right in its middle which, in a split second, shuffled all the debris to the sides, creating a clean surface. With all his armor's strength, Gustave pushed himself from the ceiling and landed on the surface. The surface changed its form, and engulfed Gustave in a protective cocoon that continued the downward motion into the rim of the base. It was like a one-man projectile, carrying him down into the bowels of the secret part of the base under the pool.

Gustave felt a strong impact as he landed on a solid surface. He knew exactly where he was. The intelligent technologies in the room began connecting with his armor. One by one they each gave a direct link to their status and purpose. Expecting a large base, Gustave found out the place was nothing more than just a large room.

Although he could not see much, his memory was updated with the room's structure which instantaneously gave away the whereabouts of the device. As it yielded an unknown device which his armor knew was there but could not connect to. His armor revealed there were two unknown devices.

As hard as he could, Gustave instructed the cocoon to open up in a lattice form, with only several microns apart from each string. The light going through the cocoon allowed him to see through it.

There were three bots. Although their shape was similar to the others he had seen on the ship, there was something very different about them. They looked rugged, ready to battle.

They began floating toward him, trying to dismantle the cocoon. It was a terrifying moment as he tried keeping the cocoon together while they were tearing it a part. The particles cracked and exploded as they received conflicting instructions. He felt them trying to get to him, he felt them trying to infiltrate his brain and entire nervous system with a powerful persuasive forces but he battled them with all his strength.

More than anything, pain, unlike anything he had ever experienced had begun forcing itself into his body. He could not see it, but his armor informed him they were using powerful rays that penetrated his body forcing organic tissues to separate.

The pain was unbearable. Yet instead of it causing him to retreat, he screamed and continued the effort to defend himself.

One of the bots got close. Close enough to engage in hand to hand combat. The armor quickly informed Gustave, which caused him to react quickly. From within the cocoon, he formed a sword.

In a sudden movement, he released an opening, and launched it in a swinging motion towards the bot. It tore it apart, and again, another swinging motion, and another and another until the bot was sliced into many pieces.

The other bots did not seem to care, or understand the change in the dynamics of the fight. They remained on their course to get closer to him.

The other bot was taken down in the same way.

Part of the cocoon left to defend from the other and the other part provided both protection and an attack opening through which Gustave used to cut the bot to slices of useless technology.

The last one was much easier. Gustave, not requiring the added protection of the cocoon, reformed it into thin atomic razors organized into a cubical lettuce shape, and launched it toward the machine. In just under a second, it entered the bot's body and expanded it, creating what might look like abstract pieces of art, divided into different canvases and arranged in equal sizes, each one a sharp as a finely honed razor blade the size of a dinner plate. When the bot was nothing but useless metallic pieces, all its parts ceased moving.

And then silence.

Gustave fell to the ground. He was still in pain. Torn from the inside, bruised and cut, his skin was stained with fresh blood from some sections where his body was fully exposed.

Exhausted, he momentarily lost consciousness.

For several moments, his body lay on the ground without moving. His body was being rebooted by the armor. Torn body tissue was being corrected and reconnected by new cells which were rapidly created to promote fast healing. The armor's rejuvenating abilities were hard at work. Slowly, the sounds of explosions and the alarms from the base were reaching his awakening consciousness. They became less and less muffled.

He opened his eyes.

The sliced body of one of the bots lay close to him. Out of fear, he regained enough strength to raise up and continue his objectives.

The first; to retrieve the device and the second was to destroy the facility.

Seeing that there weren't many instruments in the room, his second objective changed. Why would he destroy the place before he learned about all the machinery? First he must secure the devices.

The device from whose spherical center extended thousands of pins of varying lengths looked extremely odd. It had a tubular shape on both sides that looked like they were connected, although there was dead space between them. Light did not shine through it, neither was it a solid. It was as if there was consolidated emptiness in-between that kept all the parts together. It was rather small in size, or rather small enough to carry. However, two of them might prove to be too difficult, not because of their weight, which oddly enough had no weight what-so-ever. The shape seemed to be too delicate.

Gustave ordered the object which used to be the transformable rod back out from the bot. It came out, making a screeching high-pitched sound.

He formed it into the shape of a box in which he carefully inserted the two devices. The walls of the box were extruded to hold the two devices in place. Spikes reached gently around the objects securing their shape.

Running from one device to another he made contact with each to extract tiny communication software he had designed to retrieve the entire schematics of its construct.

It was then when he noticed one of the devices. Unlike the rest, he knew it all too well. It was the same one he remembered from his childhood. The same one he had activated back in the lab of his father. These were the same entities who had broken into the lab. It was they who had caused his father to lose his job in the army, and it was they who had killed his friend. No one can be trusted. Not even the Angelonians. But at least he knew who was to blame. Not some technology thirsty thugs, but the entire Galactic Union.

He called for the toolbox which K'ta gave him back on the ship. Ever since he got there, it had floated high in the air, undetectable by any human device, and too far away to be noticed by the alien base.

The toolbox came down within his reach.

Gustave closed down the remaining opening of the box forming two handles on one of its sides which he gripped. The tool box, which was now active, began glowing with an intensive blue light. It was time for him to fly out, before this thing exploded.

Controlling the nanonites of the box he took flight to the air. Looking down, he saw an intense blue light expanding from beneath the ground. The light vanished. All that remained of the facility was gray-looking, metallic rich rock. Even if they tried to study the giant solid, they would find nothing because it had all fused with the desert sand. It was as if this structure, and everything around it had never existed.

He flew very far from the base. In the distance he could see the army far below aimlessly trying to fight an invisible underground enemy while digging, shooting the ground with explosives trying to control the invisible intruders from entering the base.

"K'ta?" Gustave opened a link to the ship. He had no problems now that neither the army nor AMET was on his tail.

K'ta was in the room with his team. They were deep into a heated political discussion which of course featured no yelling or arguments, just positive reaffirmation about their rightful actions against the Galactic Union. Ever since they lost all contact with Gustave and had nothing to do but wait, they had used their time to engage in lengthy discussions to dissipate the stress.

K'ta, mid-speech, received the link invitation. The team knew there was news.

"Gustave! Is it you? Are you all right?"

"I'm fine, thank you," Gustave said, who was still in pain and not in a very good mood.

"I have your device, and need to be extracted; you have a lock on my position?"

"Wonderful!" K'ta shouted as he clapped his hands together. The team could not hear the conversation as he was not vocalizing it through his mouth. All they saw was a clap and a smiling face. They knew right away.

"We are on our way. . ." K'ta turned to his team with a smile. "He has it! The mission

is successful! We've done it!" He continued, "Bor, set a course to Gustave. We have to retrieve him as fast as possible, Milka, look for any chatter on the link, we must be certain they are not after us. Nell, the armor reports Gustave is in bad shape, please prepare for medical assistance."

They all nodded and rapidly assumed emergency retrieval positions.

* * *

Gustave landed on a sand dune. It was dark, but the moon had risen and cast golden light everywhere. He opened the box and inspected the devices for any damages. Everything seemed to have been preserved in perfect condition. He removed one of the devices from the box. It felt strange holding it in his hand. He felt it, he saw it, but it posed no added weight on his hands, it was as if he was holding air or an object in a virtual computer simulation, only he could actually feel its shapes.

The other device? It did not exist. Not as far as they knew. As far as he was concerned, it belonged to him and the people of earth. He gazed at the box and removed a section from it. The section curved itself into an improvised shovel and began digging a deep hole into the ground.

Once complete, he instructed the box to rearrange itself and close down without the separated part which he needed to fill up the hole afterward. The box closed, and entered itself into the cavity.

He had just enough time to sit and wait until the ship arrived. Bruised, bleeding and filled with pain he tried to remain calm.

A minute later the ship arrived. He couldn't see it but he sensed its presence. A ray of light peeked from an opening out of the darkness of the sky. The gravity around him changed, causing the light to bend and focus as if it was some sort of a ray. He again had the odd feeling of being upside down but ignored it, knowing everything was soon to be over and that they could fix whatever damage was caused to his body from the attack in the alien base.

He was on board. The team awaited him with a change of clothes. K'ta embraced him with his arms, but Gustave did not have any more strength left in him. He stayed on the floor.

Nell, smiled at him and whispered, "Thank you for coming back". She softly touched his cheeks, patting him for comfort.

Gustave smiled back at her and with a soft voice said, "I missed you very much, Nell. . . it was all worth it to see you again." He collapsed into deep sleep.

The bright white floor was tainted by the blood that trickled from Gustave's body.

There was very little time to waste.

CHAPTER 48

Catepet was relaxing in his favorite cushioned chair that automatically reclined itself and conformed to his body shape, whenever he moved, even slightly. He leaned his head back on the head rest and glanced around the room, one of his favorites. The colors that graced the walls and altered themselves much like the colors of a soothing sunset were restful to watch and the ideal soporific. The millwork was the glossy white of cumulous clouds and a suffused glow emitted from the whiteness of the door frames and the adjacent trim, like an electronic picture frame. The soft rose and pink and fuchsia of the walls had a gently moving wavy texture that was mesmerizing as it changed constantly, like the tides of the ocean.

Magnificent statues were randomly placed strategically throughout the open-air terrace that abutted the sitting room of a high-ranking personage such as Catepet. Each of the eight hand-carved marble-like statuettes were exact replicas of ancient works of art that were safe guarded under lock and key near the capitol. Those allowed Catepet were beautifully staged with a ceiling track light focused on each one. On the other side of the mosaic tile floor of the terrace was a mineral banister, waist-high, and beyond that, the land dropped away in a sheer cliff of blue and turquoise outcroppings, at the base of which the white froth of the endless surf furnished its eternal pulsing, like the heartbeat of the earth itself. Catepet looked over the magnificent view and smiled when he saw his new ship anchored below, her tentacle-like sails furled neatly as she moved gently with the wind. Catcpet took a deep breath and realized he was a happy person.

Catepet's eupohoric mood was short-lived as his electronic blocking resource which was set to prevent any interruptions even official messages and alerts, was by-passed by an invasive and frightening intelligence report. Rushing uninvited and unhampered into his brain was the overwhelming message stating their mission had completely failed. The terrifying news had passed through all protocols and had flooded every brain cell it could find without regard for position or rank of the recipients. The effect was instantaneous.

Catepet shouted for his first lieutenant to stand by for instructions. He stood up and tried to control his fury as the walls of his favorite room ceased undulating and became rigid and cold, as he was projecting he wanted them to appear. He frowned as his brain synapses fired more rapidly than ever and he summoned the members of his council for a meeting, as soon as possible.

After quickly changing his outfit, Catepet rushed to his transport vessel. Since this was a G.U. emergency, all channels of transportation were given direct order to dedicate all resources for the transport of the members of the council, as was needed. The Agora was thousands of light years away, yet most of them would probably make it there in a matter of minutes, as distances within the galaxy were not the issue, only timing.

* * *

Every member of the council was dispirited and deeply concerned. They all knew what had to be done. It was decided to hunt for the Petna, the ship which carried the Angelonian insurgents and attempt to seize the devices. In doing so, they knew they might compromise the identity of their infiltrator, however, that was a risk they were willing to take. The Angelonian insurgents must not have the miraculous technology in their hands. The biobots never did call home. There should have been an instantaneous connection from the first contact with Gustave. He seemed to have disabled the program somehow and they had to bypass his maneuvers.

It was decided Gustave would be retrieved with the

team and deported from earth. He would pose less risk in a rehabilitation facility under the close watch of the union instead of roaming free on earth. Killing him or any of the rest of the team was not even brought to the discussion table. It would be impossible to comprehend such a thing by their society. However, nuances and suggestions were treated with great consideration.

They set up an educational mission of the highest importance in the sun's system region. An anomaly was reported that required direct examination by G.U. teams. Of course, this was merely a public cover-up for sending out several ships with sensitive scientific equipment which was capable of distant exploration or destruction depending on how it was used.

CHAPTER 49

Gustave was dreaming of a magical flight he was taking, lying down in the middle of a large, wispy pink cloud, strands of which stroked his face and left streaks of warmth wherever they touched his cheeks. He struggled to stay asleep and enjoy the comfort of the feeling forever, when his subconscious prodded him awake. He realized even through the haze of deep sleep the faint scent of gardenias was actually Nell's natural scent and what he had thought was part of a cloud was actually the touch of her hand as she tenderly stroked his face. He inhaled deeply and turned his face slightly to the left and risked opening his eyelids for a glimpse of his surroundings as his eyes searched for her face. He was suddenly aware the fierce struggles of the immediate past were fading into memory and he felt physically and mentally rejuvenated, reborn.

He wanted to remain motionless enjoying the closeness of Nell and part of him wanted to stay that way forever. . .but the industrious and competent leader part of him urged him awake. Besides, he wanted to see Nell's face. Again. Clearly.

He looked up, smiling at her profile above his head which she cradled in her lap. "Good morning, beautiful. . ." He reached up and touched the tip of her upturned nose.

She chuckled softly and enfolded his hand in hers. "You're awake! Welcome back, Gustave! And congratulations! You did it!" Her eyes shone with delight as she leaned over to kiss him lightly on the lips.

"No, WE did it, didn't we?" Gustave pushed himself up into a sitting position and kissed her firmly on her tremulous lips as long as he could. She pressed his chest with her hands, nudging him back slightly.

"What do we do now, Gustave? I can't stay here with you!"

"Why not? Surely you aren't still afraid of humans!" He leaned forward and kissed her again, pulling her close. "I can protect you, you know. Forever. . ." He tried to kiss her again but she held him at bay, smiling the whole time. "It's not that, dear Gustave. . .I have too many things to do at home. This was just the start. . ."

Gustave had no intention of letting her know he too had plans of his own. But even so he would not mind having her beside him, anyway. He stroked the soft waves of her soft hair and let his hand rest on the front of her throat, where his fingers felt the throbbing of her pulse, echoing his own.

"You can't come with me, either. . ." Nell's brain

detected emotional imbalance, but it did not choose to overcompensate. Tears filled her eyes. She was not ready to let go, but she knew she had to.

"Why can't I come with you?" He was understandably disgruntled that she did not invite him to accompany her, even though he wasn't sure he could accept her offer.

"You have a lot of things to accomplish yourself!" She wiped at her damp cheeks with the back of her hand.

"Now, now, stop crying, Beautiful. . . I have a gift for you, but you'll have to smile again to get it. . ." He wasn't sure if his need to comfort her was because he missed her so badly or because he couldn't bear to see someone as pretty as she was crying. He straightened up into a fully seated position and cupped her face in both of his palms. Looking deeply into her eyes, he eased his mouth onto her soft lips and pressed them with his own in an emotionally charged kiss neither one had expected. They both closed their eyes, losing themselves in the merging of their heartbeats and their souls, aware there was a third entity present and it was the purest love they had for one another. Gustave transferred all the data he had collected from the instrumentation in the alien facility into her brain's receptors, taking only a few seconds to do so. Their mutual love and desire was actualized in an erotic but gently caring ecstasy, making them both reel with the power of it and also with humble gratitude at having found one another. Nell opened her eyes for a moment, then realized the scope of the information he was transferring to her, and only to her, she closed her eyes again and let herself absorb all he wanted to give her as well as opening herself up to him as deeply as she could. She knew she loved him with all her being and her heart and brain told him so. She also let him know his priceless information was safe with her.

Nell instantaneously perceived how to use the device and also knew this knowledge would help promote her to a very high rank, high enough to be awarded the command of her very own research facility, which would most likely be committed to getting the remote matter- assembler to work smoothly and error-free. She was so excited she could hardly breathe.

Suddenly, they both heard the sounds of several people approaching and knew it was K'ta and the rest of the team coming to congratulate Gustave. They were only seconds away from entering and Nell and Gustave shared the same thoughts. They could not risk letting the team see them in a loving embrace, at least not yet. They mutually agreed by thought transmission and by the time the team had entered, the two were discreetly apart and smiling a welcome at the newcomers.

K'ta walked in first. The grin on his face gave off a distinctive aura of friendly warmth. Bor and Milka followed in his footsteps and they were both happy to see him. Gustave stood up and was a little shaky at first, but after holding on to the edge of his cot for a few moments, he regained his balance.

"We are so happy to see you well, Gustave," K'ta

said, and the rest of the team nodded in agreement. "What was it like?"

"I'm happy to see all of you as well," Gustave replied. He was still a little lightheaded from standing up. "What was what like?" he answered, trying to keep his balance.

"The mission!" K'ta laughed. "In the shape you were in when we picked you up, I can't imagine the horrors you went through to get the device. What was the secret base like?"

"It wasn't easy, I'm…" He was suddenly reminded of what he found on the secret base. The prototypes from his childhood were used to work on that project. He couldn't trust them anymore so he had to make every effort to leak only necessary information to project a fake sense of trust in them. "The room was large but it was nothing more than a room, and I expected more of a base. They were able to penetrate my shield and caused me a lot of pain; how was that possible?"

K'ta looked at Milka, expecting her to arrive with answers.

"We're not quite certain, Gustave. . . My only explanation is they reprogrammed the nanonites on the fly. If that was the case, however, I'm not sure why they held on so long, they could have killed you in seconds having this ability." Milka said. She looked confused.

"I hope I will not experience any more circumstances like this again; I need some help with the practice rod you gave me K'ta. I used it as an additional shield. They must have focused a lot on programming it at the same time. But one by one, all three bots kept getting closer to me for some odd reason. You really are not accustomed to fighting, are you?"

"I must admit it was very clever of you, Gustave, although I don't remember allowing you to remove it from our ship. We put violence to rest hundreds of years ago; I suppose we were lucky in that sense. . ."

There was a moment of awkward silence. Gustave should have probably not mentioned stealing the practice rod, yet he was certain that considering it was most likely the one thing that kept him alive, and for being directly responsible for defeating the alien bots it should be fine.

"So, what's next? When are you leaving to go back to your space?" Gustave looked at each face in the group.

K'ta called for a group of chairs to be placed next to each person's position. The entire room, the bed on which he slept, the instruments and even the walls reformed themselves to accommodate the sitting arrangement. The morphing was very quick and then they all sat down.

"We are leaving soon, but not before we send you off with what we promised, Gustave. You did your part and now you must be thirsting for what we have promised." K'ta's tone was serene. His composed posture left no room for doubt that they were just about done with their exchange of technology.

Gustave still remained distrustful. "Just as we

talked about?" Gustave smiled. "May I request specific things, or will I have no say as to what will be released to us earthlings?"

Milka shrugged. Gustave noticed her but the attention of others was quickly focused on K'ta.

"What do you have in mind? What could humans benefit from most, Gustave?"

Gustave thought for a second. He knew he had already been given a technology that could eliminate any forthcoming financial issues he might have in the future, and not only that, the same technology would clean up the earth quite nicely. The next thing on his mind was space travel, but he was certain the Angelonians would not give even an explanation about how they travelled so fast in the vast spaces of the galaxy. Weapons were out of the question, but he had a few good ideas up his sleeve just for that anyway.

The opposite to warfare would be healing. Humans were a fragile specie. If he could cure sickness, diseases or generally help people live longer and better, it will be the next step for human beings. Not only that, this could bring him riches beyond what he could have possibly have foreseen. He looked at each person's face before speaking. "You know, twice I was brought up here to be fixed. I am pretty certain I would have been dead if it wasn't for the treatment I received here." The team looked at Gustave, hanging on every word. "After every time, I felt rejuvenated, as if my body was younger, under less stress and I generally felt great. I think the best thing for humans right now is something to treat ailments and injuries that is less barbaric than cutting up organs, using poisons to treat cancerous cells and many other methods of treatment which sometimes work and sometimes don't. I think what I'm asking for is for regenerative healing technology."

K'ta looked at Nell. It was her line of work, yet he felt strongly against it. "I'm sorry Gustave but we cannot provide you with this technology yet" K'ta chanted.

"Why not? We have been working on regenerative healing for years, we're just very slow at it. What could be so deeply risky for you to provide me with this?" Gustave stood his ground.

K'ta sighed. He wasn't quite sure why he shouldn't but was arming himself with a response. Yet before he could reply Gustave cut in—not in speech but he activated the viewing screen which began assembling mid-air out of the ship's nanobots. He was not supposed to have the ability to communicate with the ship. Nell had a self- conscious, embarrassed smirk on her face, but the rest of the team were taken aback.

"How are you…" K'ta said.

Again, Gustave paid most of his attention to himself, trying to illustrate his point. He began projecting images onto the screen. "Tell me, K'ta, when did you last see pictures of people suffering this much?"

On the screen, a montage of people mourning for their dead, kids in wheelchairs suffering from horrendous cancers. The display only got more and more gruesome. Looking at them, he could see they were distanced from having to know the pain of losing someone. They weren't however lacking in imagination of how tragic such an experience might be.

"Millions die. Ten times the ill ones get so sick they won't be able to cope with life. Many of them will have no pleasure of having any access to medical care. Are you prepared to tell me that this doesn't affect you? Are you telling me that after you stole technology that could help your cause to help humans against the bad judgment of the G.U you are suddenly going to let many of us perish through horrifying means?"

"Enough!" K'ta raised his voice. The screen evaporated.

"Not easy to watch is it?" Gustave continued, "If it's hard to watch, think how we feel, having these images as our reality.

"You are not ready for such technology, Gustave, there is too much anger and there is too much internal conflict and barbaric wars between humans. If someone got a hold of that technology…"

Gustave felt the urge to cut in again.

"Have you ever seen an injured animal other than myself, K'ta? You surely know that on earth, injured, beaten or discouraged animals are a lot more aggressive. It is then where they fear the most and it is then when they become over protective, and certainly violent."

K'ta breathed in, to collect enough air to respond, yet Gustave did not gave him any room to jump into the conversation. "Tell me K'ta, what's the point of warfare if you can't kill or hurt someone to make a point?"

K'ta thought for a moment and said, "Your wars are started by people who seek to destroy others for their ways of life which do not follow that of their own. I don't think they are afraid."

"Nonsense. Indeed they are directed via those outlets of justification but are fueled by the masses, mostly those who have very little and who are easily influenced into believing their governing bodies will be fair regarding their conditions once their targets are achieved. You cut the fuel, and you cut the burning flame. In all of our society, it is the sick and the poor who are more violent. Lacking education, they are very susceptive to a further destructive way of life. It can be viewed both within the countries and in international warfare. As an observer, you must agree."

"You've won that argument Gustave. Yet how will you be able to convince those who are overly passionate to realize that?"

"In time, K'ta in time. Introducing anything new is difficult for us humans. But we do strive to maximize our total utility. Eventually everyone can be helped."

A few moments passed when suddenly everyone's attention was shifted toward the sound of the ship's alarms. Gustave, having an armor which constantly examined and evaluated danger while being connected to some of the ship's systems, received the same message.

A coordinate was perceived close by. An armada was approaching them.

"Gustave, there's no time to explain. We must escape." K'ta spoke hurriedly. The room morphed again and they all rose to their feet.

"A great leader in earth's history once said 'healthy citizens are the greatest asset any country can have'. Gustave, you got what you asked for. Now, it's important you leave this ship immediately! Nell, provide him with the entire human medical tech, and be quick about it."

As the tactical officer, Milka found the urge to take charge of the situation they were in. "K'ta, if I may, it will be extremely unsafe for Gustave on earth. He will be much better off with us on the ship."

K'ta was not ready to be second guessed by his own people. He had a good idea the G.U would try to avoid landing on earth under all circumstances and would do as much as it takes to not step foot on it again. They all followed strict protocols and guidelines. Passing any of them would not be attempted by any politician and more than anyone, by a respected commanding officer of an expedition.

"Out of the question Milka! Go with Boris and help us plot an evasion course! At once!" K'ta ran out of the room as he spoke over his shoulder. There was no good bye or good luck. He simply raced out, leaving the rest of their team to follow his footsteps and attend to each of their responsibilities.

Nell approached Gustave. "Follow me Gustave, hurry, there is not much time"

They both left the room. From the corridor, Gustave noticed the fleet of biobots on the bottom deck of the ship scrambling around. They were preparing for something, although he did not know what were they planning to do to defend their ship.

"What's going to happen if they catch all of you, Nell?" Gustave asked.

"I'm not sure, Gustave. If they do catch us, then I will most likely be forbidden from ever stepping into a long distance shuttle again. It could be very long before I see you again."

Nell spoke in haste. She was busy with packing nanonites, rushing around, something which she was never too keen on doing, and at the same time making arrangements for the ship-earth transport as well as collecting all the information on human treatments and transferring them to Gustave's memory.

They made their way into a very bright small and circular shaped room.

She kissed him and said, "Thank you, Gustave, it was all worth it. . ."

Before he could react, he felt as if all his joints were paralyzed. Moments later, he lost his vision and speech.

He suddenly found himself on the floor of his apartment. His mind, still churning and trying to digest all that had happened before he returned there suddenly received a packet of information. The healing technology was safely and completely stored in his memory, available for him to access. He was ready to move on to the next step, now that he was back on earth.

Part Three

CONQUER

CHAPTER 50

Harry sat in the office overlooking the factory below through a massive glass viewing window next to the Plexiglas door. The room, high above the production line that in his mind resembled a nuclear test facility, was very spacious. Everything was in place, shiny instruments and robotic hands stationed next to conveyor belts were motionless, ready to begin work at any moment. It was quite lonely up there but Harry didn't mind.

Chris walked in from the corridor. "Gustave's back on the radar."

"And?" Harry asked in anticipation.

"And he told me he was visiting his parents and on his way here to start her up. About time. . ."

Harry lowered the book he was reading and placed it on the table. "We'd better inform security. . . they don't know him personally just yet. I would hate to delay him any longer. I think we've already waited long enough."

Harry's computer station featured all the master security monitors. The large table accommodated much of the equipment and computers that were connected to other levels of security. The entire facility, designed by

Harry himself, housed a very sophisticated system that was modeled after the same security systems which he was accustomed to using for AMET.

A proximity sensor located in a distant corner of the property of the land was activated by an approaching vehicle.

Harry received a call from the head of security requesting further instructions. It was the first time in days that a vehicle had approached the area and the first time when a vehicle was not scheduled to arrive.

"This must be Gustave. . ." Harry whispered to himself.

Chris, overlooking the screen connected to a camera located close to the sensor noticed a fast moving black sports car that zoomed in swiftly. Not just any sports car but a Morgan.

"That's Gustave all right," Chris said smiling.

Harry picked up the hand set of the phone and pressed the intercom button. "Do not shoot or disable the vehicle. Prepare the entire team for a frontal encounter. Hold for further instructions until we come in."

"Yes sir," a man's voice replied.

He placed the phone back in its socket and rose from his chair. "I don't know about you Chris, but I'm damned excited."

"Yeah, I always wanted to see one up-close!" Chris laughed. "Indeed, it's about time!"

* * *

Gustave could see the facility as he approached the guarded entrance. He was smiling with anticipation himself, as he realized this was the first time he would actually see something he had envisioned in all of his most elaborate fantasies. A company of his own, a large facility where he was to be the honcho who drives in with a fancy car, nodded at respectfully by a security guard and allowed to enter a palace of innovation and wealth.

As he approached the gates he was greeted with a far less welcoming party than he had expected. There were twenty guards aiming heavy artillery and machine guns directly at his newly purchased vehicle. Watch towers equipped with machined sniper rifles and company marked security vehicles were on alert above the entire formation. His armor calculated the fire power to be enough cause for alarm to the point where he had to calm himself down, or more so, to calm his armor down, knowing that he was in no danger, unless both of his trusted allies had betrayed him. The thought did pop up in his head, but he knew Chris well enough to know that nothing of that sort would ever happen between them.

An unarmed security guard, put his hands up in the air to signal the car to slow down and stop. "Please stop the car for inspection, sir." A voice from a megaphone reverberated in the air. It was loud enough to drown out the deep mechanical sound of the engine.

He complied.

The Guard, armed with a heavy-duty weapon and wearing a bullet proof vest, approached the vehicle slowly. He held an electronic tablet used to communicate with the security database. The guard looked at the tablet and then at Gustave.

"Good afternoon, sir. I was instructed to detain you until Mr. Escher and Mr. Timpleton could welcome you properly. . ."

"Very well." Gustave answered calmly. "Tell me, why are you pointing those weapons toward me, knowing who I am?"

"Protocol for entry to everyone that gets close at all times, regardless of rank or level in the company, sir."

"Harry has done well. . ."

"Yes, sir."

From a distance, a truck with flapping tarpaulin approached, raising a cloud of dust behind it. A text message on Gustave's phone read, "We're coming we're coming! And you'd better let me drive it, Buster!"

Gustave laughed, knowing they both shared the same enthusiasm for special, exotic cars. Knowing his might cause some envy in Chris, he ordered another one in white, especially for Chris in his favorite color. He would surprise him later. He was too excited about seeing the facility and examining every inch of his new home.

* * *

After a thorough examination of the lay-out, Gustave made his way to the fabrication lab. The lab was a key feature in the facility. It allowed Gustave to communicate with software, design, and prototype anything he could ever possibly envision. There were a few things missing necessary for the development and production of the crud nanonites required for the healing technology which the Angelonians had provided, yet he knew what he required, and he knew the company would first need to start generating a large profit margin to allow for the purchase and design of the kind of fabrication he wanted.

Combining the information they gave him with the strange insight he had into the complete structure of advanced nanonites technology, he was certain things should be fairly easy to bring up to the level of the Angelonians'standards.

After spending several hours in the lab, it was time for the machines to get to work, producing the first of many core reactors that would be shipped from the in-house factory.

There was no need for human touch for the production of the entire line. Everything would be automated, everything assembled via robotic arms and precise automated machinery.

This reduced the costs down the line but more than anything it eradicated most if not all of the risks for leaks.

Gustave emerged from the lab and called Harry to meet him in the office.

Still learning the area, it took him a little more time than he had expected to find his own office but eventually he finally made it.

Harry was waiting outside the door. "You found it!"

"Took me some time, but here we are…" Gustave laughed. He hadn't had a chance to use his own office yet, but he was looking forward to spending a lot of time behind that cherry-wood desk. The offict was spacious, lavish, slick and modern. Chris knew Gustave all too well and obviously knew what type of furnishings he would like.

For the first time he sat in his ergonomic leather swivel chair. He felt at home, and a sense of satisfaction filled him with pride and confidence. "Just a few more hours until we can try the new prototypes. . .please have a seat Harry, I have several questions."

Harry sat down in the arm chair across from Gustave, on the other side of his desk. "Of course! Anything specific on your mind? How do you like what we've done with the facility?"

"You've done a wonderful job, Harry, both of you have. We just have to make it more comfortable for us to live in, but I'm sure this could be easily arranged. Now, I've been away for some time; what happened with AMET? I have not seen a mention in today's news."

"You got rid of them for now, of that I have no doubt. The news? One by one, each report, each document you've exposed, got dismissed as a hoax. There was no evidence backing anything that was written. They said it was some genius lunatic that glued random facts together in a schizophrenic fashion. The public was outraged at first, the media enjoyed the turmoil, but after courts and trials failed at convicting most of the high officials, there was not much to report. Some of the people did get some jail time, and will stay there for a while but mostly for tax fraud charges and nothing more. That's where things got shifted toward political frauds, money laundering with the army, and a few other interesting things which were not surprisingly reported accurately. Gustave, the network of politicians and army officials is extended everywhere, especially in the news media. These things are hushed up frequently, often well before they even reach the public. It was smart of you to get the information widely available to everyone but this only created a large group of conspiracy theorists rather than shedding light on the true colors of the organization. Politicians are never to be trusted, they are elected to represent the citizen's voice but always turn to their own agendas through a network based on greed and fear."

Gustave was disappointed. He was hoping for a much needed change, a change that would make the battleground for his campaign much easier to navigate but that was not to be.

"Very soon it will all change. . ."

"What do you have in mind Gustave?" Harry looked worried. He was aware of Gustave's powers and his association with the aliens and knew that if anyone, Gustave, soon to be the owner of unlimited resources, would have the ability to act on his intentions.

"Harry, you have a strong military experience, quite a substantial one actually. I didn't choose you just so you would have a nice desk position in my company. No, I'll need you for much more than that. You see, I'm not a big fan of how things are run here on earth. No one seems to like the conditions on this planet much, except those who are in power, and even they would like to sculpt the world to fit their patterns. I have my own intentions, not only to bring new technology that will give us earth residents a better place to live in, but will assure us a position among the stars."

"I'm not sure I understand."

Gustave leaned back in his chair and said, "This world is a complete mess. We are considered savages by the other races."

"Why do they keep coming here, though?"

"The ones that look like us? They come here for the same reason we would go visit caves. Or find it amusing to visit theme parks of the Wild West, ancient Rome, or go visit Egypt and marvel at their grand achievements despite their low tech solutions to difficult problems. It's fascinating."

"And the ones that don't look like us?" Harry asked.

Gustave didn't know the answer to his question, to delay a response he asked, "To which ones do you refer?"

"The gray ones, for example, the Krill visited us more than anyone else, they were very helpful to us according to the agency, well, at least until they cut all connection with us…"

Gustave laughed, "The Krill are Angelonian robots–Very sophisticated ones but robots nonetheless."

"You mean that…"

"I mean the Angelonians have good reasons not to land here on earth. For one, they are afraid of our unpredictable nature and on the other hand, they are absolutely incapable of harming us, not directly at least."

Harry tried to assimilate all the information Gustave was revealing. He had joined the agency a long time ago, but had not had access to the databases until several months ago. He read as much as he could from the documents released to the public by Gustave—The reports, the encounters and the many documents profiling the species, none of which had much information about the aliens themselves other than their categories, their shapes, and vehicles— Being on the dark side of the conspiracy organization for so many years, he was aching to learn more, and Gustave seemed to have obtained a substantial amount of information.

"What do the others want with us? How many are there?"

Gustave had to stop Harry. For one, he did not know the answers to these questions.

"None of that is important right now. We have to focus on earth before we look up to the stars, Harry. And once the time is right, believe me when I say you will not only have the answers to these questions, you would have had the ability to find out about them for yourself. There is great room for expansion in this company, Harry. You will have all the benefits of not only being a part of them, but taking an active part in changing the course of history of this planet. My question is, are you ready to be a part of that global change?"

Harry stood up out of respect for the gravity of the responsibility facing them both. "Yes Gustave. I am ready and prepared to do whatever it takes"

"Even if that meant a complete conquest over Earth and the forging of one unified world government?"

Harry was terrified by the idea. He wasn't sure if he was standing in front of a lunatic super villain dictator with ambitions to rule earth, or the next hegemon of earth. He was certainly not prepared to follow someone with these sorts of ambitions. He swallowed and cleared his throat, then spoke the only words that occurred to him to be apropos. "Excuse me?"

CHAPTER 51

After several hours of intense conversation, Gustave and Harry had covered nearly every aspect of the situation. And in those hours, Gustave had succeeded in assuaging Harry's doubts. Harry's background in the military helped Gustave carefully forge the plan which spanned across both military and political fronts, both presenting several key elements which had to be treated with the utmost care.

There were two outcomes foreseeable to the campaign. One resulting in a complete and utter failure and the other a complete mess. Being who he was, Harry suspected the last.

Gustave summoned Chris to the fabrication lab where the three met to discover the machines had completed the prototypes. Several cores stood there, waiting to be inserted into the already manufactured battery shells, which were a marvel of engineering in their own right that had yet to be realized on earth. Gustave had no doubt the cores would work. He had run many simulations using his alien-earth-made hybrid computer.

"Harry, Chris. Please, each of you grab one core

and help me take them to the main room." Gustave was holding one of the cores in his hands. It was a fairly light octahedron-shaped fixture. It had no other features other than a very dark brushed-chrome enclosure which had no screws or any other openings.

"It can't explode can it?" Chris asked in a sincere tone. He knew that this could power up a car or a house for several years, so something in there must have some sort of incredible energy stored.

Gustave laughed nervously. "Oh yes, it can. But worry not, it will implode, and then only in the event if it encounters a force that tries to open it. It's very strong shell and will not shatter under many G's of impact neither will it cause any harm to any one in its proximity. It's completely safe!"

"No one will be able to reproduce it that way. . . very smart!" Chris said.

"Correct. The casing will not allow it to be opened without the entire core being destroyed and inner deflectors don't allow for any type of waves to bounce back in case anyone wished to examine the inside using remote access."

While the aliens provided the technology, as well as several material mixtures to allow for a very strong build, Gustave himself designed and developed the extra protection against industrial theft. It was very easy for him to implement several technologies he had access to through his armor and bring them into his design using what was available. All he needed to do was to ask himself the right questions and the armor and the computer hybrid did the rest.

They walked to the main room. The shells, although not as sophisticated as the cores, were essential to the entire output process of the core's energy. They featured an opening into which the cores were to be precisely inserted. Once inside, Gustave rotated the octahedron into the right position where it locked into place and confirmed its level of activity through a high pitched sound. The battery powered up. It was obvious through the light emitted from the shell itself, which was bright orange and made it look as if it were incredibly hot.

"Behold the future. Beautiful isn't it?" Gustave marveled at the device. For a moment he felt as if it were he who had invented the technology, forgetting those who had given it to him as an offering of peace. Both Chris and Harry were amazed by the display of light and the dim thunder sound of the battery.

"Go ahead. Place yours in the other shells too and follow me. . ."

They inserted the cores into shells, then they both followed Gustave to the power section of the factory. A part of Gustave's instructions and blueprints required the electricity area of the factory be fitted with an odd looking cabinet, which was specially made by a factory in Austria, connected to the main power lines. Once opened, it revealed a grid where many holes shaped to match the outlines of the batteries, allowed for the devices to be inserted.

Gustave examined one of the switches outside the cabinet and inserted one battery. "Go ahead, insert yours." He gestured for Chris and Harry to do the same.

The two of them placed the batteries they were holding into matching grooves, then he walked to the main power toggle and said, "Harry, Please let security know we are switching on power. I wouldn't want them to be jumpy."

Harry made the call.

"You see, these devices recognized the requested power output. They will automatically adjust to the needs and requirements of whatever it is they are connected to through several resistance tests that happen in split seconds. There is no need to manufacture every different type of power generators to many different systems." While speaking, he shut off the main electricity to the factory. Generators automatically kicked in but he quickly disabled them as well. He then toggled the main switch adjacent to the battery cabinet. The entire factory came back to life.

Chris, incredulous, placed his hands on his hips. Harry stroked his beard. They both were awestruck.

"Not only will we save on the electric bill, no one will be able to hack into our systems through those power grids. I've had that happen to me before, but it won't happen with this beauty." Gustave smiled, very pleased with himself.

CHAPTER 52

It was several months before enough units were ready to ship to the public. A decision was made first to approach the public and only then, when the demand was high both from the news media and the consumers, were they to contact car companies' regulation organizations and other comparable groups to evoke sales or to voluntarily test their device.

In the meantime, the team had designed several other devices built to be operational with their batteries. These were things that would make the transfer to their core power technology a lot easier and much more accessible to the mass market.

When they finally approached the media, they were disregarded as a hoax. However, after many live demonstrations, free samples to universities and countless other efforts it was clear the Global Technology Products Corporation, or GTP Co. as they named their company, changed the world.

The stock market collapsed under the news. Each day brought with it another catastrophe as a result of weary stock holders getting rid of their stocks anchored by the energy market. Oil companies tumbled one after another, even though there had not been one device by GTP shipped for the masses demanding its supply.

It was important to remind the public frequently and repeatedly inform them of the company's intentions so Gustave authorized the following Press Release:

"We will be shipping in several months. It takes both time and a lot of effort to manufacture this technology. I don't see why GTP should be accused of causing any harm to the economy while all we are doing is making this planet a better place to live in. Fingers ought to be pointed towards economic speculators and the stock market in general."

To the countless demands for factory tours, Gustave replied, "A certain few will be allowed in but under no circumstance will we allow a public viewing of our factory. The factory is a private and restricted area. Any unauthorized attempts to break in will encounter heavy security measures and will conclude with a legal repercussions and, if necessary, a lethal security force!"

And many attempts there were. Mercenaries, spies, and other buffoons hired to penetrate the facility by oil tycoons, energy companies, and other organizations were all caught. No matter how much money Gustave had left in the bank, it was necessary for him to request enormous loans which were spent equally on buying more raw materials and reinforcing security. Although no one was allowed into the factory itself, many patrolled the surrounding areas while others took charge of keeping an eye on those who surrounded it and others kept a close eye on those.

The procedure was to report anything suspicious. With the promise of great rewards, it was impossible for one single security person or even a few to plot anything as others would be quick to report to the authorities and receive a grateful bonus.

Those who got caught were quickly thrown out of the facility, but not before their entire operation was exposed to the media and the police alongside incriminating evidence.

While in the beginning those attempts made Gustave extremely angry he eventually warmed up to them, enjoying the interrogating and submitting the people to the police with evidence that eventually led to the people who were in charge of the plot. One by one they all got caught and with them large corporation executives, charged with conspiracy and attempts of corporate espionage, faced heavy fines, none of which they could afford considering the economic turmoil and/or long jail times.

Several days before they were to ship their first order, Harry ran into Gustave's office. He was out of breath and his face was flushed dark red.

"We have a problem!" Harry burst through the door as if it weren't there.

"Jeez, you scared me!" Gustave jumped from his chair. "What is it?"

"One of the contractors who built this place submitted some designs to another corporation." Harry was breathing heavily from the panic.

"The virus…" Still trying to gather his breath he continued, "The virus you implanted onto the CAD drawings was picked up by a signal from another location. . ."

"File number? Did you get the file number?"

"Hold on. . ." Harry leaned over the computer keyboard and retrieved the file number through the file distribution sever. "Bastards!" Even though there was no way to back-engineer the manufacturing of the battery through it, it was an important file nonetheless. Harry began chanting the number but was stopped by Gustave.

"I think we played nice until now. This will have to be treated differently."

"Gustave, we're very close to shipping products, we can't be involved with anything that is not done by the books!"

"But we can't let it slide either, can we now? What if others managed to evade the program that was supposed to delete these files automatically? What if they all start selling these to one group?"

"Well, we can do some counter-intelligence. We contact them anonymously and try to see if they got anything, at the same time we contact people in the black market and announce we have some information on GTP. See what comes up. We detain the people that take the bait. We'll keep them for some time. Scare them a little.

It will create fear among them. That is the best way to go about it. Can I have the liberty to send some men on that mission?"

Gustave thought for a few moments. Harry did make a good point. While he preferred to weed out all these companies in another way, it would be best if they could keep from having any bad publicity.

"Good idea. Go ahead and keep me updated with the progress. Harry, I can't emphasize enough how important it is we find these people."

"You can count on me, sir!" Harry, his color almost back to normal, raced out of the office, his lab coat flying behind him like an airborne rudder.

* * *

Several days passed. The company launched its first armada of shipments. Each truck carried tens of thousands of core-power batteries; their destinations were sea ports and airports to be carried outside the country or transferred within intercontinental routes.

The machines manufactured the devices faster than trucks could load them up. There were strict protocols by which truck drivers were allowed to approach the base. While they waited in a designated area, trucks came out of the facility to load secured crates onto the outside trucks. Coming back into the facility required a thorough inspection of every inch of the vehicle. The entire process was designed to prevent even a glitch or a bump that could potentially risk the entire operation.

Large computer companies, car manufacturers, housing companies, and various governmental contracts provided GTP with an unimaginable influx of cash. The privately held corporation was now the only company in history to have more wealth than several countries combined. GTP and Gustave were mentioned every second in media in every part of the world.

In an effort to redeem the company's overwhelming presence in the financial world, Gustave, together with several financial firms, bought out failing companies and distributed some of the company's wealth toward rejuvenating the world's nose-diving economy.

The tactic was quite simple. A buyout of a failing company, complete renovation and allocation of its workers toward other tasks, even though some were anything but happy about their new assignments. However that didn't stop Gustave from gaining the positive fame he so desperately sought with numerous public relations' efforts.

The company grew larger and larger, and with it many of its newly built facilities flourished across the world. It was important for the company to have a global footprint. Of course, none of the other facilities featured any production of GTP's technology but instead were assigned other products to manufacture.

It took less than a year for new laboratories to be opened several miles outside GTP's main facility. The labs' facility accommodated structures for testing and fabricating new technology, most of which would later be used for the production of nanonites. Gustave carefully planned the production of the nanonites and did hire a fleet of scientists to work on the smart materials. He often gave them directions and provided schematics showing how to approach the production of the new smart materials however, he kept most of the important formulas and operating details to himself, such as nano-mechanics, movements, and especially methods by which these tiny molecule-sized materials could communicate with each other. Testing out viral manufacturing was crucial to the process. His main challenge was to figure out a way to create stem bots—nanonites which would manufacture their own kind out of raw materials.

Eventually, he realized it was all coming together.

Chris was relocated to the corporate offices in the city, where he took charge of all financial aspects of the business, such as the company's wealth, accounting departments, as well as all new business ventures. Harry was nowhere to be seen. He worked on a remote island which Gustave had bought with cash under an anonymous name. It was agreed the authorities, through various under the table arrangements, would not venture into the area. Any attempt of satellite spying was quickly dispersed as Gustave, having the ability to connect to all satellites specifically programmed a blind spot. The army, after many spying attempts sending in repair crews or launching new satellites, always stumbled upon the same blind spot.

First-hand attempts at unauthorized surveillance also met with failure. Navy ships malfunctioned, as their electronics were taken over by sophisticated defense systems on the island. Divers got caught and were sent away peacefully. Gustave and Harry had no intention of creating any more conflicts than they were already experiencing.

The Army, one of Gustave's biggest consumers, showed modest impatience with the company. Gustave kept in close touch with their senior officers on a regular basis; they frequently requested factory visits for what they termed' quality inspection', often waiving the option to back out of large future purchases if Gustave would not allow them some access, but Gustave did not fear those threats. On the contrary, he often joked about them with other high-ranking officials.

One would say GTP changed the world not only because they became the leader in the global economy but also the first in human history that had the largest beneficial impact on human lives. Yet the world was soon going to change once more. Only this time, the change would alter the fabric of society itself.

CHAPTER 53

Gustave was extremely glad to be back in his luxurious apartment, which occupied an entire floor of the GTP building towering over the city. After he finished unpacking and straightening up, he relaxed in his chair. He had checked through his email messages, noting any updates on his projects. There were numerous invitations to events, galas, and charity fundraisers jamming his inbox. After several years of attending similar events, he was tired of such shallow gatherings with fake smiles and a generous check-book.

And then there were the events which spawned a media hoopla, several of those in which he found himself dodging bullets from assassins and other scum. He had known this might happen, because he had been going after the oil companies which were surely to seek revenge, and he had requested no photographers or videographers attend any event to which he was invited. Or at least, he tried making certain they disappeared before he was to appear.

All cameras featured some form of distance-measurement sensors to calculate focal length accurately in one form or another, which made it very easy to locate them and disable their electronics.

People knew there was more technology in GTP's hands than they would like disclosed yet fear of the man who could actually purchase an entire country if he so desired made publishers nervous about printing propaganda against him. It wasn't that such propaganda didn't occur on the internet, yet many people who had experienced a positive impact by the GTP corporate, didn't want to bother Gustave's peculiar camera-shy status.

Gustave didn't want the cameras for other obvious reasons. He knew when he was to be facing an assassin, his armor would cause so much stir it would be impossible for people to ignore his abilities. It wasn't the right time to reveal them to the public, but the day was approaching.

Gustave had invited Chris and Harry, who had just came back from the island after a long stay, to drop in for a friendly visit. It felt nice to look forward to the company of the two associates in private again because he was about to reveal to them the regeneration technology. While they both knew bits and pieces about what Gustave was working on, they had no complete picture or much information to fill in the details.

Gustave's apartment, in addition to having massive areas of open space was organized very neatly with dark wood and stylish Swedish modern furniture which complimented some pale grey Berber carpeting in several spaces, and light ash flooring on others. The clean lines of the sleek furniture pieces, most made of highly-polished teak, were a lot like Gustave himself: nothing superfluous anywhere, ready for heavy work at a moment's notice, no useless clutter taking up valuable time or space. What little metal was visible on the furnishings was brushed chrome and an occasional splash of vivid color added just the right touch of warmth. The throw pillows on the long sofa facing the wall of glass overlooking the bubbling fountain shooting up from the middle of the artificial lake below picked up the colors in the Picasso original on the wall behind, which in turn echoed the brilliance of a sunset. Gustave, being an avid enthusiast of design, arranged his living space with much care, with no consideration of costs, since there really was no problem with expense. And it most certainly showed, although unlike many incredibly wealthy people, he deliberately avoided ostentatious display.

The house phone on the console near the door rang, indicating a call from the floor desk. It was the security guard announcing Harry's arrival.

"Right on time, very well! Show him right up. . ." He smiled in anticipation and made his way to the kitchen where a specially crafted electric wine storage unit stood next to the refrigerator. He felt certain Chris, who didn't need any invitation, would follow shortly so he prepared the toasting glasses.

Moments later the doorbell rang.

Gustave opened the door to discover both Harry and Chris who lived on the floor below. They had synchronized their entrance.

"Ah! Gentleman, a toast awaits!" Shaking hands with Chris, he then turned his attention to Harry. "Great to have you back in civilization Harry! And I admire your new mustache!" He gave him a manly hug.

"Glad to be back Gustave!" His friends smiled with pleasure at seeing Gustave again.

"Please come in, make yourself at home. . ." Gustave, dressed in comfortable chocolate brown silk slacks with a lemon-yellow cashmere sweater walked toward the kitchen, returning in a few moments with a bottle of Perrier-Jouët and three Champagne flutes. Pouring the golden colored beverage into the glasses, he raised his in a toast. "We're ready for the next GTP product, guys!" He said jubilantly. "Santé!" he cheered, and drank from his glass.

Harry and Chris were not prepared for such news, but they joined Gustave in the toast, clinking their glasses against his.

"Gustave, I don't mean to be a wet blanket but is this the auspicious moment to finally find out what it is?" Chris enquired.

Gustave seemed a little too cheery. He poured himself another drink and quickly drank most of that as well. " Well, you are just about to see it working for yourselves!" He looked at them with a crooked grin. "Follow me to my study! Another refill?"

They both nodded in acknowledgment.

* * *

The study was equipped with computers, silent servers and scores of other gadgetry which Gustave had accrued. The room looked to be in disarray, but on second glance, even the disarray was organized. Everything was in its place, as Gustave wanted it to be.

In the center of the room a solid aluminum machine stood on a table, doughnut shaped; it resembled a miniaturized MRI and was connected to a computer screen.

"I present you with the Semi Auto-regenerative tissue repair unit, SARTRU-1." Gustave grinned proudly and bowed at the waist with a flourish of his hands.

"What exactly does it do Gustave?" Chris' mouth was agape and his eyes were stretched wide.

"What we have here is the future of medicine, of course this is a miniature prototype, and they will actually be much larger eventually."

The two men moved closer to the device to inspect it in more detail.

"What does it do?" Chris was still unsure what he was looking at.

Gustave was expecting them to ask questions and instead of answering them he thought it would be a good idea simply to show them how the device works, in fact, that was the reason for his drinking a bit more than usual. "I better show you. Come close will you?"

Gustave then turned to another table and picked up a clean paring knife. The next phase was the tricky bit—to convince the nanonites in his armor to move as he needed to an unprotected area in his hand— the other part was to somehow block his armor's automatic defense from disallowing any sharp object to harm his body.

"I'm going to cut myself and you'll see in a moment."

"You are going to do what?" Harry's face was the color of white marble.

"I'm going to insert this knife into the left palm of my hand and show you how this machine works," Gustave repeated.

Harry, after seeing Gustave being shot at by bullets, was taken aback to think this was even possible. "Gustave, this is crazy, it's a prototype, you said so yourself, what if it doesn't work?"

"Then I'll look pretty silly, won't I?" Gustave laughed.

Chris was very quiet. He wasn't sure how he should have reacted to what Gustave was about to do. The thought of offering his hand to test the machine did pass through his mind and yet it did just pass through. It wasn't because he did not believe it will work, it was merely that having his hand cut and bleeding seemed all too uncomfortable.

After much concentration and effort Gustave

managed to insert the knife through his skin and deep into his hand, making a painful cut. Taking the knife out with the other hand, proved to be a little more painful than he had imagined. It was stuck in the table, and considering he tried to be quick about getting it in there, he used much force his armor projected quite an amount of torque.

After moments of consideration he did the only thing he could have done which was to remove the foreign object from his hand. While his alcohol intake did dull some of the pain, he still sustained an abundance of pain, enough to cause him to cry out through clenched teeth.

Blood was gushing from his hand which was painfully throbbing from the open wound. Not a moment too soon, he asked Harry to go to the screen and press the start button.

"Which one is that, Gustave?"

"That big green button that says START!" he yelled.

The machine began its processing. It moved forward and backward on a slide groove emitting strong light and ozone-like odors.

"I pre-programmed it to the type of injury I have, and it is now scanning to assess the tissue and nerve damage. . ."

The machine stopped. The screen flickered with imagery and a lot of information about the damage caused by the blade. It even assessed the force of impact and the type of blade used to reach its recommended type of treatment.

Still bleeding, and holding his hand tightly to stop the blood flow he asked, "What does it say? How many pallets? Harry!"

"It asks for one pallet; what is that?"

"I'll explain in a moment. On the table, you see a small container; use a rubber glove to open it and insert one into the sucking hole on the right, here. . ." he pointed with his nose.

Harry opened the container to see several dozens of pill-shaped pallets gray in color and extremely heavy for their size.

He inserted a pallet to the small opening which, until Gustave told him its whereabouts, he had not even noticed.

Through the aluminum metal they saw lights in many shapes and colors sequenced in a dazzling display. A moment later a loud high pitched sound gushed out of the machine, as if air escaped from a container in one single blow.

The area between the hand and the empty space of the circular tube suddenly darkened, as if a small cloud of dust emerged from the machine.

The gray fog rapidly began disappearing as if it was being sucked into Gustave's hand.

The pain quickly stopped. It wasn't that the wound healed just yet, but the smart particles blocked pain which was unnecessary to treat the wound. The bleeding also stopped.

Retrieving his hand from the machine he then brought it closer for the two to examine.

It was healing rapidly. Since pain was no longer an issue, Gustave used his other thumb for spreading the exposed flesh for better visibility.

It almost looked as though the inside of his hand was metallic. Slowly, the metallic color disappeared as more and more tissues got reconnected and repaired. The wound was clearly healing from the inside out and slowly closing.

Chris closed his mouth and managed to whisper, "It worked!"

"Just wait a second. . ." Gustave intoned with his palm still open.

From his hand they noticed gray dust being collected and piled, as it was coming out from the inside of his hand while forming a gray pallet, the same size and shape that it was when Harry had inserted it.

"Indeed it does!" Gustave smiled as he handed Chris the pallet. "This one will have to be reset and treated in a micro nutrients solution, but you get the picture. Now, who besides me needs another drink?"

They both looked at Gustave. Without speaking a word, they raised their glasses in an admiring salute.

Back in the living room, the three men sat down on the comfortable sofas which were organized neatly around an electronic fireplace.

Chris, who had too many questions to be asked,

took a sip from his glass before asking, "To what extent can it treat people? Are we talking about diseases and cancer as well? What does it cost to manufacture on a large scale?"

Gustave replied, "It will be able to cure any damages caused by a disease but it won't get rid of the disease itself just yet. Cancer, yep, very much so, all types of it in fact. It will replace damaged tissue, fix it, and rearrange mutated cells down to their core. The machine is quite capable of diagnosing mutated, deformed and damaged tissue. It needs the proper guidance though, because it's not fully automated. I don't expect it to replace the medical profession but just used as a diagnostic tool to fix the human body."

"And the costs?"

"This is where it gets interesting Chris, the costs for each machine will be quite substantial, yet we should probably subsidize them heavily. It will be good for our image."

Chris's face soured. "Good for our image? You found a cure for everything, what more do you need to prove than that? We can't lose money on this, Gustave. We can afford to lose money, but have to think about further expansion."

"Oh, I'm quite certain we'll make that money, and quite a bit of it from the pallet sales. They can be sold at high value compared to their production costs. The nanobots need only be produced once and then replenished with the proper nutrients. I'm quite sure you will be able to figure out a price that will make them profitable to our company and yet affordable to the consumers. Oh yeah, I have to mention these smart microbots do reproduce when instructed to, so we shouldn't have to worry about the costs of their production one bit."

"Yes, I can see that working out from a business point of view, Gustave. But how is it even possible? I'm still in disbelief. I've seen you invent some crazy ideas but you've never before had any interest in medical technologies or the human body."

Gustave had expected this comment. "Chris, this was a combined effort with a group whose identity I'd like under wraps for now."

"And what are their shares? What sort of agreement will we be entering with them?" Chris was worried.

Gustave glazed at Harry and pointed at Chris with a grin on his face "Look at him, always worried about business! I like that! I expect nothing less. Chris, I can assure you that in time you will find out who they are, well before anyone else does, and our agreements have already been fulfilled. They wanted nothing to do with the business and the company."

"I'm not sure I understand. . ." Chris said. It seemed unrealistic, that a participating party would want nothing to do with the profits that would come out of this technology, and if not profit, at least the recognition.

Gustave, noticing Chris was still dissatisfied,

continued. "They will get the recognition in time, when the time is right, until then, I'm telling you it will all be all right! Don't worry about it!"

"And when will we, and by we, I mean us, when will Harry and I have the pleasure of knowing who these people are?"

"I suspect shortly after we release the technology to the public."

"The army will want their hands on these, I can guarantee you that. . ." Harry whispered.

"No doubt they will," Chris agreed.

Gustave rose stiffly from his chair and made his way to the kitchen, speaking over his shoulder. "But they won't get any exclusivity I'll tell you that; everyone will be able to buy this. Everyone."

Harry knew the reasons behind his remark. He knew Gustave had sowed the first seedlings of the grand scheme of things several years earlier.

Perhaps he had been preparing for this day for quite some time now, but preparations were merely something to pass the time and to help eliminate the fear the day might bring.

CHAPTER 54

Humans don't welcome change gracefully, not even a change for the better. While some might embrace it from the start, the vast majority will have to be gradually acclimatized to the change, sometimes after a lengthy passage of time. Pointing a finger at them would do no good as it could be equally argued that everyone fears the unknown. Some will eagerly jump ahead and see it as an adventure and others will follow. There is no point in saying one way is better than the other. The jumpers of the group might foolishly put too much trust in unseen forces to save them from the unknown, and the followers might as well be labeled as too inhibited. And then there is a group of people who at one point decided they did not have the right either to follow or to jump and lead, but chose to engineer whatever it is they expect others to jump into or follow.

Gustave belonged to that group.

There was no bone in his body that opposed the idea of forging the world the way he felt was best and most advantageous for all concerned. Regardless of the good natured ideologies on which the edifice of his global plans were built, he possessed an unfortunate and tragic trait, common among the many others of his group - Omni foresight – which was a grand vision accepting no failure and with it, an almost stupendous lack of risk management. That is to say their vision was falsely ensconced comfortably under many layers of self-reassurance.

After an incredible amount of labor to bring it to market, receive all the necessary approvals from the different administrations (quite often, Gustave pulled strings and greased palms), the healing machine was brought to the public.

As Gustave estimated, it didn't take long before the company began generating profit solely from the pallets. The demand was high, and more and more uses were found for the healing powers of the technology, which no laboratory technicians could analyze. While it served as a very affordable solution to treat people efficiently it was also used for keeping people alive much longer than under standard medicine. There were unwanted side effect however, but not from the machine itself. People worried less about injuring themselves or others and thus crime rates went through the roof.

To Gustave it seemed illogical. In his mind, if people knew they would not be able to hurt each other seriously they would probably, at one point or another, resolve disputes and reach reasonable resolutions via other means, yet people proved him wrong. For them it was like an all-you-can-eat buffet. Then again, people were more compelled to tell about their disputes but most of the low life criminals did not see that far, other than having shorter penal sentences.

Gustave approached this scenario by donating large amounts of money to the police in many cities to help curtail the rising crime rate. While it took considerable time, the more patrol on the streets and more people living to tell the story of a crime, resulted in illegal activities declining eventually to levels never seen before. Of course, jails and penitentiaries grew in numbers and became more populated, yet Gustave, under a charitable subsidiary of GTP, provided funding as well as astonishing amounts of cash donations to keep criminals off the streets. He did request some to be transferred to a rehabilitation facility constructed by GTP to test non-physical rehabilitation studies on prisoners.

While officials did not object, the media featured this development in headlines for a week until reporters were invited to the facilities to examine the methods, the prisoners, and their accommodations.

Everyone lacked the capacity to know Gustave was doing human testing on the mind- freeze technology, which he managed to coax out of Nell. He tried combining it with several other methods to keep criminals from wanting to commit a violent act and perhaps in doing so, speed up the methods by which the Angelonians used to cause their kind to avoid physical confrontation, but he kept failing. Humans were really hard-wired to protect themselves, however they saw fit and regardless of whether they were right or not. The general conclusion was this would have to be an evolutionary process. Some of the technology developed at the institute was to be used for other purposes, such as short term and long range mind anesthesia, and the ability to recognize and profile violent tendencies. With unlimited finances it was easy to acquire connections of the highest order in political circles. The entire world functioned on GTP

products, cxcept for much of the petroleum-controlled parts of the Middle East where GTP products were forbidden. Entire economies thrived under the safety of GTP.

Gustave, with the help of Chris, sought after and purchased controlling shares in many companies, which in turn gave GTP access to many different markets.

Many admired the GTP brand and considered Gustave to be the savior of humankind, a title for which the opponents of Gustave and GTP used to propagate alongside other not so favorable names. And there were quite a few of those.

There were the followers, the jumpers, the leaders, and, of course, the one remaining group completing the spectrum of animal attitude toward change, those who shunted off all change disregarding it as dangerous and hostile to their way of life. While these animals faded away from the pages of history, erased by the ever-changing lines of evolution, their type never became extinct as it was often a social trait forged by their collective surroundings rather than the environment itself.

* * *

"Sir, Mister and Mrs. Eisenstein are here to see you. . ."

The voice was that of Heather, Gustave's personal assistant. Gustave, leaning back in his office chair, observed the people below through the one-way glass of his office wall, said, "Send them up, please."

Heather was an outstanding young woman. Tall and poised, with piercing smoky blue eyes that projected an extremely dismissing, haughty look of disinterest in anything but her work, was not merely a very bright young woman but commanded respect with her regal appearance. She almost looked artificial, like a manmade human-sized Barbee. She traveled frequently with Gustave to business meetings.

It wasn't through any clandestine means that Gustave was able to locate such talent however it did take a bit of an effort to convince Heather to join the team. Her salary did not resemble that of an assistant but was more like that of an executive officer in a large corporation. While she did prove to be useful in taking and fielding calls, she had much more talent beyond just that. She was in charge of much of the day-to-day operation of the company. Her personality had an intricate integument, like the cross-section of a 14-layer cake. Each layer wrapped around the adjacent ones to form a very strong yet flexible structure. She was perfect, especially now that Gustave could not be bothered with running the company.

"Gustave?" Heather's voice came through the intercom.

"Yes, dear. . ." Gustave replied in a conciliatory tone.

"We have the meeting with the boys at four, remember?"

"Yes, and after that we're going out for dinner, I remember". The com went silent for a moment. "Is everything arranged for my speech next week?"

"Yes, all the leaders confirmed, their arrival times double- checked. . ."

"And the press?"

"Of course, I've got it covered, Gustave"

"Banners and all identity products are printed?"

"I said I have it covered Gustave, sir. . ." Heather couldn't keep the sarcastic tone out of her voice. She had the privilege of speaking to Gustave more familiarly than anyone else. Of course, this had to do with the fact that they occasionally slept together. They both realized the sexual tension between them and decided it would lead nowhere if they did not act upon it to get it off their minds.

Both were quite comfortable with this arrangement as they enjoyed the company of each other, both professionally and physically. Yet there were not many emotions involved in their arrangement, which was what made it work well.

Gustave had to make sure everything was in place for the press meeting. It would be then when he would reveal his plans for the future and disclose astonishing news to the world.

"And the tablets? You've ordered the tablets?"

There was no reply on the com. Heather had hung up, pretending she didn't hear his last query.

Gustave rose from his seat to greet his parents. He opened the doors to his office and saw his parents with Heather who had appeared to greet them as they walked out of the elevator.

It was the first time they had visited the building.

"Mom!" Gustave ran with open arms to his mother. After the hug he smiled at his father.

"You both are finally here!"

"It's the first time you invited us in your office, Gustave," Saul said.

"I don't see you anymore, Gustave; we have an armada of security outside the new house but that's the only reminder I get that I have a son. . ." Sarah said.

"I'm busy mom, I barely have time for myself these days. " Gustave was always impervious to his mother's guilt trips.

"You know, I saw a friend of yours the other day

at the grocery store, a friend from high-school, lovely girl you brought home once, Leanne. . . She said she hasn't seen you for more than a year, and that's not the way to treat a lady friend of yours! She's such a pretty girl. . ."

"Mom, I said I was busy, not much time for friends either."

"That's a poor excuse, Gustave," Saul said.

"Oh come on, Dad. Have a seat! We have lots to talk about. . ."

Gustave gestured for his parents to follow him to the sofas arranged next to his work desk. The sectional modern ultra-suede sofas were luxurious and comfortable. On the glass coffee table an elegant, sleek wine decanter containing mineral water awaited. Gustave filled two glasses and placed them on the table. The parents slowly made their way to the sofa as they examined the design of the place which was minimalistic in nature yet had various colorful focal statements.

"How are you faring the new house? Getting used to the space?"

"Yes, dear, although it's a little too big for us two, especially now that you don't visit much."

There it was; another attempt of a guilt trip. Gustave had grown quite fond of those over the years. They always brought his spirit up instead of making him feel guilty. It showed that she cared and loved him and that was all he got out of them.

"Mom, very soon I'll have a lot more time, I'm

changing the world you know, and it's not easy!"

"And we're so proud of you for doing that, dear."

That brought an unexpected moment of shock. Never in his life had he heard those words uttered from either of them. Perhaps it was the driving force behind his ambitions, where they always kept pushing him to make something of himself and for that he thanked them but not without some well-disguised momentary feelings of resentment.

"Mom, I'm about to do something bigger then this. . ." Gustave said sweeping his open arms across the vast view from the large window. "I'm about to change the world as we know it. I haven't been very honest with you two for some time now and I'm very sorry for that but I had good reasons…more water?"

There was a lot to discuss. At first they didn't believe him much. But after Gustave showed them his capabilities, as well as describing in detail some of the work Saul had participated in at the base. After his father confirmed his involvement with alien technology the picture became clear. That is not to say they showed much support for his future plans. After letting them know little bits and pieces he assured them it would all turn out fine, but he requested they take shelter on a private island until things cooled down.

He sent them off with an unlimited credit card and requested they buy everything they needed, furniture included, to make themselves comfortable for a few months.

He gave them a number to call to reach people who would take care of all the rest.

"You are ready to go?" Heather buzzed Gustave on the intercom.

"Give me a few moments," Gustave replied. He had to digest some of the words that were thrown his way during the conversation with his parents. He was about to embark on a hefty mission which up until now he had had no doubts of its outcome, only now he saw what might go wrong. He gathered his thoughts and came to the conclusion he would never be able to forgive himself after going this far and not proceeding to try to get to the finish line. . .

But would history forgive him for trying? That remained to be seen.

He grabbed his coat and spoke into the intercom, "I'm coming, Heather. . ."

CHAPTER 55

Months after Gustave's parents had visited, the facility was up to full production output. The plant had grown larger and larger and was spread out in several different locations, miles from each other, yet all enclosed behind a concrete wall that ran four-hundred and fifty feet in length, and eight-hundred feet in height. Inside the wall, Gustave had incorporated one of his old designs for an embedded security grid technology that sounded an alarm if breached and also provided the precise location of the breach. Access to Building One was the same as before, not permitted to anyone unauthorized and heavily secured through all the measures necessary.

Ordinary workers, such as scientists and administrators, were quite content with their salaries and their relaxed schedules to the point where it was unlikely they would bite the hand that fed them so handsomely, yet they feared Building One, and knew very well not to step within a foot of the restricted perimeters. Gustave had called a meeting in the main conference room of Building One, which is where everything had started. He thought it fitting to meet there and discuss the proposed events for the next quarter and beyond.

Chris, wearing a polo shirt with the GTP crest on the front, sat at the end of a long conference table across from Harry, who remained pensive and quiet, dignified in his silk suit, studying his fingernails. A wide paneled door at the far end of the massive room opened and Gustave, followed by Heather, walked in.

"Excellent. We're all here." Gustave smiled at his staff and holding Heather's elbow, escorted her to the front of the room and she sat down next to Chris. Gustave looked out over the heads of the people that had helped make his dream come true.

"We haven't much time here gentleman so we'd better get to it. . ." Gustave placed the thick file folder on the top of the rostrum. He leaned forward and looked directly at Chris.

"Chris, I have to be fully honest with you considering I haven't been thus far." Gustave was trying to think of ways to soften the blow but there was no way in which he could achieve telling Chris what he needed to hear in a more tactful manner. "Next week, as you already know, we are to have our largest press conference so far. Representatives from media of all parts of the world are expected. I am about to propose a unification of all earth under one governing body. . . I won't lie to you any more. . . I'm about to propose that governing body will be controlled by me, or actually by us."

Chris burst into spontaneous laughter. "Oh, that's

good, that's good!" He slapped the top of the table with his hand, looking at the other people in the room. "Are you pulling our leg? You are, aren't you? My God, you're not joking, are you?" He looked at Gustave with a serious expression, then burst out laughing again. "Oh, you are good, all of you! This is insane!"

Not that it was in any way necessary, but the rest couldn't resist joining in the amusement which, for the moment, seemed contagious.

"All right, that's enough. . .I need for all of you to be serious! In all solemnity this is what we're going to do. . ." Gustave tried not to look smug.

Heather had known all along, piecing facts together one by one as she helped with the preparation of the press conference. She remained calm and calculating, and supportive of the plan.

"There will still be outside governments, subordinates of the Union, but they will have no final say in managing their countries, which will be up to us and the enforcers of the Code of Behavior and Practices for the Civilian which I have brought with me here. . ."

"What are you talking about Gustave, what is this?" Chris looked at Gustave then at Harry with astonishment.

"Chris, more than a year ago I disappeared for a while if you remember. I told you I was away for some personal, work-related ordeal. That was true, only I should probably tell you that I was on a mission on behalf of an alien race called Angelonians. As a payment for my cooperation they rewarded me with some technology and the promise that they would be back to give me much more in time. I, on the other hand, took a little more than they wanted to give. You see, after learning why they wanted to help the humans and who they were, and especially where they came from, I had a vision of a different earth. One that could join the other highly advanced races on other planets."

Neither Chris not Heather were prepared for the words that came out of Gustave's mouth, as they were words one would usually associate with a mentally ill person.

"Gustave, I think you need a vacation, all this hard work is…"

"Enough!" Gustave was shaking with anger. "I apologize, Chris, please let me finish." The severity of his tone alone caused Chris much distress.

"Many of the races see humans as barbaric, savage beings that are still in an early stage of their development. Some Angelonians see it in a different light, and believe we humans are somehow related to them and they want to help us."

"Gustave, you really expect me to believe this nonsense? Come on! You think that I, no, you think anyone in my position will believe this story? Harry, help me out here. . ."

Harry revealed no emotion whatsoever.

"I enlisted Harry from the AMET organization

right before I destroyed it; he can confirm at least some of that truth."

Chris glanced at Harry surreptitiously.

"The battery, the healing device, they are both their technology with some of my modifications. Did you really think I was able to do such things by myself?"

"You know, Gustave, I have never doubted, you were some sort of a genius on some levels, but seeing what you are telling me now, I see that you really are one! Geniuses all tend to lose it at one point or another. Please tell me you are joking here, if not we are in trouble. Please tell me..."

Gustave had just about had enough. There was no other way to convince Chris otherwise except by demonstrating his power.

The conference table was made of extremely heavy teak, and weighed several hundred kilograms. It served as an easy way to quiet him down. Gustave rose from his chair, went to the far corner of the table and lifted it off the floor with one hand. The room was tall enough to give the table a space to stand on end, almost to the ceiling.

"As you can see, I was retrofitted with some of their technology to help them with their mission. I have an incredible amount of strength, regeneration abilities and can pretty much connect to anything with an electronic pulse to control it with a brain interface." He slowly lowered the conference table back to its original level on the floor.

Chris, still awed by the display, was finally without

words.

Gustave then opened a small box he removed from the pocket of his suit. Opening it, many tiny particles swarmed out of the box and up in the air and began forming a color picture.

He felt it was necessary to relay some of his memory onto the screen to show Chris who the Angelonians were and the ship he had visited as well as memory of his conflicts with AMET. The proof seemed incontrovertible. While most of the imagery could have been generated in CGI, the technology that was used to display those images did not seem real enough to be human yet was real enough to feel, as the particles generated small amounts of air turbulence as they were moving at an incredible speed to accommodate fast frame rates, as small as they were.

"Gustave, what are you going to do?" Chris' voice was barely a whisper.

"I already told you what we are to do."

"There's no 'we' here Gustave, I cannot be a part of this, you've gone mad"

"After everything you saw here and…"

Gustave was quickly interrupted "No, I can't be a part of a war, I will not see us fall after getting to where we are now. What, you think people will just give themselves to you? Are you intimating the governments of the world will say, 'okay Gustave, here are the keys to my country, and when you take over the god damned world, do you mind cleaning up after yourself'?" The sarcastic tone with which

Chris spoke was barely tolerant. Gustave was not expecting such an expression of emotion and yet Chris, out of respect or fear was hesitant about speaking in a harsher tone.

"No Chris, we are expecting to enforce our rule and are well prepared."

"We? Who's in on this? Are your friends from space taking part in it?"

"No Chris, we are alone on this; they are busy with their own stuff."

"You realize that no one will believe you, if they even show up? Do you realize that they will be the only ones to be able to stop this from going toward a world-wide war?"

"I do, Chris, But they will not show up in time of danger, and even if they did, they look like humans. Come Chris, you must see the plan and then decide if you want to be part of our history. I won't leave you without a choice. I owe you that much. But I must convince you to stay with me and you must listen, you owe me that much!"

CHAPTER 56

The ballroom of the Four Season's Hotel was elegant and regal as would befit the world leaders in attendance. Covered with luxurious ivory-colored satin panels, the walls reflected the twinkling lights of the five-foot tall crystal chandeliers hanging gracefully from the heavily carved ceilings. The napery and accompanying bone china pattern, etched crystal goblets, and the gold-plated flatware were designed according to standards suitable for a royal French palace. The setting and its amenities were perfect for hosting world leaders and respected members of the press. The news media was important, not only because they were there to cover the event, but Gustave had made sure Heather had purchased live time-slots from various channels of the big networks. In doing so they would not only compliment the leaders of the world but the world would have the opportunity to witness the event.

Each seat was accompanied by a digital tablet inserted into a monogrammed leather cover affixed to a small arm rest. The logo appeared again across the entrance, and above the foyer as well as on flags which were featured in key locations on the main stage and in discreet positions against the walls around the ballroom.

The logo was somewhat of a vertical ambigram—a typographical representation of the letters: U.n.I.O.n which could be read upside down or from the bottom up, yet it was a little more abstract than a typical ambigram design.

The politicians were greeted warmly by reporters who were standing impatiently outside the hotel. There were no protestors to be seen in the proximity of the entrance, as the public had no access into the entire street. A few groups assembled in surrounding streets which were certain to be routes through which many of the invited personages would use.

The evening began with fine wines and delectable gourmet hors d'oeuvres, including Russian caviar, ostrich liver marinated in Brazilian coffee, Chinese 100-year-old pheasant eggs in sauterne sauce, and escargot flown in from Paris. Gustave made an effort to mingle in the crowd some of whom he had already met and some who were eager to meet him. He had grown accustomed to the protocols of high society, having participated in intellectual, and political events in the past year, most of which were dedicated toward establishing strong connections. The evening seemed to have had an unusually good start even though some knew it was likely to end on a very different chord.

A melodious, harmonious sound thrummed from the PA system after which a female voice announced, "Ladies and gentlemen, please be kind enough to make your way into the main ballroom. You will find your seat number on the brass plaque on the back of your chair, which corresponds to your invitation number found inside your engraved invitation."

The instructions were repeated twice more.

It didn't take long for the guests to find their seat. It seemed everyone was equally eager to find out why they were invited and why so many members from different countries were in attendance.

The lights dimmed, revealing the strong colors of the flags that featured the unique logo.

In the background, busy cameramen and news reporters hustled around to get everything prepared for the live broadcast which was about to begin. Considering the momentous event and the billions of people watching, they had everything to gain and even more to lose if they failed to report or transmit a live video feed.

Gustave walked onto the stage, perspiration trickling down from his left temple.

The crowed began clapping their hands loudly, then the applause turned to cheers and the cheers turned into a standing ovation.

Gustave's confident appearance belied his insecurity.

He raised his hand and spoke into the small microphone which was clamped on his shirt.

"Thank you, thank you. Please, sit down"

The audience grew expectantly quiet as everyone sat down.

* * *

The press stormed into the hotel lobby after listening to the broadcast. Many of the politicians stormed out of the ballroom not thirty minutes after Gustave's Union announcement.

While some abstained from talking and sidled to their cars in haste, others gave quick responses and followed their peers. Some remained to shake Gustave's hand, promising a complete allegiance to the Union. Not surprisingly, they were the ones who had the least to lose. Their political skin wasn't thick enough to hide the insightful mind beneath. More than a couple dozen electronic tablets remained in the room, some stomped on, some broken in half, and it was clear they felt no allegiance to The Union.

Knowing the unnecessary risk involved, neither Chris, nor Harry attended the speech. They were far away on their way to the island. Heather remained with Gustave.

"How are we getting out of here, Gustave?" Heather's voice quivered with uneasy fear as she contemplated the unruly crowds. "They have police outside to arrest us. . ."

"I don't know about you, Heather, but I thought we should make a run for it through the front door while the cameras are rolling. . ."

"They'll shoot at us!"

Gustave pulled a small cube from his pocket. "Yes I know. . . it's time the world becomes acquainted with

Union technology. . . maybe then we'll get some advocacy. Come. . ."

They walked rapidly out of the lobby doors. The press was evacuated after receiving strict instructions from the police outside. The place was in such disorder it was difficult to remember how organized the place was before. And of course, outside a perimeter was arranged. It was surprising to observe just how fast the crowds had acted.

"Come out with your hands up!" The loud demand was made through a megaphone.

The bright lights made it difficult to see just how many police officers were on location. Gustave's armor however, had filled him in on all the details. There were a hundred and twenty-three officers on the ground, snipers positioned on roof tops miles away, not to mention the sharpshooters waiting on several military and police helicopters which hovered above the scene.

"Put your hands in the air, sir!" A policeman shouted.

Gustave thought it would be advisable to try and reason with them, especially since cameras were recording his every move. "I wish you no harm and I advise you to disperse and go home! You are providing a fine service to the public, but are following the wrong chain of command!" Gustave shouted as loudly as he could project his voice.

There was a moment of silence. Gustave, disconnected all communication to both the police headquarters and the military channels. He wanted the people to make their own judgment.

"This is your last warning, put your Goddamned hands in the air! You are under arrest!" The voice was strained. The man was under obvious pressure.

Heather, feeling uncomfortable and extremely unsafe began raising her hands.

"Put your hands down, Heather, right now!" Gustave's tone had changed as he spoke in a hoarse whisper. His anger toward their opponent's decision was clearly evident beneath the layers of control. "Whatever you do, stay very close to me, do you hear me, don't run outside of my radius. Now, slowly walk with me. . ."

"Sir, we will shoot, we will SHOOT!"

At that moment a trigger was squeezed.

In this scenario, the armor did not calculate trajectories of bullets and the reaction time based on the sound of the fire but by analyzing muzzle flashes which was much faster.

After almost instantaneously calculating and evaluating risk, it sent instruction to the micro-protection films produced out of nanonites to fly against the object, creating a miniature wall which no metallic object known to men could penetrate. Since it was too fast to see in action, all that could be seen was a spark, a flattened metallic square and a falling bullet. It looked as if there was some sort of an energy field, yet there was nothing of that sort. The metallic square wall, roughly the width and height of the bullet, with some extra bleed space on the sides remained in the air for not more than a split second before returning to the cube Gustave held in his hand, to be reprogrammed and sent back to interfere with another trajectory.

Now that more and more shots were fired, the cube exhausted an enormous number of those micron-thin protective shields which flew instantaneously against the many shots fired.

The only thing bothering Gustave was the noise coming from the guns as they released a massive amount of energy into the air. The smell of smoke permeated everything around them.

"Tear gas!" Someone screamed the dreaded words.

The armor raised every alarm possible to flee the area. Gustave and Heather began feeling a stinging irritation in their eyes. While the armor began treating Gustave's central nervous system with messages counteracting the side-effects of the tear-causing gas, Heather was under no such protection.

"Gustave, help me! I can't breathe!" She tried gasping for air. "Make them stop, please!"

Gustave was struggling himself, on one hand some of the effects of the tear gas still penetrated through the protective treatment and on the other the treatment made him have less in control over his armor which made him look clumsy and vulnerable. It was just the right opportunity they were looking for.

They began shooting again.

While the armor excelled at multitasking there was always the ultimate human error factored in when controlling it, without which it was impossible to function correctly. The neural link was under extreme stress overflowing with messages, counter- messages and superfluous of sub-conscious activities necessary for the control over the armor.

There were protocols embedded in the armor for stimuli-overflow scenarios.

Should the neural link be severed under any circumstance, it would be the logical next step to disconnect any further instruction from the biological operator and function as a machine. A machine with one purpose only, which was to protect the operator against any harm in an offensive manner seeing that all other defensive options were futile.

The news cameras mostly recorded blurs. The night time setting of the cameras required slower shutter speeds to accommodate for the lack of light. What they did record was astonishing. In less than a minute, severed and broken limbs of soldiers and police officers were spotted next to destroyed machine guns. A mechanical news stand flew in the air and hit one of the helicopters hovering above. The other helicopter, trying to escape had no luck either as the damaged helicopter slammed into the other. They both crashed into an office building which erupted in a response of shattered glass. Much of the hysterical crowd had run far enough away that there was a minimal number of injured people except for the few who were either dazed and stayed to watch, or those unfortunate ones who attempted following their orders.

And then there was silence.

Gustave's body was slumped on the ground and was exposed to the cameras which kept on rolling. Most of the gray suit he had been wearing earlier was lost and the parts that remained were adhering to the stickiness of his bleeding wounds. There was no more danger spotted. His armor quickly surrendered the control to Gustave which showed a promising chance of recovering. As he slowly regained consciousness, his wounds began miraculously to heal.

Gustave stood up, ignoring his lack of clothing, his memory knowledgeable of every possible movement that had been made on his behalf. He stared at Heather's lifeless body and knew it was beyond any repair, even by the advanced technology of his healing device. He longed to avenge her death but was too weak and too confused. Instead he picked up her lifeless body and staggered toward the camera.

The camera was transmitting to the news headquarters, but the feed to the public had been cut much earlier. He would have none of that. Releasing all censorship software which was set to stop the video feed from rolling into the TV sets of the viewers, he raised Heather's body in front of the nearest camera with a glowing red light.

"Look what your weapons did, look at the brutality by which she was murdered, I've done you nothing but good and this is how you repay me?"

Tears trickled down his cheeks. It was he who caused her death. It was he who was supposed to protect her but he had failed to do so.

"You have no option other than to comply with The Union's CBPC book. Any army, policing force or citizen of earth resisting the Code will be considered hostile to the Union and will be subjected to severe punishment."

He slowly eased Heather's body onto the ground. From the distance, the penetrating sounds of police sirens and military vehicles were heard approaching rapidly.

Gustave gazed at the camera once more. "It is in your best interests to surrender peacefully".

A flying vehicle landed on to the ground. The vehicle which was intended to gracefully provide an escape for Gustave and Heather landed. It resembled a flying disk. Very much like the design he saw in the Angelonians mother ship only with a modified engine which it clearly lacked. It was being maneuvered through floating nano-bots unlike the alien technology which was running in parts through some sort of magneto-gravity propulsion as well as with the help of the mysterious Throb-String Drive.

In any case, the floating nano-bots provided an impressive flight, at least impressive enough to alarm the public and prevent the air-force from taking retaliatory action.

CHAPTER 57

Phue, one of several selected members of the committee, received the news from the observatory. The observatory served as the eyes for the committee and was in charge of keeping track of and providing new intelligence for all ongoing investigations.

The news was alarming enough to request an open link with Catepet. The link was granted.

The sheer magnitude of the amount of bad news coming from earth rankled everyone on the committee, yet this seemed to have foreshadowed all that had been previously discussed.

Phue was not too satisfied to be the bearer of the news, but he had no choice but to do his job in an intuitive manner.

"We have a severe issue on Earth Catepet. . ."

"Would you care to elaborate?" Catepet prompted. He was busy enough with processing the Angelonian insurgents after the capture of their ship and the news of more leaked technology was something that will have to be brought into consideration while assessing the crew's punishment, something that was rarely done in the past centuries and was extremely difficult to approach, as any punishment would be scrutinized and advocated against by most members.

"Do you remember the report on Gustave's assessment?" Through his database access Phue pulled up the specific document in question and made sure it was available through the Link.

Catepat retrieved the document and began skimming through it in his head.

"Perhaps," Catepat allowed.

Phue continued, "He showed extreme statistical probability for becoming hostile toward his surroundings"

Catepat nodded in agreement. He then removed the document from memory's view and shifted his attention to Phue, "We were too damned late grabbing him from their hands, Phue, enough with the introductions, what is the situation on that damned rock?"

"He's just proclaimed jurisdiction of his rule over Earth. . . He built an army for that sole purpose, an army with more of our technology than we originally had expected he would own, had we failed to retrieve the insurgents in time. You better see this."

Phue exchanged the entire observation with Catepat. All of the events of the evening alongside much of the surrounding news were instantaneously transferred into his memory.

"He has access to Nanonites and is about to

change the governing body of that planet!" He paused for a moment and then continued, "None of this has been discussed in the committee as an option for failure. Phue we are about to experience a lot of scrutiny so you'd better prepare the rest for a counter-speech. The Prometheus advocates are not going to like this one bit."

"Understood, right away" Phue responded.

The link was severed.

Catepat sat in his chair smiling. His plan had worked out just as he expected, and he had Milka to congratulate for a job well done.

While he had lost the most important objective of the mission, which was the retrieval of the devices, the Prometheus treaty was breached in such a severe manner that new changes will have to be initiated to treat the situation accordingly. In doing so, he would gain a free hand to treat the Angelonians in the manner he had previously set out to do.

At last, he had some good news to take to his true superiors.

CHAPTER 58

"The U.N meeting today, scheduled to disperse in two hours, will outline the next phase. We are told at six P.M a decision will be made after which a public announcement will follow. We are joined now by our senior correspondent in Geneva, Ms. Michelle Peterson. Michelle?"

"Thank you, Greg, I am standing outside the United Nations complex waiting to hear any developments on the response to Gustave's Union address. We do not have any official response just yet but it's important to note that our reporters have spotted key army officials accompanying political figures from around the world. Generals from the U.S and the British Royal Air-Force, as well as commanding officers of special NATO forces are all attending the summit. It's too early to tell, Greg, but it looks from here like there will be an armed response. Greg?"

"All across the country we've been seeing large riots and demonstrations in front of government buildings; the GTP building demonstration has so far resulted in several casualties after the building had been shut down. We have several other casualty reports from riots across the nation and in other parts of the world. How do you think the U.N is going to address the current civilian heat wave?"

"Greg, as I said we should have the full details on it in a matter of hours, however, we did receive a reply from Senator Peel stating while they request the public remain calm, they intend to increase police attendance in several areas and will try to disperse riots peacefully with as few casualties as possible. We have a clip. . ."

"We request the people be patient, we will not stand for the demands of Gustave, no government will request their citizens revoke their religion; may God be with us all."

"He seems to address specific sections of the code, Michelle?"

"That's correct, Greg. The code, which demands for a complete separation of all religious doctrines and state viewpoints, is one of the biggest causes of rioting around the world. In the states we are seeing a lot of activity against the forbidding of owning, manufacturing, and distribution of weapons as the catalyst for many riots. There are groups banning all GTP products, including any form of transportation or medical devices used in hospitals but we are told by officials this may cause even bigger problems for government and police enforcement necessary for supporting the city infrastructures.

We are now joined by Stanley Blair from the Wall Street Journal,. . ."

"Hi, Greg, thank you for having me."

"Mr. Blair, the Dow fell today to its lowest point in three years, followed by the Nasdaq and the footsie one-hundered, do we have any indication of a recovery or should we expect an even steeper trend in the next few weeks?"

"That's a very good question Greg. . . The entire GTP upper management directors have arrest warrants and GTP's founder is expecting to be restrained by a very long jail sentence for public disturbance, resisting arrest, and multiple charges for battery of a police officer."

"We have no indication of what might happen to the company, but our best estimates are that GTP and all its assets will be seized by the government and that control will be shifted toward a board of trustees. We are not certain just why, other than global tension, the market would respond in such a hard way, considering all GTP's subsidiaries were privatized and removed from listings. I think we have yet to see it fall as low as it can, but that depends on the U.N announcement later this evening."

"You've mentioned the market falling even farther pending the decision of the U.N; just how low can we expect it to fall?"

"It's hard to tell, Greg, the last time we saw such a steep fall was when GTP announced the Power Core which caused an economic crises led by the fall of the European and North American petroleum market. If Gustave has his way, we should expect a massive fall in GDP of several key countries which will directly affect the overall economic output.

There are also the ridiculous demands for dispersing and the disassembly of all military across the world which will surely have a snowball effect on the entire world economy, especially when we are talking about millions of people losing their jobs. This could prove to be the most difficult request, umm, demand Gustave has set in his Code."

"Thank you, Mr. Blair, next, we will be joined by Christopher Fowler live, from the GTP complex in New York.

We will be right back after the following messages."

CHAPTER 59

The island had no connection to GTP; it was built as a safe place to accommodate his campaign headquarters as well as serving as the training ground for the army of a thousand robots. Of course, none of the robots have seen the light of day as their training ground was underneath the island. The robots, highly capable, probabilistic machines were built from designs and schematics stolen from Nell. They were not as perfect as the Angelonian Biobots, but were much more resilient. Their artificial brains were carefully modeled after the Biobotical engineering of the Angelonian bots, however Gustave saw fit to equip them with a shielding that very much resembled his armor. The training was quite simple. It only took one prototype to connect to several simulations which Harry managed to get a hold of from previous army contractors and when one brain learned how to react to every possible scenario thrown at him, the rest copied with the exact memory of the original one.

The machine did not need to learn how to follow orders. It did, however have to be trained how to work among hundreds of others in unison, as well as how to share its resources with the group when several collaborative efforts had to take place.

For the time being, they stood in a tranquil state at their stations which were nothing more than pods that kept them in order. Several specially re-enforced machines stood on guard in the room where Gustave kept the device he had stolen, where it had remained untouched for several years. The structures on the islands resembled an army base on one hand, and on the other a luxurious fortress of villas. Gustave had anticipated living there until the campaign was over when he planned to relocate to an area where he had designed a complex to accommodate the Union's governance offices—a center that would help propel the human kind into an era of order and peace. Until then, the comfort and safety of the structure which featured every possible defense mechanism would have to do.

Gustave was concentrating very hard as he was making his approach to a landing pad; he signaled the mainframe of his arrival which calibrated the exact landing window where the security would be opened briefly to allow for the approach of his vehicle.

"Harry, are you there?" Gustave linked himself to the communication system that gave him a direct link to a communicator device Harry was requested to wear at all times.

"Welcome back Gustave. . . I'm truly sorry to learn about Heather."

"I'm coming over. . ."

Everything on the island was connected to Gustave's armor. It was the first structure that like the Angelonian ship featured a direct link to his neural interface and every device on the property without any special need for hacking. The programming of the devices was done via Gustave's hybrid computer which seemed to have been more proficient at designing other devices than Gustave could have possibly have imagined. He made his way to Harry who was sitting in the control room that loomed above all other structures on the island.

Harry stood up when Gustave entered the room.

"Gustave, they have seized all buildings, bank accounts, and assets of GTP, the security man showed no resistance to the army, just as you instructed."

"I'm starting to regret asking them to do so, Harry" Gustave paused for a moment and sat down, motioning for Harry to do the same.

"The factories have…"

". . .All been imploded as programmed, Gustave, damned shame if you ask me, but surely was necessary. . ."

"These bastards, they have deficiency in judging intent, what are they going to do without the healing pallets, what are they going to do without energy? Did they think that far ahead?"

"That remains to be seen, Gustave, there is still the U.N Press release in less than an hour; we'll have to wait and see. . ."

"Oh, Harry, you and I both know how this will turn out. If this is what it's going to take, then so be it!" Gustave stopped himself from causing any further augmentation to his temper. "Chris must be on the fritz with all that, where is he? I can't get his com's signal. . ."

Harry's face froze. He felt as if the entire world had collapsed on top of him. For a moment he felt heavy and unable to speak. He gasped for air while realizing something had gone very wrong in the transport. He finally gathered himself together and asked, "Chris isn't here?"

Gustave was not prone to anxiety attacks, but when he checked the entry log of the island, he noticed he was the only one who had signed in.

"Harry!"

Harry was pulling at the thin threads of his hair with his fingers and did not speak much, instead, kept mumbling repeatedly, "no, no, no, no…".

"Where are my parents, Harry?" Gustave's armor kicked in a calming instrument but Gustave quickly stopped it on the spot.

"They took them!"

* * *

The entire world's attention was shifted toward the press release which was now underway to begin its broadcast. The U.N Security Council and representatives from all members were sitting down in their chairs while the Secretary-General was preparing to address the world. For once, members from countries which were not a part of the westernized world were also seen in the crowd.

At least in that sense, Gustave achieved something that has yet to have been accomplished in history: where all representatives of countries of the world were attending one meeting to address one mutual future which they all now shared. The world was about to learn if this mutual cause will be another world war against a common enemy.

The regular rooms where most meetings and public addressing took place were too small to accommodate the number of attendees. Instead they met at a hall which was organized to meet the demands for both security and a large audience.

The secretary began his speech.

"Today we have reached a cooperative plateau that many before us have dreamt of for many years. However, it is because of these unfortunate circumstances we have gathered to decide upon the fate of the world and human kind. I am standing here before you as many have stood before me and will say that not today and not ever will the people of this planet shall ever again tolerate the ignorance and forceful threats of one man's will.

"We have always wanted to advance and promote human rights and under these circumstances I am standing here today to embody our conclusion that we are now facing humanity's biggest threat to its values of life, to its values of human rights, and most of all, to the values of our freedom.

"Our countries have been built and forged through hundreds, if not thousands of years of development of governance and policies. While many of these policies were challenged throughout history, it was our ambition to protect these core values which eventually prevailed.

While we will continue to challenge rules, regulations, and policies we will not stand for anyone who challenges our ambition, we will not be silenced by an individual seeking to destroy our core values of life and exercising the right to think for ourselves and to act upon our need for freedom.

"We remain in our strong stance there is no evidence that neither GTP nor its founder Gustave Eisenstein have any relations to extraterrestrial beings living outside of our planet.

"We remain in a strong stance there is no shred of evidence that such extraterrestrial beings exist.

"While General Technology Products and Gustave Eisenstein gave us access to technology which changed the world, we will not comply by his rule or governance, we will not submit to a lunatic seeking control of the world.

"The governments of the world refuse to hear any further demands and we are prepared to do whatever it takes, to protect our freedoms.

"If it's war that one shall seek then to war we are

prepared to go when that man is a heresiarch, then he and his followers shall feel the might of our sword and the force of our bullets and the failure of their challenge on our system of beliefs. We request the citizens of earth remain calm and composed. There is no need to fear that man, for we have united here today to bring him to justice under our laws and our humane rule."

CHAPTER 60

"Can you trace the electronics on the ship?" Harry asked. It seemed almost impossible to try and help Gustave in his current state of mind.

"Don't you think I've tried that?" Gustave shouted.

"I'm sorry, Gustave"

Gustave was not thinking clearly; as it stood he had only one ally. He knew he should not have acted that way. Harry wasn't offended, to the contrary, he felt like it was, in some way his fault for not checking the arrival of Chris and Gustave's parents earlier.

"I've found nothing Harry, nothing. There is no chatter on any military channels. How can that be? There must be some trace for an operation. . ."

" This sounds a lot like secret ops to me, I know because I've commanded a few such missions. There would be no file nor would any knowledge of the mission be exposed to any party other than those directly involved. It is likely there will be similar action without any trace. The package would not be reported on delivered until it came to the base, and even then it would be in an unconventional area."

"What if this was a civilian action?" Gustave was trying to control his rising panic.

"Then look for it as if they were trafficked like drugs, you might then find some trace. Civilians, not matter how good they might be, have no experience in complete undercover operations. I can almost say for certain this was done by professionals. . ."

"I am not going to dismiss the option that this was done in a civilian operation, damn it!"

"Okay, what do they have to gain by kidnapping them? This will be used against you to either blackmail you or to try to stop you from taking over the world. . . I've personally dealt with thousands of attempts from corporate or civilians having a try at GTP, and I'm almost certain none of them finally found a way to cut through your security. And that's actually good news for us, with a little luck to help. . ."

Gustave abstained from destroying a communication module as he heard those words, "To what luck do you refer exactly?"

"They will be detained, questioned and used as a bargaining chip, which means they have no clue as to our abilities just yet, then there will be a deal and…" Harry was interrupted by a beep. The U.N's latest news press was released to a projector screen generated in mid- air.

They both gazed at the screen contemptuously.

Gustave called for the monitor to evaporate. "There is no need to watch the rest, they want a war, they asked for it and they shall receive it, idiots! Harry, send the command to the floaters, we are going in."

"What? Now?"

"Yes, now! We must not give them any more time to prepare for a global war!"

"Understood. Where are we going first?

Gustave was sending orders through a command module built into one of the surfaces of the room while at the same time sending messages through his neural interface. "We are going everywhere: North America, England, France, China, Japan and Russia. The more fronts they are fighting on the less chance they have of operating in combined forces. We will give them no opportunity to unite in war against the Union."

Harry considered their situation. In all the history of warfare there was only one thing that gave an advantage of one army over the other and that was the ability to attack at several fronts. He knew the ability of the robot soldiers quite well. He knew it would take a lot more than an entire brigade to defeat even just one robot. While they might have a better chance in fighting as a massive combined force, they will have none of that chance available to them if they were fighting alone, on their own ground.

"Harry, I'm leaving you here to watch over the Eastern hemisphere campaign. I'm going to have the pleasure of joining the Western campaign."

Harry looked confused. "Are you actually going in there?"

"The only weapon they have against me is gas. On the trip here I've calibrated my defense armor to deal with that. While the nostrils and mouth will take care of any harmful airborne molecules, I modified my eyes which were until now the only part in my body that remained without protection. Not any more."

Gustave quickly demonstrated. His eyes turned gray for a moment and then slid open to reveal the cavities of the eye sockets.

"It was necessary for them to be completely replaced with nanonites. But my vision is as good as it was before if not better. I don't know why they didn't think of that earlier when they fixed me up with the armor in the first place."

"You replaced your own eyes?" Harry said, still shocked by the gruesome display.

"I did what was necessary; I will not stand for being crippled ever again by human weaponry." Gustave's nostrils flared. It was not an easy decision to make, but with taking control and conquering over his old vulnerability he found it easier to cope with the loss of Heather.

* * *

The robots, for the first time came out from their underground barracks. It was a site Gustave was more proud of than anything else he had achieved until that moment. The display of their green brushed chrome shells was breathtaking as the reflection of the setting sun caused rays of all colors to fill the sky. Each robot mimicked the structure of a very large human being only there were clearly many attributes which caused them to look much more intimidating and a lot harder to control.

They were aligned in order, none of which carried any visible weapon yet ready for boarding the floaters which quickly rose from the ground through separate underground hangars that opened up. Each floater was designed to carry the heavy machines into and out of combat. The shapes of their hulls resembled a stretched metallic sphere out of which several cubical spaces grew.

It was the hybrid computer that had designed them which resulted in a sparse efficient structure that would provide safety and agility to the transported goods- the result actually looked menacing, Gustave thought, seeing them for the first time. And considering he was used to seeing odd things, especially after visiting the aliens, they would fulfill their purpose better that way, ugly in design yet beautifully intimidating in every other respect.

The robots boarded the ships. One by one, they took their positions in each ship. It was like watching ants on speed. The organization of their boarding was flawless, the hierarchy of their virtual command was clear. Seven ships, one hundred and forty in each ship. They all waited for the launch command by Gustave.

"Harry, it's time. Keep me constantly updated, we

must not fail!"

Gustave joined one of the two floaters which were designated to reach the western front.

The robots showed no life signs as they were lifted up into the air while the ship's doors closed. Unlike soldiers, they did not require much communication until they needed new instructions. Gustave went over the plan in his head. The best he could come up with was to warn the public of his invasion if the government did not release its hold on his parents and Chris. He had no access to their location nor had he received any threats or instructions as to how he might be able to bargain for their lives. He knew one thing was certain, and he tried not to think too hard about it. Should they be harmed, it wouldn't be the Code that would stop humanity from ever engaging in more wars, it would be the imagery of the devastation and the stench of dead bodies that would follow wherever his Army of a Thousand walked that would be embedded in the memory of humankind, which would never again engage in war.

CHAPTER 61

The Prometheus committee was stationed in one of the remote corners of the high governance complex in the G.U. Agora. The structure loomed in the distance out of which spotlights glittered to reveal large statues standing guard around the perimeter. While the Prometheus name was named after the Human Greek god, the committee was in charge of the protection of all G.U. technology across the entire galaxy. It was the Angelonians constant visitation to Earth that caused the facility to be opened but it was also instigated by a group of political figures from the Angelonian trade organization to protect their commercial interests.

The committee had become the controlling interest overseeing the entire distribution of G.U. technologies, and was also in charge of royalties, commissions, and many of the other trades across the galaxy, governed by industrial lobbyists who were often promoted to the highest levels of command.

Catepet stood before the committee. The news from Earth resonated across the chamber.

"Catepet, it is because of your great history of service to us we do not wish to revoke your position. But you have failed us. Do you wish to make a statement before we proceed?" It was impossible to identify the voice. No one knew those in charge and neither were they meant to be seen or heard. The voice was modified and altered to sound like a whisper with some hard-to-recognize natural overtones.

"We have consistently underestimated the Angelonians. Their tests on humans resulted in much more advanced mutations than we were able to predict, your Greatness," Catepat prompted.

To support his argument, he instantly linked them through a buffering link to documentation on Gustave and other humans who were descendants of Angelonian human tests.

There were several moments of silence.

"We will allow. . ." the voice whispered.

There was no requirement to show any more evidence than he already had for the committee to analyze the situation.

"This committee is forced to infringe on its highest and most important agreement. You must correct the situation on earth, yet under no circumstance are you allowed to reveal our existence. You will retrieve the Human, dismantle his army through discretionary means and will bring him before us for judgment and deactivation."

This was the first time in the history of the G.U.

that the order for the elimination or harmful intention toward a living thing was issued. The committee and much of its order were well above other political involvement.

"Well understood, your Greatness," Catepet said.

"Your discretion is of extreme value to us, Catepet. . . you will comply and enjoy a career with us or fail and will be sent to exile from the political grounds. . ."

"I will not fail this time, your Greatness, thank you for…"

He was disturbed by the voice which shouted a forceful whisper: "Leave!"

Catepet ran out. There was no time to waste.

"Phue, arrange an audience with Nell for me, immediately!"

Phue answered, "She is in her lab and will be instructed to wait for your arrival. . ."

It was still unknown what to make of the crew. They were kept on constant watch but were allowed to continue their previous activities as long as they kept out of contact with each other. There was no arrest or imprisonment for members of the G.U., especially for those who were productive members of any organization that was either politically or scientifically involved.

Catepet stepped onto a transport pad. There was no time to walk. He sent instructions to the electronic float which instantly zoomed toward its destination.

The pads traveled at great speed. However, to an untrained eye it looked as if they had no mechanism to protect the people traveling on them, except that the mechanism used a sophisticated gravity pointer keeping anyone on board trapped between four gravity poles which kept them stabilized and safe.

* * *

The lab's wall parted before Catepet entered the room.

Nell received limited access to the Link, which perhaps was one of the most gruesome punishments they could have given her until further notice when she would be free to roam it again. Until she heard the wall breach she did not know Catepet was coming, thus was unable to prepare for the visit.

"I need information, Nell!"

Nell quickly covered herself. She was wearing a revealing gown which stiffened and changed color. She knew they were likely to get caught eventually, yet nothing prepared her for the humiliation she had had to undergo the past several years or so. "And what information would that be?" She looked around, trying to appear casual and unconcerned.

"You scum!" The use of foul language was extremely uncommon among members of the G.U., yet this wasn't the first time she had been called that name.

Nonetheless, it was painful to hear. Her immediate physical reaction to scornful language shortened her breath. She gasped for air and tried hard to protect herself from further use of bad language.

"I need the sequence of his armor. . ." Catepet said, pointing a finger to her direction.

Nell, who was sitting in a chair, removed the programming rod from her hand and looked at Catepet, her eyes bright with emotion.

She missed Gustave, she missed his touch and his silly ways, and there was much to tell him that she couldn't. She wondered how he was doing. It was impossible for her to track his progress, and she was relieved to know he was still alive, otherwise Catepet would not have been standing in front of her. But why did he need the armor's security sequence. Was he captured? She couldn't bear the thought.

Catepet could not resist her beauty. Regardless of his position, there was something more to her than he had ever met in an Angelonian. As hard as he tried to avoid any feeling of mercy, he was still touched by her beauty and her vulnerability.

"I'm going to correct everything you did on Earth and bring him back here. I hope you understand I am doing this in your best interests because if the issues with the humans continues, we'll all be sentenced." He moved closer to her and she moved farther away.

"Nell, there are even talks of lifetime expulsion from the G.U. and the Link, so help me help you, Nell!",

He raised his voice while clenching his teeth. "I am . . .". He paused and calmed down a little, "…I'm being as forward and as helpful to you as I can."

"What has happened on Earth?" she asked.

"Gustave has claimed rule over their world with an army. He's using our technology to enforce his laws on innocent lives. Is that what you had in mind? Letting him loose like that?"

Nell began crying. All her hopes for reuniting with Gustave were lost. If she gave away the sequence for his armor, Gustave was sure to be eliminated, but if she didn't, she would bring a severe punishment to herself and her team.

Catepet, for a moment disconnected Nell from the Link.

She suffocated. The overbearing feeling of disconnection from the real world felt like she was deprived of air while being crushed under the weight of thousand suns.

He then restored the Link.

In that moment she felt alive again, she felt free. The access to the information link was as freeing and exhilarating like no other feeling can be. Deprivation from it meant cold and lonely emptiness which darkened the soul.

The moment of ecstasy of being returned to the Link subsided. She knew what had to be done. She knew she must give him the sequence to the armor or be responsible for crimes against her peers.

She transferred him the codes.

"You've done well my dear, I'm going to destroy Gustave and then make sure your people will never set foot in Human space. But you just might be lucky enough, depending on how nice you will be to me when I get back, that you will stay amongst us. Alive. "

Catepet zoomed out of the lab, closing the wall behind him.

Nell knew she had just fallen for the deception of that awful man. She knew she made a mistake, as her team was to be punished regardless of her efforts to keep them safe.

There was only one thing she could do to remedy the situation, and that was to take her own life.

CHAPTER 62

The armies landed across the world. Each one was positioned in key spots next to government buildings, and in particular where army headquarters were located. While there had been some resistance from security, the robots did not react to the projectiles which were shot at them because none provided any serious risk.

Gustave noticed while the robots remained stationary, the army communication lines were busy sending troops of tanks, helicopters, and soldiers to the urban battlefield. After sending a global message across all television networks to instruct and advise people to remain in their houses and wait peacefully until a resolution has been achieved, he felt at ease with himself that he had made an effort to avoid any unnecessary bloodshed. The synthesized voice coming out of the television sets was deep and intimidating. It sounded as if a choir of a thousand men were chanting their request. Of course, that didn't stop rioting groups that came to defend their country.

Gustave landed in front of the U.N building. He was wearing the same suit he helped develop for the army, yet this one was modified and perfectly fitted with Union colors: a combination of red, black and white, indicating he was the leader of that army. While the suit served as an added protection, he was also tired of replacing clothes every time he was being shot at and it added the comfort of not needing to find cover while being almost naked.

More shots were fired. But he waited for the larger weapons to arrive before making any further movement. And there it came: the first rocket, the second and third and fourth. The robots moved a little by the force of the impact but quickly returned to their previous position.

"Harry, what's your status?" Gustave asked calmly.

"We are seeing some heavy fire; they brought everything they've got in Russia. In England, we have heavy army presence. The French police are still shooting using small arms. Asia, large carriers have shot ballistics from sea. There is a lot of damage to the surroundings. Do you think it's…"

"Yeah, it's time. Send them the order." Gustave responded.

Before Gustave could give the order to his robots, an F-35 passed by and shot a missile into the building. The building collapsed next to the robots which struggled to escape from under the debris. Gustave, who had equipped his suit with nanonites, escaped being crushed by the falling building.

He waited for more troops to arrive at the scene. It was important to make a proper statement. He gave the order.

The robots began walking towards the U.N building, subjected to heavy fire; it seemed as if nothing could penetrate their heavy armor. The fighter-jets kept losing controls as they attempted to approach to the war zone.

All army machinery and electronics were lost. Nothing was left but screens which uttered: "Surrender peacefully or be eliminated. Free the prisoners and bring them to me. . ."

Foot soldiers were the only entities left with any capacity to show any resistance.

Foot soldiers and unreasonable civilians who had come to the rescue and fought alongside their servicemen were the only line of offense against the Union army.

A concern arose after people began realizing they were not being shot at. They began approaching the army.

Each Robot began emitting a strong paralyzing wave that resonated through the human's bodies, causing complete paralysis. Their nervous systems were overloaded with excruciating pain which caused them to fall on the spot, and some who resisted that pain also experienced involuntary tremors which rendered them useless.

The energy wave stopped. There was a limit to how long they could be subdued under the effect of the wave before crucial life-supporting organs would start to fail.

The astringent weapon had its effect.

The fire had ceased.

"Harry, I'm bringing their communications back

up, let's see if now they are more willing to talk. . ." Gustave intoned.

"Copy that, we are still being fired upon here. . ." Harry responded.

"You know what to do, Harry?"

"Understood. . ."

"There is no weapon or soldier that will be able to take us down. Your army is completely disabled yet none are hurt. What say you? Do keep in mind that our communications are being broadcast to the public; are you willing to negotiate peacefully?"

There was no reply.

Gustave, tapped into the entire army's communications and began listening to the absurd suggestions brought by army command. He decided to bring some of their conversations to light, so the public would realize their government cared little about the citizens.

"Send the nukes! Send the nukes! I don't care how many people live in that area, send the Goddamned nukes!"

Gustave responded, "Citizens of the Union, that was your previous president. All those talks about protecting humanity, core values, freedoms, protection of life and humanitarian causes, where are they now? Is it human life they are trying to preserve or is it their governance and rule, rules which allow them to eliminate entire cities without much thought? Luckily for you!" He stopped, realizing he was disconnected from the AF1 channel, then he continued, "Sorry, now that they are listening again. . . I've disarmed all nuclear heads, you have no way to project them to the cities, and even if you throw them in my direction with your bare hands seeing you have no way to fire them up, they still would not explode. Agree to the surrender terms and I will allow you to coexist with the Union. Refuse and you will be eliminated."

There was no reply from the command.

Gustave was willing to give it some time, after all, these people were not capable of making sound and logical decisions.

A voice was heard on the channel, "We are bringing the prisoners to you to discuss negotiation terms."

After that message another one ensued, complimented by the confirmation of the location of his parents and Chris. Harry was right, it was the remains of AMET that reunited under covert ops. It seemed all his efforts to disperse that organization were futile and yet he couldn't help but smile with amusement. "They will be useful for the Union," he said to himself.

CHAPTER 63

Afterlife servers were always busy accommodating millions of residents. While the software was fairly stable it was never flawless. It was originally created by Angelonians, one of the only species that continued to grow old mentally to the point where some preferred to retire from life in normal space and some decided to keep on going yet felt like they exhausted their capacity to stay awake, after hundreds of years. Afterlife was the perfect solution: A retirement home where they could continue their work, regardless of time and resources and where they had the option to shut down for extended periods until they regained interest with the outside world.

The place, where no rules were necessary, required very little supervision. The only restrictions were access and the ability to change someone else's profile settings which never seemed to have been an issue.

The comfort of secrecy and freedom of movement provided all the protection needed for the Angelonian rebels against the Prometheus committee to meet and discuss future missions, as well as provide training and education to new generations. The original creators of the system were, in fact, part of that rebellion because they believed it took more than dumb luck to play with their evolution and that of the humans.

There were a few restrictions to the system, however. Visitation periods were governed by the G.U. to ensure everyone from the outside world got an identical provisioned amount of visiting hours without disturbing the equilibrium between normal space and the system.

Nell, under severe sanctions, knew she would not only have less time to be connected but was most likely to be retrieved rapidly as her passage through the Link was constantly monitored.

There was only one thing she could do and that was to retire from normal space and continue her work through the protection of Afterlife citizenship and the benefit of being part of the rebellion.

* * *

The team as well as the high consul were shocked when they received the news of Nell's death. It was rare for a citizen of the Union to take their own life, yet facing the accusations and trial she was to undergo certainly made sense for someone losing their mind regardless of the neural stabilizers which sometimes can be damaged from long space exercises such as the one she had embarked on in her mission.

Waking up in afterlife was immediate. There was no fatigue, no sweat from dreaming the night before but merely an on, or off state. She skipped the orientation module and quickly contacted command. There was not much time to waste.

"I'm here," She intoned with her thought. It was standard procedure to use proxy communications as a way to communicate with other members. She was quickly transmitted to the Gap-a zone which had unlimited space yet was unobservable by people from the normal space, where the rebellion had tactical and training complexes.

"Nell, we are so sorry for the loss of your body. We welcome you here with open arms." Beta Teacher said. Beta Teacher was one of the most prolific teachers for the advancement of Angelonian ideologies and was considered to be the most important figure in their organization. His skin was dark, and his eyes generated brilliant warmth that lit up the room. Of course, some thought he changed his appearance settings to accommodate the odd glow from the eyes but the old ones attested he was just as brilliant looking in normal space.

"Knowledge and evolution are the sworn enemies of the deteriorating corruption still left in this universe, we are here to enlighten and to teach and to accelerate the deterioration of the corruption through vigilance. You are most welcome here. . ."

"Thank you Beta Teacher, I've missed you dearly. I've done something terribly wrong but if I act quickly we can hope to fix it. . . I need your help." She immediately dumped the entire batch of data into his memory.

"Come child, we haven't much time!" he said.

CHAPTER 64

The helicopter landed in an empty parking lot across from the building. Gustave was happy to see his parents safe and unhurt. Their helicopter also carried several armed men which kept their guns aimed directly at their heads.

Gustave calculated the trajectory of the projectiles which would have to hit directly at the brain stems to disable a man well before they had the opportunity to fire their guns.

Another man followed them out of the helicopter, and judging by his insignia and medals, he was a general. The army radio was silent, although Gustave did keep the lines open. That gave him some cause for alarm. The general who looked to be in his late fifties came out with his hands up.

"That's very wise general, but command your men to lower their guns!" Gustave pointed.

" Hold on a moment, why don't we just talk?" the man said.

"That's exactly what I intend for us to do, but the moment I…"

The general had the audacity to interrupt Gustave. "I know, I know, the moment we squeeze any trigger you will go 'berserk'. Boom Bang, I gotchya."

Gustave squinted his eyes in disbelief. It seemed the man did not take him seriously enough.

"The helicopter?" Gustave said.

"What about it?" The general shrugged his shoulders. His thick western accent was even more appalling than his attitude.

"Get the hell away from it and move closer, slowly!" Gustave shouted.

"You got it, son" The general commented.

Something was off. The armor informed Gustave there were snipers positioned on roof tops approximately fifteen hundred yards away.

"Harry, are you watching this?" Gustave transferred the message silently to the control room.

"Yes, Gustave. . ."

"I've given you access to the observation satellite, I'm sending you positions to lock on and transfer the feed to the broadcast," Gustave spoke through to the communications.

Harry clicked on the computer to insert the feed to the broadcast. Before sending the command he quickly gazed again on the screen. He suddenly observed an unmistakable signal the spotter gave the sniper. He shouted, "Gustave, they are about to…"

The escape command came right after Gustave

was surrounded by snipers across all buildings. They intended to shoot him in the eyes, not realizing he was not vulnerable anymore in that organ. While he tried to stay in his spot there were so many of them he had to move to another position. As he moved, two shots were fired. Yet these were not registered as a threat. The ballistics showed a calculated rout to hit both his parents. He ran as fast as he could and sent for protective nano-films to try and stop the bullets.

Then he froze. And cried out in agonizing pain.

"Hurts doesn't it? Your armor is disassembling itself from within, gosh that must hurt!" A voice laughed.

It continued, "I must thank you. You've ruined the factories, and all I have to do is destroy the robots and take you out with them..."

Gustave, lying on the ground in pain, didn't recognize the voice that came directly from his neural link yet he ignored chose to ignore it. All he saw was the bleeding bodies of his parents. He couldn't fight it, he was unable to move. And the pain was only getting stronger and stronger.

"Shoot him! Shoot him!" The general shouted. He noticed Gustave's body twisted and changed in a revealing manner, enough for him to see he was finally defenseless and likely to be susceptible to bullets. "Shoot him!" he shouted again.

The bullets were shot. The soldiers knew well enough not to attempt to aim at his body but his head. The bullets struck his head and slowly bounced off.

Gustave suddenly felt he had control of his armor again. Something seemed to have changed. He was still in much pain, but none of that mattered. He leaped forward and with as much force as he had, flattened his palm and swiveled around to make a long vertical opening from the neck down into the stomach of each of the soldiers who were standing at attention. He then grabbed their spinal cord, forcefully disconnected it and stabbed each in the head with another man's spinal cord.

He got to the third soldier who began to retreat and grabbed him in his hand. He stuck his nails into the skin of his hand and plucked the flesh from the bone. The soldier screamed in pain while holding his hand which had very little flesh remaining.

The General ran to the helicopter, but Gustave instructed one of the robots to chase him and hold him until further notice. Gustave took the bleeding bodies of his parents to the floater.

As the floater took to the air he sent a final command.

Harry shouted, "No, no, no, don't do it please Gustave! The fate of…" Before he was able to finish his bagging, Gustave cut the communication link.

The command followed: Eliminate all resistance.

* * *

The world went into panic whereupon the robots began the destruction of cities wherever they were visited with resistance. Soldiers, men and women went into the streets to fight the invading army which crushed and tore apart anyone stupid enough to be in their way.

In a matter of hours, millions of lives of resisting forces were lost. Low-tech explosives left cities in ruins.

Gustave, who was still waiting for the healing machines to work on his parents, heard the destruction from the distance. Keeping an eye on the progress of his army of a thousand robots he made sure minimal civilian life was lost. Yet he cared not for those who charged with guns against the army. These were violent people which would be of no good use for the new civilization. They would breed and train more like themselves, he assured himself.

Who was the man in the voice? What did he do to my armor? Gustave focused. What stopped him?

He asked the right question and immediately received the report. It seemed that Nell was still watching over him after all.

CHAPTER 65

After several weeks, the fighting stopped. Not because the resistance did but because Gustave instructed his robots to remain firmly in their spots as observers and not combatants. It was in the midst of the cease-fire that the public called for their leaders to submit to the Union.

There was no other option.

The Middle-East showed no intention of accepting the rule of the new government. But Gustave was certain they would in time.

Gustave called for a meeting to organize the massive reconstruction plans for resurrecting the ruined cities. He made a point of promising the new citizens of the Union, a new world and new accommodations in better, newly built cities of the future, a future which he reminded them will be without crime or hunger.

The world might have served as a final battleground, but while the war was won in one campaign, Gustave knew that winning over the world was far from being a reality.

Once won, the new world would be highly qualified to join the other civilizations living on distant planets among the stars. Although how he was going to achieve that, Gustave was not quite certain, but he had a plan.

THE END

NOTES

The Angelonian specie has undergone several Post Singularity Genomic revolutions. The exact periods of the revolutions are debatable and are hard to track down after an inexplicable attack of all general records in the Angelonian Library of Information deleted all references containing historical keywords. In the past hundred years the data has been left to restore itself using adaptive association and cross referencing with other keywords, and more information has been restored. Although the time is not certain, it is well accepted that the pioneers aimed at perfecting the Angelonian genetic code which followed by enhancing it later and eventually evolving the specie to have built-in interfaces that allowed complete control over electronic instrumentations.

After-Life- After- life mainframe was developed as an inexpensive option for retirement. The brain is carbon copied and digitalized. After the personality is extracted it is assigned with an AL citizenship and transferred into a constantly maintained mainframe into which it is at liberty to continue living, working and maintaining a connection with its family members and friends through arranged virtual visitation hours (amount of visits depend on the plan the personality chose prior to their carbon copying). The personalities are able to customize their living spaces with no limitations, as well as communicate and interact with others on the After-Life system. There are countless cities and communities in the system. Some were created by the developers and others by the citizens of After-Life. The AL system has been the subject for much scrutiny, although it is fully acceptable and widely used by billions of users.

Armor Vision – The user neurophotonic interface linking between the dermal skeleton and the brain acts in a very different way than human technology. When information is being quarried it is retrieved through memory allocation in the brain rather than a visual, Heads-Up-Display fashion. To explain it more, consider thinking about your last meal. Envision what it is you ate, the texture, color, shapes, and tastes. You are most likely to envision these details quite vividly. But before It was asked from you to remembering that meal, that memory wasn't "there" only to come to mind in detail when you retrieved it from your memory. Using the armor resemble this process, only information is brought much more vividly. It projects pictures, sounds, calculations and many other factors into the user's memory, as if they experienced and learned it. In this way, there is no need to be obstructed by looking at screens, following visual stimulus which can betime consuming and inefficient.

ABOUT THE AUTHOR

Inventor, science author and serial entrepreneur David M. Sternberg has been involved in many technology and telecommunications start-ups as well as research projects. He is also a dedicated philanthropist that believes advancing technology through academics and connecting the world via better communications methods will improve the human race and help forging a better future for our specie. He is passionate about cognitive neuropsychology and artificial intelligence and spends most his time working on development and facilitation of information systems and telecommunication technologies.

11404041R00333

Made in the USA
Charleston, SC
22 February 2012